A TIME TO REMEMBER

Also by Rosamunde Pilcher

A TIME TO REMEMBER

The Empty House

AND

The Day of the Storm

ROSAMUNDE PILCHER

THOMAS DUNNE BOOKS

ST. MARTIN'S GRIFFIN

NEW YORK

THE EMPTY HOUSE. Copyright © 1973 by Rosamunde Pilcher. THE DAY OF THE STORM. Copyright © 1975 by Rosamunde Pilcher. All rights reserved. Printed in the United States of America. For information, address St. Martin's Press, 175 Fifth Avenue, New York, N.Y. 10010.

www.thomasdunnebooks.com
www.stmartins.com

ISBN 978-1-250-10645-2 (trade paperback)

Our books may be purchased in bulk for promotional, educational, or business use. Please contact your local bookseller or the Macmillan Corporate and Premium Sales Department at 1-800-221-7945, extension 5442, or by e-mail at MacmillanSpecialMarkets@macmillan.com.

First Edition: November 2016

D 10 9 8 7 6 5

THE EMPTY HOUSE

1

t was three o'clock on a Monday afternoon in July, sunny and warm, the hay-scented air cooled by a sea breeze which blew in from the north. From the top of the hill, where the road wound up and over the shoulder of Carn Edvor, the land sloped down to distant cliffs; farmland, ribboned with yellow gorse, broken by outcrops of granite, and patchworked into dozens of small fields. Like a quilt, thought Virginia, and saw the pasture fields as scraps of green velvet, the greenish gold of new-cut hay as shining satin, the pinkish gold of standing corn as something soft and furry, to be stroked and touched.

It was very quiet. But when she closed her eyes the sounds of the summer afternoon obtruded, singling themselves out, one by one, for her attention. The humming of the wind, soft in her ears, stirred the bracken. A car climbed the long hill from Porthkerris, changed gear, came on up the road. From farther away came that pleasant summer-sound, the bee-murmur of combine harvesters. She opened her eyes and counted three, all minimized by distance to toy-size, scarlet and tiny as the models that Nicholas pushed around his nursery carpet.

The approaching car appeared over the crest of the hill, driven very slowly, its occupants, including the driver, staring from open windows at the marvellous view. Their faces were red with sunburn, spectacles glinted, arms bulged in sleeveless blouses, the car seemed packed with humanity. As it passed the lay-by where Virginia had left her own car, one of the women in the back looked up and saw her watching them from the hillside. For a startling second their eyes met, and then the car had gone, around the next corner and away to Land's End.

Virginia looked at her watch. A quarter past three. She sighed and stood up, dusted grass and bracken fronds from the seat of her white jeans, walked back down the hill to her car. The leather seat was griddle-hot with sunshine. She turned the car and started back towards Porthkerris, her mind filled with random images. Of Nicholas and Cara, incarcerated in the alien London nursery, taken to Kensington Gardens each day by Nanny; to the Zoo and the Costume Museum and suitable films by their grandmother. It would be hot in London, stuffy and airless. She wondered if they had cut Nicholas's hair. She wondered if she should buy him a model combine harvester and send it to him with some suitable, informative, maternal letter.

> *Today I saw three of these working in the fields at Lanyon,*
> *and I thought of you and thought you would like a model*
> *so that you could see how it worked.*

A letter for Lady Keile to read approvingly aloud because Nicholas, every inch a male, saw no reason in puzzling out his mother's writing if his grandmother was ready and willing to read it aloud to him. She thought of the other letter, the one from her heart.

> *My darling child, without you and Cara I am without rea-*
> *son, aimless. I drive around in the car because I can think*
> *of nothing else to do, and the car takes me to places that I*
> *used to know, and I watch and wonder who it is who drives*
> *the monster combine, turning out the hay bales, square and*
> *strong as neatly tied parcels.*

The old farmhouses with their great barns and outbuildings were strung along the five miles of coast like uncut stones on a rugged necklace, so that there was no telling where the fields of Penfolda finished and those of the next farm started. And so distant were the combines that it was impossible to guess at the identity of the men who drove them, or the tiny figures who walked behind, forking the bales into rough stooks to stand and dry in the midsummer sun.

She was not even sure that he still lived here, that he still farmed Penfolda, and yet could not imagine him existing anywhere else in the world. She let her mind's eye, like the lens of some great camera, zoom down on to the busy scene. The figures sprang into focus, huge and clear, and he was there, high at the wheel of the combine harvester, shirt sleeves rolled back from brown forearms, his hair tousled by the wind. And because there was danger in moving in so close, Virginia swiftly presented him with a wife, pictured her walking across the fields with a basket, flasks of tea, and perhaps a fruit cake to eat, and she wore a pink cotton dress and a blue apron and her long bare legs were brown.

Mrs. Eustace Philips. Mr. and Mrs. Eustace Philips of Penfolda.

The car nosed over the crest of the hill, and the bay and the white beaches and the distant headlands spread out before her, and far below, spilling down to around the blue goblet of the harbour, were the clustered houses and the Norman church tower of Porthkerris.

Wheal House, where the Lingards lived, and with whom Virginia was staying, lay on the far side of Porthkerris. If she had been a stranger, new to the district and visiting it for the first time, she would have followed the main road which led right down into the town and out the other side, and consequently become hopelessly ensnared in crawling traffic and hordes of aimless sightseers who spilled off the narrow pavements, or stood about at strategic corners, sucking ice-creams, choosing postcards and gazing in shop windows filled with brass piskies and pottery mermaids and other horrors considered suitable as souvenirs.

But, because she was not a stranger, Virginia turned off the road long before the houses started and took the narrow, high-hedged lane that wound up and over the hill which stood at the back of the town. It was the long way home, by no means a short cut, but eventually emerged out on the main road again, through a tunnel of wild rhododendrons and not fifty yards from the main entrance to Wheal House.

There was a white-barred gate and a rough drive that ran up between hedges of pink-flowered escallonia. The house was neo-Georgian, pleasingly proportioned, with a pedimented porch over the front door. The drive swept up between shaven green lawns and flower-beds heavy with the scent of wallflowers, and as Virginia parked the car in the shade of the house, there was a sharp cacophony of barking, and Dora, Alice Lingard's old spaniel, emerged from the open front door where she had been lying, for coolness, on the polished floor of the hall.

Virginia stopped to pat her and speak to her and then went indoors, taking off her sunglasses because after the bright day outside, the house seemed pitch dark.

Across the hall the garden doors stood open to the patio, which, facing south and trapping all the sun, was a favourite spot of Alice's in all but really wintry weather. Today, because of the heat, she had unrolled the split cane awnings, and the bright canvas chairs and the low tables, already set out with tea things, were narrowly striped by the shadow patterns which they cast.

On the table in the middle of the hall lay the afternoon's mail. Two letters for Virginia, both with London postmarks. She laid down her handbag and her glasses and picked them up. One from Lady Keile and one from . . . Cara. The italic letters, which she learned at school, were painfully formed, dearly familiar.

> *Mrs. A. Keile,*
> *c/o Mrs. Lingard,*
> *Wheal House,*
> *Porthkerris,*
> *Cornwall.*

No mistakes, no mis-spellings. Virginia wondered if she had managed by herself or whether Nanny had had to help. With the letters in her hand she went on across the hall and out to where her hostess sat, reclining gracefully on a long chair, with some sewing in her lap. She was making a cushion cover, stitching silk cord around the edge of the coral velvet square, and the colour lay in her lap like some huge fallen rose petal.

She looked up. "There you are! I was wondering what had happened to you. I thought perhaps you'd got stuck in a traffic jam."

Alice Lingard was a tall, dark woman in her late thirties, her firmly-built figure belied by long and slender arms and legs. She was what Virginia always thought of as a middle-aged friend, not middle-aged in the strictest sense of the word, but belonging to that generation which lay half-way between Virginia and Virginia's mother. She was, in fact, a lifelong family friend, and years ago had been a small brides-maid at Virginia's mother's wedding.

She herself had married, eighteen years or so ago, Tom Lingard, then a young man on the verge of taking over the small family busi-ness of Lingard Sons which specialized in the manufacture of heavy engineering machinery in the nearby town of Fourbourne. Under Tom's chairmanship the firm had expanded and prospered, and after a series of successful take-over bids now controlled interests which spread from Bristol to St. Just, and included mining rights, a small shipping business and the sale of agricultural machinery.

They had never had children, but Alice had diverted her natural domestic talents to her house and garden, and over the years had transformed what had once been a fairly unimaginative establishment into an enchanting house and a garden which was constantly being photographed and written about by the Garden Editors of the gloss-ier magazines. Ten years ago, when Virginia and her mother had come to Cornwall to spend Easter with the Lingards, the work had only just started. This time, having not visited Wheal House during the intervening years, Virginia had scarcely recognized the place. Every-thing had been subtly altered, straight lines curved, outlines and bound-aries magically removed. Trees had grown up, casting long shadows on smooth lawns which seemed to spread as far as the eye could see. The old orchard had been transformed to a wild garden tangled with all the sweetest of old-fashioned roses, and where once had drilled rows of runner beans and raspberry canes, now stood magnolias, creamy petalled, and heady-scented azaleas taller than a man could reach.

But, domestically, the patio was Alice's most successful project, neither house nor garden, but with the combined charm of both. Geraniums spilled from terrace pots, and up a trellised wall she had started to train a dark purple-flowered clematis. She had lately decided that she would also grow a vine, and was currently picking the brains of both friends and reference books, to decide on the best way to set about doing this. Her energies appeared to be endless.

Virginia pulled up a chair and dropped into it, surprised to find how hot and tired she felt. She shucked off her sandals and propped up her bare feet on to a handy stool. "I didn't go to Porthkerris."

"You didn't? But I thought you'd gone to the post office."

"I only wanted some stamps. I can buy them another time. There were so many people and so many buses and so much crushed and sweating humanity that I got claustrophobia and never stopped. Just went on driving."

"I can lend you stamps," said Alice. "Let me pour you some tea." She laid down her sewing and sat up to reach for the teapot. Steam rose from the delicate cup, fragrant, refreshing.

"Milk or lemon?"

"Lemon would be delicious."

"So much more refreshing, I think, on a hot day." She handed Virginia the cup and lay back again. "Where did you drive?"

"Um? . . . oh, the other way . . ."

"Land's End?"

"Not so far. I only got as far as Lanyon. I parked the car in a lay-by and climbed the hill for a bit and sat in the bracken and looked at the view."

"So beautiful," said Alice, threading her needle.

"They're cutting hay on the farms."

"Yes, they would be."

"It never changes, does it? Lanyon, I mean. No new houses, no new roads, no shops, no caravan parks." She took a mouthful of scalding hot lapsang suchong and then, with care, laid the cup and saucer down on the paved floor beside her chair. "Alice, does Eustace Philips still farm Penfolda?"

Alice stopped sewing, and put up a hand to take off her dark glasses and stare at Virginia. There was a puzzled frown between her dark brows.

"What do you know about Eustace Philips? How do you know him?"

"Alice, your memory is appalling. It was you yourself who took me out there, you and Tom, for an enormous barbecue on the cliffs at Penfolda. There must have been at least thirty people and I don't know who organized it, but we cooked sausages over a fire and drank beer out of a barrel. Oh, surely you remember, and then Mrs. Philips gave us tea in her kitchen!"

"Now you remind me, of course I do. It was bitterly cold but quite beautiful and we watched the moon rise from behind Boscovey Head. I do remember. Now, who was it who threw that party? It certainly wasn't Eustace, he was always too busy milking cows. It must have been the Barnets—he was a sculptor and had a studio for a couple of years in Porthkerris before he went back to London. His wife wove baskets or belts or something, terribly folksy, and they had a lot of children who never wore shoes. They were always thinking up the most original parties. It must have been the Barnets . . . How extraordinary! I hadn't thought about them in years. And we all went out to Penfolda." But here her memory let her down. She looked at Virginia blankly. "Or did we? Who went to that party?"

"Mother didn't come. She said it wasn't up her street . . ."

"How right she was."

"But you and I and Tom went."

"Of course. Bundled up in sweaters and socks. I'm not sure I didn't wear a fur coat. But we were talking about Eustace. How old were you, Virginia? Seventeen? Fancy your remembering Eustace Philips after all these years."

"You haven't answered my question. Is he still at Penfolda?"

"As the farm belonged to his father, and *his* father, and as far as I know *his* father before that, do you really think it likely that Eustace would up sticks and depart?"

"I suppose not. It's just that they were cutting hay this afternoon and I wondered if it was he who drove one of the combines. Do you ever see him, Alice?"

"Hardly ever. Not because we don't want to, understand me, but
he's a hard-working farmer, and Tom's so busy being a tycoon, that
their paths don't often cross. Except sometimes they meet at the hare
shoot, or the Boxing Day meet . . . you know the sort of thing."

Virginia picked up her tea-cup and saucer, and observed, minutely,
the rose painted upon its side.

"He's married," she said.

"You say that as though you were stating an irrefutable fact."

"Aren't I?"

"No, you're not. He never married. Heaven knows why. I always
thought he was so attractive in a sun-burned, D. H. Lawrence-ish sort
of way. There must have been a number of languishing ladies in Lanyon, but he resisted the lot. He must like it that way."

Eustace's wife, so swiftly imagined, as swiftly died, a wraith blown
to nothing by the cold wind of reality. Instead, Virginia saw the Penfolda kitchen, cheerless and untidy, with the remains of the last meal
abandoned on the table, dishes in the sink, an ashtray filled with cigarette stubs.

"Who looks after him?"

"I don't know. His mother died a couple of years ago I believe . . . I
don't know what he does. Perhaps he's got a sexy housekeeper, or a
domesticated mistress? I really don't know."

And couldn't care less, her tone implied. She had finished sewing
on the silk cord, now gave a couple of neat firm stitches and then broke
the thread with a little tug. "There, that's done. Isn't it a divine colour?
But it's really too hot to sew." She laid it aside. "Oh dear, I suppose I
must go and see what we'll have for dinner. What would you say to a
delicious fresh lobster?"

"I'd say 'pleased to see you.'"

Alice stood up, unfolding her long height to tower over Virginia.
"Did you see your letters?"

"Yes, they're here."

Alice stooped to pick up the tray. "I'll leave you," she said, "to read
them in peace."

Keeping the best to the last, Virginia opened her mother-in-law's
letter first. The envelope was dark blue, lined with navy blue tissue.

The writing-paper was thick, the address blackly embossed at its head.

32 Welton Gardens, S.W.8.

My dear Virginia,

I hope you are enjoying this wonderful weather, quite a heatwave and into the nineties yesterday. I expect you are swimming in Alice's pool, such a joy not having to drive to the beach every time you want to swim.

The children are both well and send their love. Nanny takes them into the park every day and they take their tea with them and eat it there. I took Cara to Harrods this morning to buy some new dresses, she is getting so tall and was quite out of her old ones. One is blue with appliquéd flowers, the other pink with a little smocking. I think you would approve!

Tomorrow they are going to tea with the Manning-Prestons. Nanny is looking forward to a good gossip with their Nanny, and Susan is just the right age for Cara. It would be nice for them to be friends.

My regards to Alice, and let me know when you decide to come back to London, but we are managing beautifully, and don't want you to cut short your holiday at all for any reason. You really were due for one.

Affectionately,
Dorothea Keile

She read the letter twice, torn by conflicting emotions. Double meanings sprang at her from between the meticulously-penned, well-turned sentences. She saw her children in the park, the baked London grass turned yellow in the heat, trodden and tired, and fouled by dogs. She saw the white-hot morning sky high above the roof tops and the little girl being fitted into dresses that she would neither like nor want, but would be too polite to reject. She saw the Manning-

Prestons's tall, terraced house, with the paved garden at the back
where Mrs. Manning-Preston held her famous cocktail parties, and
where Cara and Susan would be sent to play while the Nannies talked
about knitting patterns and what a terror Nanny Brigg's little charge
was going to be. And she saw Cara standing silent, petrified with shyness, and Susan Manning-Preston treating her with contempt because
Cara wore spectacles and Susan thought she was a ninny.

And "we are managing beautifully." The statement seemed to
Virginia completely ambiguous. Who was "we"? Nanny and the grandmother? Or did it include the children, Virginia's children? Did they
let Cara sleep with the old Teddy that Nanny swore was unhygienic?
Did they remember always to leave the light on so that Nicholas could
get himself to the bathroom in the middle of the night? And were
they ever left alone, disorganized, dirty, untidy, to play secret, pointless games in small corners of the garden, with perhaps a nut or a
leaf, and all the imaginings that were contained within their small,
clever, bewildering brains?

She found that her hands were shaking. She was a fool to get into
this state. Nanny had looked after the children since they were born,
she knew all their idiosyncrasies and nobody could cope with Nicholas's sudden rages better than she.

(But should he have such rages? At six, shouldn't he have grown out
of them? What frustration sparks them off?)

And Nanny was gentle with Cara. She made dolls' clothes and knitted scarves and sweaters for the teddies out of left-over bits of wool.
And she let Cara wheel her doll's perambulator into the park; over
the crossing by the Albert Memorial, they went. (But did she read to
Cara, the books that Cara loved? *The Borrowers* and *The Railway Children*
and every word of *The Secret Garden*.) Did she love the children, or
simply possess them?

These were all familiar questions which, lately, had been raising
themselves with ever-increasing frequency within the confines of
Virginia's own head. But never answered. Knowing that she was evad-
ing a vital issue, she would shelve her own anxiety, always with some
excuse to herself. I can't think about it now, I'm too tired. Perhaps in
a couple of years when Nicholas goes away to Prep. school, perhaps

then I'll tell my mother-in-law that I don't need Nanny any longer; I'll say to Nanny it's time to go, to find another new baby to look after. And perhaps just now I'm too emotional, I wouldn't be good for the children; they're better with Nanny: after all, she's been looking after children for forty years.

Like a familiar sedative the well-worn excuses came pat, blunting Virginia's uneasy conscience. She put the blue letter back into its expensive envelope and turned, in relief, to the second one. But the relief was short-lived. Cara had borrowed her grandmother's writing-paper, but the sentences this time were neither meticulously penned nor well-turned. The ink was blotched and the lines ran down the side of the paper as though the words were tumbling hopelessly downhill.

> *Darling Mother,*
>
> *I hope you are having a good time. I hope it is nise wether. It is hot in London. I have to go and have tea with Susan Maning Preston. I dont no what we will play. Last night Nicholas screemed and Granny had to give him a pil. He went all red. One of my dolls eyes has come out and I cant find it. Please will you rite to me soon and tell me when we are going back to Kirkton.*
>
> > *With love from Cara.*
>
> *P.S. Dont forget to rite.*

She folded the letter and put it away. Across the garden, across the lawns, the blue of Alice's swimming-pool glimmered like a jewel. The cooling air was filled with bird-song and the scent of flowers. From inside the house she could hear Alice's voice talking to Mrs. Jilkes, the cook, doubtless about the lobster which they were going to eat for dinner.

She felt helpless, totally inadequate. She thought of asking Alice to have the children here, and in the next instant knew that it was impossible. Alice's house was not designed for children, her life did not cater for their inclusion. She would be irritated beyond words by Cara forgetting to change her gum-boots, or by Nicholas kicking his football into the treasured flower-borders, or drawing "pictures" on the wallpaper. For without Nanny, he would doubtless be impossible because he was always twice as naughty without her to keep an eye on him.

Without Nanny. Those were the operative words. On her own. She had to have them on her own.

And yet the very thought filled her with dread. What would she do with them? Where would they go? Like feelers her thoughts probed around, searching for ideas. A hotel? But hotels here would be filled to the brim with summer visitors and terribly expensive. Besides, Nicholas in a hotel would be as nerve-racking as Nicholas at Wheal House. She thought of hiring a caravan, or camping with them on the beach, like the summer migration of hippies, who lit fires of driftwood and slept curled up on the chilly sand.

Of course, there was always Kirkton. Some time, she would have to go back. But all her instincts shied away from the thought of returning to Scotland, to the house where she had lived with Anthony, the place where her children had been born, the only place they thought of as home. Thinking of Kirkton, she saw tree shadows flickering on pale walls, the cold northern light reflected on the white ceilings, the sound of her own feet going up the uncarpeted, polished stairway. She thought of clear autumn evenings when the first skeins of geese flew over, and the park, in front of the house, sweeping down to the banks of the deep, swift-flowing river . . .

No. Not yet. Cara would have to wait. Later, perhaps, they would go back to Kirkton. Not yet. Behind her a door slammed, and she was jerked back to reality by the arrival of Tom Lingard, back from work. She heard him call Alice, then drop his brief-case on the hall-table, and come out to the patio in search of his wife.

"Hallo, Virginia." He bent and dropped a kiss on the top of her head. "All alone? Where's Alice?"

"Interviewing a lobster in the kitchen."

"Letters from the children? All well? Well done, that's great . . ."
One of Tom's idiosyncrasies was that he never bothered to wait for an

answer to any of his questions. Virginia sometimes wondered if this was the secret of his outstanding success. "What have you been doing all day? Lying in the sun? That's the job. How about coming and having a swim with me now? The exercise'll do you good after all this lazing about. We'll get Alice to come too . . ." He went, spring-footed and bursting with energy, back into the house and down the passage towards the kitchen, bellowing for his wife. And Virginia, grateful for directions, stood up and collected her mail and went indoors, obediently, and upstairs to her bedroom to change into a bikini.

2

The solicitors were called Smart, Chirgwin and Williams. At
least, those were the names on the brass plate by the door, a
plate which had been polished so long and so hard that the letters
had lost their sharpness and were quite difficult to read. There was a
brass knocker on the door, too, and a brass door knob, as smooth and
shining as the plate, and when Virginia turned the knob and opened
the door, she stepped into a narrow hall of polished brown linoleum
and shining cream paint and it occurred to her that some hard-
working woman was using up an awful lot of elbow grease.

There was a glass window, like an old-fashioned ticket-office with
INQUIRIES written over it, and a bell to press. Virginia pressed the
bell and the window flew up.

"Yes?"

Startled, Virginia told the face behind the window that she wanted
to see Mr. Williams.

"Have you got an appointment?"

"Yes. It's Mrs. Keile."

"Just a moment, please."

The window slammed down and the face withdrew. Presently a
door opened and the face reappeared, along with a well-upholstered
body and a pair of legs that went straight down into sturdy lace-up
shoes.

"If you'd like to come this way, Mrs. Keile."

The building which housed the solicitors' office stood at the top of the hill which led out of Porthkerris, but even so Virginia was taken unawares by the marvellous view which leapt at her as soon as she walked into the room. Mr. Williams's desk stood in the middle of the carpet and Mr. Williams was, even now, getting to his feet behind it. But, beyond Mr. Williams, a great picture-window framed, like some lovely painting, the whole jumbled, charming panorama of the old part of the town. Roofs of houses, faded slate and whitewashed chimneys, tumbled without pattern or order down the hill. Here a blue door, there a yellow window; here a window-sill bright with geraniums, a line of washing gay as flags, or the leaves of some unsuspected and normally unseen tree. Beyond the roofs and far below them was the harbour, at full tide and sparkling with sunshine. Boats rocked at anchor and a white sail sped out beyond the shelter of the harbour wall, heading for the ruler line of the horizon where the two blues met. The air was clamorous with the sound of gulls, the sky patterned with their great gliding wings and as Virginia stood there, the church bells from the Norman tower struck up a simple carillon and clock chimes rang out eleven o'clock.

"Good morning," said Mr. Williams, and Virginia realized that he had already said this twice. She tore her attention from the view and tried to focus it on him.

"Oh, good morning. I'm Mrs. Keile, I . . ." But it was impossible. "How *can* you work in a room with a view like that?"

"That's why I sit with my back to it . . ."

"It's breathtaking."

"Yes, and quite unique. We're often asked by artists if they can paint the harbour from this window. You can see the whole structure of the town, and the colours are always different, always beautiful. Except, of course, on a rainy day. Now—" his manner changed abruptly as though anxious to get down to work and to waste no more time— "what can I do for you?" He drew a chair forward for her.

Trying to stop looking out of the window and to concentrate on the matter in hand, Virginia sat down. "Well I've maybe come to quite the wrong person, but you see I can't find an estate agent anywhere in the town. And I looked in the local paper for a house to rent, but there didn't seem to be one. And then I saw your name in the telephone book, and I thought perhaps you might be able to help me."

"Help you find a house?" Mr. Williams was young, very dark, his eyes frankly interested in the attractive woman who faced him across his desk.

"Just to rent . . ."

"For how long?"

"A month . . . my children go back to school the first week in September."

"I see. Well, we don't actually *deal* in this sort of thing, but I could ask Miss Leddra if there's anything that she could suggest. But of course this is the high season, and the town is already packed to the gunwales with visitors. Even if you do find something, I'm afraid you'll have to pay a fairly steep rent."

"I don't mind."

"Well, just a moment . . ."

He left her and went out, and Virginia heard him speaking to the woman who had let her in. She got up and went back to the window, and opened it wide and laughed as a furious gull flew crossly off the sill where he had been perching. The wind off the sea was cool and fresh. A pleasure boat packed with passengers started off across the harbour and suddenly Virginia longed to be on board, irresponsible, sunburned, wearing a hat with KISS ME written on it and screaming with laughter as the first waves sent the boat rocking.

Mr. Williams came back. "Can you wait a moment? Miss Leddra's making a few inquiries . . ."

"Yes, of course." She returned to her chair.

"Are you staying in Porthkerris?" Mr. Williams asked conversationally.

"Yes. I'm staying with friends. The Lingards up at Wheal House."

His previous manner had been neither off-hand nor familiar, but all at once he was almost deferential.

"Oh yes, of course. What a charming place that is."

"Yes. Alice has made it lovely."

"Have you been there before?"

"Yes. Ten years ago. But I haven't been since."

"Are your children with you?"

"No. They're in London, with their grandmother. But I want to get them down here with me, if I can."

"Is London your home?"

"No. It's just that my mother-in-law lives in London." Mr. Williams waited. "My home . . . that is, we live in Scotland."

He looked delighted . . . Virginia could not think why it should delight him that she lived in Scotland. "But how splendid! What part?"

"In Perthshire."

"The most beautiful. My wife and I spent a holiday there last summer. The peace of it all, and the empty roads and the quiet. How could you bear to come away?"

Virginia had opened her mouth to tell him when the discussion was mercifully interrupted by the arrival of Miss Leddra, bearing a sheaf of papers.

"Here it is, Mr. Williams. Bosithick. And the letter from Mr. Kernow saying that if we could find a tenant for August he'd be willing to rent. But only to a *suitable* tenant, Mr. Williams. He's very firm about that point."

Mr. Williams took the papers and smiled at Virginia over the top of them.

"Are you a suitable tenant, Mrs. Keile?"

"It depends. On what you're offering me, doesn't it?"

"Well, it's not actually in Porthkerris . . . thank you, Miss Leddra . . . but not too far away . . . out at Lanyon actually . . ."

"Lanyon!"

She must have sounded appalled, for Mr. Williams sprang at once to Lanyon's defence. "But it's a most charming spot, quite the most beautiful bit of coastline left anywhere."

"I didn't mean that I didn't like it. I was just surprised."

"Were you? Why?"

He was too sharp, like a beady-eyed bird. "No reason, really. Tell me about the house."

He told her. It was an old cottage, neither distinguished nor beautiful, but with a small claim to fame in that a famous writer had once lived and worked there during the nineteen-twenties.

Virginia said, "Which?"

"I beg your pardon?"

"Which famous writer?"

"Oh, I'm sorry. Aubrey Crane. Didn't you know that he spent some years in this part of the world?"

Virginia did not. But Aubrey Crane had been one of the many authors of whom Virginia's mother did not approve. She remembered her mother's chill expression, lips pursed, whenever his books were mentioned; remembered them being returned swiftly to the library before the young Virginia could get her eyes on them. For some reason this seemed to make the cottage called Bosithick even more desirable. "Go on," said Virginia.

Mr. Williams went on. Despite its age Bosithick had been modernized to a certain degree—there was now a bathroom and a lavatory and an electric cooker.

"Who does it belong to?" Virginia asked.

"Mr. Kernow is the nephew of the old lady who used to own the house. She left it to him, but he lives in Plymouth so he uses it just for holidays. He and his family intended coming down for the summer, but his wife fell ill and can't make the trip. As we are Mr. Kernow's solicitors, he put the matter in our hands, with the instructions that, if we did let the house, it must be to a tenant who can be trusted to take care of it."

"How big is it?"

Mr. Williams perused his papers. "Let's see, a kitchen, a sitting-room, a downstairs bathroom, and a hall, and three rooms upstairs."

"Is there a garden?"

"Not really."

"How far is it from the road?"

"About a hundred yards down a farm lane as far as I can remember."

"And could I have it right away?"

"I can see no objection. But you must see it first."

"Yes, of course . . . when can I see it?"

"Today? Tomorrow?"

"Tomorrow morning."

"I'll take you out myself."

"Thank you, Mr. Williams." Virginia stood up and made for the door, and he had to make a little rush to get there and open it before she did.

"There's just one thing, Mrs. Keile."

"What's that?"

"You haven't asked what the rent is."

She smiled. "No I haven't, have I? Goodbye, Mr. Williams."

Virginia said nothing to Alice and Tom. She did not want to have to put into words what was, at best, only a vague idea. She did not want to be drawn into an argument, to be persuaded either that the children were best left in London with their grandmother or that Alice could disregard the possible destruction that they might perpetrate at Wheal House and would insist on having them there. When Virginia had found somewhere for them all to live, she would present Alice with what she had done as a *fait accompli*. And then Alice would maybe help her take the biggest hurdle of all, which was to persuade the grandmother to let the children come to Cornwall without Nanny. At the very prospect of this ordeal, Virginia's imagination turned and ran, but there were other and smaller obstacles to be overcome first, and these she was determined to do by herself.

Alice was a perfect hostess. When Virginia told her that she would be out for the morning it never occurred to Alice to quiz her as to what she intended doing. She only said, "Will you be in for lunch?"

"I don't think so . . . Better say not . . ."

"I'll see you at tea time, then. We'll have a swim together afterwards."

"Heaven," said Virginia. She kissed Alice and went out, got into her car and drove down the hill into Porthkerris. She parked the car near the station and walked to the solicitors' office to pick up Mr. Williams.

"Mrs. Keile, I couldn't be more sorry, but I'm not going to be able to come out with you this morning to Bosithick. An old client is coming down from Truro and I must be here to see her; I do hope you understand! But here are the keys of the house, and I've drawn a fairly detailed map of how to find it . . . I don't think you could go wrong. Do you mind going on your own, or would you like to take Miss Leddra with you?"

Virginia imagined the daunting presence of the formidable Miss Leddra and assured Mr. Williams that she'd manage perfectly on her own. She was given a ring of large keys, each with a wooden label. Front Door, Coal Shed, Tower Room. "You'll need to watch out for the lane," Mr. Williams told her, as they went together towards the door. "It's fairly bumpy and although there's no room to turn by the gate of Bosithick itself, you can manage easily if you carry on down the lane; you'll come to an old farmyard and you can turn the car there. Now, you're sure you'll be all right . . . I couldn't be more sorry about this, but I'll be here, of course, waiting to hear what you think of the place. Oh, and Mrs. Keile . . . it's been empty for some months. Try not to be influenced if it feels a little dingy. Just throw open a few windows and imagine it with a nice cheerful fire."

Slightly discouraged by these parting remarks, Virginia went back to her car. The keys of the unknown house weighed heavy as lead in her handbag. All at once, she longed for company, and even considered, for a mad moment, returning to Wheal House to make a true confession to Alice and persuade her to come out to Lanyon and lend a little moral support. But that was ridiculous. It was just a little cottage, to be viewed, and either rented or rejected. Any fool . . . even Virginia . . . could surely do that.

The weather was still beautiful and the traffic still appalling. She crawled, one of the long queue of cars, down into the depths of town and out the other side. At the top of the hill where the roads forked, the traffic thinned a little and she was able to put on some speed and pass a line of dawdling cars. As she went up and over the moor and the sea dropped and spread beneath her, her spirits rose. The road wound like a grey ribbon through the bracken-covered hill-side; to her left towered the great outcrop of Carn Edvor stained purple with heather, and on her right the country swept away down to the sea, the familiar patchwork of fields and farms, that she had sat and watched only two days before

She had been told by Mr. Williams to look out for a clump of wind-leaning hawthorns by the side of the road. Beyond this was a steep corner and then the narrow farm track which led down towards the sea. Virginia came upon it and turned the car down into it, no more than a stony lane high-hedged with brambles. She went into bottom gear and edged cautiously downhill, attempting to avoid bumps and potholes and trying not to think about the damage that the prickly gorse bushes were inflicting on the paintwork of her car.

There was no sign of any house, until she turned a steep corner and was instantly upon it. A stone wall, and beyond, a gable and a slated roof. She stopped the car in the lane, reached for her handbag and got out. There was a cool, salty wind blowing in from the sea, and the smell of gorse. She went to open the gate, but the hinges were broken and it had to be lifted before she could edge through. A path of sorts led down towards a flight of stone steps and so to the house, and Virginia saw that it was long and low with gables to the north and the south, and at the north end, looking out over the sea, had been added an extra room with a square tower above it. The tower imparted an oddly sanctified look to the house which Virginia found chilling. There was no garden to speak of, but at the south end a patch of unmown grass blew in the wind and two leaning poles supported what had once been a washing line.

She went down the steps and along a dank pathway that led along the side of the house towards the front door. This had once been painted dark red and was scarred with splitting sun blisters. Virginia took out the key and put it in the keyhole and turned the door knob and the key together and the door instantly, silently, swung inwards. She saw a tiny flight of stairs, a worn rug on bare boards, smelt damp and . . . mice? She swallowed nervously. She hated mice, but now that she had come so far there was nothing for it but to go up the two worn steps and tread gingerly over the threshold.

It did not take long to go over the old part of the house, to glance in at the tiny kitchen with its inadequate cooker and stained sink; the sitting-room cluttered with ill-matching chairs. An electric fire sat in the cavern of the huge old fireplace, like a savage animal at the mouth of its lair. There were curtains of flimsy cotton hanging at the windows, fly-blown and dejected, and a dresser packed with cups and plates and dishes in every sort of size and shape and state of dilapidation.

Without hope, Virginia went upstairs. The bedrooms were dim with tiny windows and unsuitable, looming pieces of furniture. She returned to the top of the stairs, and so up another pair of steps, to a closed door. She opened this, and after the gloom of the rest of the house, the blast of bright, northern light by which she was immediately assailed, was dazzling. Stunned by it, she stepped blindly into an astonishing room, small, completely square, windowed on three walls, it stood high above the sea like the bridge of a ship, with a view of the coastline that must have extended for fifteen miles.

A window-seat with a faded cover ran along the north side of this room. There was a scrubbed table, and an old braided rug and in the centre of the floor, like a decorative wellhead, the wrought-iron banister of a spiral staircase which led directly down to the room beneath, the "Hall" of Mr. Williams's prospectus.

Cautiously Virginia descended, to a room dominated by an enormous *art nouveau* fireplace. Off this was the bathroom; and then another door, and she was back where she'd started, in the dark and depressing sitting-room.

It was an extraordinary, a terrible house. It sat around her, waiting for her to make some decision, contemptuous of her faintness of heart. To give herself time, she went back up to the tower room, sat on the window-seat and opened her bag to find a cigarette. Her last. She would have to buy some more. She lit it and looked at the bare scrubbed table, and the faded colours of the rug on the floor, and knew that this had been Aubrey Crane's study, the workroom where he had wrestled out the lusty love stories that Virginia had never been encouraged to read. She saw him, bearded and knickerbockered, his conventional appearance belying the passions of his rebellious heart. Perhaps in summertime, he would have flung wide these windows, to catch all the scents and sounds of the countryside, the roar of the sea, the whistle of the wind. But in winter it would be bitterly cold, and he would have to wrap himself in blankets, and write painfully with chilblained fingers mittened in knitted wool . . .

Somewhere in the room a fly droned, blundering against the window-pane. Virginia leaned her forehead on the cool glass of the window and stared sightless at the view and started one of the interminable ding-dong arguments she had been having with herself for years.

I can't come here.

Why not?

I hate it. It's spooky and frightening. It's got a horrible atmosphere.

That's just your imagination.

It's an impossible house. I could never bring the children here. They've never lived in such a place. Anyway, there's nowhere for them to play.

There's the whole world for them to play in. The fields and the cliffs and the sea.

But looking after them . . . the washing and the ironing, and the cooking. And there's no refrigerator, and how would I heat the water?

I thought that all that mattered was getting the children to yourself, away from London.

They're better in London, with Nanny, than living in a house like this.

That wasn't what you thought yesterday.

I can't bring them here. I wouldn't know where to begin. Not on my own like that.

Then what are you going to do?

I don't know. Talk to Alice, perhaps I should have talked to her before now. She hasn't children of her own, but she'll understand. Maybe she'll know about some other little house. She'll understand. She'll help. She has to help.

So much, said her own cool and scathing voice, *for all those strong resolutions.*

Angrily, Virginia stubbed out the half-smoked cigarette, ground it under her heel and got up and went downstairs and took out the keys and locked the door behind her. She went back up the path to the gate, stepped through and shut it. The house watched her, the small bedroom windows like derisive eyes. She tore herself from their gaze and got back into the safety of her car. It was a quarter past twelve. She needed cigarettes and she was not expected back at Wheal House for lunch, so, when she had turned the car, and was driving back up on to the main road again, she took not the road to Porthkerris, but the other way, and she drove the short mile to Lanyon village, up the narrow main street, and finally came to a halt in the cobbled square that was flanked on one side by the porch of the square-towered church and on the other by a small whitewashed pub called The Mermaid's Arms.

Because of the fine weather, there were tables and chairs set up outside the pub, along with brightly coloured sun-umbrellas and tubs of orange nasturtiums. A man and a woman in holiday clothes sat and drank their beer, their little boy played with a puppy. As Virginia approached, they looked up to smile good morning, and she smiled back and went past them in through the door, instinctively ducking her head beneath the blackened lintel.

Inside it was dark-panelled, low-ceilinged, dimly illuminated by tiny windows veiled in lace curtains; there was a pleasant smell, cool and musty. A few figures, scarcely visible in the gloom, sat along the wall, or around small wobbly tables, and behind the bar, framed by rows of hanging beer-mugs, the barman, in shirtsleeves and a checkered pullover, was polishing glasses with a dishcloth.

"... I don't know 'ow it is, William," he was saying to a customer who sat at the other end of the bar, perched disconsolately on a tall stool, with a long cigarette ash and half a pint of bitter, "... but you put the litter bins up and nobody puts nothing into them ..."

"Ur ..." said William, nodding in sad agreement and sprinkling cigarette ash into the beer.

"Stuff blows all over the road, and the County Council don't even come and empty them. Ugly old things they are, too, we'd be better without them. Managed all right without them before, we did ..." He finished polishing the glass, set it down with a thump and turned to attend to Virginia.

"Yes, madam?"

He was very Cornish, in voice, in looks, in colouring. A red and wind-burned face, blue eyes, black hair.

Virginia asked for cigarettes.

"Only got packets of twenty. That all right?" He turned to take them from the shelf and slit the wrapper with a practised thumb-nail. "Lovely day, isn't it? On holiday, are you?"

"Yes." It was years since she had been into a pub. In Scotland women were never taken into pubs. She had forgotten the atmosphere, the snug companionship. She said, "Do you have any Coke?"

He looked surprised. "Yes, I've got Coke. Keep it for the children. Want some, do you?"

"Please."

He reached for a bottle, opened it neatly, poured it into a glass and pushed it across the counter towards her.

"I was just saying to William, here, that road to Porthkerris is a disgrace . . ." Virginia pulled up a stool and settled down to listen. ". . . All that rubbish lying around. Visitors don't seem to know what to do with their litter. You'd think coming to a lovely part like this they'd have the sense they was born with and take all them old bits of paper home with them, in the car, not leave them lying around on the roadside. They talk about conservation and ecology, but, my God . . ."

He was off on what was obviously his favourite hobby-horse, judging by the well-timed grunts of assent that came from all corners of the room. Virginia lit a cigarette. Outside, in the sunny square, a car drew up, the engine stopped, a door slammed. She heard a man's voice say good morning, and then footsteps came through the doorway and into the bar behind her.

". . . I wrote to the MP about it, said who was going to get the place cleaned up, he said it was the responsibility of the County Council, but I said . . ." Over Virginia's head he caught sight of the new customer. " 'Allo, there! You're a stranger."

"Still at the litter bins, Joe?"

"You know me, boy, worry a subject to death, like a terrier killing a rat. What'll you have?"

"A pint of bitter."

Joe turned to draw the beer, and the newcomer moved in to stand between Virginia and lugubrious William, and she had recognized his voice at once, as soon as he spoke, just as she had known his footfall, stepping in over the flagged threshold of The Mermaid's Arms.

She took a mouthful of Coke, laid down the glass. All at once her cigarette tasted bitter; she stubbed it out and turned her head to look at him, and she saw the blue shirt, with the sleeves rolled back from his brown forearms, and the eyes very blue and the short, rough, brown hair cut like a pelt, close to the shape of his head. And because there was nothing else to be done she said, "Hallo, Eustace."

Startled, his head swung round and his expression was that of a man who had suddenly been hit in the stomach, bemused and incapable. She said, quickly, "It really is me," and his smile came, incredulous, rueful, as though he knew he had been made to look a fool.

"Virginia."

She said again, stupidly, "Hallo."

"What in the name of heaven are you doing here?"

She was aware that every ear in the place was waiting for her to reply. She made it very light and casual. "Buying cigarettes. Having a drink."

"I didn't mean that. I mean in Cornwall. Here, in Lanyon."

"I'm on holiday. Staying with the Lingards in Porthkerris."

"How long have you been here?"

"About a week . . ."

"And what are you doing out here?"

But before she had time to tell him, the barman had pushed Eustace's tankard of beer across the counter, and Eustace was diverted by trying to find the right money in his trouser pocket.

"Old friends, are you?" asked Joe, looking at Virginia with new interest, and she said, "Yes, I suppose you could say that."

"I haven't seen her for ten years," Eustace told him, pushing the coins across the counter. He looked at Virginia's glass. "What are you drinking?"

"Coke."

"Bring it outside, we may as well sit in the sun."

She followed him, aware of the unblinking stares which followed them; the insatiable curiosity. Outside in the sunshine he put their glasses down on to a wooden table and they settled, side by side on a bench, with the sun on their heads and their backs against the whitewashed wall of the pub.

"You don't mind being brought out here, do you? Otherwise we couldn't say a word without it being received and transmitted all over the county within half an hour."

"I'd rather be outside."

Half turned towards her, he sat so close that Virginia could see the rough, weather-beaten texture of his skin, the network of tiny lines around his eyes, the first frosting of white in that thick brown hair. She thought, *I'm with him again.*

He said, "Tell me."

"Tell you what?"

"What happened to you." And then quickly: "I know you got married."

"Yes. Almost at once."

"Well, that would have put paid to the London Season you were dreading so much."

"Yes, it did."

"And the coming-out dance."

"I had a wedding instead."

"Mrs. Anthony Keile. I saw the announcement in the paper." Virginia said nothing. "Where do you live now?"

"In Scotland. There's a house in Scotland . . ."

"And children?"

"Yes. Two. A boy and a girl."

"How old are they?" He was really interested, and she remembered how the Cornish loved children, how Mrs. Jilkes was for ever going dewy-eyed over some lovely little great-nephew or niece.

"The girl's eight and the boy's six."

"Are they with you now?"

"No. They're in London. With their grandmother."

"And your husband? Is he down? What's he doing this morning? Playing golf?"

She stared at him, accepting for the first time the fact that personal tragedy is just that. Personal. Your own existence could fall to pieces but that did not mean that the rest of the world necessarily knew about it, or even bothered. There was no reason for Eustace to know.

She laid her hands on the edge of the table, aligning them as though their arrangement were of the utmost importance. She said, "Anthony's dead." Her hands seemed all at once insubstantial, almost transparent, the wrists too thin, the long almond-shaped nails, painted coral pink, as fragile as petals. She wished suddenly, fervently, that they were not like that, but strong and brown and capable, with dirt engrained, and fingernails worn from gardening and peeling potatoes and scraping carrots. She could feel Eustace's eyes upon her. She could not bear him to be sorry for her.

He said, "What happened?"

"He was killed in a car accident. He was drowned."

"*Drowned?*"

"We have this river, you see, at Kirkton . . . that's where we live in Scotland. The river runs between the house and the road, you have to go over the bridge. And he was coming home and he skidded, or misjudged the turn, and the car went through the wooden railings and into the river. We'd had a lot of rain, a wet month, and the river was in spate and the car went to the bottom. A diver had to go down . . . with a cable. And the police eventually winched it out . . ." Her voice trailed off.

He said gently, "When?"

"Three months ago."

"Not long."

"No. But there was so much to do, so much to see to. I don't know what's happened to the time. And then I caught this bug—a sort of 'flu, and I couldn't throw it off, so my mother-in-law said that she'd have the children in London and I came down here to stay with Alice."

"When are you going away again?"

"I don't know."

He was silent. After a little he picked up his glass and drained his beer. As he set it down he said, "Have you got a car here?"

"Yes." She pointed. "The blue Triumph."

"Then finish that drink and we'll go back to Penfolda." Virginia turned her head and stared at him. "Well, what's so extraordinary about that? It's dinner time. There are pasties in the oven. Do you want to come back and eat one with me?"

". . . Yes."

"Then come. I've got my Land-Rover. You can follow me."

"All right."

He stood up. "Come along, then."

3

She had been to Penfolda once before, only once, and then in the cool half-light of a spring evening ten years before.

"We've been invited to a party," Alice had announced over lunch that day.

Virginia's mother was immediately intrigued. She was immensely social and with a seventeen-year-old daughter to launch into society one only had to mention a party to capture her attention.

"How very nice! Where? Who with?"

Alice laughed at her. Alice was one of the few people who could laugh at Rowena Parsons and get away with it, but then Alice had known her for years.

"Don't get too excited. It's not really your sort of thing."

"My dear Alice, I don't know what you mean. Explain!"

"Well, it's a couple called Barnet. Amos and Fenella Barnet. You may have heard of him. He's a sculptor, very modern, very *avant-garde*. They've taken one of the old studios in Porthkerris, and they have a great number of rather unconventional children."

Without waiting to hear more Virginia said. "Why don't we go?" They sounded exactly the sort of people she was always longing to meet.

Mrs. Parsons allowed a small frown to show between her beautifully aligned eyebrows. "Is the party in the studio?" she inquired, obviously suspecting doctored drinks and doped cigarettes.

"No, it's out at Lanyon at a farm called Penfolda, some sort of a

barbecue on the cliffs. A camp fire and fried sausages . . ." Alice saw
that Virginia was longing to go. ". . . I think it might be rather fun."

"I think it sounds terrible," said Mrs. Parsons.

"I didn't think you'd want to come. But Tom and I might go, and
we'll take Virginia with us."

Mrs. Parsons turned her cool gaze upon her daughter. "Do you
want to go to a barbecue?"

Virginia shrugged. "It might be fun." She had learned, long ago,
that it never paid to be too enthusiastic about anything.

"Very well," said her mother, helping herself to lemon pudding. "If it's
your idea of an amusing evening and Alice and Tom don't mind taking
you along . . . but for heaven's sake wear something warm. It's bound
to be freezing. Far too cold, one would have thought, for a picnic."

She was right. It was cold. A clear turquoise evening with the shoulder of Carn Edvor silhouetted black against the western sky and a
chill inland wind to nip the air. Driving up the hill out of Porthkerris, Virginia looked back and saw the lights of the town twinkling far
below, the ink-black waters of the harbour brimming with shimmering reflections. Across the bay, from the distant headland, the lighthouse sent its warning signal. A flash. A pause. A flash. A longer
pause. Be careful. There's danger.

The evening ahead seemed full of possibilities. Suddenly excited,
Virginia turned and leaned forward, resting her chin on crossed arms
on the back of Alice's seat. The unpremeditated gesture was clumsy
and spontaneous, a reflection of natural high spirits that were normally battened firmly down under the influence of a domineering
mother.

"Alice, where is this place we're going?"

"Penfolda. It's a farm, just this side of Lanyon."

"Who lives there?"

"Mrs. Philips. She's a widow. And her son Eustace."

"What does he do?"

"He farms, silly. I told you it was a farm."

"Are they friends of the Barnets?"

"I suppose they must be. A lot of artists live out around this part of
the world. Though I've no idea how they could ever have met."

Tom said, "Probably at The Mermaid's."

"What's The Mermaid's?" Virginia asked.

"The Mermaid's Arms, the pub in Lanyon. On a Saturday night all the world and his wife go there for a drink and a get-together."

"Who else will be at the party?"

"Our guess is probably as good as yours."

"Haven't you *any* idea?"

"Well . . ." Alice did her best. ". . . Artists and writers and poets and hippies and drop-outs and farmers and perhaps one or two rather boring and conventional people like us."

Virginia gave her a hug. "You're not boring or conventional. You're super."

"You may not think we're quite so super at the end of the evening. You may hate it, so grit your teeth and reserve your judgment."

Virginia sat back, in the darkness of the car, hugging herself. *I shan't hate it.*

There were headlights like fireflies, coming from all directions, converging on Penfolda. From the road the farmhouse could be seen to be blazing with light. They joined the queue of assorted vehicles which bumped and groaned their way down a narrow, broken land and eventually were directed into a farmyard which had been turned temporarily into a car park. The air was full of voices and laughter as friends greeted friends, and already a steady trickle of people were making their way over a stone wall and down over the pasture fields towards the cliffs. Some were wrapped in rugs, some carried old-fashioned lanterns, some—Virginia was glad all over again that her mother had not come—a clanking bottle or two.

Someone said, "Tom! What are you doing here?" and Tom and Alice dropped back to wait for their friends, and Virginia went on, loving the feeling of being alone. All about her the soft, dark air smelled of peat and sea-wrack and wood-smoke. The sky was not yet empty of light and the sea was of so dark a blue that it was almost black. She went through a gap in a wall and saw, below her, at the bottom of the field, the golden flames of the fire, already ringed with lanterns and the shapes and shadows of about thirty people. As she came closer, faces sprang suddenly into focus, illuminated in firelight, laughing

and talking, everybody knowing everybody. There was a barrel of
beer, propped on a wooden stand, from which brimming glasses were
being continually filled, and there was the smell of potatoes cooking
and burning fat, and somebody had brought a guitar and begun to
play and gradually a few people gathered about him and raised uncertain voices in song.

> *There is a ship*
> *And she sails the sea,*
> *She's loaded deep*
> *As deep can be.*
> *But not as deep*
> *As the love I'm in ...*

A young man, running to pass Virginia, stumbled in the dusk and
bumped into her. "Sorry." He grabbed her arm, as much to steady
himself as her. He held his lantern high, the light in her face. "Who are
you?"

"Virginia."

"Virginia who?"

"Virginia Parsons."

He had long hair and a band around his forehead and looked like
an Apache.

"I thought it was a new face. Are you on your own?"

"N ... no. I've come with Alice and Tom ... but ..." She looked
back. "I've lost them ... they're coming ... somewhere ..."

"I'm Dominic Barnet ..."

"Oh ... it's your party ..."

"No, my father's, really. At least he's paid for the barrel of beer
which makes it his party and my mother bought the sausages. Come
on ... let's get something to drink," and he grabbed her arm with an
even firmer grip and marched her down into the seething, noisy firelit circle of activity. "Hey, Dad ... here's someone who hasn't got a
drink ..."

A huge bearded figure, medieval in the strange light, straightened
up from the tap of the barrel. "Well, here's one for her," he said, and

Virginia found herself holding an enormous mug of beer. "And here's a sausage." The young man whisked one nearly off a passing tray and handed it to her, impaled on a stick. Virginia took that too, and was just about to embark upon some polite social conversation when Dominic saw another familiar face across the circle of firelight, yelled "Mariana!" or some such name, and was away, leaving Virginia once more alone.

She searched in the darkness for the Lingards but could not find them. But everyone else was sitting, so she sat too, with the enormous beer mug in one hand and the sausage, still too hot to eat, in the other. The firelight scorched her face and the wind was cold on her back and blew her hair all over her face. She took a mouthful of beer. She had never drunk beer before and immediately wanted to sneeze. She did so, enormously and from behind her an amused voice said, "Bless you."

Virginia recovered from the sneeze and said, "Thank you," and looked up to see who had blessed her, and saw a large young man in corduroys and rubber boots and a massive Norwegian sweater. He was grinning down at her and the firelight turned his brown face to the colour of copper.

She said, "It was the beer that made me sneeze."

He squatted beside her, took the mug gently from her hand and laid it on the ground between them. "You might sneeze again and then you'd spill it all and that would be a waste."

"Yes."

"You have to be a friend of the Barnets."

"Why do you say that?"

"I haven't seen you before."

"No, I'm not. I came with the Lingards."

"Alice and Tom? Are they here?"

"Yes, somewhere."

He sounded so pleased that the Lingards were here that Virginia fully expected him to go, then and there, in search of them, but instead he settled himself more comfortably on the grass beside her, and seemed quite happy to remain silent, simply watching in some amusement, the rest of the party. Virginia ate her sausage, and when she had finished and he still had said nothing, she decided that she would try again.

"Are you a friend of the Barnets?"

"Um . . ." His attention interrupted, he turned to look at her, his eyes a clear and un-winking blue. "Sorry?"

"I wondered if you were a friend of the Barnets, that's all."

He laughed. "I'd better be. These are my fields they're desecrating."

"Then you must be Eustace Philips."

He considered this. "Yes," he said at last. "I suppose I must be."

Soon after that he was called away . . . some of his Guernseys had wandered in from a neighbouring field and a batty girl who had drunk too much wine thought that she was being attacked by a bull and had thrown a pretty fit of hysterics. So Eustace went to put the matter to rights, and Virginia was presently claimed by Alice and Tom, and although she spent the rest of the evening watching out for him, she did not see Eustace Philips again.

The party, however, was a wild and memorable success. Near midnight, with the beer finished, and the bottles going round, and the food all eaten and the fire piled with driftwood until the flames sprang twenty feet high or more, Alice suggested gently that perhaps it might be a good idea if they went home.

"Your mother will be sitting up thinking you've either been raped or fallen into the sea. And Tom's got to be at the office at nine in the morning and it really is getting bitterly cold. What do you say? Have you had enough? Have you had fun?"

"Such fun," said Virginia, reluctant to leave.

But it was time to go. They walked in silence, away from the firelight and the noise, up the slopes of the fields towards the farmhouse.

Now, only one light burned from a downstairs window, but a full moon, white as a plate, sailed high in the sky, filling all the night with silver light. As they came over the wall into the farmyard, a door in the house opened, yellow light spilled out over the cobbles, and a voice called out across the darkness. "Tom! Alice! Come and have a cup of tea or coffee—something to warm you up before you go home."

"Hallo, Eustace." Tom went towards the house. "We thought you'd gone to bed."

"I'm not staying down on the cliffs till dawn, that's for certain. Would you like a drink?"

"I'd like a whisky," said Tom.

"And I'd like tea," said Alice. "What a good idea! We're frozen. Are you sure it's not too much trouble?"

"My mother's still up, she'd like to see you. She's got the kettle on . . ."

They all went into the house, into a low-ceilinged, panelled hall, with a flagged slate floor covered with bright rugs. The beams of the roof scarcely cleared the top of Eustace Philips's head.

Alice was unbuttoning her coat. "Eustace, have you met Virginia? She's staying with us at Wheal House."

"Yes, of course—we said hallo," but he scarcely looked at her. "Come into the kitchen, it's the warmest place in the house. Mother, here are the Lingards. Alice wants a cup of tea. And Tom wants whisky and . . ." He looked down at Virginia. "What do you want?"

"I'd like tea."

Alice and Mrs. Philips at once busied themselves, Mrs. Philips with the teapot and the kettle, and Alice taking cups and saucers down from the shelves of the painted dresser. As they did this they discussed the Barnets' party, laughing about the girl who thought the cow was a bull, and the two men settled themselves at the scrubbed kitchen table with tumblers and a soda siphon and a bottle of Scotch.

Virginia sat too, wedged into the broad window-set at the head of the table, and listening to, without actually hearing, the pleasant blur of voices. She found that she was very sleepy, dazed by the warmth and comfort of the Penfolda kitchen after the bitter cold of the outdoors, and slightly fuzzy from the unaccustomed draught beer.

Sunk into the folds of her coat, hands deep in its pockets, she looked about her and decided that never had she been in a room so welcoming, so secure. There were beams in the ceiling, with old iron hooks for smoking hams, and deep window-sills crammed with flowering geraniums. There was a huge stove where the kettle simmered, and a cane chair with a cat curled in its seat, and there was a Grain Merchant's calendar and curtains of checked cotton and the warm smell of baking bread.

Mrs. Philips was small as her son was large, grey-haired, very neat. She looked as though she had never stopped working from the day she was born and would have it no other way, and as she and Alice moved about the kitchen, deft and quick, gossiping gently about the unconventional Barnets, Virginia watched her and wished that she could have had a mother just like that. Calm and good-humoured with a great comforting kitchen and a kettle always on the boil for a cup of tea.

The tea made, the two women finally joined the others around the table. Mrs. Philips poured a cup for Virginia and handed it to her, and Virginia sat up, pulling her hands out of her pockets and took it, remembering to say "Thank you."

Mrs. Philips laughed. "You're sleepy," she said.

"I know," said Virginia. They were all looking at her, but she stirred her tea and would not look up because she did not want to have to meet that blue and disconcerting gaze.

But eventually it was time to go. With their coats on again, they stood, crowded in the little hallway. The Lingards and Mrs. Philips were already at the open front door when Eustace spoke from behind Virginia.

"Goodbye," he said.

"Oh." Confused, she turned. "Goodbye." She began to put out her hand, but perhaps he did not see it, for he did not take it. "Thank you for letting me come."

He looked amused. "It was a pleasure. You'll have to come back again, another time."

And all the way home, she hugged his words close as though they were a marvellous present that he had given her. But she never came back to Penfolda.

Until today, ten years later, and a July afternoon of piercing beauty. Roadside ditches brimmed with ragged robin and bright yellow coltsfoot, the gorse was aflame and the bracken of the cliff-tops lay emerald against a summer sea the colour of hyacinths.

So engrossed had she been in her business of the day, collecting keys, and finding the cottage at Bosithick, and considering such practical questions as cookers and fridges and bedclothes and china, that all the heaven-sent morning had somehow gone unnoticed. But now it was part of what had suddenly happened and Virginia remembered long ago, how the lighthouse had flashed out over the dark sea, and she had been, for no apparent reason, suddenly excited and warm with a marvellous anticipation.

But you're not seventeen any longer. You're a woman, twenty-seven years old and independent, with two children and a car and a house in Scotland. Life doesn't hold that sort of surprise any longer. Everything is different. Nothing ever stays the same.

At the top of the lane which led down to Penfolda was a wooden platform for the milk churns, and the way sloped steep and winding between high stone walls. Hawthorns leaned distorted by the winter winds, and as Virginia followed the back of Eustace's Land-Rover around the corner of the house, two collies appeared, black and white, barking and raising a din that sent the brown Leghorn hens squawking and scuttling for shelter.

Eustace had parked his Land-Rover in the shade of the barn and was already out of it, toeing the dogs gently out of the way. Virginia put her car behind his and got out as well, and the collies instantly made for her, barking and leaping about and trying to put their front paws on her knees and stretching up to lick her face.

"Get down . . . get down, you devils!"

"I don't mind . . ." She fondled their slim heads, their thick coats. "What are their names?"

"Beaker and Ben. That's Beaker and this is Ben . . . shut up, you, boy! They do this every time . . ."

His manner was robust and cheerful as though during the course of the short drive he had decided that this was the best attitude to adopt if the rest of the day was not to become a sort of wake for Anthony Keile. And Virginia, who did not in the least want this to happen, gratefully took her cue from him. The dogs' noisy welcome helped to break the ice, and it was in an entirely natural and easy fashion that they all went up the cobbled path together, and into the house.

She saw the beams, the flagged floor, the rugs. Unchanged.

"I remember this."

There was a smell of hot pasties, mouth-watering. He went in through the kitchen door, leaving Virginia to follow behind, and across to the stove, whisking an oven cloth off a rack as he passed, and crouching to open the oven.

"They aren't burnt, are they?" she asked anxiously. Fragrant smoky smells issued out.

"No, just right."

He closed the oven door and stood up.

She said, "Did you make them?"

"Me? You must be joking."

"Who did?"

"Mrs. Thomas, my housekeeper ... like a drink, would you?" He went to open a fridge, to take a can of beer from the inside of the door.

"No, thank you."

He smiled. "I haven't got any Coke."

"I don't want a drink."

As they spoke, Virginia looked about her, terrified that anything in this marvellous room should have been altered, that Eustace might have changed something, moved the furniture, painted the walls. But it was just as she remembered. The scrubbed table pulled into the bay of the window, the geraniums on the window-sills, the dresser packed with bright china. After all these years it remained the epitome of everything a proper kitchen should be, the heart of the house.

When they had taken over Kirkton and were doing it up, cellar to attic, she had tried to get a kitchen like the Penfolda one. Somewhere comfortable and warm where the family would congregate, and drink tea and gossip round the scrubbed table.

"Who wants to go into a kitchen?" Anthony had asked, not understanding at all.

"Everybody. A farmhouse kitchen's like a living-room."

"Well, I'm not going to live in any kitchen, I'll tell you that."

And he ordered stainless steel fitments and bright Formica worktops and a black and white chequered floor that showed every mark and was the devil to keep clean.

Now Virginia leaned against the table and said with deep satisfaction, "I was afraid it would have changed, but it's just the same."

"Why should it have changed?"

"No reason. I was just afraid. Things do change. Eustace, Alice told me that your mother had died ... I'm sorry."

"Yes. Two years ago. She had a fall. Got pneumonia." He chucked the empty can neatly into a trashbucket and turned to survey her, propping his length against the edge of the sink. "And how about your own mother?"

His voice held no expression; she could detect no undertones of sarcasm or dislike.

"She died, Eustace. She became very ill a couple of years after Anthony and I were married. It was dreadful, because she was ill for so long. And it was difficult, because she was in London and I was at Kirkton . . . I couldn't be with her all the time."

"And I suppose you were all the family she had?"

"Yes. That was part of the trouble. I used to visit her as often as I could, but in the end we had to bring her up to Scotland, and eventually she went into a nursing home in Relkirk, and she died there."

"That's bad."

"Yes. And she was so young. It's a funny thing when your mother dies. You never really grow up till that happens." She amended this. "At least, I suppose that's how some people feel. You were grown up long before then."

"I don't know about that," said Eustace. "But I know what you mean."

"Anyway, it was all over years ago. Don't let's talk about miserable things. Tell me about you, and Mrs. Thomas. Do you know, Alice Lingard said you'd either have a domesticated mistress or a sexy housekeeper? I can't wait to meet her."

"Well, you'll have to. She's gone to Penzance to see her sister."

"Does she live at Penfolda?"

"She has the cottage at the other end of the house. This used to be three cottages, you know, in the old days, before my grandfather bought the place. Three families lived here and farmed a few acres. Probably had half a dozen cows for milking and sent their sons down the tin mines to keep the wolf from the door."

"Two days ago," said Virginia, "I drove out to Lanyon and sat on the hill, and there were combine harvesters out, and men haymaking. I thought one of them was probably you."

"Probably was."

She said, "I thought you'd be married."

"I'm not."

"I know. Alice Lingard said that you weren't."

After he had finished his beer, he took knives and forks from a drawer and began to lay the table but Virginia stopped him. "It's too nice indoors. Couldn't we eat the pasties in the garden?"

Eustace looked amazed, but said, "All right," and found her a basket for the knives and forks and plates and the salt and pepper and glasses, and he eased the piping hot pasties out of the oven on to a great flowered china dish, and they went out of a side door into the sunshine and the untidy little farmhouse garden. The grass needed cutting and the flower-beds were brimming with cheerful cottage flowers, and there was a washing line, flapping with bright white sheets and pillow-cases.

Eustace had no garden furniture so they sat on the grass, tall with daisies and plantains, with the dishes of their picnic spread about them.

The pasties were enormous, and Virginia had only eaten half of hers, and was defeated by the remainder, by the time that Eustace, propped on an elbow, had consumed the whole length of his.

She said. "I can't eat any more," and gave him the rest of hers, which he took and placidly demolished. He said, through a mouthful of pastry and potato: "If I weren't so hungry, I'd make you eat it, fatten you up a bit."

"I don't want to be fat."

"But you're much too thin. You were always small enough, but now you look as though a puff of wind would blow you away. And you've cut your hair. It used to be long, right down your back, flowing about in the wind." He put out a hand and circled her wrist with his thumb and forefinger. "There's nothing of you."

"Perhaps it was the 'flu."

"I thought you'd be enormous after all these years of eating porridge and herrings and haggis."

"You mean, that's what people eat in Scotland."

"It's what I've been told." He let go of her wrist and peacefully finished the pasty, and then began to collect the plates and the basket and carry everything indoors. Virginia made movements as though to help, but he told her to stay where she was, so she did this, lying back in the grass and staring at the straight grey roof on the barn, and the seagulls perched there, and the scudding shapes of small, white fine-weather clouds, blown from the sea across the incredibly blue sky.

Eustace returned, carrying cigarettes and green eating apples and a Thermos of tea. Virginia lay where she was, and he tossed her an apple and she caught it, and he sat beside her again, unscrewing the cap of the Thermos.

"Tell me about Scotland."

Virginia turned the apple, cool and smooth, in her hands.

"What shall I tell you?"

"What did your husband do?"

"How do you mean?"

"Didn't he have a job?"

"Not exactly. Not a nine-to-five job. But he'd been left this estate..."

"Kirkton?"

"... Yes, Kirkton ... by an uncle. A great big house and about a thousand acres of land, and after we'd got the house in order, that seemed to take up most of his time. He grew trees, and farmed in a rather gentlemanly way ... I mean, he had a grieve—a bailiff you'd call him—who lived in the farmhouse. Mr. McGregor. It was he who really did most of the work, but Anthony was always occupied. I mean ..." she finished feebly ... "he seemed to be able to fill in his days."

Shooting five days a week in the season, fishing and playing golf. Driving north for the stalking, taking off for St. Moritz for a couple of months every winter. It was no good trying to explain a man like Anthony Keile to a man like Eustace Philips. They belonged to different worlds.

"And what about Kirkton now?"

"I told you, the grieve looks after it."

"And the house?"

"It's empty. At least, the furniture's all there, but there's nobody living in it."

"Are you going back to this empty house?"

"I suppose so. Some time."

"What about the children?"

"They're in London, with Anthony's mother."

"Why aren't they with you?" asked Eustace, sounding not critical, merely curious, as though he simply wished to know.

"It just seemed a good idea, my coming away on my own. Alice Lingard wrote and asked me to come, and it seemed a good idea, that's all."

"Why didn't you bring the children too?"

"Oh, I don't know . . ." Even to herself her own voice sounded elaborately casual, unconvincing. "Alice doesn't have any children and her house isn't geared for them . . . I mean, everything's rather special and rare and breakable. You know how it is."

"In fact, I don't, but go on."

"Anyway, Lady Keile likes having them with her . . ."

"Lady Keile?"

"Anthony's mother. And Nanny likes going there because she used to work for Lady Keile. She was Anthony's own Nanny when he was a little boy."

"But I thought the children were quite big."

"Cara's eight and Nicholas is six."

"But why do they have to have a Nanny? Why can't you look after them?"

Over the years Virginia had asked herself that question time without number, and had come up with no sort of an answer, but for Eustace to voice it, unasked, out of the blue, filled her with a perverse resentment.

"What do you mean?"

"Just what I say."

"I do look after them. I mean, I see a lot of them . . ."

"If they've just lost their father, surely the one person they need to be with is their mother, not a grandmother and an old inherited Nanny. They'll think everybody's deserting them."

"They won't think anything of the sort."

"If you're so sure, why are you getting so hot under the collar?"

"Because I don't like you interfering, airing your opinions about something you know nothing about."

"I know about you."

"What about me?"

"I know your infinite capacity for being pushed around."

"And who pushes me around?"

"I wouldn't know for sure." She realized with some astonishment that, in a cold way, he was becoming as angry as she. "But at a rough guess I would say your mother-in-law. Perhaps she took over where your own mother left off?"

"Don't you dare to speak about my mother like that."

"But it's true, isn't it?"

"No, it's not true."

"Then get your children down here. It's inhuman leaving them in London for the summer holidays, in weather like this, when they should be running wild by the sea and in the fields. Take your finger out, ring up your mother-in-law and tell her to put them on a train. And if Alice Lingard doesn't want them at Wheal House, because she's afraid of the ornaments getting broken, then take them to a pub, or rent a cottage . . ."

"That's exactly what I intend doing, and I didn't need you to tell me."

"Then you'd better start looking for one."

"I already have."

He was momentarily silenced, and she thought with satisfaction: That took the wind out of his sails.

But only momentarily. "Have you found anything?"

"I looked at one house this morning but it was impossible."

"Where?"

"Here. In Lanyon." He waited for her to tell him. "It was called Bosithick," she added ungraciously.

"Bosithick!" He appeared delighted. "But that's a marvellous house."

"It's a terrible house"

"Terrible?" He could not believe his ears. "You do mean the cottage up the hill where Aubrey Crane used to live? The one that the Kernows inherited from his old aunt."

"That's the one, and it's creepy and quite impossible."

"What does creepy mean? Haunted?"

"I don't know. Just creepy."

"If it's haunted by the ghost of Aubrey Crane you might have quite an amusing time. My mother remembered him, said he was a dear man. And very fond of children," he added with what seemed to Virginia a classic example of a *non sequitur.*

"I don't care what sort of a man he was, I'm not going to take the house."

"Why not?"

"Because I'm not."

"Give me three good reasons . . ."

Virginia lost her patience. "Oh, for heaven's sake . . ." She made as if to get to her feet, but Eustace, with unexpected speed for such a large man, caught her wrist in his hand and pulled her back on to the grass. She looked angrily into his eyes and saw them cold as blue stones.

"Three good reasons," he said again.

She looked down at his hand on her arm. He made no effort to move it and she said, "There's no fridge."

"I'll lend you a meat-safe. Reason number two."

"I told you. It's got a spooky atmosphere. The children have never lived anywhere like that. They'd be frightened."

"Not unless they're as hen-brained as their mother. Now, number three."

Desperately she tried to think up some good, watertight reason, something that would convince Eustace of her nameless horror of the odd little house on the hill. But all she came out with was a string of petty excuses, each sounding more feeble than the last. "It's too small, and it's dirty, and where would I wash the children's things, and I don't even know if there's an iron for the ironing or a lawn-mower to cut the grass. And there's no garden, just a sort of washing green place, and inside all the furniture is so depressing and . . ."

He interrupted her. "These aren't reasons, Virginia, and you know they're not. They're just a lot of bloody excuses."

"Bloody excuses for *what?*"

"For not having a show-down with your mother-in-law or the old Nanny or possibly both. For making a scene and asserting yourself and bringing your own children up the way you want them to go."

Fury at him caught in her throat, a great lump that rendered her speechless. She felt the blood surge to her cheeks, she began to tremble, but although he must have seen all this, he went calmly on, saying all the terrible things that the voice in the back of her head had been saying for years, but to which she had never had the moral courage to pay any attention.

"I don't think you can give a damn for your children. You don't want to be bothered with them. Someone else has always done the washing and the ironing and you're not going to start now. You're too bloody idle to take them for picnics and read them books and put them to bed. It's really nothing to do with Bosithick. Whatever house you found, you'd be sure to find something wrong with it. Any excuse would do provided you never have to admit to yourself that you can't be bloody bothered to take care of your own children."

Before the last word was out of his mouth, she was on her feet, tearing her arm free of his grip.

"It's not true! It's none of it true! I do want them! I've been wanting them ever since I got here . . . !"

"Then get them here, you little fool . . ." He was on his feet too, and they were shouting at each other across three feet of grass as though it were a desert.

"That's what I'm going to do. That's just exactly what I'm going to do."

"I'll believe that when you do it!"

She turned and fled and was into her car before she remembered her handbag, still lying on the kitchen table. By now in floods of tears, she was out of the car and running into the house to retrieve it before Eustace reached her again. Then back to the car and turning it furiously, dangerously in the narrow confines of the farmyard, then back up the lane, with a roar of the engine and a great spattering of loose gravel from the back wheels.

"Virginia!"

Through tears, through the driving-mirror she saw him standing far behind her. She jammed her foot on the accelerator and swung out on to the main road without bothering to wait and see if anything was coming. By good chance it wasn't, but she didn't slow down all the way back to Porthkerris, down into the town and up the other

side, parking the car on the double yellow lines outside the solicitors'
office and leaving it there while she ran inside.

This time she did not ring the bell, nor wait for Miss Leddra, but
went, like the wind, through the outer office to fling open wide the
door of Mr. Williams's room, where Mr. Williams was rudely interrupted in the course of interviewing an autocratic old lady from Truro
about the seventh set of alterations to her will.

Both Mr. Williams and the old lady, silenced by astonishment,
stared, open-mouthed. Mr. Williams, recovering first, began to scram-
ble to his feet. "Mrs. Keile!" But before he could say another word
Virginia had flung the keys of Bosithick on to his desk and said, "I'll
take it. I'll take it right away. And as soon's I've got my children, I'm
moving in!"

4

Alice said, "I'm sorry Virginia, but I think you're making the most terrible mistake. What's more, it's a classic mistake and one so many people make when they suddenly find themselves alone in the world. You're acting on impulse, you haven't really thought about this at all . . ."

"I have thought about it."

"But the children are fine, you know they are, settled and happy with Nanny and your mother-in-law. The life they're leading is simply an extension of life at Kirkton, all the things they know and that helps them to feel secure. Their father's dead, and nothing's ever going to be the same for them again. But if there have to be changes, at least let them happen slowly, gradually; let Cara and Nicholas have time to get used to them."

"They're my children."

"But you've never looked after them. You've never had them on your own, except the odd times when Nanny could be persuaded to take a holiday. They'll exhaust you, and honestly, Virginia, at the moment I don't think you're physically capable of doing it. After all, that's why you came here, to recuperate from that loathsome 'flu, and generally have a little peace and quiet, give yourself time to get over the bad things that have been happening. Don't deprive yourself of that. You're going to need all your resources when you do eventually go back to Kirkton and start picking up the threads and learning to live without Anthony."

"I'm not going to Kirkton. I'm going to Bosithick. I've already paid the first week's rent."

Alice's expression stopped being patient and became exasperated.

"But it's so ridiculous! Look, if you feel so strongly about having the children down here, then have them by all means, they can stay here, but for heaven's sake let Nanny come too."

Only yesterday the idea could have been tempting. But now Virginia never even let herself consider it.

"I've made up my mind."

"But why didn't you *tell* me? Why didn't you discuss it with me?"

"I don't know. It was just something I had to do on my own."

"And where *is* Bosithick?"

"It's on the Lanyon road . . . You can't see it from the road, but it's got a sort of tower . . ."

"The place where Aubrey Crane lived? But, Virginia, it's ghastly. There's nothing there but moor and wind and cliffs. You'll be totally isolated!"

Virginia tried to turn it into a joke. "You'll have to come and see me. Make sure the children and I aren't driving each other slowly insane."

But Alice did not laugh, and Virginia, seeing her frown and the disapproving set of her mouth, was suddenly, astonishingly reminded of her own mother. It was as though Alice was no longer Virginia's contemporary, her friend, but had swung back a generation and from that lofty height was telling the young Virginia that she was being a fool. But perhaps, after all, this was not so strange. She had known Rowena Parsons long before Virginia was born, and the fact that she had no children of her own to contend with meant that her attitudes and opinions remained rigidly unchanged.

She said at last, "It isn't that I want to interfere, you know that. But I've known you all your life, and I can't stand to one side and watch you do this insane thing."

"What's so insane about having your children on holiday with you?"

"It's not just that, Virginia, and you know it. If you take them away from Lady Keile and Nanny without their approval, which I doubt very much you'll get, there's going to be one devil of a row."

Virginia felt sick at the thought of it. "Yes, I know."

"Nanny will probably take the most terrible umbrage and give in her notice."

"I know . . ."

"Your mother-in-law will do everything she can to stop you."

"I know that too."

Alice stared at her, as though she were staring at a stranger. Then suddenly, she shrugged and laughed, in a hopeless sort of way. "I don't understand. What made you suddenly so determined?"

Virginia had said nothing about her encounter with Eustace Philips and had no intention of doing so.

"Nothing. Nothing in particular."

"It must be the sea air," said Alice. "Extraordinary what it does for people." She picked a fallen newspaper off the floor, began folding it meticulously. "When are you going to London?"

"Tomorrow."

"And Lady Keile?"

"I'll phone her tonight. And Alice, I am sorry. And thank you for being so kind."

"I haven't been kind, I've been critical and disapproving. But somehow, I always think of you as someone young and helpless. I feel responsible for you."

"I'm twenty-seven. And I'm not helpless. And I'm responsible for myself."

Nanny answered the telephone. "Yes?"

"Nanny?"

"Yes."

"It's Mrs. Keile."

"Oh, hallo! Do you want to speak to Lady Keile?"

"Is she there? . . ."

"Just a moment and I'll get her."

"Nanny."

"Yes."

"How are the children?"

"Oh, they're very well. Having a lovely time. Just gone to bed." (This was slipped in quickly in case Virginia should ask to speak to them.)

"Is it hot?"

"Oh, yes. Lovely. Perfect weather. Hold on and I'll tell Lady Keile you're there."

There were the sounds of Nanny putting down the receiver, her footsteps going across the hall, her distant voice. "Lady Keile!"

Virginia waited. *If I was a woman who was taking to drink I would have one in my hand, right now. A great tall tumbler of dark-coloured whisky.* But she wasn't and her stomach lay heavy with impending doom.

More footsteps, sharp neat, unmistakable. The receiver was lifted once more.

"Virginia."

"Yes, it's me."

The situation was hideously complicated by the fact that Virginia had never known what to call her mother-in-law. "Call me Mother," she had said kindly, as soon as Virginia and Anthony were married, but somehow this was impossible. And "Lady Keile" was worse. Virginia had compromised by only corresponding by postcard or telegram, and always calling her "you."

"How nice to hear you, dear. How are you feeling?"

"I'm very well . . ."

"And the weather? I believe you're having a heatwave."

"Yes, it's unbelievable. Look . . ."

"How is Alice?"

"She's very well, too . . ."

"And the darling children, they've been swimming today—the Turners have got a delicious pool in their garden, and invited Cara and Nicholas over for the afternoon. What a pity they're in bed; why didn't you call earlier?"

Virginia said, "I've got something to tell you."

"Yes?"

She closed her hand around the receiver until her knuckles ached. "I've been able to find a little cottage, quite near here. It's near the sea, and I thought it would be nice for the children if they came down and we spent the rest of the holidays together."

She paused, waiting for comment but there was only silence.

"The thing is, the weather is so beautiful and I feel so guilty enjoying it all on my own . . . and it would be good for them to have some sea air before we all have to go back to Scotland and they have to go back to school."

Lady Keile said, "A cottage? But I thought you were staying with Alice Lingard?"

"Yes, I am. I have been. I'm calling from Wheal House now. But I've taken this cottage."

"I don't understand."

"I want the children to come down and spend the rest of the holidays with me. I'll come up tomorrow in the train to fetch them."

"But what sort of a cottage?"

"Just a cottage. A holiday cottage . . ."

"Well, if that's what you want . . ." Virginia began to breathe a sigh of relief. ". . . But it seems hard luck on Nanny. It's not often she gets the chance of being in London and seeing all her own friends." The relief swiftly died. Virginia went back into the attack again.

"Nanny doesn't have to come."

Lady Keile was confused. "I'm sorry, the line's not very clear. I thought you said Nanny didn't have to come."

"She doesn't. I can look after the children. There's not room for her anyway. I mean there isn't a bedroom for her, or a nursery . . . and it's terribly isolated, and she'd hate it."

"You mean you intend taking the children *away* from Nanny?"

"Yes."

"But she'll be most terribly upset."

"Yes, I'm afraid she will, but . . ."

"Virginia . . ." Lady Keile's voice was upset, distressed. "Virginia, we can't talk about this over the telephone."

Virginia imagined Nanny on the upstairs landing, listening to the one-sided conversation.

"We don't need to. I'm coming up to London tomorrow. I'll be with you about five o'clock. We can talk about it then."

"I think," said Lady Keile, "that that would be best."

And she rang off.

The next morning Virginia drove to Penzance, left her car in the station park and caught the train to London. It was another hot, cloudless morning and she had not had time to reserve a seat, and, despite the fact that she managed to get hold of a porter and tip him handsomely, he could only find her an empty corner in a carriage that was already uncomfortably full. Her fellow passengers were going home at the end of their annual holidays, grumpy and disconsolate at the thought of returning to work, and resentful at leaving the sea and the beaches on such a perfect day.

There was a family, a father and mother and two children. The baby slept damply in its mother's arms, but as the sun climbed higher into the unwinking sky and the train rattled northwards through the shimmering heat of a midsummer noon, the elder child became more and more fractious, whining, grizzling, never still, and grinding his dirty sandalled feet on to Virginia's every time he wanted to look out the window. At one point, in order to keep the child quiet, his father bought him an orangeade, but no sooner was the bottle opened than the train lurched and the entire contents went all over the front of Virginia's dress.

The child was promptly slapped by his distracted mother and roared. The baby woke up and added his wails to his brother's. The father said, "Now look what you've done," and gave the child a shake for good measure, and Virginia, trying to mop herself up with face tissues, protested that it didn't matter, it couldn't be helped, it didn't matter at all.

After a good deal of screaming the child subsided into hiccuping sobs. A bottle was produced from somewhere and stuffed into the baby's mouth. It sucked for a bit, and then stopped sucking, struggled into a sitting position and was sick.

And Virginia lit a cigarette and looked firmly out of the window and prayed, "Don't let Cara and Nicholas ever be like that. Don't let them ever be like that on a railway journey, otherwise I shall go stark, staring mad."

London was airless and stuffy, the great cavern of Paddington Station hideous with noise and aimless, hurrying crowds. As soon as she was off the train Virginia, carrying her suitcase, and filthy and crum-

pled in her stained, sticky dress, walked the length of the platform to
the booking-office and, like a secret agent making sure of his escape
route, bought tickets and reserved three seats on the Riviera for the
following morning. Only then did she return to the taxi rank, wait in
the long queue, and finally capture a cab to take her home.

"Thirty-two Melton Gardens, please. Kensington."

"OK. 'op in."

They went down by Sussex Gardens, across the park. The brown
grass was littered with picnicking families, children in scanty clothes,
couples entwined beneath the shade of trees. In Brompton Road there
were window boxes bright with flowers, shop windows filled with
clothes "For Cruising," the first of the rush hour crowds was being
sucked, a steady stream of humanity, down Knightsbridge Underground.

The cab turned into the network of quiet squares that lay behind
Kensington High Street, edged down narrow roads lined with parked
cars, and finally turned the corner into Melton Gardens.

"It's the house by the pillar box."

The taxi stopped. Virginia got out, put her case on the pavement,
opened her bag for the fare. The driver said, "Thanks very much," and
snapped up his flag, and Virginia picked up her case and turned towards
the house and, as she did so, the black-painted door opened and her
mother-in-law waited to let her in.

She was tall, slim, immensely good-looking. Even on this breathless day she looked cool and uncrushed, not a wrinkle in her linen
dress, not a hair out of place.

Virginia went up the steps towards her.

"How clever of you to know I was here."

"I was looking out of the drawing-room window. I saw the taxi."

Her expression was friendly, smiling, but quite implacable, like the
matron of a lunatic asylum come to admit a new patient. They kissed,
touching cheeks.

"Did you have a terrible journey?" She closed the door behind
them. The cool, pale-coloured hall smelt of beeswax and roses. At the
far end steps led down to the glass side door, and beyond it could be
seen the garden, the chestnut tree, the children's swing.

"Yes, it was ghastly. I feel filthy and a revolting child spilt orange juice all over me." The house was silent. "Where are the children?"

Lady Keile began to lead the way upstairs to the drawing-room. "They're out with Nanny. I thought perhaps it would be better. They won't be long, not more than half an hour. That should give us time to get this all thrashed out."

Treading behind her, Virginia said nothing. Lady Keile reached the top of the stairs, crossed the small landing and went in through the drawing-room door and Virginia followed her, and, despite her anxiety of mind, was struck, as always, by the timeless beauty of the room, the perfect proportions of the long windows which faced out over the street, open today, the fine net curtains stirring. There were long mirrors, filling the room with reflected light and these gave back images of highly polished antique furniture, tall cabinets of blue and white Meissen plates, and the flowers with which Lady Keile had always surrounded herself.

They faced each other across the pale, fitted carpet. Lady Keile said, "We may as well be comfortable," and lowered herself, straight as a ramrod, into a formal, wide-lapped French chair.

Virginia sat too, on the very edge of the sofa, and tried not to feel like a domestic servant being interviewed for a job. She said, "There really isn't anything to thrash out, you know."

"I thought I must have misunderstood you on the telephone last night."

"No, you didn't misunderstand me. I decided two days ago that I wanted the children with me. I decided it was ridiculous, me being in Cornwall and them in London, specially during the summer holidays. So I went to a solicitor and I found this little house. And I've paid the rent and I've got the keys. I can move in right away."

"Does Alice Lingard know about this?"

"Of course. And she offered to have the children at Wheal House, but by then I'd committed myself and couldn't go back."

"But Virginia, you *surely* can't mean that you want them without Nanny?"

"Yes, I do."

"But you'll never manage."

"I shall have to try."

"What you mean is that you want the children to yourself."

"Yes."

"Are you sure you aren't being a little . . . selfish?"

"*Selfish?*"

"Yes, selfish. You're not thinking of the children, are you? Only yourself."

"Perhaps I am thinking of myself, but I'm thinking of the children too."

"You can't be if you intend taking them away from Nanny."

"Have you spoken to her?"

"I had to, of course. She had to have some idea of what I understood you wanted to do. But I hoped I would be able to change your mind."

"What did she say?"

"She didn't say very much. But I could tell that she was very upset."

"Yes, I'm sure."

"You must think of Nanny, Virginia. Those children are her life. You must consider her."

"With the best will in the world I don't see that she comes into this."

"Of course she comes into it. She comes into everything that we do. Why, she's family, she's been part of the family for years, ever since Anthony was a tiny boy . . . and the way she's looked after those babies of yours, she's devoted herself, given her life to them. And you say she doesn't come into this."

"She wasn't my Nanny," said Virginia. "She didn't look after me when I was a little girl. You can't expect me to feel quite the same about her as you do."

"You really mean to say you feel no sort of loyalty towards her? After letting her bring up your children? After virtually living with her for eight years at Kirkton? I must say you fooled me. I always thought there was a very happy atmosphere between you."

"If there was a happy atmosphere it was because of me. It was because I gave in to Nanny over every little thing, just to keep the peace. Because if she didn't get her own way, she would go into a sulk that would last for days, and I simply couldn't bear it."

"I always imagined you were the mistress of your own home."

"Well, you were wrong. I wasn't. And even if I'd plucked up the courage to have a row with Nanny, and asked her to leave, Anthony would never have heard of it. He thought the sun rose and fell on her head."

At the mention of her son's name Lady Keile had gone a little pale. Her shoulders were consciously straight, her clasped hands tightened in her lap. She said, icily, "And I suppose now that no longer has to be considered."

Virginia was instantly repentant. "I didn't mean that. You know I didn't mean that. But I'm left now. I'm on my own. The children are all I have. Perhaps I'm being selfish, but I need them. I need them so badly with me. I've missed them so much since I've been away."

Outside, across the street, a car drew up, a man began to argue, a woman answered him in anger, her voice shrill with annoyance. As though the noise were more than she could stand, Lady Keile stood up and went over to close the window.

She said, "I shall miss them too."

If we had ever been close, thought Virginia, I could go now and put my arms around her and give her the comfort she is longing for. But it was not possible. Affection had existed between them, and respect. But never love, never familiarity.

"Yes, I'm sure you will. You've been so wonderfully good to them, and to me. And I'm sorry."

Her mother-in-law turned from the window, brisk again, emotion controlled. "I think," she said, making for the bell-pull which hung at the side of the fireplace, "that it would be a good idea if we were to have a cup of tea."

The children returned at half past five. The front door opened and shut and their voices rose from the hall. Virginia laid down her teacup and sat quite still. Lady Keile waited until the footsteps had passed the landing outside the drawing-room door and were on their way upstairs to the nursery. Then she got up and went across the drawing-room and opened the door.

"Cara. Nicholas."

"Hallo, Granny."

"There is someone here to see you."

"Who?"

"A lovely surprise. Come and see."

Much later, after the children had gone upstairs for their bath and supper, after Virginia herself had bathed and changed into a clean cool silk dress, and before the gong rang for dinner, she went upstairs to the nursery to see Nanny.

She found her alone, tidying away the children's supper things and straightening the room before she settled to her nightly session with the television.

Not that the room needed straightening, but Nanny could not relax until every cushion was plump and straight on the sofa, every toy put away, and the children's dirty clothes discarded, and clean ones set out for the following morning. She had always been like this, revelling in the orderly pattern of her own rigid routine. And she had always looked the same, a neat spare woman, over sixty now, but with scarcely a trace of grey in her dark hair which she wore drawn back and fastened in a bun. She appeared to be ageless, the type that would continue, unchanging, until she was an old woman when she would suddenly become senile and die.

She looked up as Virginia came into the room, and then hastily away again.

"Hallo, Nanny."

"Good evening."

Her manner was frigid. Virginia shut the door and went to sit on the arm of the sofa. There was only one way to deal with Nanny in a mood and that was to jump right in off the deep end. "I'm sorry about this, Nanny."

"I don't know what you mean, I'm sure."

"I mean about my taking the children away. We're going back to Cornwall tomorrow morning. I've got seats on the train." Nanny folded the checked tablecloth, corner to corner into perfect squares. "Lady Keile said she'd spoken to you."

"She certainly mentioned something about some hare-brained scheme . . . but it was hard to believe that my ears weren't playing me tricks."

"Are you cross because I'm taking them, or because you're not coming too?"

"Who's cross? Nobody's cross, I'm sure . . ."

"Then you think it's a good idea?"

"No, that I do not. But what I think doesn't seem to matter any more, one way or the other."

She opened a drawer in the table and laid the cloth away, and shut the drawer with a little slam which instantly betrayed her scarcely-banked rage. But her face remained cool, her mouth primly set.

"You know that what you think matters. You've done so much for the children. You mustn't think I'm not grateful. But they're not babies any longer."

"And what is that meant to convey, if I might ask?"

"Just that I can look after them now."

Nanny turned from the table. For the first time, her eyes met Virginia's. And as they watched each other, Virginia saw the slow, angry flush spread up Nanny's neck, up her face, up to her hair line.

She said, "Are you giving me my notice?"

"No, that's not what I intended at all. But perhaps, now we've started to discuss it, it would be the best thing. For your sake as much as anyone else's. Perhaps it would be better for you."

"And why would it be better for me? All my life I've given to this family, why, I had Anthony to look after from the beginning, and there was no reason why I should come up to Scotland and take care of your babies, I never wanted to go, to leave London, but Lady Keile asked me, and because it was the family, I went, a real sacrifice I made, and this is all the thanks I get . . ."

"Nanny . . ." Virginia interrupted gently when Nanny paused for a breath ". . . It would be better for you because of this. For that very reason. Wouldn't it be better to make a clean break, and maybe have a new baby to take care of, a new little family? You know how you always said a nursery wasn't a nursery without a little baby, and Nicholas is six now . . ."

"I never thought I'd live to see the day . . ."

"And if you don't want to do that, then why not speak to Lady Keile? You could maybe make some arrangement with her. You get on so well together, and you like being in London, with all your friends . . ."

"I don't need you to give me any suggestions, thank you very much . . .

given up the best years of my life ... bringing up your children ...
never expected any thanks ... never would have happened if poor
Anthony ... if Anthony had been alive ..."

It went on and on, and Virginia sat and listened, letting the invec-
tive pour over her. She told herself that this was the least she could do.
It was over, it was done, and she was free. Nothing else mattered. To
wait, politely, for Nanny to finish was no more than a salute of respect,
a tribute paid by the victor to the vanquished after a bloodthirsty but
honourable battle.

Afterwards, she went to say good night to the children. Nicholas
was already asleep, but Cara was still deep in her book. When her
mother came into the room, she looked up slowly, dragging her eyes
away from the printed page. Virginia sat on the edge of her bed.

"What are you reading now?"

Cara showed her. "It's *The Treasure Seekers.*"

"Oh, I remember that. Where did you find it?"

"In the nursery bookcase."

Carefully, she marked the place in her book with a cross-stitched
marker she had made herself, closed it and put it down on her bedside
table. "Have you been talking to Nanny?"

"Yes."

"She's been funny all day."

"Has she, Cara?"

"Is something wrong?"

It was hard to be so perceptive, so sensitive to atmosphere when
you were only eight years old. Especially when you were shy and not
very pretty and had to wear round steel spectacles that made you look
like a little owl.

"No, nothing's wrong. Just different. And new."

"What do you mean?"

"Well, I'm going back to Cornwall tomorrow morning in the
train, and I'm going to take you and Nicholas with me. Will you like
that?"

"You mean ..." Cara's face lit up. "We're going to stay with Aunt
Alice?"

"No, we're going to stay in a house on our own. A funny little house called Bosithick. And we're going to have to do all the housekeeping ourselves and the cooking . . ."

"Isn't Nanny coming?"

"No. Nanny's staying here."

There was a long silence. Virginia said, "Do . . . you mind?"

"No, I don't mind. But I expect she will. That's why she's been so funny."

"It's not easy for Nanny. You and Nicholas have been her babies ever since you were born. But somehow I think you're growing out of Nanny now, like you grow out of coats and dresses . . . You're both old enough to look after yourselves."

"You mean, Nanny's not going to live with us any more?"

"No, she's not."

"Where will she live?"

"She'll maybe go and find another little new baby to take care of. Or she may stay here with Granny."

"She likes being in London," said Cara. "She told me so. She likes it much better than Scotland."

"Well, there you are!"

Cara considered this for a moment. Then she said, "When are we going to Cornwall?"

"I told you. Tomorrow on the train."

"When will we leave?" She liked everything cut and dried.

"About half past nine. We'll get a taxi to the station."

"And when are we going back to Kirkton?"

"I expect when the holidays are over. When you have to go back to school." Cara remained silent. It was impossible to tell what she was thinking. Virginia said, "It's time to go to sleep now . . . we've got a long day tomorrow," and she leaned forward and gently unhooked Cara's spectacles and kissed her good night.

But as she went towards the door, Cara spoke again.

"Mummy."

Virginia turned. "Yes."

"You came."

Virginia frowned, not understanding.

"You came," said Cara again. "I said to write to me, but you came instead."

Virginia remembered the letter from Cara, the catalyst that had started everything off. She smiled. "Yes," she said. "I came. It seemed better." And she went out of the room, and downstairs to endure the ordeal of a silent dinner in the company of Lady Keile.

5

Virginia awoke slowly, to a quite unaccustomed mood of achievement. She felt purposeful and strong, two such alien sensations that it was worth lying for a little, quietly, to savour them. Pillowed in Lady Keile's incomparably comfortable spare bed, lapped in hemstitched linen and cloudy blankets, she watched the early sunshine of another perfect summer morning seep in long strands of gold through the leafy branches of the chestnut tree. The bad things were over, the dreaded hurdles somehow cleared, and in a couple of hours she and the children would be on their way. She told herself that after last night she would never be afraid to tackle anything, no problem was insurmountable, no problem too knotty. She let her imagination move cautiously forward to the weeks ahead, to the pitfalls of coping with Cara and Nicholas single-handed, the discomfort and inconvenience of the little house she had so recklessly rented for them, and still her good spirits remained undismayed. She had turned a corner. From now on everything was going to be different.

It was half past seven. She got up, revelling in the fine weather, the sound of bird-song, the pleasant, distant hum of traffic. She bathed and dressed and packed and stripped her bed and went downstairs.

Nanny and the children always had breakfast in the nursery and Lady Keile hers on a tray in her bedroom, but this was a perfectly ordered household and Virginia found that coffee had been set out for her on the dining-room hotplate, and a single place laid at the head of the polished table.

She drank two cups of scalding black coffee and ate toast and marmalade. Then she took the key from the table to the hall and let herself out of the front door into the quiet morning streets and walked down to the small old-fashioned grocer's patronized by Lady Keile. There she laid in sufficient provisions to start them off when they eventually got back to Bosithick. Bread and butter and bacon and eggs and coffee and cocoa, and baked beans (which she knew Nicholas adored, but Nanny had never approved of) and tomato soup and chocolate biscuits. Milk and vegetables they would have to find when they got down there, meat and fish could come later. She paid for all this, and the grocer packed it for her in a stout cardboard carton and she walked back to Melton Gardens with her weighty load carried before her in both arms.

She found the children and Lady Keile downstairs; no sign of Nanny. But the small suitcases, doubtless perfectly packed, were lined up in the hall, and Virginia dumped the carton of groceries down beside them.

"Hallo, Mummy!"

"Hallo." She kissed them both. They were clean and tidy, ready for their journey, Cara in a blue cotton dress and Nicholas in shorts and a striped shirt, his dark hair lately flattened by a hairbrush. "What have you been doing?" he wanted to know.

"I've been buying some groceries. We probably won't have time to go shopping when we get to Penzance; it would be terrible if we didn't have anything to eat."

"I didn't know till this morning when Cara told me. I didn't know till I woke up that we were going in the train."

"I'm sorry. You were asleep last night when I came in to tell you and I didn't want to disturb you."

"I wish you had. I didn't know until *breakfast*." He was very resentful.

Smiling at him, Virginia looked up at her mother-in-law. Lady Keile was drawn and pale. Otherwise she looked, as always, perfectly groomed, quite in charge of the situation. Virginia wondered if she had slept at all.

"You should telephone for a taxi," said Lady Keile. "You don't want to risk missing the train. It's always best to be on the early side. There's a number by the telephone."

Wishing that she had thought of this herself Virginia went to do as she was told. The clock in the hall struck a quarter past nine. In ten minutes' time the taxi was there and they were ready to leave.

"But we have to say goodbye to Nanny!" said Cara.

Virginia said, "Yes, of course. Where is Nanny?"

"She's in the nursery." Cara started for the stairs, but Virginia said, "No."

Cara turned and stared, shocked by the unaccustomed tone of her mother's voice.

"But we *have* to say goodbye."

"Of course. Nanny will come down and see you off. I'll go up now and tell her we're just on our way. You get everything together."

She found Nanny determinedly occupied in some entirely unnecessary task.

"Nanny, we're just going."

"Oh, yes."

"The children want to say goodbye."

Silence.

Last night Virginia had been sorry for her, had, in a funny way, respected her. But now all she wanted to do was take Nanny by her shoulders and shake her till her stupid head fell off. "Nanny, this is ridiculous. You can't let it end this way. Come downstairs and say goodbye to them."

It was the first direct order she had ever given to Nanny. The first, she thought, and the last. Like Cara, Nanny was obviously shaken. For a moment she stalled, her mouth worked, she seemed to be trying to think up some excuse. Virginia caught her eye and held it. Nanny tried to stare her out, but was defeated, her eyes slid away. It was the final triumph.

"Very well, madam," said Nanny and followed Virginia back down to the hall, where the children rushed at her in the most gratifying way, hugged her and kissed her as though she were the only person in the world they loved, and then, with this demonstration of affection safely over, ran down the steps and across the pavement and into the waiting taxi.

"Goodbye," said Virginia to her mother-in-law. There was nothing more to be said. They kissed once more, leaning cheeks, kissing the air. "And goodbye, Nanny." But Nanny was already on her way up to the nursery again, fumbling for her handkerchief and blowing her nose. Only her legs were visible, treading upstairs, and the next moment she had reached the turn of the landing and disappeared.

She need have had no fear about her children's behaviour. The novelty of the train journey did not excite, but silenced them. They had not often been taken on holiday, and never to the seaside, and when they travelled to London to stay with their grandmother had been bundled into the night train already dressed in their pyjamas and had slept the journey away.

Now, they stared from the window at the racing countryside as though they had neither of them ever seen fields or farms or cows or towns before. After a little, when the charm of this wore off, Nicholas opened the present Virginia had bought for him at Paddington and smiled with satisfaction when he saw the little red tractor.

He said, "It's like the Kirkton one. Mr. McGregor had a Massey Fergusson just like this." He spun the wheels and made tractor noises in the back of his throat, running the toy up and down the prickly British Railway upholstery.

But Cara did not even open her comic. It lay folded on her lap, and she continued to stare out of the window, her bulging forehead leaning against the glass, her eyes intent behind her spectacles, missing nothing.

At half past twelve they went for lunch and this was another adventure, lurching down the corridor, rushing through the scary connections before the carriages came apart. The dining-car they found enthralling, the tables and the little lights, the indulgent waiter and the grown-up-ness of being handed a menu.

"And what would madam like?" the waiter asked, and Cara went pink with embarrassed giggles when she realized that he was speaking to her, and had to be helped to order tomato soup and fried fish, and to decide the world-shaking problem of whether she would eat a white ice-cream or a pink.

Watching their faces Virginia thought: Because it's new and exciting to them, it's new and exciting for me. The most trivial, ordinary occurrences will become special because I shall see them through

Cara's eyes. And if Nicholas asks me questions that I can't answer, I shall have to go and look them up and I shall become informed and knowledgeable and a brilliant conversationalist.

The idea was funny. She laughed suddenly, and Cara stared and then laughed back, not knowing what the joke was, but delighted to be sharing it with her mother.

"When did you first come on this train down to Cornwall?" Cara asked.

"When I was seventeen. Ten years ago."

"Didn't you come when you were a little girl my age?"

"No, I didn't. I used to go to an aunt in Sussex."

Now, it was afternoon and they had the compartment to themselves. Nicholas, charmed by the adventure of the corridor, had elected to stay out there, and could be seen straddle-legged, trying to adjust his small weight to the rocking of the train.

"Tell me."

"What? About Sussex?"

"No. About coming to Cornwall."

"Well, we just came. My mother and I, to stay with Alice and Tom Lingard. I'd just left school, and Alice wrote to invite us, and my mother thought it would be nice to have a holiday."

"Was it a summer holiday?"

"No. It was Easter. Spring time. All the daffodils were out and the railway cuttings were thick with primroses."

"Was it hot?"

"Not really. But sunny, and much warmer than Scotland. In Scotland we never really have a proper spring, do we? One day it's winter and the next day all the leaves are out on the trees and it's summer time. At least that's the way it's always seemed to me. In Cornwall the spring is quite a long season . . . that's why they're able to grow all the lovely flowers and send them to Covent Garden to be sold."

"Did you swim?"

"No. The sea would have been icy."

"But in Aunt Alice's pool?"

"She didn't have a pool in those days."

THE EMPTY HOUSE
69

"Will we swim in Aunt Alice's pool?"

"Sure to."

"Will we swim in the sea?"

"Yes, we'll find a lovely beach and swim there."

"I . . . I'm not very good at swimming."

"It's easier in the sea than in ordinary water. The salt helps you to float."

"But don't the waves splash into your face?"

"A little. But that's part of the fun."

Cara considered this. She did not like getting her face wet. Without her spectacles things became blurred and she couldn't swim with her spectacles on.

"What else did you do?"

"Oh, we used to go out in the car, and go shopping. And if it was warm we used to sit in the garden, and Alice used to have friends to tea, and people for dinner. And sometimes I used to go for walks. There are lovely walks there. Up to the hill behind the house, or down into Porthkerris. The streets are all steep and narrow, so narrow you could scarcely get a car down them. And there were lots of little stray cats, and the harbour, with fishing boats and old men sitting around enjoying the sunshine. And sometimes the tide was in and all the boats were bobbing about in the deep blue water, and sometimes it was out, and there'd be nothing but gold sand, and all the boats would be leaning on their sides."

"Didn't they fall over?"

"I don't think so."

"Why?"

"I haven't any idea," said Virginia.

There had been a special day, an April day of wind and sunshine. On that day the tide was high, Virginia could remember the salt smell of it, mixed with the evocative sea-going smells of tar and fresh paint.

Within the shelter of the quay the water swelled smooth and glassy, clear and deep. But beyond the harbour it was rough, the dark ocean flecked with white horses and, out across the bay, the great seas creamed against the rocks at the foot of the lighthouse, sending up spouts of white spray almost as high as the lighthouse itself.

It was a week since the night of the barbecue at Lanyon, and for once Virginia was on her own. Alice had driven to Penzance to attend some committee meeting, Tom Lingard was in Plymouth, Mrs. Jilkes, the cook, had her afternoon off and had departed, in a considerable hat to visit her cousin's wife, and Mrs. Parsons was keeping her weekly appointment with the hairdresser.

"You'll have to amuse yourself," she told Virginia over lunch.

"I'll be all right."

"What will you do?"

"I don't know. Something."

In the empty house, with the empty afternoon lying, like a gift, before her, she had considered a number of possibilities. But the marvellous day was too beautiful to be wasted, and she had gone out and started walking, and her feet had taken her down the narrow path that led to the cliffs, and then along the cliff path, and down to the white sickle of the beach. In the summer this would be crowded with coloured tents and ice-cream stalls and noisy holiday-makers with beach balls and umbrellas, but in April the visitors had not started to arrive, and the sand lay clean, washed by the winter storms, and her footsteps left a line of prints, neat and precise as little stitches.

At the far end, a lane leaned uphill and she was soon lost in a maze of narrow streets that wound between ancient, sun-bleached houses. She came upon flights of stone steps and unsuspected alleys and followed them down until all at once she turned a corner out at the very edge of the harbour. In a dazzle of sunshine she saw the bright-painted boats, the peacock-green water. Gulls screamed and wheeled overhead, their great wings like white sails against the blue, and everywhere there was activity and bustle, a regular spring-cleaning going on. Shop-fronts were being white-washed, windows polished, ropes coiled, decks scrubbed, nets mended.

At the edge of the quay a hopeful vendor had set up his ice-cream barrow, shiny white, and lettered seductively "Fred Hoskings, Cornish Ice-cream, The Best Home-made" and Virginia suddenly longed for one, and wished she had brought some money. To sit in the sunshine on such a day and lick an ice-cream seemed, all at once, the height of luxury. The more she thought about it the more desirable it seemed, and she even went through all her pockets in the hope of finding some forgotten coin, but there was nothing there. Not so much as a half-penny.

She sat on a bollard and gazed disconsolately down on to the deck of a fishing boat where a young boy in a salt-stained smock was brewing up tea on a spirit lamp. She was trying not to think about the ice-cream when, like the answer to a prayer, a voice spoke from behind her.

"Hallo."

Virginia looked around over her shoulder, pushing her long dark hair out of her face, and saw him standing there, braced against the wind, with a package under his arm, and wearing a blue polo-necked sweater that made him look like a sailor.

She stood up. "Hallo."

"I thought it was you," said Eustace Philips, "but I couldn't be sure. What are you doing here?"

"Nothing. I mean, I just came for a walk, and I stopped to look at the boats."

"It's a lovely day."

"Yes."

His blue eyes gleamed, amused. "Where's Alice Lingard?"

"She's gone to Penzance . . . she's on a committee . . ."

"So you're all alone?"

"Yes." She was wearing worn blue sneakers, blue jeans and a white cable-stitch sweater, and felt miserably convinced that her naivete was painfully obvious not only in her clothes but her lack of small-talk as well.

She looked at his package. "What are *you* doing here?"

"I came in to pick up a new rick cover. The wind last night blew the old one to ribbons."

"I expect you're going back now."

"Not immediately. How about you?"

"I'm not doing anything. Just exploring, I suppose."

"Don't you know the town?"

"I've never got this far before."

"Come along then, I'll show you the rest of it."

They began to walk back along the quay, in no hurry, their slow paces matched. He caught sight of the ice-cream barrow and stopped to talk.

"Hallo, Fred."

The ice-cream man, resplendent in a white starched coat like a cricket umpire, turned and saw him. A smile spread across features browned and wizened as a walnut.

"'Allo, Eustace. 'Ow are you?"

"Fine. How's yourself?"

"Oh, keeping not too bad. Don't often see you down 'ere. 'Ow are things out at Lanyon?"

"All right. Working hard." Eustace ducked his head at the barrow. "You're early out. There's nobody here yet to buy ice-creams."

"Oh well, early bird catches the worm I always say."

Eustace looked at Virginia. "Do you want an ice-cream?"

She could not think of any person who had offered her, so instantly, exactly what she wanted most.

"I'd love one, but I haven't any money."

Eustace grinned. "The biggest you've got," he said to Fred, and reached his hand into the back pocket of his trousers.

He took her the length of the wharf, up cobbled streets at whose existence she had never even guessed, through small, surprising squares, where the houses had yellow doors and window-boxes, past little courtyards filled with washing-lines and flights of stone steps where the cats lay and sunned themselves and attended to their ablutions. They came out at last on to a northern beach which lay with its face to the wind, and the long combers rolled in jade green with the sun behind them, and the air was misted with blown spume.

"When I was a boy," Eustace told her, raising his voice above the wind, "I used to come here with a surf-board. A little wooden one my uncle made me, with a face painted on the curve. But now they have these Malibu surfboards, made of fibreglass they are and they surf all year round, winter and summer."

"Isn't it cold?"

"They wear wet suits."

They came to a sea wall, curved against the wind with a wooden bench built into its angle and here Eustace, apparently deciding that they had walked far enough, settled himself, his back to the wall and his face to the sun and his long legs stretched in front of him.

Virginia, consuming the last of the mammoth ice-cream, sat beside him. He watched her, and when she had demolished the final mouthful and was wiping her fingers on the knees of her jeans he said, "Did you enjoy it?"

His face was serious but his eyes laughed at her. She didn't mind. "It was delicious. The best. You should have had one too."

"I'm too big and too old to go walking round the streets licking an ice-cream."

"I shall never be too big or too old."

"How old are you?"

"Seventeen, nearly eighteen."

"Have you left school?"

"Yes, last summer."

"What are you doing now?"

"Nothing."

"Are you going to University?"

She was flattered that he should imagine she was so clever. "Goodness, no."

"What are you going to do, then?"

Virginia wished that he had not asked.

"Well, eventually, I suppose, next winter I'll learn how to cook or do shorthand and typing or something gruesome like that. But you see my mother has this bee in her bonnet about being in London for the summer and going to all the parties and meeting all the right people and generally having a social whirl."

"I believe," said Eustace, "it's called 'Doing the Season.'"

His tone of voice made it very clear that he thought as little of the idea as she did.

"Oh, don't. It gives me the shivers."

"It's hard to believe, in this day and age, that anybody bothers any more."

"I know, it's fantastic. But they do. And my mother's one of them. She's already met some of the other mothers and had ghastly tea parties with them. She's even booked a date for a dance, but I'm going to try my hardest to talk her out of that one. Can you think of anything worse than having a coming-out dance?"

"No, I can't, but then I'm not a sweet seventeen-year-old." Virginia made a face at him. "If you feel so strongly about it why don't you dig in your toes, tell your mother you'd rather have the price of a return ticket to Australia or something?"

"I already have. At least I've tried. But you don't know my mother. She never listens to anything I say, she just says that it's so *important* to meet all the right people, and be asked to all the right parties and be seen at all the right places."

"You could try getting your father on your side."

"I haven't got a father. At least I never see him; they were divorced when I was a baby."

"I see." He added, without much heart: "Well, cheer up—who knows—you might enjoy it."

"I shall hate every moment of it."

"How do you know?"

"Because I'm useless at parties, and I get tongue-tied with strangers, and I can never think of anything to say to young men."

"You're thinking of plenty to say to me," Eustace pointed out.

"But you're different."

"How am I different?"

"Well, you're older. I mean you're not young." Eustace began to laugh and Virginia was embarrassed. "I mean you're not really young, like twenty-one or twenty-two." He was still laughing. She frowned. "How old *are* you?"

"Twenty-eight," he told her. "Twenty-nine next birthday."

"You are lucky. I wish I was twenty-eight."

"If you were," said Eustace, "you probably wouldn't be here now."

All at once it turned dark and cold. Virginia shivered, and looked up and saw that the sun had disappeared behind a large grey cloud, the vanguard of a bank of dirty weather which was blowing in from the west.

"That's it," said Eustace. "We've had the best of the day. It'll be raining by this evening." He looked at his watch. "It's nearly four o'clock, time I made for home. How are you getting back?"

"Walking, I suppose."

"Do you want a ride?"

"Have you got a car?"

"I've got a Land-Rover, parked round by the church."

"Won't I be taking you out of your way?"

"No. I can go back to Lanyon over the moor."

"Well, if you're certain . . ."

Driving back to Wheal House, Virginia fell silent. But it was a natural, companionable silence, comfortable as an old shoe, and had nothing to do with being shy or unable to think of anything to say. She could not remember when she had felt so at ease with a person— and certainly never with a man whom she had known such a short time. The Land-Rover was an old one, the seats worn and dusty and there were stray scraps of straw lying about the floor and a faint smell of farmyard manure. Virginia did not find this in the least offensive— rather, she liked it because it was part of Penfolda.

She realized that she wanted, above all things, to go back there. To see the farm and the fields in daylight, to inspect the stock and be shown around, perhaps to be allowed to see the rest of the farmhouse and be asked to tea in that enviable kitchen. To be accepted.

They came up the hill out of the town, where the houses of the old residential area had all been turned into hotels, with gardens bull-dozed into car parks, and glassed-in porches. There were sun-rooms and palm trees, dismal against the grey sky, and municipal flower-beds planted with straight rows of daffodils.

High above the sea, the road levelled out. Eustace changed into top gear and said, "When are you going back to London?"

"I don't know. In about a week."

"Do you want to come out to Penfolda again?"

This was the second time that day that he had offered her what she craved most. She wondered if he were psychic.

"Yes, I'd love to."

"My mother was very taken with you. Not often she sees a new face. It would be nice for her if you'd come and have a cup of tea with her."

"I'd like to come."

"How would you get out to Lanyon?" asked Eustace, his eyes on the road ahead.

"I could borrow Alice's car. I'm sure if I asked her she'd let me borrow it. I'd be very careful."

"Can you drive?"

"Of course. Otherwise I wouldn't borrow the car." She smiled at him. Not because it was meant to be a joke, but because all at once she felt so good.

"Well, I'll tell you," said Eustace in his deliberate way. "I'll have a word with my mother, find out which day suits her best, give you a ring on the telephone. How would that be?"

She imagined waiting for the call, having it come, hearing his voice over the wire. She almost hugged herself with pleasure.

"It would be all right."

"What's the number?"

"Porthkerris three two five."

"I'll remember that."

They had reached home. He turned into the white gates of Wheal House and roared up the drive between the hedges of escallonia.

"There you are!" He stopped with a great jerk of brakes and a splattering of gravel. "Home safely, just in time for tea."

"Thank you so much."

He leaned on the wheel, smiling at her. "That's all right."

"I mean, for everything. The ice-cream and everything."

"You're welcome." He reached across and opened the door for her. Virginia jumped down on to the gravel, and as she did so, the front door opened and Mrs. Parsons emerged, wearing a little suit of raspberry-red wool, and a white silk shirt, tied like a stock at the neck.

"Virginia!"

Virginia swung around. Her mother came across the gravel towards them, immaculate as always, but her hair, short and dark, blew casually in the wind and had obviously not been attended to that afternoon.

"Mother!"

"Where have you been?" The smile was friendly and interested.

"I thought you were at the hairdresser."

"The girl who usually does me is in bed with a cold. They offered me another girl of course, but, as she's the one who usually spends her days sweeping hair off the floor, I declined with thanks." Still smiling, she looked beyond Virginia to where Eustace waited. "And who is your friend?"

"Oh. It's Eustace Philips . . ."

But now Eustace had decided to get out of the car. He jumped down on to the gravel and came around the front of the Land-Rover to be introduced. And, hating herself, Virginia saw him through her mother's eyes; the wide powerful shoulders beneath the sailor's sweater, the sun-burned face, the strong, calloused hands.

Mrs. Parsons came forward graciously. "How do you do."

"Hallo," said Eustace, meeting her eye with an unblinking blue gaze. Her hand was half-way out to shake his, but Eustace either didn't see this or chose to ignore it. Mrs. Parsons's hand dropped back to her side. Her manner became, subtly, a fraction more cool.

"Where did Virginia meet *you*?" The question was harmless, even playful.

Eustace leaned against the Land-Rover and crossed his arms. "I live out at Lanyon; farm Penfolda . . ."

"Oh, of course, the barbecue. Yes, I heard all about it. And how nice that you met up again today."

"By chance," said Eustace, firmly.

"But that makes it even nicer!" She smiled. "We're just going to have tea, Mr. Philips. Won't you join us?"

Eustace shook his head. His eyes never left her face. "I've got seventy cows waiting to be milked. I'd better be getting back . . ."

"Oh, of course. I wouldn't want to keep you from your work." Her tone was that of the lady of the house dismissing the gardener, but she continued to smile.

"I wouldn't let you," said Eustace, and went to get back into the car.

"Goodbye, Virginia."

"Oh. Goodbye," said Virginia faintly. "And thank you for bringing me home."

"I'll ring you up some time."

"Yes, do that."

He gave a final salute with his head, then started the engine, put the Land-Rover into gear, and without a backward glance, shot away, down the drive and out of sight, leaving Virginia and her mother standing, staring after him, in a cloud of dust.

"Well!" said Mrs. Parsons, laughing, but obviously nettled.

Virginia said nothing. There did not seem to be anything to say.

"What a very basic young man! I must say, staying down here, one does meet all types. What's he going to ring you up about?"

The tone of her voice implied that Eustace Philips was something of a joke, a joke that she and Virginia shared.

"He thought perhaps I might go out to Lanyon and have tea with his mother."

"Isn't that marvellous? Pure Cold Comfort Farm." It began, very lightly, to rain. Mrs. Parsons glanced at the lowering sky and shivered. "What are we doing, standing out here in the wind? Come along, tea's waiting . . ."

Virginia thought nothing of the shiver, but the next morning her mother complained of feeling unwell, she had a cold, she said, an upset stomach, she would stay indoors. As the weather was horrible nobody questioned this, and Alice laid and lit a cheerful fire in the drawing-room, and by this Mrs. Parsons reclined on the sofa, a light mohair rug over her knees.

"I shall be perfectly all right," she told Virginia, "and you and Alice must just go off and not bother about me at all."

"What do you mean, we must just go off? Where is there to go off to?"

"To Falmouth. To lunch at Pendrane." Virginia stared blankly. "Oh, darling, don't look so gormless, Mrs. Menheniot asked us ages ago. She wanted to show us the garden."

"Nobody ever told me," said Virginia, who did not want to go. It would take all day to get to Falmouth and back again and have lunch and see the boring garden. She wanted to stay here and sit by the telephone and wait for Eustace to ring.

"Well, I'm telling you now. You'll have to change. You can't go out for lunch dressed in jeans. Why not wear that pretty blue shirt I bought for you? Or the tartan kilt? I'm sure Mrs. Menheniot would be amused by your kilt."

If she had been any other sort of a mother Virginia would have asked her to listen for the telephone, to take a message. But her mother did not like Eustace. She thought him ill-mannered and uncouth, and her smiling reference to Cold Comfort Farm had put the official stamp of disapproval upon him. Since his departure his name had not been mentioned, and although, during dinner last night, Virginia had tried more than once to tell Alice and Tom about her chance encounter, her mother had always firmly overridden the conversation, interrupting if necessary, and steering it into more suitable channels. While she changed, Virginia debated what to do.

Eventually, dressed in the kilt and a canary yellow sweater, with her dark hair brushed clean and shining, she went along to the kitchen to find Mrs. Jilkes. Mrs. Jilkes was a new friend. One wet afternoon she had taught Virginia to make scones, at the same time regaling her with a great deal of gratuitous information concerning the health and longevity of Mrs. Jilkes's numerous relations.

"'Allo, Virginia."

She was rolling pastry. Virginia took a scrap and began, absently, to eat it.

"Now, don't go eating that! You'll fill yourself up, won't have no room for your lunch."

"I wish I didn't have to go. Mrs. Jilkes, if a phone call comes through for me, would you take a message?"

Mrs. Jilkes looked coy, rolling her eyes. "Expecting a phone call are you? Some young man, is it?"

Virginia blushed. "Well, all right, yes. But you will listen, won't you?"

"Don't you worry, my love. Now, there's Mrs. Lingard calling . . . time you was off. And I'll keep an eye on your mother, and give her a little lunch on a tray."

They did not return home until half past five. Alice went at once to the drawing-room, to inquire for Rowena Parsons's health, and to tell her all that they had done and seen. Virginia had made for the stairs, but the instant the drawing-room door was safely closed, turned and sprinted down the kitchen passage.

"Mrs. Jilkes!"

"Back again, are you?"

"Was there a phone call?"

"Yes, two or three, but your mother answered them."

"Mother?"

"Yes, she had the phone switched through to the drawing-room. You'll have to ask her if there are any messages."

Virginia went out of the kitchen, and back down the passage, across the hall and into the drawing-room. Across Alice Lingard's head, her eyes met and held her mother's cool gaze. Then Mrs. Parsons smiled.

"Darling! I've been hearing all about it. Was it fun?"

"It was all right." She waited, giving her mother the chance to tell her that the telephone call had come through.

"All right? No more? I believe Mrs. Menheniot's nephew was there?"

". . . Yes."

Already the image of the chinless young man was so blurred that she could scarcely remember his face. Perhaps Eustace would ring to-morrow. He couldn't have phoned today. Virginia knew her mother. Knew that, however much she disapproved, Mrs. Parsons would be meticulous about such social obligations as passing on telephone messages. Mothers were like that. They had to be. Because if they didn't live by the code of behaviour which they preached, then they lost all right to their children's trust. And without trust there could be no affection. And without affection, nothing.

The next day it rained. All morning, Virginia sat by the fire in the hall, pretending to read a book, and flying to answer the telephone each time it rang. It was never for her; it was never Eustace.

After lunch her mother asked her to go down to the chemist in Porthkerris to pick up a prescription. Virginia said she didn't want to go.

". . . It's pouring with rain."

"A little rain won't hurt you. Besides, the exercise will do you good. You've been sitting indoors all day, reading that silly book."

"It's not a silly book . . ."

"Well, anyway, reading. Put on some wellingtons and a raincoat and you won't even notice the rain . . ."

It was no good arguing. Virginia made a resigned face and went to find her raincoat. Trudging down the road towards the town, the pavements dark and grey between the dripping trees, she tried to face up to the unthinkable possibility that Eustace was never going to ring her.

He had said that he would, certainly, but it all seemed to depend on what his mother said, when she would be free, when Virginia would be able to borrow the car and drive herself out to Lanyon.

Perhaps Mrs. Philips had changed her mind. Perhaps she had said, "Oh Eustace, I haven't got time for tea parties . . . what were you thinking of, saying she could come out here?"

Perhaps, having met Virginia's mother, Eustace had changed his own mind about Virginia. They said that if you wanted to know what sort of a wife a girl was going to turn into, you looked at her mother. Perhaps Eustace had looked and decided that he did not like what he saw. She remembered the challenge in his unblinking blue eyes, and that final bitter exchange.

"I wouldn't want to keep you from your work."

"I wouldn't let you."

Perhaps he had forgotten to telephone. Perhaps he had had second thoughts. Or perhaps—and this was chilling—Virginia had misconstrued his friendliness, unburdened all her problems, and so aroused his sympathy. Perhaps that was all it was. That he was sorry for her.

But he said he would telephone. He said he would.

She collected the prescription and started home once more. It was still raining. Across the street from the chemist stood a call-box. It was empty. It would all be so simple. It wouldn't take a moment to look up his number, to dial. She had her purse in her pocket, with coins to pay for the call. *It's Virginia*, she would say, and make a joke of it, teasing him. *I thought you were going to ring me up!*

She almost crossed the road. At the edge of the pavement she hesitated, trying to pluck up the courage to take the initiative in a situation which was beyond her.

She imagined the conversation.

"Eustace?"

"Yes."

"This is Virginia."

"Virginia?"

"Virginia Parsons."

"Oh, yes. Virginia Parsons. What do you want?"

But at this point her courage turned on its heels and fled, and

Virginia never crossed the road to the telephone box, but carried on up the hill with the rain in her face and her mother's pills deep in the pocket of her waterproof coat.

As she came in through the front door of Wheal House she heard the telephone ringing, but by the time she had got her wellingtons off the ringing had stopped, and by the time she burst into the drawing-room, her mother was just putting down the receiver.

She raised her eyebrows at her breathless daughter.

"Whatever's wrong?"

"I . . . I thought it might be for me."

"No. A wrong number. Did you get my pills, darling?"

"Yes," said Virginia dully.

"Sweet of you. And the walk has done you good. I can tell. Your cheeks are quite pink again."

The next day Mrs. Parsons announced out of the blue that they must return to London. Alice was astonished. "But, Rowena, I thought you were going to stay at least another week."

"Darling, we'd love to, but you know, we do have a very busy summer to put in, and a lot of arrangements and organization to be seen to. I don't think we can sit here enjoying ourselves for another week. Much as I would adore to."

"Well, anyway, stay over the week-end."

Yes, stay over the week-end, Virginia prayed. *Please, please, please stay over the week-end.*

But it wasn't any use. "Oh, adore to, but we must go . . . Friday at the latest I'm afraid. I'll have to see about booking seats on the train."

"Well, it seems a shame, but if you really mean it . . ."

"Yes, darling, I really do mean it."

Let him remember. Let him phone. There wouldn't be time to go out to Penfolda but at least I could say goodbye, I'd know that he'd meant it . . . perhaps I could say I'd write to him, perhaps I could give him my address.

"Darling, I wish you'd get on with your packing. Don't leave anything behind, it would be such a bore for poor Alice to have to parcel it up. Have you put your raincoat in?"

This evening. He'll ring this evening. He'll say, I am sorry but I've been away; I've been so busy I haven't had a moment; I've been ill.

"Virginia! Come and write your name in the visitors' book! There, under mine. Oh, Alice, my dear, what a wonderful holiday you've given us. Sheer delight. We've both adored it, haven't we, Virginia? Can't bear to go."

They went. Alice drove them to the station, saw them into their first-class carriage, the corner seats reserved, the porter being deferential because of Mrs. Parsons's expensive luggage.

"You'll come again soon," said Alice as Virginia leaned out of the window to kiss her.

"Yes."

"We've loved having you . . ."

It was the last chance. *Tell Eustace I had to go. Tell him goodbye for me.* The whistle shrilled, the train began to move. *Ring him up when you get back.*

"Goodbye, Virginia."

Send him my love. Tell him I love him.

By Truro her misery had become so obvious with sniffs and sobs and brimming tears that her mother could ignore them no longer.

"Oh, darling." She put down her newspaper. "Whatever is the matter?"

"Nothing . . ." Virginia stood at the window swollen-faced, unseeing.

"But it has to be something." She put out a hand and put it, gently, on Virginia's knee. "Was it that young man?"

"Which young man?"

"The young man in the Land-Rover, Eustace Philips? Did you break your heart over him?" Virginia, weeping, could make no reply. Her mother went on, reassuring, gentle. "I wouldn't be too unhappy. It's probably the first time you've been hurt by a man, but I assure you it won't be the last. They're selfish creatures, you know."

"Eustace wasn't like that."

"Wasn't he?"

"He was kind. He was the only man I've ever really liked." She blew her nose lustily and gazed at her mother. "You didn't like him, did you?"

Mrs. Parsons was momentarily taken aback by such unusual directness. "Well . . . let's say I've never been very fond of his type."

"You mean, you didn't like him being a farmer?"

"I never said that."

"No, but that's what you mean. You only like chinless weeds like Mrs. Menheniot's nephew."

"I never met Mrs. Menheniot's nephew."

"No. But you would have liked him."

Mrs. Parsons did not reply to this at once. But after a little she said, "Forget him, Virginia. Every girl has to have one unhappy love affair before she finally meets the right man and settles down and gets married. And this summer's going to be such fun for us both. It would be a pity to spoil it, yearning for something that probably never even existed."

"Yes," said Virginia and wiped her eyes and put her sodden handkerchief away in her pocket.

"That's a good girl. Now, no more tears." And, satisfied that she had poured oil on troubled waters, Mrs. Parsons sat back in her seat and picked up the newspaper again. But presently, disquieted, disturbed by something, she lowered the paper and saw that Virginia was watching her, unblinking, an expression in her dark eyes that her mother had never seen before.

"What is it?"

Virginia said, "He said he'd phone. He promised he'd telephone me."

"Well?"

"Did he? You didn't like him, I know. Did you take the call and never tell me?"

Her mother never hesitated. "Darling! What an accusation. Of course not. You surely didn't think . . . ?"

"No," said Virginia dully as the last flicker of hope died. "No, I never thought." And she turned to lean her forehead against the smeared glass of the train window, and the rocketing countryside, together with everything else that had happened, streamed away, for ever, into the past.

That was April. In May Virginia met up again with an old school-friend, who invited her down to the country for the week-end.

"It's my birthday, darling, too super, Mummy says I can ask any-one I like, you'll probably have to sleep in the attic, but you won't mind, will you? We're such a madly disorganized family."

Virginia, taking all this with a pinch of salt, accepted the invitation. "How do I get there?"

"Well, you *could* catch a train, and someone *could* meet you, but that's so dreadfully boring. I tell you what, my cousin's probably coming, he's got a car, he'll maybe give me a lift. I'll speak to him and see if he's got room for you. You'll probably have to squeeze in with the luggage or sit on the gear lever, but anything's better than fighting the crowds at Waterloo . . ."

Rather surprisingly, she duly arranged this. The car was a dark blue Mercedes coupé, and once Virginia's luggage had been crammed into the over-loaded boot, she was invited to squash herself into the front seat, between the girlfriend and the cousin. The cousin was tall and fair, with long legs and a grey suit and hair that curled in ducks' tails from beneath the brim of his forward-tilted brown trilby hat.

His name was Anthony Keile.

6

Travel-worn and tired, and with all the problems of Bosithick still to be faced, Virginia got out of the train at Penzance, took a lungful of cool sea air, and was thankful to be back. The tide was low, the air strong with the smell of seaweed. Across the bay, St. Michael's Mount stood gold in the evening sun, and the wet sands were streaked with blue, where small streams and shallow pools of seawater gave back the colour of the sky.

Miraculously, here was a porter. As they followed him and his barrow out of the station Nicholas said, "Is this where we're going to stay?"

"No, we've got to drive over to Lanyon."

"How are we going to drive?"

"I told you, I left my car here."

"How do you know it hasn't been stolen?"

"Because I can see it, waiting for us."

It took some time to pack all their belongings into the boot of the Triumph. But in the end it was all piled in, crowned by the cardboard crate of groceries, and Virginia tipped the porter and they got in, all three of them in the front seat, with Cara in the middle, and the door on Nicholas's side firmly locked.

She had put down the hood and then tied a scarf around her head, but the wind blew Cara's hair forward all over her face.

"How long will it take us to get there?"

"Not long, about half an hour."

"What does the house look like?"

"Why don't you wait and see?"

At the top of the hill she stopped the car, and they looked back to see the view, the lovely curve of Mount's Bay, still and blue, enclosed in the warmth of the day that was over. And all about them were little fields, and ditches blue with wild scabious, and they went on and dropped into a miniature valley filled with ancient oak trees, and a stream ran beneath a bridge, and there was an old mill and a village, and then the road twined up on to the moor again, and all at once the straight bright horizon of the Atlantic lay before them, glittering to the westward in a dazzle of sun.

"I thought the sea was behind us," said Nicholas. "Is that another sea?"

"I suppose it is."

"Is that our sea? Is that the one we're going to use?"

"I expect so."

"Is there a beach?"

"I haven't had time to look. There are certainly a lot of steep cliffs."

"I want a beach. With sand. I want you to buy me a bucket and spade."

"All in good time," said Virginia. "How about taking things one at a time?"

"I want to buy a bucket and spade *tomorrow*."

They joined the main road and turned east, running parallel to the coast. They left Lanyon village behind them and the road which led to Penfolda, and they climbed the hill and came to the clump of leaning hawthorns which marked the turning to Bosithick.

"Here we are!"

"But there's no house."

"You'll see."

Bumped and jarred, the car and its occupants lurched down the lane. From beneath them came sinister banging sounds, the great gorse bushes closed in at either side, and Cara, anxious for their provisions, reached back a hand to hang on to the grocery carton. They swung around the last corner with a final lurch, ran up on to the grass bank at a frightening angle, and stopped with a jerk. Virginia put on the hand-brake, turned off the engine. And the children sat in the car and stared at the house.

In Penzance there had been no wind, the air was milky and breath-lessly warm. Here, there was a faint whining, a coolness. The broken washing line stirred in the breeze and the long grass at the top of the stone hedge lay flattened like a fur coat, stroked by a hand.

And there was something else. Something was wrong. For a mo-ment Virginia stared, trying to think what it was. And then Cara told her. "There's smoke in the chimney," said Cara.

Virginia shivered, a frisson of unease, like a trickle of cold water ran down her spine. It was as though they had caught the house un-awares, they had not been expected by the nameless, unimagined beings who normally occupied it.

Cara felt her disquiet. "Is anything wrong?"

"No, of course not." She sounded more robust than she felt. "I was just surprised. Let's go and investigate."

They got out of the car, leaving the cases and groceries behind. Virginia manhandled the gate open and stood aside for the children to go through while she felt in her bag for the ring of keys.

They went ahead of her, Nicholas running, to investigate what lay around the far corner of the house, but Cara trod cautiously as though trespassing, avoiding an old rag, a broken flower-pot, her hands held fastidiously, anxious not to be asked to touch anything.

Together, they opened the front door. As it swung inwards Cara said, "Do you suppose it's Gipsies?"

"What's Gipsies?"

"Who've lit the fire."

"Let's look . . ." The smell of mice and damp had gone. Instead the house felt fresh and warm, and when they stepped into the living-room they found it bright with firelight. The whole aspect of the house was changed by this, it was sullen and depressing no longer . . . on the contrary, quite cheerful. The hideous electric fire had somehow been disposed of, and a tall rush basket stood by the hearth, piled with a good supply of logs.

What with the fire and the last of the afternoon sun filtering in through the west window, the room was very warm. Virginia went to open a window, and saw, through the open kitchen door, the bowl set on the table, piled with brown eggs, the white enamel milk pan. She went into the kitchen and stood in the middle of the floor and stared. Someone had been in and cleaned the place up, the sink was shining and the curtains laundered.

Cara stole in behind her, still cautious. "It's like fairies," she said.

"It's not fairies," said Virginia, smiling. "It's Alice."

"Aunt Alice Lingard?"

"Yes, isn't she a dear? She pretended to be so disapproving about us coming to Bosithick and then she goes and does a thing like this. But that's just like Alice. She's very kind. We'll have to go tomorrow and thank her. I'd ring up, only we haven't got a telephone."

"I hate the telephone anyway. And I want to go and see her. I want to see the swimming pool."

"If you take your bathing-suit you can have a swim."

Cara stood staring up at her mother. Virginia thought she was still thinking about swimming and was surprised when she said, "How did she get in?"

"Who?"

"Aunt Alice. We've got the keys."

"Oh. Well. I expect she got a spare key from Mr. Williams. Something like that. Now what are we going to do first?"

Nicholas appeared at the door. "I'm going to look all over the house and then I want some tea. I'm starving!"

"Take Cara with you."

"I want to stay with *you*."

"No." Virginia gave her a gentle push. "You go and tell me what you think of the rest of the house. Tell me if you don't think it the funniest house you've ever seen in your life. And I'll put the kettle on and we'll boil some eggs, and after that we'll bring all the stuff in from the car and see about unpacking and making the beds."

"Aren't the beds even made?"

"No, we've got to do it all. We're really on our own now."

Somehow, by the end of the evening they had managed to attain a semblance of order, but finding the switch for the hot-water tank and the cupboard where the sheets were kept, and trying to decide who was going to sleep in which bed, all took a very long time. For supper Nicholas wanted baked beans on toast, but they couldn't find a toaster and the grill on the cooker was fiercely temperamental, so he had baked beans on bread instead.

"We need washing-up stuff and a mop, and tea and coffee . . ." Virginia searched for a piece of paper and a pencil and started, frantically, to make a list.

Cara chimed in, ". . . And soap for the bathroom and stuff to clean the bath with, because it's got a *horrid* dirty mark."

"And a bucket and spade," said Nicholas.

"And we'll have to get a fridge," said Cara. "We haven't got anywhere to keep our food and it'll all grow a blue beard if we let it just lie about."

Virginia said, "Perhaps we could borrow a meat-safe," and then remembered who had offered to lend her one, and frowned down at her shopping list and hastily changed the subject.

When the little water tank finally heated up, they had baths in the gimcrack bathroom, Nicholas and Cara going in together, and then Virginia swiftly before the water went cold. In dressing-gowns, by firelight, they made cocoa . . .

"There isn't even a television."

"Or a wireless."

"Or a clock," said Nicholas cheerfully.

Virginia smiled and looked at her watch. "If you really want to know, it's ten past nine."

"Ten past nine! We should be in bed ages ago."

"It doesn't matter," she told them.

"Doesn't *matter*? Nanny would be furious!"

Virginia leaned back in her chair, stretched out her legs and wriggled her bare toes at the heat of the fire.

"I know," she said.

After they were in bed, after she had kissed them, and left the door open on the landing and showed them how the light worked, she left them, and went down the narrow passage and up the two steps that led to the Tower Room.

It was cold. She sat by the window and looked out across the still, shadowed fields, and saw that the peaceful sea had turned pearly in the dusk, and the sky in the afterglow of sunset was streaked in long scarves of coral. Clouds were gathered in the west. They lay, piled beyond the horizon, threaded with shafts of gold and pink light, but gradually even these last shreds of light filtered away, and the clouds turned black, and in the east a little new moon, like an eyelash, floated up into the sky.

One by one lights started to twinkle out across the soft darkness, along the whole length of the coast, from farm-houses, and cottages and barns. Here, a window burned square and yellow. There a light bobbed across a rick yard. A pair of headlights tunnelled up a lane, and headed out on to the main road towards Lanyon, and Virginia wondered if it was Eustace Philips, making for Lanyon and The Mermaid's Arms, and she wondered if he would come and see how they were getting along, or whether he would be taciturn and sulky and wait for Virginia to produce some sort of an olive branch. She told herself that it would be worth doing even this, if it were only for the satisfaction of seeing his face when he realized how well she and Cara and Nicholas were managing for themselves.

But next day it was different.

In the night the wind had got up, and the dark clouds which last evening had lain banked on the horizon, were blown inland, bringing with them a dark and drenching rain. The sound of gutters trickling and dripping, the rattle of raindrops against the glass of the window-pane were the sounds which woke Virginia up. Her bedroom was so gloomy that she had to turn on the lamp before she could read her watch. Eight o'clock.

She got out of bed and went and shut the window. The floor-boards beneath her feet were quite wet. The rain curtained everything, and she could see no more than a few yards. It was like being in a ship, marooned in a sea of rain. She hoped the children would not wake up for hours.

She dressed in trousers and her thickest jersey and went downstairs and found that the rain had come down the chimney and effectively put out the fire, and the room felt damp and chilly. There were matches, but no firelighters; wood, but no kindling. She pulled on a raincoat and went out into the rain and across to the sagging garden shed, and found a hatchet, blunt with age and misuse. On the stone front doorstep, and at considerable personal danger to herself, she chopped a log into kindling, then took some paper which had been wrapped in with their groceries, and kindled a little fire. The sticks snapped and crackled, the smoke, after one or two surly billows into the room, ran sweetly up the chimney. She piled on logs and left the fire to burn.

Cara appeared when she was cooking breakfast.

"Mummy!"

"Hallo, my love." She bent to kiss her. Cara wore sky blue shorts, a yellow tee shirt, an inadequate little cardigan. "Are you warm enough?"

"No," said Cara. Her fine, straight hair was bunched into a slide, her spectacles were crooked. Virginia straightened them.

"Go and put on some more clothes, then. Breakfast isn't ready yet."

"But there isn't anything else. In my suitcase, I mean. Nanny didn't pack anything else."

"I don't believe it!" They gazed at each other. "You mean no jeans or raincoats or gumboots."

Cara shook her head. "I suppose she thought it was going to be hot."

"Yes, I suppose she did," said Virginia mildly, mentally cursing Nanny. "But you'd have thought she knew enough about packing to put a raincoat in."

"Well, we've sort of got raincoats, but not proper ones."

She looked so worried that Virginia smiled. "Don't worry."

"What shall we do?"

"We'll have to go and buy you both some clothes."

"Today?"

"Why not? We can't do anything else in weather like this."

"How about seeing Aunt Alice and swimming in her pool?"

"We'll keep that for a finer day. She won't mind. She'll understand."

They drove through the downpour to Penzance. At the top of the hill the mist was thick and grey, swirling in the wind, parting momentarily to allow a glimpse of the road ahead, and then closing in once more so that Virginia could scarcely see the end of the bonnet.

Penzance was awash with rain, traffic and disconsolate holiday-makers, prevented by the weather from their usual daily ploy of sitting on the promenade or the beach. They clogged the pavements, stood in shop doorways, aimlessly surged round the counters of shops, looking for something to buy. Behind the steamy windows of cafés and ice-cream shops they could be seen, packed in at little tables, slowly sipping, licking, munching; spinning it out, making it last, so that as to postpone the inevitable moment when they had to go out into the rain again.

Virginia drove around for ten minutes before she found a place to leave the car. In the rain they searched the choked streets until they came to a shop where fishermen's oilskins were for sale, and huge thigh-length rubber boots and lanterns and rope, and they went in and she bought jeans for Cara and Nicholas, and dark blue Guernseys, and black oilskins and sou'westers which obliterated the children like candle-snuffers. The children put on the new oilskins and the sou'westers, then and there, but the rest of the clothes were tied up in a brown paper parcel. Virginia took the parcel and paid the bill, and with the children, stiff as robots in their new coats, blinded by the brims of the hats, she went out into the street again.

It still poured. "Let's go home now," said Cara.

"Well, while we're here, we may as well get some fish or some meat or a chicken. And we haven't any potatoes or carrots or peas. There may be a supermarket."

"I want a bucket and spade," said Nicholas.

Virginia pretended not to hear. They found the supermarket, and joined the herd-like crowds, queuing and choosing, waiting and paying, packing the parcels into carriers, lugging them out of the shop.

The gutters gurgled, water streamed from drainpipes.

"Cara, can you really carry that?"

"Yes . . ." said Cara, dragged down to one side by the weight of the carrier.

"Give half of it to Nicholas."

"I want a bucket and spade," said Nicholas.

But Virginia had run out of money. She was about to tell him that he would have to wait until the next shopping expedition, but he turned up his face under the brim of the sou'wester, and his mouth was mutinous, but his eyes huge and beginning to brim with tears. "I want a bucket and spade."

"Well, we'll buy you one. But first I'll have to find a bank and cash a cheque and get more money."

The tears, as if by magic, vanished. "I saw a bank!"

They found the bank, filled with queuing customers.

The children made their way to a leather bench and sat, exhausted, like two little old people, their chins sunk into their chests, and their legs stuck out in front of them, regardless of whom they might trip up. Virginia waited in a queue, then produced her bank card and wrote her cheque.

"On holiday?" asked the young cashier. Virginia wondered how he could still be good-tempered at the end of such a morning.

"Yes."

"It'll clear up by tomorrow, you'll see."

"I hope so."

The red bucket and the blue spade was their final purchase. Laden, they walked the long way back to the car, and for some reason it was all uphill. Nicholas, banging the bucket with the spade as though it were a drum, trailed behind. More than once Virginia had to turn and wait for him, exhort him to get a move on. Finally, she lost her patience. "Oh, Nicholas, *do* hurry," and a passing woman heard the suppressed irritation in her voice, and glanced back, her face full of disapproval at such a disagreeable and short-tempered mother.

And that was after only one morning.

It still rained. They came at last to the car, and loaded the boot with parcels, and pulled off their dripping raincoats and stuffed them into the boot, and then scrambled into the car and slammed the door, thankful beyond words to be at last sitting down and out of the rain.

"Now," said Nicholas, still banging the bucket with the spade, "do you know what I want?"

Virginia looked at her watch. It was nearly one o'clock. "Something to eat?" she guessed.

What I would like would be to go back to Wheal House and know that Mrs. Jilkes had lunch ready and waiting, and there would be a cheerful fire in the drawing-room, and lots of new magazines and newspapers and nothing to do for the rest of the afternoon except read them.

"Yes, that. But something else as well."

"I don't know."

"You've got to guess. I'll give you three guesses."

"Well." She thought. "You want to go to the loo?"

"No. At least not yet."

"You want . . . a drink of water?"

"No."

"Give in."

"I want to go to a beach this afternoon and dig. With my new bucket and spade."

The young man in the bank proved to be quite correct in his weather forecast. That evening, the wind swung around to the north, and the shredded clouds were sent bowling away, over the moors. At first small patches of sky appeared, and then these grew larger and brighter and at last the evening sun broke through, to set, triumphantly, in a welter of glorious pinks and reds.

"Red Sky At Night, Shepherd's Delight," said Cara as they went to bed. "That means it's going to be a lovely day tomorrow."

It was.

"I want to go to the beach today and dig with my bucket and spade," said Nicholas.

"You will," Virginia told him firmly. "But first we have to go and see Aunt Alice Lingard, otherwise she'll think we're the rudest, most ungrateful people she's ever known."

"Why?" said Nicholas.

"Because she got the house all ready for us and we haven't even said thank you . . . finish up your egg, Nicholas, it's getting all cold."

"I wish I could have cornflakes."

"We'll buy cornflakes," said Virginia, and Cara got the pencil and the shopping list and they wrote Cornflakes underneath Steel Wool, Peanut Butter and Caster Sugar, Splits, Jellies, Soap Powder and Cheese. Virginia had never done so much shopping in her life.

She sent them off to play while she did the breakfast dishes and went upstairs to make the beds. The children's room was awash with clothes. Virginia had always imagined they were neat and tidy, but realized now that it had simply been Nanny, who moved along behind them, picking up and putting away everything that they dropped. She gathered up the clothes, not knowing if they were dirty or clean, took a sock from the top of the chest of drawers, and carefully did not touch a crumpled paper bag with two sticky sweets in the corner.

There was also a big pigskin folder of photographs. This belonged to Cara, and had been packed by Nanny, with what intention Virginia could only guess. One side of the folder was taken up with a selection of small photographs, many of which had been taken by Cara herself, and arranged with more affection than artistry. The front of the house, rather crooked; the dogs, the farm men on the tractor; an aerial view of Kirkton, and a picture postcard or two. On the other side was an impressive studio portrait of Anthony, a head and shoulders, all lighting and angles, so that his hair looked white blond, and his jaw very square and determined. The photographer's impression was of a strong man, but Virginia knew the narrowed eyes, and the weak, handsome mouth. And she saw the striped collar of the Turnbull and Asher shirt, the discreetly patterned silk of the Italian tie, and she remembered how clothes had mattered to Anthony; just as his car was important, and the furnishings of his house and his manner of living. Virginia had always imagined that these were subsidiary considerations, and took their shape from the character of the individual. But with Anthony Keile it was the other way round, and he had invariably given the highest priority to the smallest details, as though realizing that they were the props behind his image, and without them his inadequate personality would crumble.

Carrying the armful of clothes, she went downstairs and washed them in the tiny sink. When she took these outside to peg them crookedly on to the knotted clothes-line, she found only Nicholas, alone, playing with his red tractor and a few pebbles and bits of grass. He wore his new navy-blue Guernsey and was already scarlet in the face with heat, but Virginia knew better than to suggest that it might be a good idea if he took the sweater off.

"What are you playing?"

"Nothing much . . ."

"Is the grass straw?"

"Sort of."

Virginia pegged out the last pair of pants. "Where's Cara?"

"She's inside."

"Reading, I expect," said Virginia and went in to find her. But Cara was not reading; she was in the Tower Room, sitting by the window staring sightlessly out across the fields to the sea. When Virginia appeared at the door, she turned her head slowly, bemused, unrecognizing.

"Cara..."

Her eyes behind the spectacles came into focus. She smiled. "Hallo. Is it time to go....?"

"I'm ready when you are." She sat beside Cara. "What are you doing? Thinking, or looking at the view."

"Both, really."

"What were you thinking about?"

"I was really wondering how long we were going to stay here..."

"Oh—I suppose about a month. I've taken it for a month."

"But we'll have to go back to Scotland, won't we? We'll have to go back to Kirkton."

"Yes, we'll have to go back. There's your school for one thing." She waited. "Don't you want to go?"

"Isn't Nanny coming with us?"

"I shouldn't think so."

"It'll be funny, won't it, Kirkton, without Daddy or Nanny? It's so big for just the three of us. I think that's why I like this house. It's just the right size."

"I thought perhaps you wouldn't like it."

"I love it. And I love this room. I've never seen a room like it, with the stairs going down in the middle of the floor and all the windows and the sky." She was obviously not bothered by spooky sensations. "Why isn't there any furniture, though?"

"I think it was built as a study, a workroom. There was a man who lived here, about fifty years ago. He wrote books and he was very famous."

"What did he look like?"

"I don't know. I suppose he had a beard, and perhaps he was rather untidy and forgot to do up his sock suspenders, and buttoned his suit all wrong. Writers are often very absentminded."

"What was his name?"

"Aubrey Crane."

"I'm sure he was nice," said Cara, "to have made such a pretty room. You can just sit and see everything that happens."

"Yes," said Virginia, and together they gazed out at the patchwork fields, where peaceful cows grazed, and the grass was emerald green after the rain, and stone walls and leaning gate posts were tangled with brambles which, in just a month or two, would be sweet and heavy with black fruit. Away to the west a tractor hummed. She turned her head, pressing her forehead against the window and saw the patch of scarlet, bright as a pillar-box, and the man sitting up behind the wheel, wearing a shirt as blue as the sky.

"Who's that?" asked Cara.

"That's Eustace Philips."

"Do you know him?"

"Yes. He farms Penfolda."

"Are these all his fields?"

"I expect so."

"When did you know him?"

"A long time ago."

"Does he know you're here?"

"Yes, I think so."

"I expect he'll come for a drink or something."

Virginia smiled. "Yes, perhaps he will. Now come and comb your hair and get ready. We're going to see Alice Lingard."

"Shall I put in my bathing things? Can we swim in her pool?"

"That's a good idea."

"I wish we had a swimming pool."

"What, here? There wouldn't be room in the garden."

"No, not here. At Kirkton."

"Well, we could," said Virginia, without thinking. "If you really wanted one. But do let's go, otherwise it'll be lunchtime, and we shall have done nothing but sit here and talk."

But when they got to Wheal House, they found only Mrs. Jilkes at home. Virginia had rung the bell but only as a formality, immediately opening the door and stepping into the hall with the children at her heels. She waited for the dog to start barking, for Alice's voice to say "Who is it" and Alice to appear through the drawing-room door. But she was met only by silence, broken by the slow ticking of the grandfather clock which stood by the fireplace.

"Alice?"

Somewhere a door opened and shut. And then Mrs. Jilkes came up the kitchen passage, like a ship in full sail with her starched white apron. "Who is it?" She sounded quite cross until she saw Virginia standing there with the children beside her.

Then she smiled. "Oh, Mrs. Keile, you did surprise me, I couldn't think who you were, standing there. And these are your children. My, aren't they lovely? Aren't you lovely?" she inquired conversationally of Cara, who had never been asked such a question before. She wondered if she would say "no" because she knew that she wasn't lovely, but she was too shy to say anything. She simply stared at Mrs. Jilkes.

"Cara, isn't it? And Nicholas. Brought your swimming things, too, I can see. Going to go and have a dip in the pond?" She turned back to Virginia. "Mrs. Lingard's not here."

"Oh dear."

"Been away she has, ever since you went. Mr. Lingard had to go to some big dinner in London, so Mrs. Lingard suddenly decided she'd go too. Said she hadn't been up for a bit. She'll be home this evening, though."

Virginia worked this out. "You mean, she's been away since Thursday?"

"Thursday afternoon she went."

"But . . . Bosithick . . . A fire had been lighted when we got there, and it was all clean and there were eggs and milk waiting for us . . . I thought it was Mrs. Lingard."

Mrs. Jilkes looked coy.

"No. But I'll tell you who it was, though."

"Who was it?"

"It was Eustace Philips."

"*Eustace?*"

"Well, don't sound so shocked, it's not as though he's done anything wrong."

"But how do you know it was Eustace?"

"Because he telephoned me," Mrs. Jilkes said, importantly. "Least, he telephoned Mrs. Lingard, but her being in London I spoke to him instead. And he said was anybody doing anything about you coming back to Bosithick with those children, and I said I didn't know, and told him Mrs. Lingard was away, and he said, 'Well, never mind, I'll look after it,' and that was it. Make a good job, did he?"

"You mean he came in and did all that *house-cleaning*?"

"Oh no. Eustace wouldn't know one end of a duster from the other. That would have been Mrs. Thomas. She'd scrub the flags off the floor if you'd give her half a chance."

Cara put her hand into Virginia's. "Is that the man on the tractor we saw this morning?"

"Yes," said Virginia, distracted.

"But won't he think we're terribly rude? We haven't said thank you."

"No, I know. We'll have to go this afternoon. When we get back, we'll go down to Penfolda and explain."

Nicholas was furious. "But you said I could dig on the beach with my bucket and spade!"

Mrs. Jilkes knew a rebellious voice when she heard one. She stooped towards Nicholas, hands on her knees, her face close to his, her voice seductive.

"Why don't you go and have a lovely swim? And when you come out you and your Mummy and your sister can come and eat shepherd's pie, in the kitchen with Mrs. Jilkes . . ."

"Oh, but Mrs. Jilkes . . ."

"*No.*" Mrs. Jilkes shook her head at Virginia's interruption. "It's no trouble. All waiting to be eaten it is. And I was just beginning to think that the house was somehow empty, and me rattling around in it like a pea in a drum." She beamed at Cara. "You'd like to do that, wouldn't you, my lovely?"

She was so kind that Cara's icy shyness thawed. She said, "Yes, please."

That warm Sunday afternoon they walked across the fields to Penfolda, across the stubble fields where, only a week ago, Virginia had
watched the harvesters at work; across the grassy meadows, going
from field to field by stiles made of granite steps laid across the open
ditches. As they approached the farm, they saw the dutch barns, the
gates, the concrete cattle court, the milking parlours. Cautiously opening and shutting the gates behind them they crossed the court and
came out in the old cobbled farmyard. There was the sound of scrubbing, wet bristles on stone, and Virginia went to an open door of
what looked like stables, with loose boxes, and found a man, who was
not Eustace, cleaning the place out. He wore a faded navy-blue beret
on the back of his curly grey head, and old-fashioned dungarees with
braces.

He saw her and stopped sweeping. Virginia said, "I'm sorry, I'm
looking for Mr. Philips . . ."

" 'E's around somewhere . . . up at the back of the house . . ."

"We'll see if we can find him."

They went through a gate, and along a path that led between the
farmhouse and the tangled little garden where she and Eustace had
shared the pasty. A tabby cat sat on the doorstep in a warm patch of
sun. Cara squatted to pet it and Virginia knocked on the door. There
were footsteps and the door opened, and a little round woman stood
there, cosy as an arm-chair, upholstered in a black dress and loose-
covered with a print apron. From behind her, from the kitchen, came
a good smell, the memory of a hearty Sunday dinner.

"Yes?"

"I'm Virginia Keile . . . from Bosithick . . ."

"Oh yes . . ."

A smile creased the rosy face, pushing up her cheeks into two little
bunches.

"You must be Mrs. Thomas."

"That's right . . . and these your children, are they?"

"Yes. Cara and Nicholas. We feel so bad because we never came
down to thank you. For cleaning the house I mean, and leaving the
eggs and the milk and the firewood and everything."

"Oh, that wasn't me. I just cleaned the place up a bit, opened a few windows. It was Eustace who got the logs there, took up a load on the back of the tractor . . . left the milk and the eggs at the same time. We thought you wouldn't have had time to do much before you went to London . . . dismal it is coming home to a dirty house; couldn't let you do that."

"We'd have come before, but we thought it was Mrs. Lingard . . ."

"Want to see Eustace, do you? He's up in the vegetable garden at the back, digging me a bucket of potatoes." She smiled down at Cara. "Do you like the little pussy cat?"

"Yes, she's sweet."

"She's got kittens in the barn. Do you want to go and see them?"

"Will she mind?"

"She won't mind. Come along, Mrs. Thomas will show you where to find them."

She made for the barn, with the children at her heels; not a backward glance did they spare for their mother, so intent were they on seeing the kittens. Left alone, Virginia went up on the garden path, through a wicket gate, arched in ivy. Eustace's blue shirt could be glimpsed beyond the pea-vines, and she made her way towards this and found him forking up a drill of potatoes. Round and white and smooth as sea pebbles, they were, caked in earth the same colour and consistency as rich, dark chocolate cake.

"Eustace."

He looked over his shoulder and saw her. She waited for him to smile, but he did not. She wondered if he had taken offence. He straightened up, leaning on the handle of the spade.

"Hallo," he said, as though it were a surprise to see her there.

"I've come to say thank you. And I'm sorry."

He shifted the spade from one hand to another. "What have you got to be sorry for?"

"I didn't realize it was you who'd brought the wood and lit the fire and everything. I thought it was Alice Lingard. That's why we haven't been down before."

"Oh, that," said Eustace and she wondered if there was something else she should be sorry about.

"It was terribly kind. The milk and the eggs and everything. It just made all the difference." She stopped, terrified of sounding insincere. "But how did you get into the house?"

Eustace drove the prongs of the fork into the ground, and started towards her. "There's a key here. When my mother was first married, she used to go over sometimes, do a bit of work for old Mr. Crane. His wife was ailing, my mother used to clean the place up. He gave her a key to hang on the dresser and it's been there ever since."

He reached her side, and stood, looking down at her, then he suddenly smiled, his blue eyes crinkled with amusement and she knew that her fears were unjustified, and that he bore no grudge. He said, "So you decided to take the house after all."

Ruefully, Virginia said, "Yes."

"I felt badly, saying those things, and you so upset about everything. I lost my temper, but I shouldn't have."

"You were right. It was all I needed to make me make up my own mind."

"That's why I brought up the logs and stuff . . . I thought it was the least I could do. You'll be wanting more milk . . ."

"Could you let us have it every day?"

"If someone comes and fetches it."

"I could, or one of the children. I hadn't realized, but over the fields and the stiles it's no distance at all."

They had begun to walk back towards the gate.

"Are your children here?"

"They've gone with Mrs. Thomas to see some kittens."

Eustace laughed. "They'll fall in love with them, so be warned. That little tabby got caught by a Siamese up the road, and you've never seen such pretty kittens." He opened the gate for Virginia to go through. "Blue eyes they've got and . . ."

He stopped, watching over her head as Cara and Nicholas came, slowly, carefully, out of the barn, their cupped hands held cradled to their chests, their heads bent in adoration. "What did I tell you?" said Eustace and shut the gate behind them.

The children came up the slope of the lawn, ankle deep, knee deep, in plantains and great white daisies. And all at once Virginia saw them with fresh eyes, with Eustace's eyes, as though she were seeing them for the first time. The fair head and the dark, the blue eyes and the brown. And the sun blinked on to Cara's spectacles so that they flashed like the headlights of a little car, and their new jeans, bought too big, slipped down over their hips and Nicholas's shirt-tail hung out over his firm, round little bottom.

A love-like pain caught at Virginia's throat, unshed tears prickled at the back of her eyes. They were so defenceless, so vulnerable, and for some reason it mattered so much that they should make a good impression on Eustace.

Nicholas caught sight of her. "Look what we've got, Mummy; Mrs. Thomas said that we could bring them out."

"Yes," said Cara, "and they're tiny and they've got their eyes . . ." She saw Eustace, behind her mother, and stopped dead, where she was standing, her face closed up, her eyes watching him from behind her glasses.

But Nicholas came on . . . "Look, Mummy you've got to look. It's all furry and it's got tiny claws. But I don't know if it's a boy or girl. Mrs. Thomas says she can't tell." He looked up and saw Eustace and smiled engagingly into his face. "They've stopped sucking their mother, Mrs. Thomas says, she was getting too thin, and she's put a little saucer of milk out for them, and they lap and their tongues are tiny," he told Eustace.

Eustace put out a long brown finger and scratched the top of the kitten's head. Virginia said, "Nicholas, this is Mr. Philips, you're meant to say how do you do."

"How do you do. Mrs. Thomas said that if we wanted one we could have one but we had to ask you, but you wouldn't mind, would you, Mummy? It's so little and it could sleep on my bed and I'd look after it."

Virginia found herself coming out with all the classic arguments produced by the parents of children, in the same situation as herself. *Too young to be taken from its mother yet. Still needs her to keep him warm. Only at Bosithick for the holidays, and think how he'd hate the train journey back to Scotland.*

Eustace had put down the bucket of potatoes and now went over to where Cara stood, clutching her kitten. Virginia, in agony for her, saw Eustace squat to Cara's height, loosen her fingers gently with his own. "You don't want to hold him too tight, otherwise he won't be able to breathe."

"I'm frightened of dropping him."

"You won't drop him. He wants to look out and see what's happening in the world. He's never seen sun as bright as that." He smiled at the kitten, at Cara. After a little, slowly, she smiled back, and you forgot the ugly spectacles and the bumpy forehead and the straight hair, and saw only the marvellous sweetness of her expression.

After a little he sent them to put the kittens back, and, telling Virginia to stay outside in the sunshine, went into the house with the potatoes for Mrs. Thomas, only to emerge a moment or so later with a packet of cigarettes and a bar of chocolate. They lay where they had lain before, in the long grass, and were joined there by the children.

He gave them the chocolate but talked to them like adults. What have you been doing? What did you do yesterday in all that rain? Have you been swimming yet?

They told him, voices chiming against each other, Cara, her shyness over, as eager to impart information as Nicholas.

"We bought raincoats, and we got *drenched*. And Mummy had to go to the bank to get more money, and Nicholas got a bucket and spade."

"But I haven't been to the beach to dig yet!"

"And we swam this morning at Mrs. Lingard's. We swam in her pool. But we haven't swum in the sea yet."

Eustace raised his eyebrows. "You haven't swum in the sea and you haven't been to a beach? That's all wrong!"

"Mummy says there hasn't been time . . ."

"But she promised me," Nicholas reminded of his grievance, became indignant. "She said today I could dig with the spade, but I've not been near one grain of sand."

Virginia began to laugh at him, and he became, naturally, angrier than ever. "Well, it's true, and it's what I want more than anything."

"Well," said Eustace, "if you want it more than anything, what are we doing sitting around here talking our heads off?"

Nicholas stared at Eustace, his eyes narrowed suspiciously. "You mean go to the beach?"

"Why not?"

"Now?" Nicholas could not believe his ears.

"Is there anything else you'd rather do?"

"No. Nothing. Nothing else." He sprang to his feet. "Where shall we go? Shall we go to Porthkerris?"

"No, we don't want to go there—nasty crowded place. We'll go to our own private beach, the one that nobody knows about, that belongs to Penfolda and Bosithick."

Virginia was astonished. "I didn't know we had one. I thought there was nothing but cliffs."

By now Eustace was also on his feet. "I'll show you . . . come along, we'll take the Land-Rover."

"My bucket and spade's at our house."

"We'll pick them up on the way."

"And our swimming things," said Cara.

"Those too."

He went into the house to fetch his own things, shouted a message to Mrs. Thomas, led the way through the gate and back across the farmyard. He whistled and the dogs, barking, came rushing around the side of the barn, knowing that the whistle meant a walk, smells, rabbits, maybe a swim. Everybody, including the dogs, clambered into the Land-Rover, and Cara, her shyness now quite forgotten, screamed with delight, as they lurched out of the cobbled farmyard, and went bumping and bouncing up the lane towards the main road.

"Is it far?" she asked Eustace.

"No distance at all."

"What's the beach called?"

"Jack Carley's cove. And it's not a place for babies, only for big children who can look after themselves and climb down the cliff."

They assured him hastily that they came into this category and Virginia watched Nicholas's face, and saw the joyful satisfaction upon it at being indulged, at last, in the one thing he had been wanting to do for a whole day. And what was more, doing it instantly. Not told maybe, or tomorrow, or to wait or to be patient. And she knew exactly how he felt for long ago Eustace had done the very same, performed the same miracle for the young Virginia; had bought her the ice-cream she had been yearning for, and then, out of the blue, asked her to come back to Penfolda.

7

They left the Land-Rover in the deserted farmyard below Bosithick and started to walk down towards the sea. At first, crossing the fields, they went in a bunch, four abreast, Eustace taking Nicholas by the hand because he was inclined to lag. But then the fields gave way to brambles and bracken and they fell into single file with Eustace leading the way; over crumbling stone walls and across a stream, where rushes grew shoulder high to a small person. Then over another wall, and the path disappeared beneath a jungle of green bracken. Through this they pushed their way, gorse bushes pressing in at either side. The ground all at once slid steeply away from beneath their feet, and the path zig-zagged down through the undergrowth, down to the very lip of the curving cliff. And beyond, space. Blue air. Soaring, screaming gulls, and the distant creaming of the sea.

At this point the coast seemed to fling itself out into a jagged headland, composed of great granite outcrops. Between these the turf was smooth and very green, stained with patches of purple-belled heather, and the path wound down between these outcrops and as they followed its convolutions, a little cove, sheltered and enclosed, gradually revealed itself, far below. The sea was deep and still, purple over the rocks and jade green over the sand. The beach was tiny, and backed by the remains of an old sea wall. Beyond this the land sloped up to the green wedge of the cliff, down which trickled, in a series of small waterfalls, a fresh-water stream. And above the sea wall, tucked snug against the foot of the cliff, stood the remains of a cottage; derelict, windows broken, slates torn from the roof.

They stood in a row, the four of them, buffeted by the gentle wind, looking down. It was a disturbing sensation. Virginia wondered if the children might suffer from vertigo, but neither of them seemed in the least disturbed by the dizzy emptiness of the great height.

"There's a house," said Cara.

"That was where Jack Carley lived."

"Where does he live now?"

"With the angels, I reckon."

"Did you know him?"

"Yes, I knew him. He was an old man when I was a boy. Didn't like people coming down here. Not any old people. Had a great barking dog and he used to chase them away."

"But he let you come?"

"Oh, yes, he let me come." He grinned down at Nicholas. "Do you want me to carry you, or can you manage?"

Nicholas peered out and over. The path trickled down the face of the cliff and so out of sight. Nicholas remained undismayed.

"No. I don't want to be carried, thank you. But I'd like it better if you went first."

In fact, the dogs went first, unafraid, sure-footed as goats. The humans followed at a more prudent speed, but Virginia found that the path was not as dangerous as it appeared. After the dry spell the ground was hard and firm underfoot, and in steep places, steps had been cut, shored up with driftwood or fashioned roughly out of cement.

Much sooner than she had expected they were all safely down. Above them, the cliff loomed, dark and cold in the shadow, but when they jumped down on to the beach they came out of the shade and into the sunshine, and the sand was warm, and there was the smell of tar from the little house, and no sound but the gulls and the creaming sea, and the splash of the stream.

There was an air of unreality about the little cove, as though they had somehow strayed out of time and space. The air was still, the sun burning hot, the sand white and the green water clear as glass. The

children stripped off their clothes, and took Nicholas's new bucket
and spade and went at once to the water's edge, where they began to
dig a sand castle, moated and turreted with bucket-shaped towers.

"If the tide comes in it'll wash the whole castle away," said Cara.

"No, it won't, because we're going to make a great huge moat and
then the water will go into that."

"If the tide comes in higher than the castle, it's going to wash it
away. Like King Canute."

Nicholas considered this. "Well, it won't for ages."

It was the sort of day that they would remember for the rest of their
lives. Virginia imagined them, middle-aged, reminiscing, nostalgic.

*There was a little cove and a ruined cottage and not another soul but
us. And there were two dogs and we had to climb down a suicidal path.*

Who took us?

Eustace Philips.

But who was he?

*I can't remember . . . he must have been a farmer, some sort of a
neighbour.*

And they would argue over details.

There was a stream.

No, it was a waterfall.

*There was a stream running down the middle of the beach. I can re-
member it quite clearly. And we dammed it with a sandbank.*

But there was a waterfall too. And I had a new spade.

When the tide was high, they all swam, and the water was clear and
salt and green and very cold. Virginia had forgotten her cap and her
dark hair lay sleek to her head, and her shadow moved across the peb-
bled sea-bed like some strange new variety of fish. Holding Cara, she
floated, drifting between the sea and the sky, with her eyes dazzled by
water and sunshine; and the air was cleft with screaming gulls, and
always the gentle murmur of breaking waves.

She became very cold. The children showed no signs of chill, however, so she left them with Eustace, and came out of the water, and
went to sit on the dry sand, above the high water mark.

She sat on the sand because they had brought no rug, no super-
sized bath-towels. And no comb or lipstick, or biscuits or knitting,

and no Thermos of tea, and no extra cardigan. And no plum cake or chocolate biscuits, and no money for the donkey rides or the man with the ice-cream.

She was joined at last by Cara, teeth chattering. Virginia wrapped her in a towel and began gently to dry her. "You'll soon be swimming at this rate."

Cara said, "What time is it?"

Her mother squinted up at the sun. "I suppose, nearly five . . . I don't know."

"We haven't had tea yet."

"No, nor we have. And I don't suppose we will either."

"Not have any *tea*?"

"It doesn't matter for once. We'll have supper later on."

Cara made a face, but raised no objections. Nicholas, however, was vociferous in his complaints when he realized that Virginia had brought nothing for him to eat.

"But I'm hungry."

"I'm sorry."

"Nanny always had shivery bites and you haven't got anything."

"I know. I forgot. We were in such a hurry and I never thought of biscuits."

"Well, what am I going to eat?"

Eustace caught the tail end of this conversation as he came, dripping, up the beach. "What's this?" He stopped to pick up a towel.

"I'm very hungry and Mummy hasn't brought anything to eat."

"Too bad," said Eustace unsympathetically.

Nicholas sent him a long, measured look, and turned away, headed in a sulky silence back to his digging, but Eustace caught him by an arm and pulled him gently back and held him against his knees, rubbing at him absently with the towel, rather as though he were fondling one of the dogs.

Virginia said, placatingly, "Anyway, we'll have to go soon, I expect."

"Why?" asked Eustace.

"I thought you had all those cows to milk."

"Bert's doing them."

"Bert?"

"He was at Penfolda today, cleaning out the loose boxes."

"Oh, yes."

"He used to work for my father, he's retired now, but he comes along every alternate Sunday, gives me a hand. He likes to do it, and Mrs. Thomas feeds him a good dinner, and it means I have a few hours to myself."

Nicholas became irritated by the pointless small-talk. He reared around in Eustace's hands, turned up a furious face towards him. "I am *hungry*."

"So am I," said Cara, wistful if not so vehement.

"Well, listen," said Eustace.

They listened. And heard, over the sound of the sea and the gulls, another sound. The soft drumming of an engine, putt-putt-putt, all the time coming closer.

"What is it?"

"You watch and see."

The sound grew louder. Presently around the point they saw approaching a small open boat, white with a blue stripe, riding the waves with a scud of white spray. A stocky figure stood at its stern. Putt-putt, it swung round into the shelter of the cove, and the engine idled down to a steady throb . . .

They all stared. "There you are!" said Eustace, smug as a conjuror who has brought off a difficult trick.

"Who is it?" asked Virginia.

"That's Tommy Bassett from Porthkerris. Come to pick up his lobster pots."

"But he won't have any biscuits," said Nicholas, who would never be diverted from the matter in hand.

"No. But he might have something else. Shall I go and see?"

"All right." But they sounded doubtful.

He put Nicholas aside and went back down the sand and into the sea, diving through the eye of a peacock-coloured wave, and swimming, with a strong and steady crawl, far out to where the boat bobbed. The lobster pots were already being hauled aboard. The fishermen emptied one and dropped it back, and then saw Eustace coming, and stood, watching.

"Hallo there, boy!" His voice carried across the water.

They saw Eustace catch the gunwales with his hands, hang there for a moment, and then with a heave pull himself clean out of the water and into the rocking boat.

"What a long way to swim," said Cara.

Nicholas said, "I hope he isn't going to bring back a lobster."

"Why not?"

"Lobsters have got claws."

In the boat, some discussion seemed to be taking place. But at last Eustace stood up, and they saw that he was carrying some sort of bundle. He let himself overboard and started back, swimming more slowly this time, hampered as he was by his mysterious burden. This proved to be, of all things, a string shopping-bag, but it contained, wet and dripping, a dozen gleaming mackerel.

Nicholas opened his mouth to say, "I don't like fish," but caught Eustace's eye, and closed his mouth and said nothing instead.

"I thought he might have a few," Eustace told them. "He usually puts a line out when he's coming out to the pots." He smiled down at Cara. "Ever eaten mackerel, have you?"

"I don't think so. But," said Cara, "fancy giving you the string bag." To her, this seemed far more amazing than the gift of the mackerel. "Doesn't he want it back again?"

"He didn't say he did."

"Shall we have to take them back to Bosithick."

"What would we do that for? . . . No, we cook them here . . . come on, you can come and help."

And he collected six or seven big stones, round and smooth, and built them into a ring, and he took matches, and a scrap of an old cigarette packet, and some chips of driftwood and straw, and he kindled a fire and sent the children off to find more wood and soon they had a regular bonfire going. And when the wood ash was deep and grey and burned red when you blew on it, he laid the fish there, in a row, and there was a sizzling and a spitting and presently a most delicious smell.

"But we haven't got knives and forks," said Cara.

"Fingers were made before forks."

"But it'll be hot."

She and Nicholas squatted by the fireside, hair on end, naked except for their bathing pants and a coating of sand. They looked like savages, and perfectly content.

Cara watched Eustace's clever hands. "Have you done this before?"

"What, whittled a stick?"

"No, had a fire, and cooked fish."

"Many times. This is the only way to cook mackerel, and eat it, fresh out of the sea."

"Did you use to do this when you were a boy?"

"Yes."

"Was the old man alive then? Jack Carley."

"Yes. He used to come out and sit on the beach and join in the party. Bring a bottle of rum with him and a smelly old pipe and sit there and tell us yarns so hair-raising we could never be quite sure if they were true."

"What sort of yarns?"

"Oh, adventures . . . he'd been all over the world, done everything. Been a cook in a tanker, a lumberjack, built roads and railways, worked in the mines. He was a tin miner, see. A tinner. Went off to Chile, worked there for five years or more, came home a rich man, but all his money was gone within the twelve months, and he was off again."

"But he came back."

"Yes, he came back. Back to Jack Carley's cove." Cara shivered. "You cold?"

"Nanny calls it a ghost going over your grave."

"Put on a sweater then, and that'll keep the ghosts away, and then it'll be time to eat our tea."

And seeing him with her children, Virginia thought of Anthony who had missed so much because he had never wanted to have anything to do with them. If Cara had been pretty, perhaps he would have paid attention to her . . . Cara who longed for attention and love and thought her father the most wonderful being in the world. But she was plain and shy and wore spectacles, and he never endeavoured to hide the fact that he was ashamed of her. And Nicholas . . . with Nicholas it might have been different. When he was old enough, Anthony would have taught him to shoot and play golf and fish, they would have become friends and gone about together. But now Anthony was dead, and none of this would happen and she felt sorry because they would never now remember swimming with him, they would never crouch with him round a camp fire, listening to his stories and watching his clever hands whittle wooden skewers to be used instead of forks.

The sun slipped down out of the sky, shone directly in upon them, and the sea was turned to a liquid dazzle. It would soon be evening and then it would be dark. And Jack Carley had lived here, just as Aubrey Crane had lived at Bosithick. You didn't see them. You didn't hear them. But you knew that they were still around.

It was disturbing, this awareness of the past, but somehow elemental, and so not really frightening. And it was not possible to live in this part of the world as a nervous or a timid person, for, beneath the beauty it was a savage land, and danger lurked everywhere. In the sea, deep and treacherous, with its undertows and unsuspected currents. In the cliffs and caves, so swiftly cut off and submerged by racing tides. Even the quiet fields down which they had walked this afternoon concealed unthought-of horrors; abandoned mine workings, deep pits and shafts, black as wells, lay hidden beneath the bracken. And scraps of fur and feather, and little bleached bones bore witness to the foxes who built their lairs in earthly hollows under the gorse.

And after nightfall the owl set up his predatory hooting, and the badger emerged to tunnel and scavenge. Not for him the thrill of the hunt. He was just as content to push the lid off a dustbin in the middle of the night, causing such a clatter as to waken the farmer's wife in a cold sweat of fright.

"Mummy. It's cooked." Cara's voice broke across her thoughts. She looked up and saw Cara holding a stick aloft, a fragment of fish impaled dangerously upon its point. "Come and get it *quickly* before it falls off!" Her voice was agonized, and Virginia got to her feet, dusting the sand off the seat of her bathing-suit, and went down to join in the picnic.

In the afterglow of the setting sun, with the offshore wind cool on their faces, they climbed slowly home. After the swim the children were sleepy and silent. Nicholas was not too proud to accept a piggyback from Eustace, and Virginia carried the wet bathing things and towels in the string bag which had been used for the mackerel, and helped Cara along with the other hand. They were all sandy, salty, tousled, weary, and the path was steep and the climb, up through the bracken and the treacherous undergrowth, exhausting. But at last they reached the fields at the top, and after that the going was easy. Behind them the sea, luminous, in the half-light, reflected all the colours of the sky, and ahead was Bosithick, cradled in the curve of the hill, with the road behind it flickering, every now and then, with the searchlight glare of a passing car.

Some of Eustace's cows had strayed through a gap in the hedge into the top field. In the dusk they loomed, brown and white, and made pleasant munching sounds, raising their heads to watch as the small procession walked by.

Nicholas said, leaning forward to speak into Eustace's ear, "Are you going to come back with us?"

He smiled. "Time I was getting home."

"We would like you to stay for supper."

"You've had your supper," Eustace told him.

"I thought that was tea."

"Don't tell me you've got room for more food."

Nicholas yawned. "No, maybe not."

Virginia said, "I'll make you cocoa, and you can drink it in bed."

"Yes," said Nicholas. "But it would be nice if Eustace would come and talk to us while we had our baths . . ."

Cara chimed in. "Yes, and then Mummy could get our cocoa ready, and you could talk to us."

"I'll do more than that," said Eustace. "I'll scrub the sand off your backs."

They giggled in a high-pitched fashion as though this were very funny, and as soon as they were indoors raced for the bathroom to fight over the taps. Ominous splashing sounds came from beyond the door, and Eustace, rolling up his sleeves, moved in to break it up.

Virginia heard him saying, "Quiet now, you'll sink the ship if you don't watch out."

Leaving him to it, she carried the fishy string bag out to the kitchen and emptied the bathing things and the sand-encrusted towels into the sink, and rinsed them out and wrung them, and carried them out into the dark garden, and, by feel, found the clothes-line and pegged them out, leaving them to billow and flap like ghosts in the darkness.

Back in the kitchen, she poured milk into a sauce-pan, put it on to heat, stood watching it, leaning against the cooker, yawning a little. She put up a hand to her eyes, and found that her face was rough with sand, so she took the little mirror out of her handbag, and a comb, and propped the mirror on one of the shelves of the dresser and tried to do something about her hair, but it was stiff and dry with salt, and full of sand. She thought that if there had been a shower, she would have washed it, but the idea of putting it under a tap was somehow all too difficult, too complicated. In the inadequate light her reflection gazed back at her from the round mirror, and there were freckles across the bridge of her nose, but her eyes were shadowed, dark as two holes in her face.

The milk rose in the pan. She made the two mugs of cocoa, put them on a tray, started upstairs with them. She saw that the bathroom was empty, a trail of damp towels and footprints led upstairs. She heard voices and came along the passage, and their bedroom door stood open.

They were inside and they did not see her. She stood and watched them. Eustace sat, with his back to her, on Cara's bed, and the children were perched on Nicholas's bed. All three heads together, Eustace was being given a guided tour of Cara's photographs.

"And this is Daddy. The big one here. He's terribly good-looking, don't you think? . . ." This was Cara, as chatty now as she could be with someone with whom she was completely at ease. "And this is our house in Scotland, that's my bedroom, and that's Nicholas's bedroom, and that's the nursery up at the top . . ."

"That's my bedroom!"

"I said it was that bedroom, silly. And this is Nanny's room, and that's Mummy's room, but you can't see the rooms at the back because they're round at the back. And this is an aerial view . . ."

"A man took it in an aeroplane . . ."

"And that's all the park and the river. And that's the walled garden."

"And that's Mr. McGregor on his tractor, and that's Bob and that's Fergie."

Eustace was beginning to lose the thread . . . "Hold on now, who are Bob and Fergie?"

"Well, Bob helps Mr. McGregor and Fergie helps the gardener. Fergie plays the bagpipes and do you know who taught him? His uncle. And do you know what his uncle is called? Muncle." Nicholas triumphantly produced the answer.

Eustace said, "Uncle Muncle."

"And this is Daddy skiing at St. Moritz, and that's all of us at a grouse shoot—at least, we went to the picnic bit, we didn't go up the hill. And that's the bit of the river where we sometimes swim, but it's not always very safe, and the stones hurt your feet. But Mummy says we can have a swimming pool, she says when we go back to Kirkton, we can have a swimming pool, just like Aunt Alice Lingard's . . ."

"And that's Daddy's car, it's a great big Jaguar. It's a . . ." Nicholas faltered. "It was a great big Jaguar." He finished bravely, "Green."

Virginia said, "Here's your cocoa."

"Oh Mummy, we were showing Eustace all the photographs of Kirkton . . ."

"Yes, I heard."

"That was very nice," said Eustace. "Now I know all about Scotland."

He stood up, as though to get out of Virginia's way, and went to put the photograph frame back on to the chest of drawers.

The children climbed into bed. "You'll have to come and see us. You'll have to come and stay. Won't he, Mummy? He can sleep in the spare room, can't he?"

"Maybe," said Virginia. "But Eustace is a busy man."

"That's it," said Eustace. "Busy. Always got plenty to do. Well . . ." He moved towards the open door. "I'll say good night."

"Oh, good night, Eustace. And thank you for taking us to that lovely place."

"Don't dream about Jack Carley."

"Even if I do I shan't be frightened."

"That's the way. Good night, Nicholas."

"Good night. I'll see you in the morning."

Virginia said to him, "Don't go. I'll be down in a moment."

He said, "I'll wait downstairs."

The cocoa was duly consumed, between yawns. Their eyes drooped. At last they lay down and Virginia kissed them good night. But when she kissed Nicholas he did a surprising thing. Most undemonstrative of children, he put his arms around her neck and held her cheek down against his own.

She said, gently, "What is it?"

"It was a nice place, wasn't it?"

"You mean the little beach?"

"No. The house where Eustace lives."

"Penfolda."

"Will we go back?"

"Sure to."

"I loved that little kitten."

"I know you did."

"Eustace is downstairs."

"Yes."

"I shall hear you talking." His voice was filled with satisfaction. "I shall hear you go talk, talk, talk."

"Will that be cosy?"

"I think so," said Nicholas.

They were near to sleep, but still she stayed with them, moving quickly about the room, picking up stray clothes and folding them and putting them, neat as Nanny, across the seats of the two rickety cane chairs. This done, she went to close the window a little, for the night air was growing chill, to draw the skimpy curtains. The room, by the meagre light of the bedside lamp was all at once enclosed, safe, soft with shadows, the only sound the ticking of Cara's clock and the breathing of the children.

She was filled, in that moment, with love. For her children; for this strange little house; for the man, downstairs, who waited for her. And aware, too, of a marvellous sense of completion, of rightness. It will be the first time, she thought, that Eustace and I have been alone, with all the time in the world. Just the two of us. She would light the fire for company and draw the curtains and make him a jug of coffee. If they wished, they could talk all night. They could be together.

Cara and Nicholas were sleeping. She turned off the light and went downstairs to unexpected and surprising darkness. For an incredulous moment she thought that Eustace had changed his mind and already gone, but then she saw that he stood by the window, smoking, watching the very last of the light fade from the sky. A little of this light was reflected upon his face, but when he heard her footstep he turned, and she could see no expression on his face, only shadows.

She said, "I thought you'd gone."

"No. I'm still here."

The darkness disturbed her. She reached for the lamp on the table and switched it on. Yellow light was thrown, like a pool, between them. She waited for him to speak, but when he said nothing, simply stood there, smoking, she began to fill the silence with words.

"I . . . I don't know about supper. Do you want something to eat? I don't even know what time it is."

"I'm all right."

"I could make you some coffee . . ."

"You haven't got a can of beer?"

She made a helpless gesture. "I haven't, Eustace. I'm sorry. I never bought any. I never drink it." That sounded priggish, as though she disapproved of beer. "I mean, I just don't like the taste." She smiled, trying to turn it into a joke.

"It doesn't matter."

The smile collapsed. Virginia swallowed. "Are you sure you wouldn't like coffee?"

"No, thank you." He began to look about for somewhere to stub out his cigarette. She found him a saucer and put it on the table, and he demolished the stub as through he had a personal, vicious grudge against it.

"I must go."

"But . . ."

He turned towards her, waiting for her to finish. She lost her nerve. "Yes. It's been a good day. It was kind of you to give up your day for us and show us the cove and . . . everything." Her voice sounded high-pitched and formal as though she were opening a sale of work. "The children loved it."

"They're good children."

"Yes. I . . ."

"When are you going back to Scotland?"

The abruptness of the question, the coldness of his voice, were shocking. She was suddenly cold, a shiver of apprehension trickling down her spine like a stream of icy water.

"I . . . I'm not sure." She took hold of the back of one of the wooden chairs, leaning against it as if for support. "Why do you ask?"

"You're going to go back."

It was a statement, not a question. Faced with it, Virginia's natural diffidence leapt to the worst conclusion. Eustace expected her to go, even wanted her to go. She heard herself telling him, with marvellous lightness, "Well, some time, of course. After all, it's my home. The children's home."

"I hadn't realized until this evening that it was such a considerable property . . ."

"Oh, you mean, Cara's photographs . . ."

"But then, you have plenty of people to help you run it."

"I don't run it, Eustace."

"Then you should. Learn something about farming. You'd be surprised how much there is to it. You should take an interest, start up something new. An Aberdeen Angus herd. Did your husband ever think of doing that? You can sell a good bull at the Perth sales for sixty, seventy thousand pounds?"

It was like a conversation in a nightmare, mad and pointless. She said, "Can you?" but her mouth was dry and the words scarcely made any sound at all.

"Of course. And who knows, one day you may have built up something really great to hand on to that boy of yours."

"Yes."

He said again, "I must go." The trace of a smile crossed his features. "It was a good day."

But Virginia remembered a better one, that other day she had spent with Eustace, the spring afternoon of sun and wind when he had brought her an ice-cream and finally driven her home. And he had promised to telephone her, and then forgotten, or perhaps he had changed his mind. She realized that she had been waiting, all afternoon, for him to tell her what really happened. She had been expecting him to bring up the subject, perhaps as a story for the children to share, or as a scrap of harmless nostalgia to be remembered, over the years, by two old friends. But he had said nothing. And now she would never know.

"Yes." She let go of the chair and straightened up, folding her arms across her chest as though she were trying to stay warm. "A special day. The kind that people never forget."

He moved towards her, around the edge of the table, and Virginia turned away from him and went to open the door. Cool air, smelling sweet and damp, flooded in from a night arched in a sapphire sky, bright with stars. Out of the darkness a curlew sent up its long mournful cry.

He was beside her. "Good night, Virginia."

"Good night, Eustace."

And then he was going down the steps, away from her, over the wall and down the fields towards the old farmyard where he had left his car. The dusk swallowed him. She closed the door and locked it and went back to the kitchen and took the children's cocoa mugs and washed them, slowly and carefully. She heard his Land-Rover go grinding up past the gate, up the lane towards the main road, heard the sound of the engine die away into the quiet night, but she never looked up from what she was doing. When the mugs were dry, the tea towel folded and there was nothing more to do, she found that she was exhausted. She turned off the lights and went slowly upstairs and undressed and climbed into bed. Her body lay slack, but the inside of her head behaved as though she had been living on black coffee for a week.

He doesn't love you.

I never thought he did.

But you were beginning to think so. After today.

Then I was wrong. We have no future together. He made that very clear.

What did you imagine was going to happen?

I imagined that he would be able to talk about what happened ten years ago.

Nothing happened. And why should he remember?

Because I did. Because Eustace was the most important person, the most important thing that ever happened to me.

You didn't remember. You married Anthony Keile.

They were married in London, in July; Virginia in a cream satin dress with a six foot train and a veil that had belonged to Lady Keile's grandmother, and Anthony in a grey frock-coat and an immaculately cut pair of sponge-bag trousers. They emerged from St. Michael's, Chester Square, with bells jangling, sun shining, and a small retinue of beribboned bridesmaids extorting *oohs* and *aahs* of admiration from the thin crowd of inquisitive women who had realized that there was a wedding going on, and hung about to see what turned up when the doors were opened.

The excitement, the champagne, the pleasures of being loved and congratulated and kissed kept Virginia going until it was time to go upstairs and change. Her mother was there, ubiquitous, efficient, to unzip the clinging satin and unpin the borrowed tiara and the filmy veil.

"Oh, my dear, it all went off so beautifully, and you really did look enchanting, even though perhaps I shouldn't say anything so conceited about my own child . . . Darling, you're shivering, you're surely not cold?"

"No. I'm not cold."

"Change your shoes, then, and I'll help you on with your dress."

It was rose pink, with a tiny petalled hat to match, a charming useless ensemble that she would never wear again. She imagined coming back from her honeymoon, still wearing paper silk and pink petals, a little crushed by now, and going brown at the edges. (But of

course they couldn't go brown, they weren't real, they were pretence
petals . . .)

"And your suitcase is in the boot of Anthony's car, such a good idea
taking a taxi round to the flat and picking the car up there, then you
have none of this terrible horse-play with kippers and old shoes."

A roar, a galloping of feet, came from the passage outside the bedroom. Anthony's voice was raised in a comic sound like a hunting
horn. "There! He sounds as though he's ready." She kissed Virginia
briskly. "Have a good time, my darling."

The door burst open, and Anthony stood there, wearing the suit
that he had chosen to go away in, and with a large sun hat on the top
of his head. He was considerably drunk.

"Here she is! We're off to the South of France, my love, which is why
I am wearing this hat."

Mrs. Parsons, laughing indulgently, removed it, smoothed his
hair with her long fingers, straightened his tie. She might have been
the bride, not Virginia, who stood and watched this little ceremony
with a face that held no expression whatsoever. Anthony held out a
hand to her. "Come on," he said. "Time we went."

The hired car, awash in confetti, took them back to the Parsonses'
flat, where Anthony's car was waiting for them. The plan had been
that they should get straight into his car and drive to the airport, but
Virginia had a latch-key in her purse, and instead, they let themselves
in and went into the kitchen, and she tied an apron around the pink
silk dress, and Anthony sat on the table and watched while she brewed
him up a jug of black coffee.

For their honeymoon they had been lent a villa in Antibes. By their
second day Anthony had met an old friend; by the end of the first
week, he knew everyone in the place. Virginia told herself that this
was what she had expected, was what she wanted. Anthony's gregari-
ous instincts were part of his charm, and one of the things that had
attracted her to him in the first place. Besides, after one day it became
very obvious that they were going to find it hard to think of things to
say to each other. Conversation at meals was inclined to be distinctly
sticky. She realized then, that they had never been alone together
before now.

There was a couple, called Janey and Hugh Rouse; he was a writer and they had rented a house at Cap Ferrat. Janey was older than Virginia and Virginia liked her, and found her easy to talk to. Once, sitting on the terrace at the Rouses' house, waiting for the men to come up from the rocks, Janey had said, "How long have you known Anthony, honey?" She had lived, as a child, in the States, and although she did not speak with an American accent, her speech was spattered with words and phrases which instantly gave her origins away.

"Not very long. I met him in May."

"Love at first sight, hm?"

"I don't know. I suppose so."

"How old are you?"

"Eighteen."

"That's awfully young to settle down. Not that I can see that Anthony settling down too much for a few years yet."

"He'll have to," Virginia told her. "You see, we're going to live in Scotland. Anthony's been left this estate, Kirkton . . . it used to belong to an uncle who was a bachelor. And we're going to go and live there."

"You mean, you think Anthony will spend all his time tramping around in a tweed suit with mud on his boots?"

"Not exactly. But I can't believe that living in Scotland is going to be quite the same as living in London."

"It won't," said Janey, who had been there. "But don't expect the simple life, or you'll be disappointed."

But Virginia did expect the simple life. She had never seen Kirkton, never been to Scotland for that matter, but she had once spent an Easter holiday with a schoolfriend who lived in Northumberland and somehow she imagined that Scotland would be rather like that, and that Kirkton would be a low-ceilinged, rambling, stone farmhouse, with flagged floors, and worn Turkey carpets, and a dining-room with a great log fire and hunting prints on the walls.

Instead, she was presented with a tall, square, elegantly proportioned Adam house, with sash windows full of reflected sunshine, and a flight of stone stairs which led, from the carriage sweep, up to the front door.

Beyond the gravel was grass, and then a ha-ha wall, and then the park, landscaped with giant beeches, sloping down to the distant silver curve of the river.

Overwhelmed, silent, Virginia had followed Anthony up the steps and through the door. The house was empty, old-fashioned and unfurnished. Between them they were going to do it up. To Virginia the task seemed daunting, but when she said as much Anthony overrode her.

"We'll get Philip Sayer on to it, he's this interior decorator my mother got to do the house in London for her. Otherwise we'll make the most ghastly mistakes and the place will be a mess."

Virginia privately thought she preferred her own ghastly mistakes to somebody else's impeccable taste—it was more homely; but she said nothing.

"And this is the drawing-room, and then the library beyond. And the dining-room, and there are kitchens and stuff downstairs."

The room soared and echoed, the icy prisms of crystal chandeliers glinted, dependent from ornately decorated ceilings. There was panelling and marvelous cornices over the tall windows. There was dust and a distinct feeling of chill.

They mounted to the first floor up a curved stairway, airy and elegant, and their steps echoed on the polished treads and through the empty house. Upstairs, there were bedrooms, each with its own bathroom, dressing-rooms, linen rooms, housemaid's cupboards, even a boudoir.

"What would I do with a boudoir?" Virginia wanted to know.

"You can come and boud in it, and if you don't know what that means, it's French for sulk. Oh, come on, take that horrified expression off your face and look as though you're enjoying yourself."

"It's just so big."

"You talk as though it were Buckingham Palace."

"I've never been in such a big house. I certainly never thought I would live in one."

"Well, you're going to, so you'd better get used to it."

Eventually they were outside again, standing by the car, staring up at the elegant front elevation, regularly spaced with windows. Virginia put her hands deep in the pockets of her coat and said, "Where's the garden?"

"What do you mean?"

"I mean flower-beds and stuff. Flowers. You know. A garden."

But the garden was a half-mile away, enclosed in a wall. They drove there and went inside and found a gardener and rows of fruit and vegetables like soldiers, waiting to be picked off.

"This is the garden," said Anthony.

"Oh," said Virginia.

"What's that meant to mean?"

"Nothing. Just oh."

The interior decorator duly arrived. Hard on his heels came vans and lorries, builders, plasterers, painters, men with carpets, men with curtains, men in pan-technicons which spilled out furniture like cornucopias, endlessly, as though they would never run out.

Virginia let it all happen. "Yes," she would say, agreeing to whatever shade of velvet Philip Sayer was suggesting. Or "Yes" when he thought of Victorian brass bedsteads in the spare room, and thick white crochet bedcovers. "Terribly Osborne, my dear, you know, Victorian Country Life."

The only time that she had raised her voice with an independent idea was over the kitchen. She wanted it like the one she remembered, the marvellous room at Penfolda with its air of stability, the suggestion in the air of good things cooking, the cat in the chair and the geraniums crowded on the window-sill.

"A farmhouse kitchen! That's what I want. A farmhouse kitchen's like a living-room."

"Well, I'm not going to live in any kitchen, I'll tell you that."

And she had let Anthony have his way because, after all, it was not her house, and it was not her money which paid for the stainless steel sinks, and the black and white floor and the patent self-cleaning cooking unit with eye-level grill, and a spit for broiling chickens.

It was finished and Virginia was pregnant.

"How marvellous for Nanny!" said Lady Keile.

"Why?"

"Well, darling, she's in London, doing temporary work, but she's longing, but longing for a new baby. Of course she won't be all that keen on leaving London, but she's bound to make friends, you know what this Nanny's network's like, better than the English Speaking Union I always say. And that top floor is *meant* to be a nursery, you can tell by the gate at the top of the stairs, and the bars on the windows. Gorgeously sunny. I think pale blue, don't you? For carpets, I mean, and then French chintz curtains . . ."

Virginia tried to stand up for herself. To say, *No. I will look after my own baby.* But she was so sick carrying Cara, so weak and unwell, that by the time she once again felt strong enough to cope with the situation and stand on her own two feet, the nursery had been decorated and Nanny was there, established, rigid, immovable.

I'll let her stay. Just until the baby's born and I'm on my feet again. She can stay for a month or two, and then I'll tell her that she can go back to London because I want to look after my baby for myself.

But by then, there were further complications. Virginia's mother, in London, complained of pains and tiredness; she thought she was losing weight. Virginia at once went south to see her, and after that, her loyalties were torn between her baby in Scotland and her mother in London. Travelling up and down in the train it became very clear that it would be madness to get rid of Nanny until Mrs. Parsons had recovered. But of course, she didn't recover and, by the time the whole ghastly nightmare was over, Nicholas had arrived and, with two babies in the nursery, Nanny was dug in for good.

At Kirkton they were surrounded, within a radius of ten miles or so, by a number of entertaining neighbours. Young couples with time and money to spare, some with young children like the Keiles', all with interests which matched Anthony's.

For appearances' sake, he put in a certain amount of time on the farm, talking to McGregor, the grieve, finding out what McGregor thought should be done, and then telling McGregor to do it. The rest of the day was his own, and he used it to the full, doing exactly what he wanted. Scotland is a country geared to the pleasures of menfolk, and there was always shooting to be got, grouse in the summer, and partridges and pheasants in the autumn and winter. There were rivers to be fished and golf courses and a social life which was even gayer than the one he had left behind in London.

Virginia did not fish or play golf and Anthony would not have invited her to join him even if she had wanted to. He preferred the company of his men-friends, and she was expected to be present only when they had been invited specifically as a couple. To a dinner or a dance, or perhaps to lunch before a point-to-point, when she would go through agonies trying to decide what to put on, and inevitably turn up in what everybody had been wearing last year.

She was still shy. And she didn't drink so there seemed no artificial way of getting over this terrible defect. The men, Anthony's friends, obviously thought her a bore. And their wives, though kind and friendly, terrified her with their private jokes and their incomprehensible references to places and persons and events known only to them. They were like a lot of girls who had all been to the same school.

Once, driving home after a dinner party, they quarrelled. Virginia had not meant to quarrel but she was tired and unhappy, and Anthony was more than a little drunk. He always seemed to drink too much at parties, almost as though it were a social grace that was expected of him. This evening it made him aggressive and bad-tempered.

"Well, did you enjoy yourself?"

"Not particularly."

"You certainly didn't look as though you did."

"I was tired."

"You're always tired. And yet you never seem to do a thing."

"Perhaps that's why I'm tired."

"And what does that mean?"

"Oh, nothing."

"It has to mean something."

"All right, it means that I get bored and lonely."

"That's not my fault."

"Isn't it? You're never there . . . sometimes you're not in the house all day. You have lunch in the club at Relkirk . . . I never see you."

"OK. Me and about a hundred other chaps. What do you suppose their wives do? Sit and mope?"

"I've wondered what they do with their time. You tell me."

"Well, they get around, that's what. They see each other, take the children to Pony Club meets, play bridge; I suppose, garden."

"I can't play bridge," said Virginia, "and the children don't want to ride ponies, and I would garden only there isn't a garden at Kirkton, just a four-walled prison for flowers, and a bad-tempered gardener who won't let me so much as cut a bunch of gladioli without asking him first."

"Oh, for heaven's sake . . ."

She said, "I watch other people. Ordinary couples, sometimes on Saturdays in Relkirk. Doing the shopping together in the rain or the sunshine, and children with them, sucking ice-creams, and they put all the parcels into shabby little cars and drive home, and they look so happy and cosy, all together."

"Oh, God. You can't want that."

"I want not to be lonely."

"Loneliness is a state of mind. Only you can do anything about that."

"Weren't you ever lonely, Anthony?"

"No."

"Then you didn't marry me for company. And you didn't marry me for my startling conversation."

"No." Coldly agreeing, his profile was stony.

"Then why?"

"You were pretty. You had a certain fawn-like charm. You were very charming. My mother thought you were very charming. She thought your mother was very charming. She thought the whole bloody arrangement was charming."

"But you didn't marry me because your mother told you to."

"No. But you see, I had to marry somebody, and you turned up at such a singularly opportune time."

"I don't understand."

He did not reply to this. For a little he drove in silence, perhaps prompted by some shred of decency not to tell her the truth, now or ever. But Virginia, having come so far, made the mistake of pressing him. "Anthony, I don't understand," and he lost his temper and told her.

"Because I was left Kirkton on condition that I was married when I took it over. Uncle Arthur thought I would never settle down, would break the place up if I moved in as a bachelor . . . I don't know what he thought, but he was determined that if I lived at Kirkton I'd do it as a family man."

"So that's why!"

Anthony frowned. "Are you hurt?"

"I don't think so. Should I be?"

He fumbled for her hand with his own . . . the car swerved slightly as his fingers closed over hers. He said, "It's all right. It may be no better, but it's certainly no worse than other marriages. Sometimes it's a good thing to be frank and clear the air. It's better to know where we both stand."

She said, "Do you ever regret it? Marrying me, I mean."

"No. I don't regret it. I'm just sorry that it had to happen when we were both so young."

One day she found herself in the house alone. Quite alone. It was Saturday, and afternoon. Mr. McGregor, the grieve, had gone to Relkirk, taking Mrs. McGregor with him. Anthony was playing golf, and Nanny and the children were out for a walk. An empty house and nothing to do. No washing to be done, no cake to be baked, no ironing, no garden to weed. Virginia walked through it, going from room to room, as though she were a stranger who had paid to see around, and her footsteps echoed on the polished staircase, and there was the tick of the clock, and everywhere order, neatness. This was what Anthony loved. This was what he had created. This was why he had married her. She ended up in the hall, opened the front door and went down the steps on to the gravel, thinking that she would maybe spy Nanny and the children in the distance; she would go to meet them, run and snatch Cara up in her arms, hug her and hold her, if only to prove that she really existed, that she was not a dream-child that Virginia had conceived, like some frustrated spinster, out of her own imagination.

But there was no sign of Nanny and, after a little, she went back up the steps and so indoors again, because there did not seem to be anywhere else to go.

There was a pretty girl, called Liz, married to a young lawyer who worked in Edinburgh. He worked in Edinburgh, but they lived only a mile or two from Kirkton, in an old, converted Presbyterian manse, with a wild garden, that was filled with daffodils in the spring, and a paddock for the ponies.

She had young children, dogs, a cat, and a parrot in a cage, but—perhaps because she missed her husband who was in Edinburgh all week, or perhaps because she was simply a girl who enjoyed people—her house was always full. Other mothers' children lolloped about on the ponies, crowded the dining-room table at teatime, played rounders on the lawn. If she didn't have whole families staying with her, then she had whole families for the day, feeding them on huge roasts of beef, and steak and kidney pies, marvellous old-fashioned puddings, and homemade ice-creams. Her drink cupboard, which must have taken a frightening beating from the hordes who passed through her hospitable doorway, was always open, always at hand for any guest in need of a little liquid refreshment.

"Help yourself," she would call through the open door, while she knocked up a three-course dinner for ten unexpected guests. "There's ice in the fridge if the ice-bucket's empty."

Anthony, naturally enough, adored her, flirted cheerfully and openly with her, put on a great show of jealousy when the week-ends came around and her husband was home.

"Get that bloody man out of the house," he would tell Liz, and she would go into gales of delighted laughter, as would everybody else who was listening. Virginia smiled, and over their heads met the eye of Liz's husband. He was a quiet young man, and though he stood there, with a glass in his hand, smiling, it was almost impossible to tell what he was thinking.

"You'll have to watch out for that husband of yours," one of the other wives said to Virginia. But she only said, "I have been, for years," and changed the subject, or turned to speak to somebody else.

One Tuesday, Anthony called her from the club in Relkirk. "Virginia. Look, I've got embroiled in a poker game, God knows when I'll be home. But don't wait, I'll get a bite to eat here. See you later."

"All right. Don't lose too much money."

"I shall win," he told her. "I shall buy you a mink coat."

"That's just what I need."

He arrived home, after midnight, stumbling up the stairs. She heard him moving about in his dressing-room, dropping things, opening and shutting drawers, swearing at some cuff-link or button.

After a little, she heard him getting into bed, and the light beyond the open door went out, and there was only darkness. And she wondered if he had chosen to sleep in his dressing-room out of consideration to Virginia, or whether there was some other, more sinister reason.

She soon knew. The society in which they moved, the narrow clique, was too small for secrets. "Virginia darling, I told you to watch out for that naughty man of yours."

"What's he done now?"

"You are marvellous, the way you never get ruffled. You obviously know all about it."

"All about what?"

"Darling, the intimate dinner party that he had with Liz."

". . . Oh, yes, of course. Last Tuesday."

"He is an old devil. I suppose he thought none of us would find out. But then Midge and Johnny Gray suddenly decided on the spur of the moment to go up to the Strathtorrie Arms for dinner, you know, there's a new manager now, and it's all frightfully dark and chic and you can get a very good dinner. Anyway, off they went, and of course there were Anthony and Liz, all snugged up in a corner. And you knew all the time!"

"Yes."

"And you don't mind?"

"No."

That was the terrible thing. She didn't mind. She was apathetic, bored by Anthony and the outrageous schoolboy charm that had, as far as Virginia was concerned, long since worn itself to shreds. And this was not the first affair. It had happened before and it would doubtless happen again, but still, it was daunting to look down the years ahead and see herself tied for ever to this tedious Peter Pan. A man so unperceptive that he could gaily embark on a clandestine involvement, and yet conduct the whole affair on what was virtually his own front doorstep.

She thought about divorce, but knew that she would never divorce Anthony, not simply because of the children, but because she was Virginia, and she could no more embark, voluntarily, upon such a course, than she could have flown to the moon.

She was not happy, but what could be the good of broadcasting her failure, her disillusion, to the rest of the world? Anthony did not love her, had never loved her. But then she had never loved him. If he had married Virginia to get his hands on Kirkton, then she had married Anthony on the rebound, in an emotional state of extreme unhappiness, and in a desperate bid to avoid the London Season that her mother had planned for her, culminating in the final nightmare of a coming-out dance.

She was not happy, but, to all intents and purposes, she had everything. A lovely house, a handsome husband, and the children. The children were worth everything. For them she would shore up her crumbling marriage, and for them she would create a world of security that they would never know again.

Anthony had been with Liz that night he was killed. He had called in at the Old Manse for a drink on his way back from Relkirk and was invited to stay for supper.

He rang Virginia.

"Liz has got the Cannons staying. She wants me to eat here and make up a four for bridge. I'll be home some time. Don't wait up."

Liz's cupboard with the whisky bottle stood open, as always. And as always Anthony helped himself liberally and with a generous hand. It was two o'clock before he started home, a black and starless night of pouring rain. It had been raining for days and the river was in spate. Afterwards the police came with tape measures and bits of chalk, and they measured the skid marks, and hung over the broken rail of the bridge and stared down into the muddy, swirling waters. And Virginia stood with them, in the drenching rain, and watched the divers go down, and there was a kindly sergeant who kept urging her to go back to the house, but she wouldn't go because, for some reason, she had to be there, because he had been her husband and the father of her children.

And she remembered what he had said, that night he told her about Kirkton. *I'm just sorry that it had to happen when we were both so young.*

8

The quiet night moved slowly past, the seconds, the minutes, the hours, measured by the ticking of Virginia's wrist-watch which she had put on the table by her bed. Now, she reached out for it and saw that it was nearly three o'clock in the morning. She got out of bed, wrapped herself in the quilt and went to sit on the floor by the open window. It was the hour before dawn, dark and very still. She could hear, a mile or more away, the gentle movement, like breathing, of the sea. She could hear the soft shufflings and munchings of the Guernseys, grazing two or three fields distant; she could hear rustlings and whisperings and creepings from hedgerow and burrow, and the hooting of a night owl.

She found that she was devilled by the memory of Liz. Liz had come to Anthony's funeral wearing a face of grief and guilt so naked that instinctively one had turned away from it, not wanting to witness such pain. Soon afterwards her husband had taken her to the South of France for a holiday and Virginia had not seen her again.

But now she knew that she must go back to Scotland and soon, if it was only to square things up with Liz. To convince Liz that no blame could ever be laid at her door, to make—as far as was humanly possible—friends with her again. She thought of returning to Kirkton and this time her imagination did not turn and run but took the journey quietly and without horror. Off the road it went, and down over the bridge and the river, and up the drive between the lush meadows of the park. It came to the curving sweep in front of the house, and went up the steps and in through the front door, and now there was no longer the old familiar sensation of loneliness, of being trapped. But simply a sadness that the lives of the people who had lived in this beautiful house had achieved no lasting cohesion, but had unravelled like a length of badly spun yarn, and finally shredded away.

She would sell the house. Somewhere, some time, her subconscious had made the decision and now presented it to her conscious mind as a *fait accompli*. How much this phenomenon had to do with Eustace, Virginia could not at the moment comprehend. Later on, no doubt, it would all work itself out. For now the relief was enormous, like the shedding of a load carried too long, and she felt grateful, as though another person had stepped in and made the decision for her.

She would sell Kirkton. Buy another house, a little house ... somewhere. Again, later on, it would all work itself out. She would make a new home, new friends, create a garden, buy a puppy, a kitten, a canary in a cage. Find schools for the children, fill the holidays with pleasures she had previously been too diffident to attempt. She would learn to ski; they would go on skiing holidays together. She would build kites and mend bicycles, let Cara read all the books she ever wanted, and go to Nicholas's sports days wearing the right sort of hat, and achieve marvellous things like winning the egg-and-spoon race.

And it would happen because she would make it happen. There was no more Eustace, no more dreams, but other good things were constant. Like pride, and resolution, and the children. The children. And she smiled, knowing that, like the arrow on the compass for ever pointing north, whatever she did and however she behaved, she was always left, facing squarely in their direction.

She was beginning to be cold. The first lightening of dawn was beginning to creep up into the sky. She got up off the floor, took a sleeping-pill and a glass of water and climbed back into bed. When she opened her eyes again the sun, high in the sky, was shining full in her face, and from downstairs came a terrible racket, a banging at the front door and a voice calling her name.

"Virginia! It's me. Alice! Wake up, or are you all dead?"

Dazed with shock and sleep, Virginia stumbled out of bed, across the floor, and hung out of the window. "Alice! Stop making such a din. The children are asleep."

Alice, foreshortened, turned up an astonished face. Her voice dropped to an exaggerated stage-whisper. "I'd begun to think you'd all passed out. It's past ten. Come down and let me in!"

Yawning, incapable, Virginia groped for her dressing-gown, pushed her feet into slippers and went downstairs, pausing at the open door of the children's room on the way. To her surprise they were still asleep, undisturbed by Alice's shouting. She thought, we must have been late last night. We must have been much later than I realized.

She unlocked the door, to let in a flood of sunshine and Alice. Alice wore a crisp blue linen dress, a silk scarf over her head. As usual she was bright-skinned, clear-eyed, maddeningly awake.

"Do you usually wake up at this hour?"

"No, but . . ." Virginia swallowed a yawn.

". . . I couldn't get to sleep last night. Eventually I took a pill. It must have knocked me out."

"And the children?"

"I didn't give them a pill, but they're still asleep. We were late, we were out all day." She yawned again, forced her eyes open. "How about some coffee?"

Alice looked amused. "You certainly look as though you'll need some. I tell you what. I'll make it, you go and get yourself woken up, and put some clothes on. It's no good talking to you when you're in this state." She laid her handbag on the table in a purposeful way. "I must say, this really isn't too bad a little house, is it? And here's the kitchen. A little poky, perhaps, but perfectly adequate . . ."

Virginia ran a bath, got into it and washed her hair. Afterwards, she went upstairs, wrapped in a towel, and took clean clothes from the drawer, and a cotton dress, as yet unworn, from the wardrobe. She pushed her feet into sandals, combed her sleek wet hair into place, and feeling clean and strangely hungry, went back downstairs to Alice.

She found her thoroughly organized, the kettle on the gas, the jug ready with the coffee, mugs laid out on the table.

"Oh, there you are . . . we're just about ready . . . I thought we'd have proper coffee; I get so fed up with this wishy-washy stuff, don't you?"

Virginia sat on the edge of the table. "When did you get back from London?"

"Last night."

"How was it? Did you have fun?"

"Yes, but I didn't come here to talk about London."

"In that case, what brought you here at ten o'clock on a Monday morning?"

"Curiosity," said Alice. "Sheer, undiluted curiosity."

"About me?"

"About Eustace Philips!"

Virginia said, "I don't understand."

"Mrs. Jilkes told me. I was scarcely in through the front door when I was hearing all about it. She said that Eustace had telephoned her while I was away to ask if anybody was getting Bosithick ready for you and the children. And she said I was in London, and he said not to bother, he'd see to it."

"Yes, that's right . . . and he did too . . ."

"But Virginia . . . You talked about Eustace, but you never told me that you'd met him again."

"Didn't I?" Virginia frowned. "No, I didn't, did I?"

"But when did you meet him?"

"That day I came out to see the cottage. Do you remember? I said I wouldn't be back for lunch. And I went to the pub in Lanyon to buy cigarettes and I met him there."

"But why didn't you say anything about it? Was there any particular reason that you didn't want me to know?"

"No." She tried to remember. "But I suppose I just didn't want to talk about him." She smiled. "It wasn't as though it had been such a friendly reunion. In fact, we had the most terrible row . . ."

"But did you *mean* to meet him again?"

"No. It just happened."

"And he remembered you? After all this time? But he'd only ever seen you that once at the barbecue."

"No," said Virginia. "I did see him again."

"*When?*"

"About a week after the barbecue. I met him in Porthkerris. We spent the afternoon together and he drove me back to Wheal House. You didn't see him because you were out that day. But my mother was there. She knew about it."

"But why was it all kept such a secret?"

"It wasn't a secret, Alice. It was just that my mother didn't like Eustace. I must say, he didn't make much of an effort to impress her, and he was rude and the Land-Rover was covered with bits of straw and mud and manure . . . not my mother's cup of tea at all. She treated the whole incident as though it were a sort of joke, but I knew that he had made her angry, and that she didn't like him."

"But you could have talked to me about him. After all, it was I who introduced you to Eustace."

"I tried, but every time I started, my mother somehow broke into the conversation or changed the subject or interrupted in some way. And . . . you mustn't forget this, Alice . . . you were her friend, not mine. I was just the little girl, out of the nursery. I never imagined for a moment that you'd take my side against hers."

"Was it a question of taking sides?"

"It would have been. You know what a snob she was."

"Oh, yes, of course, but it was harmless."

"No, Alice, it wasn't harmless. It was terribly dangerous. It affected everything she did. It deformed her."

"Virginia!" Alice was shocked.

"That's why we suddenly went back to London. You see, she knew, she guessed right away, that I was in love with Eustace."

The kettle boiled. Alice lifted it, and filled the coffee jug, and the kitchen was suffused with a delicious fresh smell. Alice drew a spoon gently across the surface of the coffee.

"And were you?" she asked at last. "In love with Eustace?"

"Of course I was. Wouldn't you have been at seventeen?"

"But you married Anthony Keile."

"Yes."

"Did you love him?"

"I . . . I married him."

"Were you happy?"

"I was lonely . . ."

"But, Virginia, I always thought . . . I mean, your mother always said . . . I thought you were so happy," Alice finished, hopeless with confusion.

"No. But it wasn't all Anthony's fault. It was my fault, too."

"Did Lady Keile know this?"

"No." Nor did she know the circumstances of Anthony's death. Nor did she know about Liz. Nor was she ever going to. "Why should she know? She used to come and stay with us, but never for more than a week at a time. It wasn't difficult to foster the illusion of an idyllically happy marriage. It was the least we could do for her . . ."

"I'm surprised Nanny never said anything."

"Nanny never saw anything she didn't want to see. And to her, Anthony was perfection."

"It can't have been easy."

"No. But like I said, it wasn't all Anthony's fault."

"And Eustace?"

"Alice, I was seventeen; a little girl, waiting for someone to come and buy her an ice-cream."

"But not now . . ." said Alice.

"No. Now I'm twenty-seven and the mother of two children. And I'm not waiting for ice-creams any longer."

"You mean, he has nothing to give you."

"And he needs nothing from me. He's self-sufficient. He has his own life. He has Penfolda."

"Have you discussed this with him?"

"Oh, Alice . . ."

"You obviously haven't. So how can you be so certain?"

"Because all those years ago, he said he'd phone me. He said that he wanted me to come out to Penfolda for tea or something, to meet his mother again. And I was going to borrow your car and drive myself out here. But you see, he never telephoned. I waited, but he never telephoned. And before there was time to find out why, or do anything about it, I'd been whisked back to London by my mother."

Alice said, "And how do you *know* he never telephoned?" She was beginning to sound impatient.

"Because he never did."

"Perhaps your mother took the call."

"I asked her. And she said there'd never been any telephone call."

"But, Virginia, she was perfectly capable of taking a call and never telling you about it. Specially if she didn't like the young man. Surely you realized that."

Her voice was brisk and practical. Virginia stared, scarcely able to believe her ears. That Alice should say such things about Rowena Parsons—Alice of all people, her mother's oldest friend. Alice, coming out with a dark truth that Virginia had never had the courage to find out for herself. She remembered her mother's face, smiling across the railway carriage, the laughing protest. *"Darling! What an accusation. Of course not. You surely didn't think . . ."*

And Virginia had believed her. She said at last, helplessly, "I thought she was telling me the truth. I didn't think she was capable of lying."

"Let's say she was a determined person. And you were her only child. She always had great ambitions for you."

"You knew this. You knew this about her and yet she was still your friend."

"Friends aren't people you particularly like for any special reason. You just like people because they're your friends."

"But if she was lying, then Eustace must have thought that I didn't want to see him again. All these years he's been thinking I simply let him down."

"But he wrote you a letter," said Alice.

"A *letter*?"

"Oh, Virginia, don't be so dense. That letter that came for you. The day before you went back to London." Virginia continued to stare blankly. "I know there was a letter. It came by the afternoon post, and it was on the table in the hall and I thought 'How nice' because you didn't get many letters. And then I went off to do something or other and when I came back the letter had gone. I presumed you'd taken it."

A letter. Virginia saw the letter. Imagined the envelope as white, the writing very black, addressed to her. Miss Virginia Parsons.

Lying unattended and vulnerable upon that round table that still stood in the centre of the hall at Wheal House. She saw her mother come out of the drawing-room, perhaps on her way upstairs, pause to inspect the afternoon's mail. She was wearing the raspberry-red suit with the white silk shirt, and when she put out her hand to pick up the letter, her nails were painted the same raspberry-red, and her heavy gold charm bracelet made a jingling sound, like bells.

She saw her frown at the writing, the black masculine writing, inspect the postmark, hesitate for perhaps a second, and then slip the envelope into the pocket of her jacket and carry on with what she was doing, unperturbed, as though nothing had happened.

She said, "Alice, I never got that letter."

"But it was there!"

"Don't you see? Mother must have taken it. Destroyed it. She would, you know. She would say, 'It's all for Virginia's sake. For Virginia's own good.'"

Illusions were gone for ever, the veil torn away. She could look back with a cool, objective regard and see her mother the way she had really been, not merely snobbish and determined, but devious too. In some odd way, this was a relief. It had taken some effort, all these years, to sustain the legend of an irreproachable parent, even though Virginia had been deceiving nobody but herself. Now, remembered, she seemed much more human.

Alice was looking upset, as though already regretting any mention of the letter.

"Perhaps it wasn't from Eustace."

"It was."

"How do you know?"

"Because if it had been from anyone else, then she would have given it back to me, with some excuse or other about opening it by mistake."

"But we don't know what was in the letter."

Virginia got off the table. "No. But I'm going to find out. Now. Will you stay here till the children wake up? Will you tell them I shan't be long?"

"But where are you going?"

"To see Eustace, of course," said Virginia, from the door.

"But you haven't drunk your coffee. I made you coffee and you haven't even drunk it. And what are you going to say to him? And how are you going to explain?"

But Virginia had already gone. Alice was speaking to an empty room, an open, swinging door. With an exclamation of exasperation, she put down her coffee cup and went to the door as though to call Virginia back, but Virginia was already out of earshot, running like a child through the tall summer grass, across the fields in the direction of Penfolda.

She took the field path because it would have taken too long to get into the car and turn it and drive back along the main road. And time was too precious to be wasted. They had already lost ten years, and there was not another moment to spare.

She was running, through a joyous morning of honey-scents and white daisies and tall grass that whipped at her bare legs. The sea was a dark, purplish blue, striped with ribbons of turquoise, and the horizon was blurred in a haze that promised great heat. She was running, long-legged, taking the steps of the stiles two at a time, and the ditches of the stubble fields brimmed with red poppies and the air was filled with the petals of yellow gorse flowers, blown to confusion, like confetti, by the sea-wind.

She came across the last field, and Penfolda lay ahead of her, the house and the long barns, and the little garden, wall-enclosed from the wind. She went over the last stile that led into the vegetable garden, and down the path and through the gate, and she saw that the cat and her half-Siamese kittens lay in the sun on the doorstep, and the front door stood open and she went indoors and called Eustace, and the house was dark after the brightness of the day outside.

"Who's that?"

It was Mrs. Thomas, carrying a duster, peering over the banister.

"It's me. Virginia. Virginia Keile. I'm looking for Eustace."

"He's just coming in from milking . . ."

"Oh, thank you." Without bothering to wait and explain, she went back out of doors, and started across the lawn, making for the cattle court and the milking parlour. But at that moment he appeared, coming through the gate that opened into the far side of the garden. He was in shirt sleeves, aproned, wearing rubber boots and carrying a polished aluminum pail of milk. Virginia stopped dead. He closed the latch of the gate behind him and looked up and saw her.

She had meant to be very sensible. To say, calmly and quietly, "I want to ask you about the letter you wrote me." But it didn't happen like that at all. For everything was said in that long moment, while they stood and looked at each other, and then Eustace set down his bucket and started towards her, and she ran down the slope of the grass and into his arms, and she was laughing, her face pressed into the front of his shirt, and he was saying, "It's all right. It's all right," just as though she were crying, not laughing. And Virginia said, "I love you," and then she burst into tears.

He said, "Of course I telephoned. Three or four times. But you were never there. It was always your mother and each time I felt more of a fool and each time she said that she'd tell you I'd called and that you'd ring me back. And I thought maybe you'd changed your mind. I thought perhaps you'd decided you had better things to do than come and have tea with someone like me and my old mother. I thought maybe your mother had talked you round. She didn't lose any love on me, not from the first moment she set eyes on me. But you knew that, didn't you?"

"Yes, I knew. And I wondered. Once, I nearly rang you up. I thought perhaps you'd forgotten . . . and then I lost my nerve. And then, out of the blue, my mother said we had to go back to London and after that, there wasn't any time. And in the train, I asked her, straight out, if you'd ever called and she said never. And I believed her. That was the terrible thing, I always believed her. I should have known. It was my fault, I should have known. Oh, Eustace, why was I such a ninny?"

They had come indoors, ostensibly to find a clean handkerchief for Virginia, and for no particular reason had stayed there, ending up, inevitably, in the kitchen, sitting at the scrubbed table, with the air filled with the smell of baking saffron bread, and the only sound to disturb them the slow ticking of the old-fashioned pendulum clock.

"You weren't a ninny," said Eustace. "You were seventeen. That was another of the things that bothered me. It would have been easy to persuade you, push you around, before you'd even had time to grow up and make up your own mind about things. That's what I said in the letter. When you never rang me back, I thought maybe you'd got cold feet. So I said that if you wanted to wait a couple of years, I'd be ready to wait too, see how we felt about things then." He grinned, ruefully. "It took some writing, I can tell you. I'd never said such things to a girl before, nor have since."

"And you thought I'd never even bothered to reply?"

"I didn't know what to think . . . And then, the next thing, I saw in the paper that you were getting married."

"Eustace, if I'd got the letter, I wouldn't have gone back to London. I'd have refused."

"You couldn't refuse, you were under age."

"I'd have had hysterics, then. A nervous breakdown. Made the most ghastly scenes. Made myself ill."

"You'd still have gone."

She knew that he was right. "But I'd have known you were there, waiting. And I would never have married Anthony. I would never have gone to Scotland. I would never have wasted all these years."

Eustace raised his eyebrows. "Wasted? They weren't wasted. What about Cara and Nicholas?"

Virginia's eyes stung with sudden tears. She said, "Now it's all too complicated."

He put his arms around her, kissed the tears away, pushed her hair back off her face. He said, "Things happen the way they're meant to. There's a pattern and a shape to everything. You look back and see it all. Nothing happens without a reason. Nothing is impossible, like meeting again, walking into The Mermaid's Arms and seeing you sitting there, just as though you'd never been away. Like a miracle."

"You didn't behave as though it were a miracle. In no time at all you were bawling at me."

"I was scared of getting hurt a second time. I was scared that I'd been mistaken about you, that all the things that were so important to your mother had become important to you, too."

"I told you. They were never important."

He took her hand in his. "After the picnic yesterday, I thought it was going to be all right. After being with you and Cara and Nicholas, and swimming and cooking the fish, and you all seeming to enjoy it so much, I thought then, coming up the cliff, that it was like being back where we started. And I thought I would be able to talk about that time, when you went back to London and I was left not knowing what had happened, and we never saw each other again. I thought we could have talked about it, perhaps made a new beginning."

"But I was thinking the same, you stupid man, and all you did was to tell me to go back to Scotland and learn how to be a farmer. I want to be farmer's wife, but I don't want to be a farmer. And I wouldn't know one end of an Aberdeen Angus herd from the other."

Eustace grinned again, faintly sheepish. "I told you, it was those photographs of Cara's. We'd seemed so close all day, and all at once I realized that we weren't close, we belonged to different worlds. We always have done, Virginia. A place like Kirkton and a little farm like Penfolda, well, you just don't talk about them in the same breath. And suddenly it seemed insane to imagine that I could ask you to leave all that, give it all up, just for the sake of being with me. Because that's all I've got to offer."

"And that's what I want. That's all I've ever wanted. Kirkton was Anthony's house. Without him to keep it going, it has no life at all. Anyway, I'm going to sell it. I decided last night. I shall have to go back, of course, break the news to everybody, put the whole thing in the lawyer's hands . . ."

"Have you thought about the children?"

"I never stop thinking about them. And they'll understand."

"It's their home."

"Penfolda's going to be their home." She smiled at the thought, and Eustace took her shoulders between his big hands and leaned forward to kiss her open, smiling mouth. "A new home and a new father," she finished when she had got her breath back.

But Eustace did not seem to be listening to her. "Talk of the devil," he said.

And Virginia heard the children, coming across the garden, talking, their voices high-pitched.

"Look, there are the kittens. Look, they're in the sun, and they haven't drunk their milk."

"Oh, leave them, Nicholas. They're having a sleep."

"This one isn't sleeping. It's got its eyes open. Look. Its eyes are open."

"I wonder where Mummy is? Mummy!"

"In here," called Eustace.

"Mummy, Aunt Alice Lingard wants to know if you're ever coming home again." Cara appeared at the kitchen door, her spectacles crooked, her hair hanging out of its slide. "She gave us some bacon and eggs, but we've been waiting and waiting and she says Mrs. Jilkes will think that she's been in a car accident, and died . . ."

"Yes," said Nicholas, appearing, hard on her heels, with a kitten spread-eagled by pin-like claws across the front of his sweater. "And we didn't wake up till ten past ten when Aunt Alice came up to see us, and we very nearly didn't have any breakfast at all, we very nearly just waited until lunch-time . . . but I was . . . so hungry . . ."

His voice trailed away. He had realized that nobody was talking but him. His mother and Eustace were simply sitting, watching him, and Cara was staring at her mother as though she had never seen her before. Nicholas was disconcerted. "Well, what's wrong? Why isn't anybody talking?"

"We're waiting for you to stop," said Virginia.

"Why?"

Virginia looked at Eustace. Eustace leaned forward to draw Cara towards him. Very gently, seriously, he set her spectacles straight. Then Nicholas saw that he was smiling.

"We've got something to tell you," said Eustace.

THE
DAY OF
THE STORM

1

I t all started on a Monday at the end of January. A dull day at a dull
time of the year. Christmas and the New Year were over and forgotten and yet the new season had not started to show its face. London
was cold and raw, the shops filled with empty hope and clothes "for
cruising." The trees in the park stood lacy and bare against low skies,
the trodden grass beneath them dull and dead, so that it was impossible to believe that it could ever again be carpeted with drifts of purple
and yellow crocus.

It was a day like any other day. The alarm woke me to darkness, but
a darkness made paler by the wide expanse of the uncurtained windows, and through them I could see the top of the plane tree, illuminated by the orange glow of distant street lights.

My room was unfurnished, except for the sofa bed on which I lay,
and a kitchen table which I was going to strip of paint when I had the
time, and polish with a coat of beeswax. Even the floor was bare,
boards stretching to the wainscotting. An orange box did duty as a
bedside table, and a second one filled in for a chair.

I put out a hand and turned on the light and surveyed the desolate
scene with the utmost satisfaction. It was mine. My first home. I had
moved in only three weeks ago but it belonged entirely to me. With it,
I could do as I pleased. Cover the white walls with posters or paint
them orange. Sand the bare floor or stripe it in colour. Already I had
started to acquire a proprietary interest in junk and antique shops,
and could not pass one without scanning the window for some treasure

that I might be able to afford. This was how the table had come into my possession, and I already had my eye on an antique gilt mirror, but had not yet plucked up the courage to go into the shop and find out how much it was going to cost. Perhaps I would hang it in the centre of the chimney breast, or on the wall opposite the window, so that the reflections of the sky and the tree would be caught, like a picture, within its ornate frame.

These pleasant imaginings took some time. I looked again at the clock, saw that it was growing late, and climbed out of bed to pad, barefooted, across the floor and into the tiny kitchen, where I lit the gas and put the kettle on to boil. The day had begun.

The flat was in Fulham, the top floor of a small terrace house which belonged to Maggie and John Trent. I had met them only at Christmas, which I had spent with Stephen Forbes and his wife Mary and their large family of untidy children, in their large and untidy house in Putney. Stephen Forbes was my boss, the owner of the Walton Street bookshop where I had been working for the past year. He had always been enormously kind and helpful towards me and when he found out, from one of the other girls, that I would be on my own for Christmas, he and Mary had immediately issued a firm invitation— more an order, really—that I should spend the three days with them. There was plenty of space, he insisted vaguely, a room in the attic, a bed in Samantha's room, somewhere, but I wouldn't mind, would I? And I could always help Mary baste the turkey and pick all those torn bits of tissue paper off the floor.

Considering it from this angle, I finally accepted, and had a wonderful time. There's nothing like a family Christmas when there are children everywhere and noise and paper and presents, and a pine-smelling Christmas tree, glittering with baubles and crooked home-made decorations.

On Boxing Night, with the children safely in bed, the Forbeses threw a grown-up party, although we still seemed to continue playing childish games, and Maggie and John Trent came to this. The Trents were young marrieds, she the daughter of an Oxford don, whom Stephen had known well in his undergraduate days. She was one of those laughing, cheerful out-going people, and after she had arrived the party went with a swing. We were introduced but we didn't manage to talk until a game of charades, when we found ourselves side by side on a sofa, trying to guess, from the most incoherent gestures, that Mary was trying to act to us, in dumb show, the title of a film. *"Rose Marie!"* somebody yelled, for no apparent reason.

"Clockwork Orange!"

Maggie lit a cigarette and sank back on the sofa, defeated. "It's beyond me," she said. She turned her dark head to look at me. "You work in Stephen's shop, don't you?"

"Yes."

"I'll come in next week and spend all my Christmas book tokens. I've been given dozens."

"Lucky girl."

"We've just moved into our first house, so I want lots of coffee table stuff so that all our friends think I'm wildly intelligent ..." Then somebody shouted, "Maggie, it's your turn," and she said "Cripes," and shot to her feet, and went stalking off to find out what she was going to have to act. I can't remember what it was, but watching her make a cheerful fool of herself, my heart warmed to her, and I hoped that I would see her again.

I did, of course. True to her word, she came into the shop a couple of days after the holiday wearing a sheepskin coat and a long purple skirt, and carrying a bulging handbag stuffed with book tokens. I wasn't serving anybody at that particular moment and I came out from behind a neat stack of shiny-jacketed novels and said, "Hallo."

"Oh, good, there you are. I was hoping I'd find you. Can you help me?"

"Yes, of course."

Together, we chose a cookery book, a new autobiography which everybody was talking about, and a marvellously expensive volume of Impressionist paintings for the legendary coffee table. All this came to a little more than the book tokens did, so she groped around in that handbag and took out a cheque book in order to pay for the balance of the amount.

"John'll be furious," she told me happily, writing out the amount with a red felt pen. The cheque was yellow and the effect quite gay. "He says we're spending far too much money as it is. There." She turned it over to write her address. "Fourteen Bracken Road, SW6." She said it aloud in case I couldn't read her writing. "I haven't got used to writing it yet. We've only just moved in. Terribly exciting, we've bought it freehold, believe it or not. At least our parents chipped in with the deposit and John managed to con some building society or other into giving us a loan for the rest. But of course because of this, we've got to let the top floor to help pay the mortgage, but still, I suppose it'll all work out." She smiled. "You'll have to come and see it."

"I'd like to." I was wrapping her parcel, being meticulous about matching the paper and folding the corners.

She watched me. "You know, it's terribly rude, but I don't know your name. I know it's Rebecca, but Rebecca what?"

"Rebecca Bayliss."

"I suppose you don't know of a nice peaceful individual who wants an unfurnished flat?"

I looked at her. Our thoughts were so close I scarcely had to speak. I tied the knot on the parcel and snapped the string. I said, "How about me?"

"You? But are you looking for somewhere to live?"

"I wasn't until a moment ago. But I am now."

"It's only a room and a kitchen. And we have to share the bath."

"I don't mind if you don't. And if I can afford the rent. I don't know what you're asking."

Maggie told me. I swallowed and did a few mental calculations and said, "I could manage that."

"Have you got any furniture?"

"No. I've been living in a furnished flat with a couple of other girls. But I can get some."

"You sound as though you're desperate to get out."

"No, I'm not desperate, but I'd like to be on my own."

"Well, before you decide you'd better come and see it. Some evening, because John and I both work."

"*This* evening?" It was impossible to keep my impatience and excitement out of my voice and Maggie laughed.

"All right," she said. "This evening," and she picked up the beautifully wrapped parcel of books and prepared to depart.

I suddenly panicked ... "I ... I don't know the address ..."

"Yes you do, silly, it's on the back of the cheque. Get a twenty-two bus. I'll expect you about seven."

"I'll be there," I promised.

Jolting slowly down the Kings Road in the bus I had to consciously damp down my enthusiasm. I was out to buy a pig in a poke. The flat might be totally impossible, too big, too small or inconvenient in some unimagined way. Anything was better than being disappointed. And indeed, from the outside, the little house was entirely unremarkable, one of a row of red brick villas, with fancy pointing around the doors and a depressing tendency towards stained glass. But inside Number 14 was bright with fresh paint and new carpets and Maggie herself in old jeans and a blue sweater.

"Sorry I look such a mess but I've got to do all the housework, so I usually change when I get back from the office. Come on, let's go up and see it ... put your coat on the banisters, John's not home yet, but I told him you were coming and he thought it was a frightfully good idea ..."

Talking all the time, she led the way upstairs and into the empty room which stood at the back of the house. She turned on the light. "It faces south, out over a little park. The people who had the house before us built an extension on underneath, so you've got a sort of balcony on its roof." She opened a glass door and we stepped together out into the cold dark night, and I smelt the leaf-smell of the park, and damp earth, and saw, ringed by lamplight from the streets all around, the stretch of empty darkness. A cold wind blew suddenly, gustily, and the black shape of the plane tree rustled and then the sound was lost in the jet roar of an aeroplane going overhead.

I said, "It's like being in the country."

"Well, next best thing perhaps." She shivered. "Let's go in before we freeze." We stepped back through the glass door, and Maggie showed me the tiny kitchen which had been fashioned out of a deep cupboard, and then, halfway down the stairs, the bathroom, which we would all share. Finally, we ended up downstairs again in Maggie's warm, untidy sitting-room, and she found a bottle of sherry and some potato crisps which she swore were stale, but tasted all right to me. "Do you still want to come?" she asked.

"More than ever."

"When do you want to move in?"

"As soon as possible. Next week if I could."

"What about the girls you're sharing with just now?"

"They'll find someone else. One of them has a sister who's coming to London. I expect she'll move into my room."

"And what about furniture?"

"Oh . . . I'll manage."

"I expect," said Maggie comfortably, "your parents will come up trumps, they usually do. When I first came to London, my mother produced the most wonderful treasures out of the attic and the linen cupboard and so . . ." Her voice died away. I watched her in rueful silence, and she finally laughed at herself. "There I go again, opening my mouth and putting my foot in it. I'm sorry. I've obviously said something idiotically tactless."

"I haven't got a father, and my mother's abroad. She's living in Ibiza. That's really why I want somewhere of my own."

"I am sorry. I should have known, you spending Christmas with the Forbeses . . . I mean, I should have guessed."

"There's no reason why you should guess."

"Is your father dead?"

She was obviously curious, but in such an open and friendly way that all at once it seemed ridiculous to close up and shut up the way I usually did when people began asking me questions about my family.

"I don't think so," I said, trying to sound as though it didn't matter. "I think he lives in Los Angeles. He was an actor. My mother eloped with him when she was eighteen. But he soon got bored with domesticity, or perhaps he decided that his career was more important than raising a family. Anyway, the marriage lasted only a few months before he upped and left her, and then my mother had me."

"What a terrible thing to do."

"I suppose it was. I've never thought very much about it. My mother never talked about him. Not because she was particularly bitter or anything, just that when something was over and in the past, she usually forgot it. She's always been like that. She only looks forward, and always with the utmost optimism."

"But what happened after you were born? Did she go back to her parents?"

"No. Never."

"You mean, nobody sent a telegram saying 'Come back all is forgiven'?"

"I don't know. I honestly don't know."

"There must have been the most resounding row when your mother ran off, but even so . . ." Her voice trailed away. She was obviously unable to understand a situation which I had accepted with equanimity all my life. ". . . what sort of people would do a thing like that to their daughter?"

"I don't know."

"You must be joking!"

"No. I honestly don't know."

"You mean you don't know your own grandparents?"

"I don't even know who they are. Or perhaps who they were. I don't even know if they're still alive."

"Don't you know anything? Didn't your mother ever say anything?"

"Oh, of course . . . little scraps of the past used to come into her conversation but none of it added up to anything. You know how mothers talk to their children, remembering things that happened and things they used to do when they were little."

"But—Bayliss." She frowned. "That's not a very usual name. And it rings a bell somehow but I can't think why. Haven't you got a single clue?"

I laughed at her intensity. "You talk as though I really wanted to know. But you see, I don't. If you've never known grandparents, then you don't miss them."

"But don't you wonder . . ." she groped for words . . . "where they *lived?*"

"I know where they lived. They lived in Cornwall. In a stone house with fields that sloped down to the sea. And my mother had a brother called Roger but he was killed during the war."

"But what did she do after you were born? I suppose she had to go out and get a job."

"No, she had a little money of her own. A legacy from some old aunt or other. Of course, we never had a car or anything, but we seemed to manage all right. She had a flat in Kensington, in the basement of a house that belonged to some friends. And we stayed there till I was about eight, and then I went to boarding school, and after that we sort of . . . moved around . . ."

"Boarding schools cost money . . ."

"It wasn't a very grand boarding school."

"Did your mother marry again?"

I looked at Maggie. Her expression was lively and avidly curious, but she was kind. I decided that, having gone so far, I may as well tell her the rest.

"She . . . wasn't exactly the marrying type . . . But she was always very, very attractive, and I don't remember a time when there wasn't some adoring male in attendance . . . And once I was away at school, I suppose there wasn't much reason to go on being circumspect. I never knew where I was going to spend the next set of holidays. Once it was in France, in Provence. Sometimes in this country. Another time it was Christmas in New York."

Maggie took this in, and made a face. "Not much fun for you."

"But educational." I had long ago learned to make a joke of it. "And just think of all the places I've seen, and all the extraordinary places I've lived in. The Ritz in Paris once, and another time a gruesomely cold house in Denbighshire. That was a poet who thought he'd try sheep farming. I've never been so glad in my life when that association came to an end."

"She must be very beautiful."

"No, but men think she is. And she's very gay and improvident and vague, and I suppose you'd say utterly amoral. Maddening. Everything is 'jokey.' It's her big word. Unpaid bills are 'jokey' and lost handbags and unanswered letters, they're all 'jokey.' She has no idea of money and no sense of obligation. An embarrassing sort of person to live with."

"What's she doing in Ibiza?"

"She's living with some Swedish man she met out there. She went out to stay with a couple she knew, and she met this guy and the next thing I knew I had a letter saying that she was going to move in with him. She said he was terribly Nordic and dour but he had a beautiful house."

"How long is it since you've seen her?"

"About two years. I eased out of her life when I was seventeen. I did a secretarial course and took temporary jobs, and finally I ended up working for Stephen Forbes."

"Do you like it?"

"Yes. I do."

"How old are you?"

"Twenty-one."

Maggie smiled again, shaking her long hair in wonderment. "What a lot you've done," she said, and she did not sound in the least bit sorry for me but even slightly envious. "At twenty-one I was a blushing bride in a beastly busty white wedding dress and an old veil that smelt of mothballs. I'm not really a trad. person, but I've got a mother who is, and I'm very fond of her so I usually used to do what she wanted."

I could imagine Maggie's mother. I said, resorting to the comfort of clichés, because I couldn't think of anything else to say, "Oh, well, it takes all sorts," and at that moment we heard John's key in the lock and after that we did not bring up the subject of mothers and families again.

It was a day like any other day, but it had a bonus attached to it. Last Thursday I had worked late with Stephen, trying to complete the last of the January stocktaking, and in return he had given me this morning off so that I had until lunchtime to my own devices. I filled it in cleaning the flat (which took, at most, no more than half an hour), doing some shopping and taking a bundle of clothes to the launderette. By eleven thirty all this domesticity was completed so I put on my coat and set off, in a leisurely way, for work, intending to walk some of the way, and maybe stand myself an early lunch before getting to the shop.

It was one of those cold, dark, damp days when it never really gets light. I walked, through this gloom, up into the New Kings Road, and headed west. Here, every other shop seems to sell either antiques or second-hand beds or picture frames, and I thought I knew them all, but all at once I found myself outside a shop which I had not noticed before. The outside was painted white, the windows framed in black, and there was a red and white awning pulled out as protection against the imminent drizzle.

I looked up to see what the shop was called and read the name TRISTRAM NOLAN picked out in neat black Roman capitals over the door. This door was flanked by windows filled with delectable odds and ends and I paused to inspect their contents, standing on the pavement bathed in brightness from the many lights which burned within. Most of the furniture was Victorian, re-upholstered and restored and polished. A buttoned sofa with a wide lap and curly legs, a sewing box, a small picture of lap dogs on a velvet cushion.

I looked beyond the windows and into the shop itself, and it was then that I saw the cherrywood chairs. They were a pair, balloon backed, with curved legs and seats embroidered with roses.

I craved them. Just like that. I could picture them in my flat, and I wanted them desperately. For a moment I hesitated. This was no junk shop and the price might well be more than I could afford. But after all, no harm could be done by asking. Before I could lose my nerve, I opened the door and went in.

The shop was empty, but the door opening and closing had rung a bell, and presently there was the sound of someone coming down the stairs, the woollen curtain that hung over the door at the back of the shop was drawn aside and a man came into view.

I suppose I had expected someone elderly and formally attired, in keeping with the ambience of the shop and its contents, but this man's appearance rocked all my vague, preconceived notions. For he was young, tall and long-legged, dressed in jeans—faded to a soft blue and clinging like a second skin—and a blue denim jacket, equally old and faded, with the sleeves turned back in a businesslike way to reveal the checked cuffs of the shirt he wore beneath it. A cotton handkerchief was knotted at his neck and on his feet he wore soft moccasins, much decorated and fringed.

That winter the most unlikely people were drifting around London dressed as cowboys, but somehow this one looked real, and his worn clothes appeared as genuine as he was. We stood and looked at each other, and then he smiled and for some reason this took me unawares. I don't like being taken unawares, and I said "Good morning" with a certain coolness.

He dropped the curtain behind him and came forward, soft footed. "Can I help you?"

He may have looked like a genuine, dyed-in-the-wool American, but the moment he opened his mouth it was clear that he was no such thing. For some reason this annoyed me. The life I had led with my mother had left me with a thick streak of cynicism about men in general, and phoneys in particular, and this young man, I decided then and there, was a phoney.

"I . . . I was going to ask about these little chairs. The balloon-back ones."

"Oh, yes." He came forward to lay his hand on the back of one. The hand was long and shapely, with spade-tipped fingers, the skin very brown. "There's just the pair of them."

I stared at the chairs, trying to ignore his presence.

"I wondered how much they were."

He squatted beside me to search for a price ticket and I saw his hair fell thick and straight to his collar, very dark and lustrous.

"You're in luck," he told me. "They're going very cheap because the leg of one has been broken and then not very professionally repaired." He straightened up suddenly, surprising me by his height. His eyes were slightly tip-tilted, and a very dark brown, with an expression in them that I found disconcerting. He made me uncomfortable and my antipathy for him began to turn to dislike. "Fifteen pounds for the pair," he said. "But if you'd like to wait and pay a little more, I can get the leg reinforced, and perhaps a small veneer put over the joint. That would make it stronger and it would look better too."

"Isn't it all right now?"

"It would be all right for you," said the young man, "... but if you had a large fat man for dinner, he'd probably end up on his backside."

There was a pause while I regarded him—I hoped coldly. His eyes were brimming, with a malicious amusement which I had no intention of sharing. I did not appreciate the suggestion that the only men who would ever come and have dinner with me would necessarily be large and fat.

I said at last, "How much would it cost me to have the leg repaired?"

"Say five pounds. That means you get the chairs for a tenner each."

I worked this out, and decided that I could just afford them.

"I'll take them."

"Good," said the young man and put his fists on his hips and smiled amiably, as though this were the end of the transaction.

I decided he was utterly inefficient. "Do you want me to pay for them now, or to leave a deposit . . . ?"

"No, that doesn't matter. You can pay for them when you collect them."

"Well, when will they be ready?"

"In about a week."

"Don't you want my name?"

"Not unless you want to give it to me."

"What happens if I never come back?"

"Then I expect they'll be sold to someone else."

"I don't want to lose them."

"You won't," said the young man.

I frowned, angry with him, but he only smiled and went to the door to open it for me. Cold air poured in, and outside the drizzle had started and the street looked dark as night.

He said, "Goodbye," and I managed a frosty smile of thanks and went past him, out into the gloom, and as I did so I heard the bell ring as he shut the door behind me.

The day was, all at once, unspeakable. My pleasure in buying the chairs had been wrecked by the irritation which the young man had generated. I did not usually take instant dislikes to people and I was annoyed not only with him, but with myself, for being so vulnerable. I was still brooding on this when I walked down Walton Street and let myself into Stephen Forbes's bookshop. Even the comfort of being indoors and the pleasant smell of new paper and printers' ink did nothing to dispel my wretched mood.

The shop was on three levels, with new books on the ground floor, second-hand books and old prints upstairs, and Stephen's office in the basement. I saw that Jennifer, the second girl, was busy with a customer, and the only other person visible was an old lady in a tweed cape engrossed in the Gardening section, so I headed for the little cloakroom, unbuttoning my coat as I went, but then I heard Stephen's heavy, unmistakeable footsteps coming up from downstairs, and for some reason I stopped to wait for him. The next moment he appeared, tall, stooping and spectacled, with his usual expression of vague benevolence. He wore dark suits that always managed to appear as though in need of a good press, and already, at this early hour, the knot of his tie had begun to slip down, revealing the top button of his shirt.

"Rebecca," he said.

"Yes, I'm here . . ."

"I'm glad I've caught you." He came to my side speaking low-voiced, so as not to disturb the customers. "There's a letter for you downstairs; it's been forwarded on from your old flat. You'd better nip down and collect it."

I frowned. "A letter?"

"Yes. Airmail. Lots of foreign stamps. It has, for some reason, an air of urgency about it."

My irritation, along with all thoughts of new chairs, was lost in a sudden apprehension.

"Is it from my mother?"

"I don't know. Why don't you go and find out?"

So I went down the steep, uncarpeted stairs to the basement, lit, on this dark day, by long strip-lights let into the ceiling. The office was marvellously untidy—as usual—littered with letters and parcels and files, piles of old books, and cardboard boxes and ashtrays which no-body ever remembered to empty. But the letter was on the middle of Stephen's blotter and instantly visible.

I picked it up. An airmail envelope, Spanish stamps, an Ibizan post-mark. But the writing was unfamiliar, pointed and spiky, as though a very fine pen had been used. It had been sent to the old flat, but this address had been crossed out and the address of the bookshop substi-tuted in large, girlish, handwriting. I wondered how long the letter had lain on the table by the front door, before one of the girls realized that it was there and had taken the trouble to forward it on to me.

I sat down in Stephen's chair and slit the envelope. Inside, two pages of fine airmail paper, and the date at the head was the third of January. Very nearly a month ago. My mind sounded a note of alarm and, suddenly frightened, I began to read.

Dear Rebecca,

I hope you do not mind me calling you by your Christian name, but your mother has spoken to me of you a great deal. I am writing because your mother is very ill. She has been unwell for some time and I wished to write to you before but she would not let me.

Now, however, I am taking matters into my own hands, and with the doctor's approval I am letting you know that I think you should come out to see her.

If you can do this, perhaps you will cable me the number of your aeroplane flight so that I can be at the airport to meet you.

I know that you are working and it may not be easy to make this trip, but I would advise you to waste no time. I am afraid that you will find your mother very changed, but her spirit is still high.

With good wishes.
Sincerely,
Otto Pedersen.

I sat in unbelief, and stared at the letter. The formal words told me nothing and everything. My mother was very ill, perhaps dying. A month ago I had been asked to waste no time but to go to her. Now it was a month later, and I had only just got the letter and perhaps she was already dead—and I had never gone. What would he think of me, this Otto Pedersen whom I had never seen, whose name, even, I had not known until this moment?

2

read the letter again, and then again, the flimsy pages rustling in my hands. I was still there, sitting at his desk, when Stephen finally came downstairs to find me.

I turned to look up at him over my shoulder. He saw my face and said, "What is it?"

I tried to tell him, but could not. Instead I thrust the letter at him, and while he took it, and read it, I sat with my elbows on his desk, biting my thumbnails, bitter and angry, and fighting a terrible anxiety.

He was soon finished reading. He tossed the letter down on the desk between us, and said, "Did you know she was ill?"

I shook my head.

"When did you last hear from her?"

"Four, five months ago. She never wrote letters." I looked up at him and said, furiously, choked by the great lump in my throat, "That was nearly a *month* ago. That letter's been lying in the flat, and nobody bothered to send it to me. She may be dead by now and I never went, and she'll think I simply didn't care!"

"If she had died," said Stephen, "then we'd have surely heard. Now, don't cry, there isn't time for that. What we have to do is get you out to Ibiza with all convenient speed, and let—" he glanced down at the letter again—"Mr Pedersen know you're arriving. Nothing else matters."

I said, "I can't go," and my mouth began to grow square and my lower lip tremble as though I were a ten-year-old.

"Why can't you go?"

"Because I haven't got enough money for the fare."

"Oh, my dear child, let me worry about that . . ."

"But I can't let you . . ."

"Yes, you can, and if you get all stiff-necked about it then you can pay me back over the next five years and I'll charge you interest, if it'll make you feel happier, and now for God's sake don't let's mention it again . . ." He was already reaching for the directory, behaving in an altogether efficient and un-Stephen-like fashion. "Have you got a passport? And nobody's going to clamp down on you for smallpox injections or anything tiresome like that. Hallo? British Airways? I want to make a reservation on the first plane to Ibiza." He smiled down at me, still fighting tears and temper, but already feeling a little better. There is nothing like having a large and kindly man to take over in times of emotional stress. He picked up a pencil and drew a sheet of paper towards him and began to make notes. "Yes. When? Fine. Can we have a reservation, please? Miss Rebecca Bayliss. And what time does it get to Ibiza? And the flight number? Thank you so much. Thank you. Yes, I'll get her to the airport myself."

He put down the receiver and surveyed, with some satisfaction, the illegible squiggles his pencil had made.

"That's it, then. You fly tomorrow morning, change planes at Palma, get to Ibiza about half-past-seven. I'll drive you to the airport. No, don't start arguing again, I wouldn't feel happy unless I saw you actually walk on to the aeroplane. And now we'll cable Mr Otto Pedersen—" he picked up the letter again—"at the Villa Margareta, Santa Catarina, and let him know that you're coming." He smiled down at me with such cheerful reassurance that I was suddenly filled with hope.

I said, "I can't ever thank you . . ."

"I don't ever want you to," said Stephen. "It's the least I can do."

I flew the next day, in a plane half-filled with hopeful winter holiday tourists. They even carried straw hats against an improbably blazing sun, and their faces, as we stepped out into a steady drizzle at Palma, were disappointed but resolutely cheerful, as though, for certain, to-morrow would be better.

The rain never ceased, all the four hours I waited in the transit lounge, and the flight out of Palma was bumpy with thick, wet clouds. But as we rose above them and headed out across the sea, the weather brightened. The clouds thinned and broke, disclosing an evening sky of robin's egg blue, and far below the crumpled sea was streaked with the pink light of the setting sun.

It was dark when we landed. Dark and damp. Coming down the gangway beneath a sky full of bright southern stars, there was only the smell of petrol, but as I walked across the puddled tarmac towards the lights of the terminal building I felt the soft wind in my face. It was warm and smelt of pines, and was evocative of every summer holiday I had ever spent abroad.

At this quiet time of the year the plane had not been full. It did not take long to get through Customs and Immigration, and—my passport stamped—I picked up my suitcase and walked into the Arrivals Lounge.

There were the usual small groups of waiting people standing about or sitting hunched apathetically on the long plastic banquettes. I stopped and looked about me, waiting to be identified, but could see nobody who looked in the least like a Swedish writer come to meet me. And then a man turned from buying a newspaper at the book-stall. Across the room our eyes met, and he folded the newspaper and began to walk towards me, pushing his paper into his jacket pocket as though it were no longer of any use to him. He was tall and thin, with hair that was either blond or white—it was impossible to tell in the bright, impersonal electric light. Before he was half way across the polished floor I smiled tentatively, and as he approached he said my name, "Rebecca?" with a question mark at the end of it, still not entirely certain that it was I.

"Yes."

"I'm Otto Pedersen." We shook hands and he gave a formal little bow as he did so. His hair, I saw then, was pale blond, turning grey, and his face was deeply tanned, thin and bony, the skin dry and finely wrinkled from long exposure to the sun. His eyes were very pale, and more grey than blue. He wore a black polo-necked sweater and a light oatmeal-coloured suit with pleated pockets, like a safari shirt, and a belt which hung loose, the buckle swinging. He smelt of aftershave and looked as clean as if he had been bleached.

Having found each other, it was suddenly difficult to find anything to say. All at once we were both overwhelmed by the circumstances of our meeting and I realized that he was as unsure of himself as I. But he was also urbane and polite, and dealt with this by taking my suitcase from me and asking if this was all my luggage.

"Yes, that's all."

"Then let us go to the car. If you like to wait at the door, I will fetch it and save you the walk . . ."

"I'll come with you."

"It's only across the road, in the car park."

So we went out together, into the darkness again. He led me to the half empty car park. Here, he stopped by a big black Mercedes, unlocked it, and tossed my case on to the back seat. Then he held the door open so that I could get in before coming around to the front of the car to settle himself beside me.

"I hope you had a good journey," he said, politely, as we left the terminal behind us and headed out into the road.

"It was a little bumpy in Palma. I had to wait four hours."

"Yes. There are no direct flights at this time of the year."

I swallowed. "I must explain about not answering your letter. I've moved flats, and I didn't get it till yesterday morning. It wasn't forwarded to me, you see. It was so good of you to write, and you must have wondered why I never replied."

"I thought something like that must have happened."

His English was perfect, only the precise Swedish vowel sounds betraying his origins, and a certain formality in the manner in which he expressed himself.

"When I got your letter I was so frightened . . . that it would be too late."

"No," said Otto. "It is not too late."

Something in his voice made me look at him. His profile was knife sharp against the yellow glow of passing street lights, his expression unsmiling and grave.

I said, "Is she dying?"

"Yes," said Otto. "Yes, she is dying."

"What is wrong with her?"

"Cancer of the blood. You call it leukaemia."

"How long has she been ill?"

"About a year. But it was only just before Christmas time that she became so ill. The doctor thought that we should try blood transfusions, and I took her to the hospital for this. But it was no good, because as soon as I got her home again, she started this very bad nose bleed, and so the ambulance had to come and take her back to hospital again. She was there over Christmas and only then allowed home again. It was after that I wrote to you."

"I wish I'd got the letter in time. Does she know I'm coming?"

"No, I didn't tell her. You well know how she loves surprises, and equally how she hates to be disappointed. I thought there was a chance that something would go wrong and you wouldn't be on the plane." He smiled frostily, "But of course you were."

We stopped at a cross-roads to wait for a country cart to pass in front of us, the feet of the mule making a pleasant sound on the dusty road, and a lantern swinging from the back of the cart. Otto took advantage of the pause to take a cheroot from the breast pocket of his jacket and light it from the lighter on the dashboard. The cart passed, we moved on.

"How long is it since you have seen your mother?"

"Two years."

"You must expect a great change. I am afraid you will be shocked, but you must try not to let her see. She is still very vain."

"You know her so well."

"But of course."

I longed to ask him if he loved her. The question was on the tip of my tongue, but I realized that at this stage of our acquaintance it would be nothing but impertinence to ask such an intimate and personal thing. Besides, what difference did it make? He had met her and wanted to be with her, had given her a home, and now, when she was so ill, was cherishing her in his own apparently unemotional manner. If that wasn't love, then what was?

After a little, we began to talk of other things. I asked him how long he had lived on the island, and he said five years. He had come first in a yacht and had liked the place so well that he had returned the next year to buy his house and settle here.

"You're a writer . . ."

"Yes, but I am also a Professor of History."

"Do you write books on history?"

"I have done so. At the moment I am working on a thesis concerned with the Moorish occupation of these islands and southern Spain."

I was impressed. As far as I could remember, none of my mother's previous lovers had been even remotely intellectual.

"How far away is your house?"

"About five miles now. The village of Santa Catarina was quite un-spoiled when I first came here. Now, however, large hotel develop-ments are planned and I fear it will become spoiled like the rest of the island. No, that is wrong. Like some parts of the island. It is still pos-sible to be entirely remote if you know where to go and have a car or perhaps a motor boat."

It was warm in the car and I rolled down the window. The soft night air blew in on my face and I saw that we were in country now, passing through groves of olives, with every now and then the glimmering light of a farmhouse window shining beyond the bulbous, spiked shapes of prickly pear.

I said, "I'm glad she was here. I mean, if she has to be ill and die, I'm glad it's somewhere like this, in the south, with the sun warm and the smell of pines."

"Yes," said Otto. And then, precisely as ever, "I think that she has been very happy."

We drove on in silence, the road empty, telegraph poles rushing to meet the headlights of the car. I saw that now we were running paral-lel to the sea, which spread to an invisible, dark horizon and was dot-ted here and there with the lights of fishing boats. Presently there appeared ahead of us the neon-lighted shape of a village. We passed a sign reading "Santa Catarina" and then were driving down the main street; the air was filled with the smell of onions and oil and grilling meat. Flamenco music flung itself at us from open doorways, and dark faces, filled with absent curiosity, turned to watch us pass. In a moment we had left the village behind us, and had plunged forward into the darkness which lay beyond, only to slow down almost immediately to negotiate a steep corner which led up a narrow lane between orchards of almond trees. The headlights bored into the darkness, and ahead I saw the villa, white and square, pierced by small, secretive windows and with a lighted lantern swinging over the great, nailed front door.

Otto braked the car and switched off the engine. We got out, Otto taking my suitcase from the back seat and leading the way across the gravel. He opened the door and stood aside and I walked in ahead of him.

We were in a hallway, lit by a wrought-iron chandelier and furnished with a long couch covered in a bright blanket. A tall blue and white jar stood by the door containing a selection of ivory-handled walking sticks and sun umbrellas. As Otto closed the front door, another opened ahead of us and a small, dark-haired woman appeared, wearing a pink overall and flat, worn slippers.

"Señor."

"Maria."

She smiled, showing a number of gold teeth. He spoke to her in Spanish, asking a question to which she replied and then, turning, introduced me to her.

"This is Maria, who takes care of us. I have told her who you are . . ."

I held out my hand and Maria took it: we made friends by smiling and nodding. Then she turned back to Otto and spoke some more. Presently he handed her my suitcase, and she withdrew.

Otto said, "Your mother has been asleep but she is awake now. Let me take your coat."

I unbuttoned it, and he helped me off with it and laid it across the end of the couch. Then he went across the floor towards yet another door, motioning me to follow. I did, and was suddenly nervous, afraid of what I was going to find.

It was the salon of the house into which he led me. A long low-ceilinged room, white-washed like the rest of the house, and furnished with a pleasing mixture of modern Scandinavian and antique Spanish.

The tile floor was scattered with rugs, there were a great many books and pictures, and in the centre of the room a round table was laid out, seductively, with neatly ordered magazines and newspapers.

A wood fire burned in a great stone fireplace, and in front of this was a bed, with a low table alongside, holding a glass of water and a jug, a few pink geraniums in a mug, some books and a lighted lamp.

This lamp and the flicker of flames provided the only light in the room, but from the door I could see the narrow shape which humped the pink blankets and the attenuated hand and arm which was extended as Otto came forward to stand on the hearth rug.

"Darling," she said.

"Lisa." He took the hand and kissed it.

"You haven't been long after all."

"Maria says you have slept. Do you feel ready for a visitor?"

"A visitor?" Her voice was a thread. "Who?"

Otto glanced up at me, and I moved forward to stand beside him. I said, "It's me. Rebecca."

"Rebecca. Darling child. Oh, how blissfully jokey." She held out both arms to me, and I knelt down beside the bed to kiss her; her body gave me no resistance or support at all, so thin was she, and when I touched her cheek it felt papery beneath my lips. It was like kissing a leaf that has long since been wrenched by the wind from its parent tree.

"But what are you doing *here*?" She looked over my shoulder at Otto, and then back at me again. She put on the pretence of a frown. "You didn't *tell* her to come?"

"I thought you would like to see her," said Otto. "I thought it would cheer you up."

"But darling, why didn't you tell me?"

I smiled. "We wanted it to be a surprise."

"But I wish I'd known, then I could have looked forward to seeing you. That's what we always used to think, before Christmas. Half the fun was anticipation." She let me go and I sat back on my heels. "Are you going to stay?"

"For a day or so."

"Oh, how utterly perfect. We can have the most gorgeous gossips. Otto, does Maria know she's staying?"

"Of course."

"And what about dinner tonight?"

"It's all arranged . . . we'll have it together, in here, just the three of us."

"Well, let's have something now. A little drinkey. Is there any champagne?"

Otto smiled. "I think I can find a bottle. In fact, I think I remembered to put one on ice for just such an occasion."

"Oh, you clever man."

"Shall I get it now?"

"Please, darling."

She slid her hand in mine and it was like holding chicken bones. "And we'll drink to being together."

He went away to fetch the champagne and we were alone. I found a little stool and pulled it up so that I could sit close to her. We looked at each other, and she could not stop smiling. The dazzling smile and the bright dark eyes were still the same, so was the dark hair that spread like a stain over the snowy pillowcase. Otherwise her appearance was horrifying. I had never known anyone could be so thin and still be alive. And to make it more unreal, she was not pale and colourless but quite brown, as though she still spent most of the day lying in the sun. But she was excited. It seemed she could not stop talking.

"So sweet of the darling man to know how much I would love to see you. The only thing is, I'm so boring just now, I don't feel like doing anything, he should have waited until I'm better and then we could have had some fun together, and gone swimming and out in the boat and had picnics and things."

I said, "I can come again."

"Yes, of course you can." She touched my face with her hand as though needing this contact to reassure her that I was really there. "You're looking gorgeous, do you know that? You've got your father's colouring, with those big grey eyes, and that corn-coloured hair. Is it corn, or is it gold? And I love the way you're doing it." Her hand travelled to the single plait which fell forward, like a rope over my right shoulder. "It makes you look like something out of a fairy story; you know, those old-fashioned books with the magical pictures. You're very pretty."

I shook my head. "No. I'm not."

"Well, you look it, and that's the next best thing. Darling, what are you doing with yourself? It's such ages since I wrote or heard from you. Whose fault was that. Mine, I suppose, I'm hopeless at writing letters."

I told her about the book shop and the new flat. She was amused by this. "What a funny person you are, building a little nest for yourself without anybody to share it with. Haven't you met anybody yet you want to marry?"

"No. Nor anyone who wants to marry me."

She looked malicious. "What about the man you work for?"

"He's married, he's got a charming wife and a brood of children."

She giggled. "That never bothered me. Oh, darling, what a dreadful mother I was to you, trailing you round in that reprehensible fashion. It's a wonder you haven't collected the most ghastly selection of neuroses or hang-ups or whatever they call them these days! But you don't look as though you have, so perhaps it was all right after all."

"Of course it was all right. I just grew up with my eyes open and that was no bad thing." I added, "I like Otto."

"Isn't he divine? So correct and punctilious and *northern*. And so blazingly intelligent . . . So lucky he doesn't want me to be intelligent too! He just likes having me make him laugh."

Somewhere, in the middle of the house, a clock struck seven, and as the last note chimed Otto came back into the room carrying a tray with the champagne bottle in a bucket of ice, and three wine glasses. We watched as he expertly loosened the cork and the golden foaming wine spilled into the three glasses, and we each took one and raised them, all of us smiling because it was suddenly a party. My mother said, "Here's to the three of us and happy times. Oh, so divinely jokey."

Later, I was shown to my bedroom, which was either simply luxurious or luxuriously simple, I couldn't decide which. A fitted bathroom led off it, so I showered, and changed into trousers and a silk shirt, and brushed my hair and replaited it, and returned to the salon. I found Otto and my mother waiting for me, Otto also changed for the evening, and Mother wearing a fresh bedjacket of powder blue with a silk shawl embroidered with pink roses flung across her knees, its long fringe brushing the floor. We had another drink and then

Maria served dinner on a low table by the fire. My mother never stopped talking—it was all about the old days when I was growing up, and I kept thinking that Otto would be shocked, but he wasn't shocked at all, he was curious and much amused and kept asking questions and prompting my mother to tell us more.

"... and that dreadful farm in Denbighshire ... Rebecca, do you remember that terrible house? We nearly died of cold and the fire smoked whenever we lit it. That was Sebastian," she explained for Otto's benefit. "We all thought he was going to be a famous poet, but he wasn't any better at writing poetry than he was at sheep farming. In fact, if anything, worse. And I couldn't think how on earth I could leave him without hurting his feelings and then luckily Rebecca got bronchitis so I had the most perfect excuse."

"Not so lucky for Rebecca," suggested Otto.

"It certainly was. She hated it just as much as I did; anyway he had a horrible dog that was always threatening to bite her. Darling, is there any more champagne?"

She ate hardly anything, but sipped glass after glass of the icy wine while Otto and I worked our way steadily through Maria's delicious, four-course dinner. When it was finished, and the dishes cleared away, my mother asked for some music, and Otto put a Brahms concerto on the record player, turned very low. Mother just went on talking, like a toy that has been overwound and will only stop whirring senselessly around the floor when it finally breaks.

Presently, saying that he had work to do, Otto excused himself and left us, first building up the fire with fresh logs and making sure that we had everything we needed.

"Does he work every evening?" I asked, when he had gone.

"Nearly always. And in the mornings. He's very punctilious. I think that's why we've got on so well because we're so different."

I said, "He adores you."

"Yes," said my mother, accepting this. "And the best bit is that he never tried to turn me into someone else; he just accepted me, with my wicked ways and my lurid past." She touched my plait again. "You're growing more like your father ... I always thought you looked like me, but you don't, you look like him now. He was very handsome."

"You know, I don't even know what his name was."

"Sam Bellamy. But Bayliss is a much better name, don't you think? Besides, having you all on my own like that, I always felt you were my child and nobody else's."

"I wish you'd tell me about him. You never have."

"There's so little to tell. He was an actor, and too good-looking for words."

"But where did you meet him?"

"He came down to Cornwall with a Summer Stock company doing open-air Shakespeare. It was all terribly romantic, dark blue summer nights and the damp, dewy smell of the grass, and that divine Mendelssohn music and Sam being Oberon.

> *Through the house give glimmering light,*
> *By the dead and drowsy fire;*
> *Every elf and fairy sprite;*
> *Hop as light as bird from brier.*

It was magical. And falling in love with him was part of the magic."

"Was he in love with you?"

"We both thought he was."

"But you ran away with him, and married him . . ."

"Yes. But only because my parents left me with no alternative."

"I don't understand."

"They disliked him. They disapproved. They said I was too young. My mother said why didn't I marry some nice young man who lived locally, why didn't I settle down and stop making an exhibition of myself? And if I married an actor, what would people say? I sometimes thought that was all she cared about, what people would say. As if it could possibly matter what anybody said."

It was, unbelievably, the first time I had ever heard her mention her mother. I said, cautiously prompting, "Didn't you like her?"

"Oh, darling, it's so long ago. It's so difficult to remember. But she stifled and repressed me. I sometimes felt she was trying to choke me with conventions. And Roger had been killed and I missed him so dreadfully. Everything would have been different if Roger had been

there." She smiled. "He was so nice. Almost too nice. A real BV right
from the very start."

"What's a BV?"

"Bitches' Victim. He always fell in love with the most impossible
girls. And finally he married one. A little blonde doll, with dolly hair
and dolly china blue eyes. My mother thought she was sweet. I couldn't
stand her."

"What was she called?"

"Mollie." She made a face as though the very word tasted bad.

I laughed. "She can't have been as bad as all that."

"I thought she was. So maddeningly tidy. Always cleaning out her
handbag or putting her shoes into trees, or sterilizing the baby's toys."

"She had a baby then?"

"Yes, a little boy. Poor child, she insisted on calling him Eliot."

"I think that's a nice name."

"Oh, Rebecca, it's sickening." It was obvious that nothing Mollie had done could find favour in my mother's eyes. "I always felt
sorry for the child, being saddled with such a dreadful name. And
somehow he lived up to it, you know how people do, and after Roger
was killed the poor scrap was worse than ever, always hanging
round his mother's neck and having to have a light on in his room at
night."

"I think you're being very unkind."

She laughed. "Yes, I know, and it wasn't his fault. He probably
turned into quite a personable young man if his mother gave him half
a chance."

"I wonder what happened to Mollie?"

"I don't know. I don't particularly care, either." My mother could
always be cruelly off-hand. "It's like a dream. Like remembering
dream people. Or perhaps—" her voice trailed away—"perhaps they
were real and I was the dream."

I felt uncomfortable, because this was too near the truth that I was
trying to keep at bay. I said quickly, "Are your parents still alive?"

"My mother died that Christmas we spent in New York. Do you
remember that Christmas? The cold and the snow and all the shops
full of the sound of 'Jingle Bells'? By the end of that Christmas I felt I

never wanted to hear that damned tune again. My father wrote to me, but of course the letter didn't reach me until months later by which time it had followed me half round the world. And then it was really too late to write and say anything. Besides, I'm so useless about writing letters. He probably thought I simply didn't care."

"Didn't you ever write?"

"No."

"Didn't you like him either?" It seemed a sorry state of affairs.

"Oh, I adored him. He was wonderful. Terribly good looking, attractive to women, frightfully fierce and frightening. He was a painter. Did I ever tell you that?"

A painter. I had imagined everything, but never a painter. "No, you never said."

"Well, if you'd had any sort of education at all you'd probably have guessed. Grenville Bayliss. Doesn't that mean anything to you at all?"

I shook my head sadly. It was terrible never to have heard of a famous grandfather.

"Well, why should it? I was never any good at trailing you round art galleries or museums. Come to think of it, I was never much good at anything. It's a wonder you've turned out so well on a solid diet of maternal neglect."

"What did he look like?"

"Who?"

"Your father."

"How do you imagine him?"

I considered the question and came up with Augustus John. "Bohemian, and bearded and rather leonine . . ."

"Wrong," said my mother. "He wasn't like that at all. He started off his life in the Navy and the Navy left an indelible stamp on him. You see, he didn't decide to be a painter until he was nearly thirty, when he threw up a promising career and enrolled at the Slade. It nearly broke my mother's heart. And moving to Cornwall and setting up house at Porthkerris simply added insult to injury. I don't think she ever forgave him for being so selfish. She'd adored queening it in Malta, and probably fancied herself as wife to the Commander-in-Chief. I must say, he was tailor-made for the part, very blue-eyed and imposing and terrifying. He never lost what was known in those days as a quarter-deck manner."

"But you weren't terrified of him?"

"No. I loved him."

"Then why didn't you go home?"

Her face closed up. "I couldn't. I wouldn't. Terrible things had been said, by all of us. Old resentments and old truths had all come boiling up, and threats were made and ultimatums handed out. And the more they opposed me, the more determined I became, and the more impossible it was, when the time came, to admit that they'd been right, and I'd been wrong, and I'd made a hideous mistake. And if I had gone home, I would never have got away again. I knew that. And you wouldn't have belonged to me any more, you'd have belonged to your grandmother. I couldn't have borne that. You were such a precious little thing." She smiled and added rather wistfully, "And we did have fun, didn't we?"

"Yes, of course we did."

"I would have liked to go back. Sometimes I very nearly did. It was such a lovely house. Boscarva it was called, and it was rather like this villa, standing square on a hill above the sea. When Otto first brought me here, it reminded me of Boscarva. But here it's warm and the winds are gentle; there, it was wild and stormy, and the garden was honeycombed with tall hedges to shelter the flower beds from the sea winds. I think the wind was the thing that my mother most hated. She used to seal all the windows and shut herself indoors, playing bridge with her friends or doing needlepoint."

"Didn't she ever do things with you?"

"Not really."

"But who looked after you?"

"Pettifer. And Mrs Pettifer."

"Who were they?"

"Pettifer had been in the Navy, too; he looked after my father and cleaned the silver and sometimes drove the car. And Mrs Pettifer did the cooking. I can't tell you how cosy they were. Sitting by the kitchen fire with them making toast and listening to the wind battering at the windows, knowing that it couldn't get in . . . it made you feel so safe.

And we used to read fortunes from the teacups . . ." Her voice trailed off, memories uncertain now. And then, "No, that was Sophia."

"Who was Sophia?"

She did not reply. She was staring at the fire, her expression far away. Perhaps she had not heard me. She said at last, "After my mother died I should have gone back. It was naughty of me to stay away, but I was never over-endowed with what is known as moral fibre. But, you know, there are things at Boscarva that belong to me."

"What sort of things?"

"A desk, I remember. A little one, with drawers down the side, and a lid that opened up. I think it's called a davenport. And some jade that my father brought home from China and a Venetian looking-glass. They were all mine. On the other hand, I moved around so much that they would just have been a nuisance." She looked at me, frowning a little. "But perhaps you don't think they are a nuisance. Have you got any furniture in this flat of yours?"

"No. Practically none."

"Then perhaps I'll see if I can get hold of them for you. They must still be at Boscarva, provided the house hasn't been sold or burned down or something. Would you like me to try and get hold of them?"

"More than anything. Not just because I need furniture, but because they belonged to you."

"Oh, darling, how sweet, too jokey the way you long for roots, and I could never bear to have any. I always felt they would just tie me down in one place."

"And I always feel that they would make me belong."

She said, "You belong to me."

We stayed talking until the early hours of the morning. About midnight, she asked me to refill her waterjug, and I found my way into the deserted kitchen and did this for her, and realized then that Otto, with gentle tact, had probably taken himself quietly off to bed, so that we could be together. And when at last her voice grew tired and her words began to trail off in a blur of exhaustion, I said that I was sleepy too, which I was, and I stood up, cramped from sitting, stretched, and put more logs on the fire. Then I took away her second pillow so that she lay, ready for sleep. The silken shawl had slipped to the floor, so I picked this up and folded it and laid it on a chair. It remained only to stoop and kiss her, turn off the lamp, and leave her there in the firelight. As I went through the door, she said, as she always used to say when I was a little girl, "Good night, my love. Goodbye until tomorrow."

The next morning I was awake early, aware of sunshine streaming through the gaps in the shutters. I got up and went to open them, and saw the brilliant Mediterranean morning. I stepped out through the open windows on to the stone terrace which ran the length of the house and saw the hill sloping down to the sea, maybe a mile distant. The sand-coloured land was veiled in pink, the first tender blossoms of the almond trees. I went back into my room, dressed, and went out again—across the terrace, down a flight of steps, and through the ordered, formal garden. I vaulted a low stone wall, and walked on in the direction of the sea. Presently, I found myself in an orchard, surrounded by almond trees. I stopped and looked up at a froth of pink blossom and beyond it a pale and cloudless blue sky.

I knew that each flower would bear a precious fruit which, when the time came, would be frugally cropped, but even so I could not resist picking a single spray, and I was still carrying this when an hour or so later, having walked to the sea and back, I retraced my steps up the hill towards the villa.

It was steeper than I had realized. Pausing for breath, I looked up at the house, and saw Otto Pedersen standing on the terrace watching my progress. For an instant we both stood still; then he moved and started down the steps, and came down the garden to meet me.

I went on more slowly, still holding the spray of blossom. I knew then. I knew before he came close enough for me to see the expression on his face, but I went on, up through the orchard, and we met at last by the little drystone wall.

He said my name. That was all.

I said, "I know. You don't have to tell me."

"She died during the night. When Maria went in this morning to wake her . . . it was all over. It was so peaceful."

It occurred to me that we were not doing much to comfort each other. Or maybe there was no need. He put out a hand to help me over the wall, and kept my hand in his as we walked together up through the garden to the house.

She was buried, according to Spanish law, that very day, and in the little churchyard in the village. There was only the priest present, and Otto and Maria and myself. When it was all over, I put the spray of almond blossom on to her grave.

I flew back to London the next morning, and Otto drove me to the airport in his car. For most of the time we travelled in silence, but as we approached the terminal he suddenly said, "Rebecca, I don't know whether this has any significance, but I would have married Lisa. I would have married her, but I already have a wife in Sweden. We do not live together, and have not done so for a number of years, but she will not divorce me because her religion will not allow it."

"You didn't need to tell me, Otto."

"I wanted you to know."

"You made her so happy. You took such care of her."

"I am glad that you came. I am glad that you saw her."

"Yes." There was, all at once, a terrible lump in my throat, and my eyes filled and brimmed with painful tears. "Yes, I am glad too."

In the terminal, my ticket and my luggage checked, we stood and faced each other.

"Don't wait," I said. "Go now. I hate goodbyes."

"All right . . . but first . . ." He felt in his jacket pocket and took out three fine, worn silver bracelets. My mother had worn them always. She had been wearing them that last night. "You must have these." He took my hand and slipped them on to my wrist. "And this." Out of another pocket came a folded wad of British notes. He pressed it into my palm and closed my fingers over it. "They were in her handbag . . . so you must have them."

I knew they hadn't been in her handbag. She had never any money in her handbag except a few coppers for the next telephone call, and some dog-eared bills, long overdue. But there was something in

Otto's face that I couldn't refuse, so I took the money and kissed him, and he turned on his heel, without a word.

I flew back to London in a state of miserable indecision. Emotionally I was empty, drained even of grief. Physically I found that I was exhausted but I could neither sleep nor face the meal that the stewardess offered me. She brought me tea and I tried to drink that, but it tasted bitter and I left it to grow cold.

It was as though a long-locked door had been opened, but only a crack, and it was up to me to open it wide, although what lay behind it was dark and fraught with uncertainty.

Perhaps I should go to Cornwall and seek out my mother's family, but the glimpses I had been given of the set-up at Porthkerris were not encouraging. My grandfather would be very old, lonely and probably bitter. I realized that I had made no arrangement with Otto Pedersen about letting him know that my mother was dead, and so there was the hideous possibility that if I went to see him, I should be the one who would have to break the news. As well, I blamed him a little for having let his daughter make such a mess of her life. I knew that she was impulsive and thoughtless, and stubborn too, but surely he could have been a little more positive in his dealings with her. He could have sought her out, offered to help, inspected me, his grandchild. But he had done none of these things, and surely this would always stand like a high wall between us.

And yet, I longed for roots. I did not necessarily want to live with them, but I wanted them to be there. There were things at Boscarva that had belonged to my mother, and so now belonged to me. She had wanted me to have them, had said as much, so perhaps I was under an obligation to go to Cornwall and claim them as my own, but to go only for this reason seemed both soulless and greedy.

I leaned back and dozed and heard again my mother's voice.

I was never frightened of him. I loved him. I should have gone back.

And she had said a name—Sophia—but I had never found out who Sophia was.

I slept at last and dreamed that I was there. But the house in my dream had no shape or form and the only real thing about it was the sound of the wind, battering its way inland, fresh and cold from the open sea.

I was in London by the early afternoon, but the dark day had lost its shape and meaning, and I could not think what I was meant to do with what remained of it. In the end I got a taxi and went to Walton Street to seek out Stephen Forbes.

I found him upstairs, going through a box of books out of an old house which had just been sold up. There was no one else with him, and as I appeared at the top of the stairs he stood up and came towards me, thinking that I was a potential customer. When he saw that I was not, his manner changed.

"Rebecca! You're back."

I stood there, with my hands in my coat pockets.

"Yes. I got in about two." He watched me, his face a question. I said, "My mother died, early yesterday morning. I was just in time. I had an evening with her, and we talked and talked."

"I see," said Stephen. "I'm glad you saw her." He cleared some books from the edge of a table, and leaned against it, folding his arms and eyeing me through his spectacles. He said, "What are you going to do now?"

"I don't know."

"You look exhausted. Why not take a few days off?"

I said again, "I don't know."

He frowned. "What don't you know?"

"I don't know what to do."

"What's the problem?"

"Stephen, have you ever heard of an artist called Grenville Bayliss?"

"Heavens, yes. Why?"

"He's my grandfather."

Stephen's face was a study. "Good Lord. When did you find that out?"

"My mother told me. I'd never heard of him," I had to admit.

"You should have."

"Is he well known?"

"He was, twenty years ago when I was a boy. There was a Grenville Bayliss over the dining-room fireplace in my father's old house in Oxford. Part of my growing up, one might say. A grey stormy sea and a fishing boat with a brown sail. Used to make me feel seasick to look at it. He specialized in seascapes."

"He was a sailor. I mean, he'd been in the Royal Navy."

"That follows."

I waited for him to go on, but he was silent. I said at last, "What am I to do, Stephen?"

"What do you want to do, Rebecca?"

"I never had a family."

"Is it so important?"

"Suddenly it is."

"Then go and see him. Is there any reason not to?"

"I'm frightened."

"Of what?"

"I don't know. Of being snubbed, I suppose. Or ignored."

"Were there dreadful family rows?"

"Yes. And cuttings off. And never darken my door again. You know the sort of thing."

"Did your mother suggest that you went?"

"No. Not in so many words. But she said there were some things that belonged to her. She thought I should have them."

"What sort of things?"

I told him. "I know it's nothing very much. Perhaps not even worth making the journey for. But I'd like to have something that belonged to her. Besides—" I tried to turn it into a joke—"they might help to fill up some of the blank spaces in the new flat."

"I think collecting your possessions should be a secondary reason for going to Cornwall. Your first should be making friends with Grenville Bayliss."

"Supposing he doesn't want to make friends?"

"Then no harm has been done. Except possibly a little bruising to your pride, but that won't kill you."

"You're rail-roading me into this," I told him.

"If you didn't want my advice, then why did you come to see me?"

He had a point. "I don't know," I admitted.

He laughed. "You don't know much, do you?" and when at last I smiled back, he said, "Look. Today's Thursday. Go home and get some sleep. And if tomorrow's too soon, then go down to Cornwall on Sunday or Monday. Just go. See how the land lies, see how the old boy is. It may take a few days, but that doesn't matter. Don't come back to London until you've done all you can. And if you can get hold of your own bits and pieces, well and good, but remember that they're of secondary importance."

"Yes. I'll remember."

He stood up. "Then push off," he said. "I've got enough to do without wasting my time running a private Tell Auntie column on your account."

"Can I come back to work when all this is over?"

"You better had. I can't manage without you."

"Goodbye then," I said.

"Au revoir," said Stephen, and as if on an afterthought, leaned forward to give me a clumsy kiss. "And Good Luck!"

I had already spent enough money on taxis, so, still carrying my case, I walked up to the bus stop and waited until one came, and lurched my way back to Fulham. Gazing, unseeing, out of the window at the grey, crowded streets, I tried to make some plans. I would go to Cornwall, as Stephen suggested, on Monday. At this time of year it shouldn't be difficult to get a seat on the train or find somewhere to stay when I finally got to Porthkerris. And Maggie would keep an eye on my flat.

Thinking of the flat made me remember the chairs I had bought before I had gone to Ibiza. That day seemed a lifetime ago. But if I did not claim them then they would be sold as the disagreeable young man had threatened. With this in mind, I got off the bus a few stops before my own so that I could call into the shop and pay for the chairs and thus be certain that they would be waiting for me when I returned.

I had steeled myself to do business once more with the young man in the blue denims, but as I let myself in and the bell rang with the opening and the closing of the door, I saw with some relief that it was not he who stood up from behind the desk at the back of the shop, but another man, older, with grey hair and a dark beard.

He came forward, taking off a pair of horn-rimmed spectacles, as I thankfully put down my suitcase.

"Good afternoon."

"Oh, good afternoon. I came about some chairs I bought last Monday. Cherrywood, balloon-back ones."

"Oh, yes, I know."

"One of them had to be repaired."

"It's been done. Do you want to take them with you?"

"No. I've got a suitcase. I can't carry them. And I'm going away for a few days. But I thought if I paid for them now, perhaps you'd keep them until I got back."

"Yes, of course." He had a charming, deep voice, and when he smiled his rather saturnine face lit up.

I began to open my bag. "Will it be all right if I write you a cheque? I've got a Bankers Card."

"That's all right . . . would you like to use my desk? And here's a pen."

I began to write. "Who shall I make it out to?"

"To me. Tristram Nolan."

I was gratified to know that it was he who owned this pleasant shop and not my mannerless, cowboy friend. I wrote the cheque and crossed it, and handed it to him. He stood, head down, reading it, and took so long that I thought I must have forgotten something.

"Have I put the date?"

"Yes, that's perfect." He looked up. "It's just your name. Bayliss. It's not very common."

"No. No it's not."

"Are you any relation to Grenville Bayliss?"

Having his name flung at me, just now, was extraordinary and yet not extraordinary at all, in the same way that a name, or a relevant item of news, will spring at you, unbidden, from a page of close print.

I said, "Yes, I am." And then because there was no reason why he shouldn't know, "He's my grandfather."

"Extraordinary," he said.

I was puzzled. "Why?"

"I'll show you." He laid my cheque down on his desk and went to pull out from behind a drop-leafed sofa table a large, sturdy oil painting in a gilt frame. He held it up, balancing one corner on his desk, and I saw that it was by my grandfather. His signature was in the corner, and the date below it, 1932.

"I've only just bought it. It needs cleaning, of course, but I think it's very charming."

I stepped closer to inspect it, and saw sand dunes in an evening light, and two young boys, naked, bent over a collection of shells. The work was perhaps old-fashioned, but the composition charming—the colouring delicate and yet somehow robust—as though the boys, vulnerable in their nakedness, were still tough, and creatures to be reckoned with.

"He was good, wasn't he?" I said, and could not hide the note of pride in my voice.

"Yes. A marvellous colourist." He put the picture back. "Do you know him well?"

"I don't know him at all. I've never met him."

He said nothing, simply stood, waiting for me to enlarge on this odd statement. To fill the silence I went on. "But I've decided that perhaps it's time I did. In fact, I'm going to Cornwall on Monday."

"But that's splendid. The roads will be empty at this time of the year, and it's a lovely drive."

"I'm going by train. I haven't got a car."

"It will still be a pleasant journey. I hope the sun shines for you."

"Thank you very much."

We moved back to the door. He opened it, I picked up my suitcase. "You'll look after my chairs for me?"

"Of course. Goodbye. And have a good time in Cornwall."

3

But the sun did not shine for me. Monday dawned grey and depressing as ever and my faint hopes that the weather would improve as the train rocketed westwards soon died, for the sky darkened with every mile and the wind got up and the day finally dissolved into pouring rain. There was nothing to be seen from the streaming windows; only the blurred shapes of hills and farmsteads, and every now and then the clustered roofs of a village flashed by, or we raced through the half-empty station of some small anonymous town.

By Plymouth, I comforted myself, it would be different. We would cross the Saltash Bridge and find ourselves in another country, another climate, where there would be pink-washed cottages and palm trees and thin winter sunshine. But of course all that happened was that the rain fell even more relentlessly; as I stared out at flooded fields and leafless wind-torn trees, my hopes finally died and I began to be discouraged.

It was nearly a quarter to five by the time we reached the junction which was the end of my journey, and the dark afternoon had sunk, already, into twilight. As the train slowed down alongside the platform, I saw an incongruous palm tree, silhouetted like a broken umbrella against the streaming sky, and the falling rain shimmered and danced in front of the lighted sign which said "St Abbotts, change for Porthkerris." The train finally stopped. I shouldered my rucksack and opened the heavy door which was instantly torn out of my grasp by the wind. The sudden impact of strong cold air, driven inland, over the dark sea, made me gasp, and with some idea of making haste I picked up my bag and jumped out on to the platform. I followed the general exodus of travellers up and over the wooden bridge to the station building on the far side. Most of the other passengers seemed to have friends to meet them, or else walked through the ticket office in a purposeful fashion, as though knowing that a car was waiting for them on the far side. Blindly, I followed them, feeling very new and strange but hoping that they would lead me to a taxi. But when I came out into the station yard, there were no taxis. I stood about, hopeful of being offered a lift, but too shy to ask for one, until the tail light of the last car, inevitably, disappeared up the hill in the direction of the main road and I was forced to return to the ticket office for help and advice.

I found a porter, stacking hen coops in a smelly parcels office.

"I'm sorry, but I have to get to Porthkerris. Would there be a taxi?"

He shook his head slowly, without hope, and then said, brightening slightly, "There's a bus. Runs every hour." He glanced up at the slow-ticking clock high on the wall. "But you've just missed one, so you'll 'ave to wait some time."

"Can't I ring up for a taxi?"

"Isn't much call for taxis at this time of the year."

I let my heavy rucksack slip to the floor and we gazed at each other, both defeated by the enormity of the problem. My wet feet were slowly congealing. As we stood there, there came, above the noise of the storm, the sound of a car, driven very fast down the hill from the road.

I said, raising my voice slightly in order to make my point, "I must get a taxi. Where could I telephone?"

"There's a box just out there . . ."

I turned to go in search of it, trailing my rucksack behind me, and as I did so I heard the car stop outside in the yard; a door slammed, footsteps ran, and the next moment a man appeared, banging the door open and shut against the icy wind. He shook himself like a dog before crossing the floor and disappearing through the open door of the Parcels Office.

I heard him say, "Hallo, Ernie. I think there's a parcel here for me. From London."

" 'Ullo, Mr Gardner. That's a dirty night."

"Filthy. The road's awash. That looks like it . . . that one over there. Yes, that's it. Want me to sign for it?"

"Oh, yes, you'll 'ave to sign. 'Ere we are . . ."

I imagined the slip of paper, smoothed on a table top, the stub of a pencil taken from behind Ernie's ear. And for the life of me I could not remember where I had heard that voice before, nor why I knew it so well.

"That's great. Thanks very much."

"You're welcome."

The telephone, the taxi, forgotten for the moment, I watched the door, waiting for him to reappear. When he did, carrying a large box stuck with red GLASS labels, I saw the long legs, the blue denims drenched in mud to the knee, and a black oilskin, beaded and running with rivulets of water. He was bare-headed, his black hair plastered to his skull, and he saw me for the first time and stopped dead, holding the parcel in front of him like an offering. In his dark eyes was first a flicker of puzzlement, and then recognition. He began to smile. He said, "Good God!"

It was the young man who had sold me the two little cherrywood chairs.

I stood open-mouthed, feeling obscurely that someone had played me a mean and unfair trick. If ever I was in need of a friend it was at this moment, and yet fate had chosen to send me, possibly, the last person on earth I ever wanted to see again. And that he should see me thus, drenched and desperate, was somehow the last straw.

His smile widened. "What a fantastic coincidence. What are you doing here?"

"I've just got off the train."

"Where are you going?"

I had to tell him. "To Porthkerris."

"Is someone coming for you?"

I very nearly lied and told him "yes." Anything to get rid of him. But I was always a useless fibber, and he would be bound to guess the truth.

I said, "No," and then I went on, trying to sound competent, as though I could take good care of myself, "I'm just going to phone for a taxi."

"It'll take hours. I'm going to Porthkerris, I'll give you a ride."

"Oh, you don't need to bother . . ."

"No bother, I'm going anyway. Is that all your luggage?"

"Yes, but . . ."

"Come on then."

I still hesitated, but he seemed to consider the matter already settled, going over to the door to open it, and holding it open with his shoulder, waiting for me to follow. So eventually I did so, edging past him, and out into the fury of the dark evening.

In the dim light I saw the Mini pick-up, parked, with the sidelights burning. Letting the door slam behind him, he crossed over to this, and gently loaded his parcel into the back, and then took my rucksack from me, and heaved this in too, covering the two bundles in a cursory fashion with an old piece of tarpaulin. I stood watching him, but he said, "Go on, get in, there's no point us both getting wet through," so I did as I was told, settling myself in the passenger seat with my bag jammed between my legs. Almost at once he had joined me, shutting his door with an almighty slam, and switching on the engine as though there were not a moment to be lost. We roared up the hill away from the station, and the next moment had turned on to the main road and were heading for Porthkerris.

He said, "Tell me more, now. I thought you lived in London."

"Yes, I do."

"Have you come down for a holiday?"

"Sort of."

"That sounds good and vague. Are you staying with friends?"

"Yes. No. I don't know."

"What does that mean?"

"Just that. It means I don't know." This sounded rude but it couldn't be helped. I felt as though I had no control over what I was saying.

"Well, you'd better make up your mind before you get to Porthkerris, otherwise you'll be spending the night on the beach."

"I . . . I'm going to stay in a hotel. Just for tonight."

"Well, that's great. Which one?"

I sent him an exasperated look and he said, reasonably enough, "Well, if I don't know which one, I can't take you there, can I?"

He seemed to have me cornered. I said, "I haven't booked in to any hotel. I mean, I thought I could do that when I arrived. There *are* hotels, aren't there?"

"Porthkerris is running with them. Every other house is a hotel. But at this time of the year most of them are closed."

"Do you know some that are open?"

"Yes. But it depends what you want to pay."

He glanced at me sideways, taking in my patched jeans, scuffed shoes, and an old fur-lined leather coat that I had worn for warmth and comfort. At the moment this garment looked and smelt like a wet dog.

"We go from one extreme to the other. The Castle, up on the Hill, where you change for dinner, and dance the foxtrot to a three-piece orchestra, right down to Mrs Kernow who does Bed and Breakfast at Number Two, Fish Lane. Mrs Kernow I can recommend. She looked after me for three months or more before I got into my own place, and her prices are very reasonable."

I was diverted. "Your own place? You mean you live here?"

"I do now. Have done for the last six months."

"But . . . the shop in the New Kings Road . . . where I bought the chairs?"

"I was just helping out for a day or so."

We came to a crossroads, and, slowing down, he turned to look at me. "Have you got the chairs yet?"

"No. But I've paid for them. They'll still be there when I get back."

"Good," said the young man.

We drove for a little in silence. Through a village, and up over a wild bit of country high above the sea; then the road leaned down again, and there were trees on either side of us. Through these, through twisted trunks and branches tortured by the wind, there presently appeared, far below us, the twinkling lights of a little town.

"Is that Porthkerris?"

"It is. And in a moment you're going to have to tell me if it's to be The Castle or Fish Lane."

I swallowed. The Castle was out of the question, obviously, but if I went to Fish Lane I would necessarily place myself under an obligation to this managing person. I had not come to Porthkerris for any other reason than to see Grenville Bayliss, and I had an uncomfortable feeling that if I once got involved with this man he would stick like a burr.

I said, "No, not The Castle . . ." meaning to suggest some other, more modest establishment, but he cut me short.

"That's great," he said, with a grin. "Mrs Kernow of Fish Lane it is, and you won't regret it."

My first impression of Porthkerris, in the dark and the gusty rain, was confused to say the least of it. The town was, on this unsalubrious evening, nearly empty of people; the deserted streets gleamed wetly with reflected light, and the gutters ran with water.

At a great speed, we plunged down into a warren of baffling lanes and alleys, at one time emerging out on to the road which circled the harbour, only to turn back once more into the maze of cobbled roads and uneven, haphazard houses.

We turned at last into a narrow street of grey terrace houses, with front doors opening flush on to the pavement.

All was seemly and respectable. Lace curtains veiled windows, and there could be glimpsed statuettes of girls with dogs, or large green pots containing aspidistras.

The car slowed at last and stopped.

"We're here." He switched off the engine, and I could hear the wind and, above its whine, the nearby sound of the sea. Great breakers thundered up on to the sand, and there was the long hiss of the retreating waves.

He said, "You know, I don't know your name."

"It's Rebecca Bayliss. And I don't know yours."

"Joss Gardner . . . it's short for Jocelyn, not Joseph." With this useful bit of information he got out of the car and rang a bell in a door and, while waiting for an answer, went to retrieve my rucksack from underneath the tarpaulin. As he heaved it out, the door opened and he turned and was illuminated in a shaft of warm light which streamed from inside the house.

"Joss!"

"Hallo, Mrs Kernow."

"What are you doing here?"

"I've brought you a visitor. I said you were the best hotel in Porthkerris."

"Oh, my soul, I don't belong to take visitors at this time of the year. But come along in now, out of the rain, what weather isn't it? Tom's down at the Coastguard lodge, been some sort of a warning up from the Trevose way, but I don't know, I haven't heard no rockets . . ."

Somehow we were all inside and the door shut and there was scarcely room for the three of us to stand in the narrow hall.

"Come along in by the fire . . . it's nice and warm, I'll get you a cup of tea if you like . . ." We followed her into a tiny, cluttered, cosy parlour. She knelt to poke the fire to life and add more coal, and for the first time I was able to take a good look at her. I saw a small, bespectacled lady, quite elderly, wearing bedroom slippers and a pinafore over her good brown dress.

"We don't really want tea," he told her. "We just want to know if you can give Rebecca a bed—for a night or so."

She stood up from the fireplace. "Well, I don't know . . ." She looked at me doubtfully, and what with my appearance and the dog-smelling coat I didn't blame her for being doubtful.

I started to open my mouth, but Joss sailed in before I could say a word. "She's highly respectable and she won't run away with the spoons. I'll vouch for her."

"Well . . ." Mrs Kernow smiled. Her eyes were pretty, a very pale blue. "The room's empty, so she may as well have it. But I can't give her supper tonight, not expecting anybody, I haven't anything in the house but a couple of little pasties."

"That's all right," said Joss. "I'll feed her."

I started to protest, but once again I was overborne. "I'll leave her here to get settled in and unpacked, and then I'll be back about—" he glanced at his watch—"seven thirty, to pick her up. That all right?" he flung casually in my direction. "You're an angel, Mrs Kernow, and I love you like a mother." He put an arm around her and kissed her. She looked delighted; then he gave me a final, cheerful grin, said, "See you," and so departed. We heard his car roaring away down the street.

"He's a lovely boy," Mrs Kernow informed me. "I had him living here three months or more . . . now come along, pick up your little bag and I'll show you your room. 'Course it'll be cold, but I've got an electric fire you can have, and the water in the tank's nice and hot if you want a bath . . . I always say you feel so mucky coming off those dirty trains . . ."

The room was as tiny as all the other rooms in this little house, furnished with an enormous double bed which took up nearly all the space. But it was clean and, presently, warm, and after Mrs Kernow had shown me where to find the bathroom she went back downstairs and left me to myself.

I went to kneel by the low window and draw back the curtains. The old frames had been jammed tight shut against the wind by rubber wedges, and the dark glass streamed with rain. There was nothing to be seen, but I stayed there anyway, wondering what I was doing in this little house, and trying to work out why Joss Gardner's sudden re-appearance in my life had left me with this unexplained feeling of unease.

needed defences. I needed to build up my confidence and my self-esteem, disliking the role of rescued waif in which I had suddenly found myself. A hot bath and a change of clothes went a long way towards restoring my composure. I did my hair, made up my eyes, splashed on the last of a bottle of expensive scent and was halfway towards being in charge again. I had already unpacked a dress from the ubiquitous rucksack and hung it hopefully to shed its wrinkles; now I put it on, a dark cotton with long sleeves, and dark stockings, very fine, and shoes with heels and old-fashioned buckles which I had found, long back, on a stall in the Portobello Road . . . As I fastened my pearl ear-rings I heard, over the rattle and bang of the gusty wind, the sound of Joss Gardner's little van, tyres drumming on the cobbles, coming up the street. It screeched to a noisy halt outside the door, and the next moment I heard his voice downstairs, calling first for Mrs Kernow and then for me.

I continued, slowly, to screw the fastening of the last ear-ring. I picked up my bag, and then my leather coat. This I had draped near the electric fire in the hope that it would dry off, but it hadn't. The heat had merely emphasized the smell of a spaniel come in from a wet walk, and it still weighed heavy as lead. Lugging it over my arm, I went down the stairs.

"Hallo, there." Joss, in the hall, looked up at me. "Well, what a transformation. Feel better now?"

"Yes."

"Give me your coat . . ."

He took it from me intending to help me on with it, and instantly became a comic weightlifter, sagging at the knees with the sheer bulk of it.

"You can't wear this, it'll drive you into the ground. Anyway it's still wet."

"I haven't got another." Still toting the coat, he started to laugh. My self-esteem began to drain away and some of this must have showed on my face, because he suddenly stopped laughing and shouted for Mrs Kernow. When she appeared, with an expression both exasperated and loving on her face, he bundled my coat into her arms, told her to dry it for me, unbuttoned and removed his own black oilskin and laid it, with a certain grace, around my shoulders.

Beneath it he wore a soft grey sweater, a cotton scarf knotted at the neck. "Now," he said, "we are ready to go." He opened the door, on to a curtain of rain.

I protested, "But you'll get wet," but he only said "Scuttle" so I scuttled, and he scuttled too, and the next instant we were back in the van, scarcely wet at all, with the doors banged tight and shut against the storm, although small puddles of rain on my seat and at my feet gave rise to the suspicion that this staunch vehicle was no longer as watertight as it had once been. But he started the noisy engine and we were away, and with the volume of water both outside and inside the car it was a little like being taken for a fast ride in a leaky motor boat.

I said, "Where are we going?"

"The Anchor. It's just round the corner. Not very smart. Do you mind?"

"Why should I mind?"

"You might mind. You might have wanted to be taken to The Castle."

"You mean to foxtrot to a three-piece orchestra?"

He grinned. He said, "I can't foxtrot. Nobody ever learned me."

We flashed down Fish Lane, around a right angled corner or two, beneath a stone archway and so out into a small square. One side of this was formed by the low, uneven shape of an old inn. Warm light shone from behind small windows spilled from a crooked doorway and the Inn sign over the door swung and creaked in the wind. There were four or five cars already parked outside, and Joss inserted the van neatly into a tidy space between two of them, turned off the engine, said, "One, two, three, run," and we both got out and sprinted the short distance between the car and the shelter of the porch.

There Joss shook himself slightly, brushed the rain from the soft surface of his sweater, took the oilskin off my shoulders and opened the door for me to go ahead of him.

It was warm inside, and low-ceilinged and smelt the way old pubs have always smelt. Of beer and pipe smoke and musty wood. There was a bar, with high stools, and tables around the edge of the room. Two old men were playing darts in a corner.

The barman looked up and said, "Hi, Joss." Joss put the oilskin up on a coat hook, and led me across the room to be introduced.

"Tommy, this is Rebecca. Rebecca, this is Tommy Williams. He's been here man and boy; anything you want to know about Porthkerris, or the people who live here, you come and ask Tommy."

We said, "How do you do." Tommy had grey hair and a lot of wrinkles. He looked as though he might be a fisherman in his spare time. We sat ourselves on two stools, and Joss ordered a scotch and soda for me and a scotch and water for himself, and while Tommy fixed these the two men began to talk, falling comfortably into conversation the way men in pubs always seem to.

"How are things going with you?" That was Tommy.

"Not too bad."

"When are you opening up?"

"Easter, maybe, with a bit of luck."

"Place finished is it?"

"More or less."

"Who's doing the carpentry?"

"Doing it myself."

"That'll save you something."

My attention wandered. I lit a cigarette and looked around me, liking what I saw. The two old men playing darts; a young couple, jeaned and longhaired, crouched over a table and a couple of pints of bitter, discussing, with avid and intense concentration—existentialism? Concrete painting? How they were going to pay the rent? Something. But it mattered, intensely, to both of them.

And then a party of four, older, expensively dressed, the men self-consciously casual, the women unwittingly formal. I guessed they were staying at The Castle, and out of boredom with the weather, per-haps, had come down the town for a spot of slumming. They seemed uncomfortable, as though they knew they looked out of place, and could scarcely wait to get back to the padded velvet comfort of the big hotel on the hill.

My eyes moved on around the room, and it was then that I caught sight of the dog. He was a beautiful dog, a great red setter, his coat hand-some and shining, his tail a silken plume of copper fur against the grey flags of the floor. He sat very still, close to his master, and every now and then the tail would move slightly in a thump of approval, a pri-vate applause.

Intrigued, I inspected the man who appeared to own this enviable creature, and found him almost as interesting as the dog. Sitting, with an elbow on the table top, and his chin resting on his fist, he presented to me a clear and unblurred profile, almost as though he were posing for my inspection. His head was well shaped, and his hair had that thick silver-fox look of a person who has started to go grey early in life. The single eye which his profile allowed me was deep set, and darkly shadowed, the nose was long and aquiline, the mouth pleasant, the chin strongly formed. And, from the length of his wrist, emerg-ing from a checked shirt cuff and the sleeve of a grey tweed jacket, and the way he disposed of his legs beneath the little table, I guessed that he was tall, probably over six feet.

As I watched him, he laughed suddenly at something his com-panion had said. This drew my attention to the other man, and I felt a shock of surprise, because, for some reason, they did not match. Where the one was slender and elegant, the other was short, fat, red of face, and dressed in a tight-fitting navy blue blazer and a shirt collar that looked as though it were about to strangle him. It was not overly warm in the pub, but there was a shine of sweat on the ruddy brow, and I saw that the dark hair had been barbered with some ingenuity, so that a long oiled lock was combed up and over, concealing what would otherwise have been a totally bald head.

The man with the dog was not smoking, but the fat man suddenly crushed out his own cigarette in the brimming ashtray on the table, as though emphasizing some point that he was making, and almost instantly reached into his pocket for a silver case and another cigarette.

But the man with the dog had decided that it was time to go. He took his hand from his chin, pushed back his shirt cuff to consult his watch, and then finished his drink. The fat man, apparently anxious to comply with the other's arrangements, hastily lit the cigarette and then tossed back his whisky. They began to get up, pushing back their chairs with a hideous scraping sound. The dog stood up, his tail swooping in exultant circles.

Standing, one so short and fat and the other so tall and slim, the two men looked more ill-assorted than ever. The thin one reached for a raincoat which had been lying across the back of his chair and slung it over his shoulders like a cloak, and then turned towards us, heading for the door. For an instant I was disappointed, because full face, his finely drawn good looks did not live up to the promise of that intriguing profile. And then I forgot about being disappointed, because he suddenly saw Joss. And Joss, perhaps sensing his presence, stopped talking to Tommy Williams and turned to see who was standing behind him. For an instant they both looked disconcerted, and then the tall man smiled, and the smile etched lines down his thin brown cheeks and creased up his eyes, and it was impossible not to be warmed by such charm.

He said, "Joss. Long time no see." His voice was pleasant and friendly.

"Hi," said Joss, not getting off his stool.

"I thought you were in London."

"No. Back again."

The creaking swing of the door caught my attention. The other man, the fat man, had quietly left. I decided that he had an urgent appointment and thought no more about it.

"I'll tell the old boy I've seen you."

"Yes. Do that."

THE DAY OF THE STORM

The deep set eyes moved in my direction, and then away again. I waited to be introduced, but nothing happened. For some reason this lack of manners on Joss's part was like a slap in the face.

At last, "Well, see you around," said the tall man, and moved off.

"Sure," said Joss.

"Night, Tommy," he called to the barman as he pushed the door open and let the dog out ahead of him.

"Good night, Mr Bayliss," said the barman.

I felt my head jerk around as though someone had pulled a string. He had already disappeared, leaving the door swinging behind him. Without thinking, I slipped off the stool to go after him, but a hand caught my arm and restrained me, and I turned to find Joss holding me back. For a surprising second our eyes clashed, and then I shook myself free. Outside I heard a car start up. Now it was too late.

I said, "Who is he?"

"Eliot Bayliss."

Eliot. Roger's boy. Mollie's child. Grenville Bayliss's grandson. My cousin. My family.

"He's my cousin."

"I didn't know that."

"You know my name. Why didn't you tell him? Why did you stop me going after him?"

"You'll meet him soon enough. Tonight it's too late and too wet and too dark for family reunions."

"Grenville Bayliss is my grandfather, too."

"I thought there was probably some connection," said Joss coolly. "Have another drink."

By now I was really angry. "I don't want another drink."

"In that case, let's go and eat."

"I don't want to eat either."

I thought that I truly didn't want to. I didn't want to spend another moment with this boorish and overbearing young man. I watched him finish his drink and get down off his stool, and for an instant I thought that he was actually going to take me at my word; was going to drive me back to Fish Lane and there dump me, un-nourished. But, luckily, he did not call my bluff, simply paid for the drinks, and without a word led the way through a door at the far end of the bar, which gave on to a flight of stairs and a small restaurant. I followed him because there didn't seem to be anything else to do. Besides, I was hungry.

Most of the tables were already occupied, but a waitress saw Joss and recognized him and came over to say good evening, and led us to what was obviously the best table in the room, set in the narrow alcove of a jutting bay window. Beyond the window could be seen the shapes of rain-washed roofs, and beyond them again the liquid darkness of the harbour, a-shimmer with reflections from the street lamps on the quay and the riding lights of fishing boats.

We faced each other. I was still deeply angry and would not look at him. I sat, drawing patterns with my finger on the table mat, and listened to him ordering what I was to eat. Apparently I was not even to be allowed the right of making my own choice. I heard the waitress say, "For the young lady, too?" as though even she were surprised by his cursory behaviour, and Joss said, "Yes, for the young lady, too," and the waitress went off, and we were alone.

After a little I looked up. His dark gaze met mine, unblinking. The silence grew, and I had the ridiculous feeling that he was waiting for me to apologize to him.

I heard myself say, "If you won't let me talk to Eliot Bayliss, perhaps you'll talk about him."

"What do you want to know?"

"Is he married?" It was the first question that came into my head.

"No."

"He's attractive." Joss acknowledged this. "Does he live alone?"

"No, with his mother. They have a house up at High Cross, six miles or so from here, but about a year ago they moved into Boscarva, to be with the old man."

"Is my grandfather ill?"

"You don't know very much about your family, do you?"

"No." I sounded defiant.

"About ten years ago Grenville Bayliss had a heart attack. That's when he stopped painting. But he always appears to have had the constitution of an ox, and he made a miraculous recovery. He didn't want to leave Boscarva, and he had this couple to take care of him . . ."

"The Pettifers?"

Joss frowned. "How do you know about the Pettifers?"

"My mother told me." I thought of the long-ago tea parties by the kitchen fire. "I never imagined they'd still be there."

"Mrs Pettifer died last year, so Pettifer and your grandfather were left on their own. Grenville Bayliss is eighty now, and Pettifer can't be far behind him. Mollie Bayliss wanted them to move up to High Cross and sell Boscarva, but the old man was adamant, so in the end she and Eliot moved in with him. Without noticeable enthusiasm, I may add." He leaned back in his chair, his long clever hands resting on the edge of the table. "Your mother . . . was she called Lisa?" I nodded.

"I knew Grenville had a daughter who'd had a daughter, but the fact that you call yourself Bayliss threw me slightly."

"My father left my mother before I was born. She never used his name."

"Where's your mother now?"

"She died—just a few days ago. In Ibiza." I repeated, "Just a few days ago," because all at once it seemed like a lifetime.

"I'm sorry." I made some sort of vague gesture, because there weren't any words. "Does your grandfather know?"

"I don't know."

"Have you come to tell him?"

"I suppose I may have to." The idea of doing so was daunting.

"Does he know you're here? In Porthkerris?"

I shook my head. "He doesn't even know me. I mean we've never met. I've never been here before." I made the final admission. "I don't even know how to find his house."

"One way and another," said Joss, "you're going to give him something of a shock."

I felt anxious. "Is he very frail?"

"No, he's not frail. He's fantastically tough. But he's getting old."

"My mother says he was frightening. Is he still frightening?"

Joss made a gruesome face, doing nothing to comfort me. "Terrifying," he said.

The waitress brought our soup. It was oxtail, thick and brown and very hot. I was so hungry that I ate it right down to the bottom of the bowl without saying another word. As I finally laid down my spoon, I looked up and saw that Joss was laughing at me.

"For a girl who didn't want to eat, you haven't done so badly."

But this time I did not rise. I pushed the empty bowl away, and leaned my elbows on the table.

"How is it that you know so much about the Bayliss family?" I asked him.

Joss had not bolted his soup as I had. Now, he was taking his time, buttering a roll, being maddeningly slow.

"It's easy," he said. "I do a certain amount of work up at Boscarva."

"What sort of work?"

"Well, I restore antique furniture. And don't gape in that unattractive fashion, it does nothing for you."

"*Restore antique furniture?* You must be joking."

"I'm not. And Grenville Bayliss has a houseful of old and very valuable stuff. In his day he made a lot of money, and he invested most of it in antiques. Now, some of the things are in a shocking state of repair, not that they haven't been polished to within an inch of their lives, but ten years ago he put in central heating and that wrecks old furniture. Drawers shrink and veneers curl and crack, and legs fall off chairs. Incidentally—" he added, diverted by the memory—"it was I who mended your cherrywood chair."

"But how long have you been doing this?"

"Let's see, I left school when I was seventeen, and I'm twenty-four now, so that makes it about seven years."

"But you had to *learn* . . ."

"Oh, sure. I did joinery and carpentry first, four years of it at a trade school in London, and then when I'd got that under my belt, I apprenticed myself for another couple of years to an old cabinet-maker down in Sussex. I lived with him and his wife, did all the dirty jobs in the workshop, learned everything I know."

I did a few sums. "That's only six years. You said seven."

He laughed. "I took a year off in the middle to travel. My parents said I was becoming parochial. My father has a cousin who runs a cattle ranch up in the Rockies, south-west Colorado. I worked as a ranch hand nine months or more." He frowned. "What are you grinning about?"

I told him. "That first time I saw you, in the shop . . . you looked like a ranch hand . . . you looked real. And somehow it annoyed me that you weren't."

He smiled. "And you know what you looked like?"

I cooled off. "No."

"The head girl of a nicely run orphanage. And that annoyed *me*."

A small clash of swords, and once more we were on opposite sides of the fence.

I eyed him with dislike as he cheerfully finished his soup; the waitress came to take away the empty plates, and to set down a carafe of red wine. I had not heard Joss ordering the wine, but now I watched him pour two full glasses and I saw the long spade-tipped fingers; I liked the idea of them working with wood and old and beautiful things, shaping and measuring and oiling and coaxing into shape. I picked up the glass of wine and against the light it glowed red as a ruby. I said, "Is that all you're doing in Porthkerris? Restoring Grenville Bayliss's furniture?"

"Good God, no. I'm opening a shop. I managed to rent these premises down on the harbour six months or so ago. I've been here, off and on, ever since. Now, I'm trying to get it into some sort of order before Easter, or Whitsun, or whenever the summer business really starts."

"Is it an antique shop?"

"No, modern, furniture, glass, textiles. But antique restoring goes on in the background. I mean I have a workroom. I also have a small pad on the top floor which is where I now live, which is why you were able to take over my room at Mrs Kernow's. One day when you've decided that I'm trustworthy you can climb the rickety stairs and I'll show it to you."

I ignored this fresh little sally.

"If you work down here, what were you doing in that shop in London?"

"Tristram's? I told you, he's a friend; I drop in and see him whenever I'm up in town."

I frowned. There were so many coincidences. Our lives seemed to be tied up in them, like a parcel well-knotted with ends of string. I watched him finish his wine and once more was visited with the unease

which I had known earlier in the evening. I knew I should ask him a
thousand questions, but before I could think of one the waitress arrived at our table once more, bearing steaks and vegetables and fried
potatoes and dishes of salad. I drank some wine and watched Joss,
and when the waitress had gone I said, "What does Eliot Bayliss do?"

"Eliot? He runs a garage up at High Cross, specializes in highly-
powered second-hand cars, Mercedes, Alfa Romeos. If you've got the
right sort of cheque book he can supply you with practically anything."

"You don't like him, do you?"

"I never said I didn't like him."

"But you don't."

"Perhaps it would be nearer the mark to say he doesn't like me."

"Why?"

He looked up, his eyes dancing with amusement. "I haven't any
idea. Now why don't you eat up your steak before it gets cold."

He drove me home. It was still raining and I was, all at once, deathly
tired. Outside Mrs Kernow's door Joss stopped the car, but left the engine running. I thanked him and said good night and began to open
the door, but before I could do so he had reached across and stopped
me. I turned to look at him.

He said, "Tomorrow. Are you going to Boscarva?"

"Yes."

"I'll take you."

"I can go alone."

"You don't know where the house is, and it's a long climb up the
hill. I'll pick you up in the car. About eleven?"

Arguing with him was like arguing with a steamroller. And I was
exhausted. I said, "All right."

He opened the door for me and pushed it open.

"Good night, Rebecca."

"Good night."

"I'll see you in the morning."

5

The wind did not drop during that night. But when I woke, the little window of my room at Mrs Kernow's gave me sight of a square of pale blue traversed by ballooning white clouds travelling at some speed. It was very cold, but bravely I got up and dressed and went downstairs in search of Mrs Kernow. I found her outside in the little yard at the back of the house, pegging out her washing on a line. At first, battling with flailing sheets and towels, she didn't see me, but when I appeared between a shirt and a modest lock-knit petticoat she gave a great start of surprise. Her own astonishment amused her, and she shook with shrill laughter, as though the two of us were a double act on the halls.

"You gave me some shock. I thought you were still asleep! Comfortable were you? That dratted wind's still around the place, but the rain's stopped, thank heaven. Want your breakfast do you?"

"A cup of tea, perhaps."

I helped her peg out the rest of the washing and then she picked up her empty basket and led the way back indoors. I sat at the kitchen table and she boiled a kettle and began to fry bacon.

"Have a good supper last night did you? Go to The Anchor? Tommy Williams keeps a good place there, always packed, winter and summer. I heard Joss bring you home. He's a lovely boy. I missed him when he moved out. Still, I go down sometimes to his new place, clean it up a bit for him, bring his washing home and do it here. Sad, a young

man like that on his own. All wrong somehow, not having someone
to take care of him."

"I should think Joss could take care of himself."

"It's not right a man doing woman's work." Mrs Kernow obviously
did not believe in Women's Lib. "Besides, he's busy enough working
for Mr Bayliss."

"Do you know Mr Bayliss?"

"Everyone knows he. Lived here nearly fifty years now. One of the
old ones, he is. And some lovely painter he was before he took ill.
Used to have an exhibition every year, and all sorts used to come down
from London, famous people, everybody. 'Course, lately we don't see
so much of him. He can't walk up and down the hill like he used to,
and it's a bit of a business Pettifer getting that great car down these
narrow lanes. Besides, in the summer, you can't move for traffic and
visitors. The place is teeming with them. Sometimes you'd think half
the population of the country is jammed into this little town."

She flipped the bacon on to a warm plate and set it in front of me.
"There now, eat that up before it gets cold."

I said, "Mrs Kernow, Mr Bayliss is my grandfather."

She stared at me, frowning. "Your grandfather?" Then, "Whose child
are you?"

"Lisa's."

"Lisa's child." She reached for a chair and slowly sat down upon it.
I saw that I had shocked her. "Does Joss know?"

It seemed irrelevant. "Yes, I told him last night."

"She was a lovely little girl." She stared into my face. "I can see her
in you . . . except that she was so dark and you're fair. We missed her
when she went, and never came back. Where is she now?"

I told her. When I had finished she said, "And Mr Bayliss doesn't
know you're here?"

"No."

"You must go now. Right away. Oh, I wish I could be there to see
the old man's face. He worshipped your mother . . ."

A tear gleamed. Quickly, before we were both awash with senti-
ment, I said, "I don't know how to get there."

Trying to tell me, she confused the two of us so much that finally she found an old envelope and the stub of a pencil and drew a rough map. Watching her I remembered Joss's promise to come at eleven o'clock and take me to Boscarva in his ramshackle van, but all at once it seemed a much better idea to go at once, on my own. Besides, last night I had been altogether too meek and compliant. It would do Joss's boundless ego no harm to arrive here and find me already gone. The thought of this happening cheered me considerably and I went upstairs to fetch my coat.

Outside I was instantly buffeted by the wind which tunnelled down the narrow street like the draught in a chimney. It was a cold wind, smelling of the sea, but when the sun burst out from behind the racing clouds the brightness was dazzling, full of glare, and overhead gulls screamed and floated, their wings white sails against the blue of the sky.

I walked and soon I was climbing. Up narrow, cobbled streets, between haphazard lines of houses. Up flights of steps, and leaning alleys. The higher I went the stronger became the wind. As I climbed the town dropped below me, and the ocean revealed itself, dark blue, streaked with jade and purple and flecked with white horses. It spread to the horizon where the sky took over, and below me the town and the harbour shrank to toy-size, to insignificance.

I stood looking at it, catching my breath, and all at once a funny thing happened. For this new place was not new to me at all, but totally familiar. I felt at home, as though I had returned to somewhere I had known all my life. And though I had scarcely thought of my mother since making the decision to come to Porthkerris, she was suddenly beside me, climbing the steep streets, long-legged, breathless, and warm with exertion as I was.

I was comforted by this sense of *déjà-vu*. It made me feel less lonely and much more brave. I went on and was glad I had not waited for Joss. His presence was disturbing, but I could not for the life of me decide why. He had, after all, been quite open with me, answering questions, giving perfectly believable reasons for his every action.

It was obvious that there was no love lost between himself and Eliot Bayliss, but I could easily understand this. The two young men would have nothing in common. Eliot, albeit unwillingly, was living at Boscarva. He was a Bayliss and the house was, for the time being, his home. On the other hand Joss's occupation in the house would give him the freedom to come and go in his own time. Be found, unexpectedly, at odd hours of the day, perhaps when his presence was neither convenient nor welcome. I imagined him on easy terms with everybody, sometimes getting in the way, and worst of all, blithely unaware of the trouble he was causing. A man like Eliot would resent this and Joss, in return, would react to his resentment.

Busy with these thoughts and the exertion of climbing, I did not observe my surroundings, but now the road levelled off beneath my feet, and I stopped to look around and take my bearings. I was on top of the hill, that was for sure. Behind and below me lay the town; ahead stretched the rugged coastline, curving away into the distance. It bordered a green country, patchworked with small farms and miniature fields, traversed by deep valleys, thick with hawthorn and stunted elm, where narrow streams channelled their way down to the sea.

I looked about me. This too was country. Or a year ago it had been. But since then a farm, perhaps, had been bought out, the bulldozers brought in, old hedges demolished, the rich earth torn up and flattened, and a new housing estate was in the process of being erected. All was raw, stark and hideous. Cement mixers churned, a lorry ground through a sea of mud, there were piles of brick and concrete, and in front of it all, like a proud banner, a hoarding which announced the man responsible for this carnage.

ERNEST PADLOW
DESIRABLE DETACHED HOUSES
FOR SALE
Apply Sea Lane, Porthkerris
Telephone Porthkerris 873

The houses were certainly detached, but only just. Scarcely three feet lay between them, and one window stared straight into another.

My heart mourned for the lost fields and the lost opportunities. As I stood there, mentally re-designing the entire project, a car came up the hill behind me, and drew to a halt in front of the hoarding. It was an old Jaguar, navy blue, and the man who stepped out of it, shutting the door behind him with a resounding thump, wore a workman's donkey jacket and carried a clip board and a lot of papers which fluttered in the wind. He turned and saw me, hesitated for only a second and then walked towards me, trying to flatten his hair down over his bald head.

"Morning." His smile was familiar as though we were old friends.

"Good morning."

I had seen him before. Last night. At The Anchor. Talking to Eliot Bayliss.

He glanced up at the hoarding.

"Thinking of buying a house for yourself?"

"No."

"You should. Get a good view up here."

I frowned. "I don't want a house."

"Be a good investment."

"Are you the foreman?"

"No." He glanced, with some pride, up at the hoarding which reared above us. "I'm Ernest Padlow."

"I see."

"Lovely site this . . ." He looked around at the devastation with some satisfaction. "Lot of people after this site, but the old girl who owned the land was a widow, and I managed to charm her into letting me have it."

I was surprised. As he spoke he reached for and lit himself a cigarette; he did not offer me one, his fingers were stained with nicotine and he seemed to me the most uncharming man I had ever met.

He turned his attention back to me. "Haven't seen you around, have I?"

"No."

"Visiting?"

"Yes, perhaps."

"It's better out of season. Not so crowded."

I said, "I'm looking for Boscarva."

Caught unawares, the bonhomie slid from his manner. His eyes were sharp as pebbles in his florid face. "Boscarva? You mean old Bayliss's place?"

"Yes."

His expression became wily. "Looking for Eliot?"

"No."

He waited for me to enlarge on this. When I didn't he tried to make a joke of it. "Well, I always say, least said, soonest mended. You want Boscarva, you go down that little lane. About half a mile. You'll see the house down towards the sea. It's got a slate roof, a big garden round it. You can't miss it."

"Thank you." I smiled politely. "Goodbye."

I turned and began to walk, feeling his eyes on my back. Then he spoke once more and I turned back. He was smiling, all friends again.

"You want a house, make up your mind quickly. They're selling like hot cakes."

"Yes, I'm sure. But I don't want one. Thank you."

The lane led downhill towards the great blue bowl of the sea, and now I was truly in the country, in a farmland of fields grazed by sweet-faced Guernseys. Wild violets and primroses grew in the grassy hedges, and the sun came out and turned the rich grass to emerald. Presently, I came around a corner and saw the white gates, set between low drystone walls; a driveway curved down, out of sight, and there were high hedges of escallonia and elm trees, tortured to unnatural shapes by the relentless winds.

I could not see the house. I stood at the open gates and looked down the drive, my courage seeping away like bathwater after the plug has been pulled out. I could not think what I was meant to do, nor what I was going to say once I had done it.

My mind was, unexpectedly and mercifully, made up for me. Down by the house, out of sight, I heard a car start up and come at some speed up the drive towards me. As it approached, a low-slung open sports car of some age and style, I stood aside to let it flash past between the gate posts and up the hill in the direction from which I had come, but still there was time to see the driver and the great red setter sitting up on the back seat, with the deliriously joyful expression of any dog being taken for a ride in an open car.

I thought that I had not been noticed but I was wrong. A moment later the car stopped with a screech of brakes and a shower of small stones flung from the back wheels. Then it went into reverse, and returned, with scarcely less speed back to the spot where I stood. It stopped, the engine was killed, and Eliot Bayliss, leaning an arm on the driving wheel, surveyed me across the empty passenger seat. He was bare-headed and wore a sheepskin car coat, and his expression was one of amusement, perhaps intrigue.

"Hallo," he said.

"Good morning." I felt a fool, bundled in my old coat, with the wind blowing stray strands of hair over my face. I tried to push them away.

"You look lost."

"No. I'm not."

He continued to regard me, frowning slightly. "I saw you last night, didn't I? At The Anchor? With Joss."

"Yes."

"Are you looking for Joss? As far as I know he's not arrived yet. That is, if he's decided to come today."

"No. I mean I'm not looking for him."

"Then who—" asked Eliot Bayliss gently—"are you looking for?"

"I . . . I wanted to see old Mr Bayliss."

"It's a little early for that. He doesn't usually appear 'til mid-day."

"Oh." I had not thought of this. Some of my disappointment must have shown in my face, for he went on, in the same gentle and friendly voice, "Perhaps I could help. I'm Eliot Bayliss."

"I know. I mean . . . Joss told me last night."

A small frown appeared between his eyebrows. He was obviously and naturally puzzled by my relationship with Joss.

"Why did you want to see my grandfather?" And when I did not reply, he suddenly leaned across to open the door of the car and said, with cool authority, "Get in."

I got in, closing the door behind me. I could feel his eyes on me, the shapeless coat, the patched jeans. The dog leaned forward to nuzzle my ear; his nose was cold and I reached over my shoulder to stroke the long, silky ear.

I said, "What's he called?"

"Rufus. Rufus the Red. But that doesn't answer my question, does it?"

I was saved by another interruption. Another car. But this time it was the Post Office van, rattling scarlet and cheerful, down the lane towards us. It stopped, and the postman rolled down the window to say to Eliot, good naturedly, "How can I get down the drive and deliver the letters if you park your car in the gateway?"

"Sorry," said Eliot, unperturbed, and he got out from behind the driving wheel and went to take a handful of mail and a newspaper from the postman. "I'll take it—it'll save you the trip."

"Lovely," said the postman. "Be nice if everyone did my job for me," and with a grin and a wave he went on his way, presumably to some outlying farmstead.

Eliot got back into the car.

"Well," he said, smiling at me. "What am I going to do with you?"

But I scarcely heard him. The pile of mail lay loosely in his lap, and on the top was an airmail envelope, postmarked Ibiza, and addressed to Mr Grenville Bayliss. The spiky handwriting was unmistakable.

A car is a good place for confidences. There is no telephone and you can't be unexpectedly interrupted. I said, "That letter. The one on the top. It's from a man called Otto Pedersen. He lives in Ibiza."

Eliot, frowning, took up the envelope. He turned it over and read Otto's name on the back. He looked at me. "How did you know?"

"I know his writing. I know him. He's writing to . . . to your grandfather to tell him that Lisa is dead. She died about a week ago. She was living with Otto in Ibiza."

"Lisa. You mean Lisa Bayliss?"

"Yes. Roger's sister. Your aunt. My mother."

"You're Lisa's child?"

"Yes." I turned to look directly at him. "I'm your cousin. Grenville Bayliss is my grandfather, too."

His eyes were a strange colour, greyish-green, like pebbles washed by some fast-moving stream. They showed neither shock nor pleasure, simply regarded me levelly without expression. He said at last, "Well I'll be damned."

It was hardly what I expected. We sat in silence because I could think of nothing to say, and then, as though coming to a sudden decision, he tossed the pile of mail into my lap, started the car up once more, and swung the wheel around so that once more we were facing the drive.

"What are you doing?" I asked.

"What do you think? Taking you home of course."

Home. Boscarva. We came around the curve of the drive and it was there, waiting for me. Not small, but not large either. Grey stone, smothered in creeper, grey slate roof, a semicircular stone porch with the door open to the sunshine, and inside a glimpse of red tiles, a clutter of flowerpots, the pinks and scarlets of geranium and fuchsia. A curtain fluttered at an open upstairs window and smoke plumed from a chimney. As we got out of the car the sun came out from behind a cloud and, caught in the spread arms of the house, sheltered from the north wind, it was suddenly very warm.

"Come along," said Eliot and led the way, the dog at his heels. We went through the porch and into a dark, panelled hallway illuminated by the big window on the turn of the stairs. I had imagined Boscarva as being a house of the past, sad and nostalgic, filled with the chill of old memories. But it wasn't like that at all. It was vital, humming with a sense of activity. There were papers lying on the table, a pair of gardening gloves, a dog's lead. From beyond a doorway came the kitchen sounds of voices and the clatter of crockery. From upstairs a vacuum-cleaner hummed. And there was a smell compounded of scrubbed stone and old polished floors, and years of woodfires.

Eliot stood at the foot of the staircase and called, "Mamma." But when there was no answer, only the continued hum of the vacuum-cleaner, he said, "You'd better come this way." We went down the hall and through a door which led into a long, low drawing room, palely panelled and sensuous with the brightness and scent of spring flowers. At one end, in a fireplace of carved pine and Dutch tiles, a newly lit fire flickered cheerfully, and three tall windows, curtained in faded yellow silk, faced out over a flagged terrace, and beyond the balustrade of this I could see the blue line of the sea.

I stood in the middle of this charming room as Eliot Bayliss closed the door and said, "Well, you're here. Why don't you take your coat off?"

I did so. It was very warm. I laid it over a chair where it looked like some great, dead creature.

He said, "When did you get here?"

"Last night. I caught the train from London."

"You live in London?"

"Yes."

"And you've never been here before?"

"No. I didn't know about Boscarva. I didn't know about Grenville Bayliss being my grandfather. My mother never told me till the night before she died."

"How does Joss come into it?"

"I . . ." It was too complicated to explain. "I'd met him in London. He happened to be at the junction when my train got in. It was a coincidence."

"Where are you staying?"

"With Mrs Kernow in Fish Lane."

"Grenville's an old man. He's ill. You know that, don't you?"

"Yes."

"I think . . . this letter from Otto Pedersen . . . we'd better be careful. Perhaps my mother would be the best person . . ."

"Yes, of course."

"It was lucky you saw the letter."

"Yes. I thought he would probably write. But I was afraid that I would have to break the news to you all."

"And now it's been done for you." He smiled, and all at once he looked much younger . . . belying those strange coloured eyes and the thick silver-fox hair. "Why don't you wait here and I'll go and find my mother and try to put her in the picture. Would you like a cup of coffee or something?"

"Only if it's not a nuisance."

"No nuisance. I'll tell Pettifer." He opened the door behind him. "Make yourself at home."

The door closed softly, and he was gone. Pettifer. *Pettifer had been in the Navy too, he looked after my father and sometimes drove the car and Mrs Pettifer did the cooking.* So my mother had told me. And Joss had told me that Mrs Pettifer had died. But in the old days she had taken Lisa and her brother into the kitchen and made hot buttered toast. She had drawn the curtains against the dark and the rain, and made the children feel safe and loved.

Alone, I inspected the room where I had been left to wait. I saw a glass-doored cabinet filled with Oriental treasures, including some small pieces of jade, and wondered if these were the ones that my mother had mentioned to me. I glanced around, thinking that perhaps I might find the Venetian mirror and the davenport desk as well, but then my attention was caught by the picture over the mantelpiece, and I went to look at it, all else forgotten.

It was a portrait of a girl, dressed in the fashion of the early 1930s, slender, flat-chested, her white dress hanging straight to her hips, her dark, bobbed hair revealing with enchanting innocence the long, slender neck. She sat, in the picture, on a tall stool, holding a single long-stemmed rose, but you could not see her face, for she was looking away from the artist, out of some unseen window, into the sunshine. The effect was all pink and gold, with sunlight filtering through the thin stuff of her white dress. It was enchanting.

Behind me the door opened suddenly and I turned, startled, as an old man came into the room, stately, bald-headed, a little stooped, perhaps; treading cautiously. He wore rimless spectacles and a striped shirt with an old-fashioned hard collar, and over it all a blue and white butcher's apron.

"Are you the young lady wanting a cup of coffee?" He had a deep, lugubrious voice, and this, with his sombre appearance, made me think of a reliable undertaker.

"Yes, if it's not too much trouble."

"Milk and sugar?"

"No sugar. Just a little milk. I was looking at the portrait."

"Yes. It's very pleasing. It's called 'Lady Holding a Rose.'"

"You can't see her face."

"No."

"Did my . . . Did Mr Bayliss paint it?"

"Oh yes. That was hung in the Academy, could have been sold a hundred times over, but the Commander would never part with it." As he said this, he carefully took off his spectacles, and was now staring at me intently. His old eyes were pale. He said, "For a moment, when you spoke, you reminded me of someone else. But you're young and she'd be middle-aged by now. And her hair was dark as a blackbird. That's what Mrs Pettifer used to say. Dark as a blackbird's wing."

I said, "Eliot didn't tell you?"

"What didn't Mr Eliot tell me?"

"You're talking about Lisa, aren't you? I'm Rebecca. I'm her daughter."

"Well." Fumbling a little he put his spectacles back on again. A faint gleam of pleasure showed on his gloomy features. "I was right then. I'm not often wrong about things like that." And he came forward, holding out a horny hand. "It's a real pleasure to meet you . . . A pleasure that I never thought I should have. I thought you'd never come. Is your mother with you?"

I wished that Eliot had made it a little easier for me.

"My mother's dead. She died last week. In Ibiza. That's why I'm here."

"She died." His eyes clouded. "I'm sorry. I'm really sorry. She should have come back. She should have come home. We all wanted to see her again." He took out a copious handkerchief and blew his nose. "And who—" he asked—"is going to tell the Commander?"

"I think . . . Eliot's gone to fetch his mother. You see, there's a letter for my grandfather in the post, it came this morning. It's from Ibiza, from the man who was . . . taking care of my mother. But if you think that wouldn't be a very good idea . . ."

"What I think won't make no difference," said Pettifer. "And whoever tells the Commander, it's not going to lessen his sorrow. But I'll tell you one thing. You being here will help a lot."

"Thank you."

He blew his nose again and put away his handkerchief.

"Mr Eliot and his mother . . . well, this isn't their home. But it was either the old Commander and me moving up to High Cross or them coming here. And they wouldn't be here if the doctor hadn't insisted. I told them we could manage all right, the Commander and me. We've been together all these years . . . but there, we're neither of us as young as we used to be, and the Commander, he had this heart attack . . ."

"Yes, I know . . ."

"And after Mrs Pettifer passed on, there wasn't anyone to do the cooking. Mind, I can cook all right, but it takes me a good part of my time taking care of the Commander, and I wouldn't want to see him going about the place looking shabby."

"No, of course not . . ."

I was interrupted by the slam of a door.

A hearty male voice called, "Pettifer!" and Pettifer said, "Excuse me a moment, miss," and went out to investigate, leaving the door open behind him.

"Pettifer!"

I heard Pettifer say, with what sounded like the greatest satisfaction, "Hallo, Joss."

"Is she there?"

"Who, here?"

"Rebecca."

"Yes, she's right here, in the sitting-room . . . I was just going to get her a cup of coffee."

"Make it two would you, there's a good chap. And black and strong for me."

His footsteps came down the hall, and the next moment he was there, framed in the doorway, long-legged, black-haired, and—it was obvious—angry.

"What the hell do you think you're doing?" he demanded.

I could feel my hackles rising, like a suspicious dog. Home, Eliot had said. This was Boscarva, my home, and whether I was here or not was nothing to do with Joss.

"I don't know what you're talking about."

"I went to pick you up and Mrs Kernow told me you'd already left."

"So?"

"I told you to wait for me."

"I decided not to wait."

He was silent, fuming, but finally appeared to accept this inescapable fact.

"Does anyone know you've arrived?"

"I met Eliot at the gate. He brought me here."

"Where's he gone?"

"To find his mother."

"Have you seen anyone else? Have you seen Grenville?"

"No."

"Has anyone told Grenville about your mother?"

"A letter came by this morning's post, from Otto Pedersen. But I don't think he's seen it yet."

"Pettifer must take it to him. Pettifer must be there when he reads it."

"Pettifer didn't seem to think that."

"I think it," said Joss.

His apparently outrageous interference left me without words, but as we stood glaring at each other across the pretty patterned carpet and a great bowl of scented narcissus, there came the sound of voices and footsteps down the uncarpeted staircase and along the hall towards us.

I heard a woman's voice say, "In the sitting-room, Eliot?"

Joss muttered something that sounded unprintable, and marched over to the fireplace where he stood with his back to me, staring down into the flames. The next instant, Mollie appeared in the doorway, hesitated for a moment and then came towards me, hands outstretched.

"Rebecca." (So it was to be a warm welcome.) Eliot, following behind her, closed the door. Joss did not even turn round.

I worked it out that by now Mollie must be over fifty, but this was hard to believe. She was plump and pretty, her fading blonde hair charmingly coiffed, her eyes blue, her skin fresh and lightly scattered with freckles which helped to create this astonishing illusion of youth. She wore a blue skirt and cardigan and a creamy silk blouse; her legs were slim and shapely and her hands beautifully manicured, decorated with pale pink fingernails, and many rings and fine gold bracelets. Scented, immaculately preserved, she made me think of a charming little tabby cat, curled precisely in the centre of her own satin cushion.

I said, "I'm afraid this is something of a shock."

"No, not a shock, but a surprise. And your mother . . . I'm so dreadfully sorry. Eliot's told me about the letter . . ."

At this Joss swung around from the fireplace.

"Where is the letter?"

Mollie turned her gaze upon him, and it was impossible to guess whether this was the first time she had realized he was there, or whether she had seen him and simply decided to ignore him.

"Joss. I didn't think you were coming this morning."

"Yes. I just got here."

"You know Rebecca, I believe."

"Yes, we've met." He hesitated, seeming to be making an effort to pull himself together. Then he smiled, ruefully, turned to lean his broad shoulders against the mantelpiece and apologized. "I'm sorry. And I know it's none of my business, but that letter that came this morning . . . where is it?"

"In my pocket," said Eliot, speaking for the first time. "Why?"

"It's just that I think Pettifer should be the one to break the news to the old man. I think Pettifer is the only person to do it."

This was greeted by silence. Then Mollie let go of my hands and turned to her son.

"He's right," she said. "Grenville's closest to Pettifer."

"That's all right by me," said Eliot, but his eyes, on Joss, were cold with antagonism. I did not blame him. I felt the same way myself—I was on Eliot's side.

Joss said again, "I'm sorry."

Mollie was polite. "Not at all. It's very thoughtful of you to be so concerned."

"None of my business, really," said Joss. Eliot and his mother waited with pointed patience. At last he took the hint, heaved his shoulders away from the mantelpiece, and said, "Well, if you'll excuse me, I'll go and get on with some work."

"Will you be here for lunch?"

"No, I can only stay a couple of hours. I'll have to get back to the shop. I'll pick up a sandwich at the pub." He smiled benignly at us all, not a trace of his former temper showing. "Thanks all the same."

And so he left us, modest, apologetic, apparently cut down to size. Once more the young workman, an employee, with a job to do.

6

Mollie said, "You must forgive him. He's not always the most tactful of men."

Eliot laughed shortly. "That's the understatement of the year."

She turned to me, explaining, "He's restoring some of the furniture for us. It's old and it had got into bad repair. He's a marvellous craftsman, but we never know when he's going to arrive or when he's going to go!"

"One day," said her son, "I shall lose my temper with him and punch his nose into the back of his neck." He smiled at me charmingly, his eyes crinkling, belying the ferocity of his words. "And I'm going to have to go too. I was late as it was, now I'm bloody late. Rebecca, will you excuse me?"

"Of course. I'm sorry, I'm afraid it was my fault. And thank you for being so kind . . ."

"I'm glad I stopped. I must have known how important it was. I'll see you . . ."

"Yes, of course you will," said Mollie quickly. "She can't go away now that she's found us."

"Well I'll leave the two of you to fix everything up . . ." He made for the door, but his mother interrupted gently.

"Eliot." He turned. "The letter."

"Oh, yes, of course." He took it from his pocket, the fateful letter, a little crumpled now, and handed it to Mollie. "Don't let Pettifer make too big a meal of it. He's a sentimental old chap."

"I won't."

He smiled again, saying goodbye to both of us. "See you at dinner."

And he was gone, whistling up his dog as he went down the hall. We heard the front door open and shut, his car start up. Mollie turned to me.

"Now," she said, "come and sit by the fire and tell me all about it."

I did so, as I had already told Joss and Mrs Kernow, only this time I found myself stumbling a little when I got to the bit about Otto and Lisa living together, as though I were ashamed of it, which was a thing which I had never been. As I talked and Mollie listened, I tried to work this out, and to understand why my mother had disliked her so much. Perhaps it was simply a natural antipathy. It was obvious that they would never have had anything in common. And my mother had never had much tolerance for women who bored her. Men, now, were different. Men were always amusing. But women had to be very special for my mother to be able to tolerate their company. No, it could not all have been Mollie's fault. Sitting across the fireside from her, I resolved that I would be friends with her, and perhaps compensate, in a small way, for the short shrift she had received from Lisa.

"And how long are you going to be able to stay in Porthkerris? Your job . . . do you have to get back?"

"No. I seem to have been given a sort of indefinite leave."

"You'll stay here, with us?"

"Well, I've got this room with Mrs Kernow."

"Yes, but you'd be much better here. There's not a lot of space, that's the only thing; you'll have to sleep up in the attic, but it's a dear little room if you don't mind the sloping ceilings and you manage not to bump your head. You see, Eliot and I seem to have filled up the guest rooms, and as well I've got my niece staying for a few days. Perhaps you'll make friends with her. It'll be nice for her to have someone young about the place."

I wondered where the niece was. "How old is she?"

"Only seventeen. It's a difficult age, and I think that her mother felt it would be a good thing if she was out of London for a little. They live there, you see, and of course she has so many friends, and there is so much going on . . ." She was obviously finding it difficult to find the

right words . . . "Anyway, Andrea's down here for a week or two to
have a little change, but I'm afraid she's rather bored."

I imagined myself at seventeen, in the unseen Andrea's shoes, staying in this warm and charming house, cared for by Mollie and Pettifer, with the sea and the cliffs on my doorstep, the countryside inviting
long walks, and all the secret crooked streets of Porthkerris waiting
to be explored. To me it would have been heaven, and impossible to
be bored. I wondered if I would have very much in common with Mollie's niece.

"Of course," she went on, "as you've probably gathered, Eliot and I
are only here because Mrs Pettifer died and really the two old men
couldn't manage on their own. We've got Mrs Thomas, she comes in
each morning to help do the housework, but I do all the cooking, and
keep the place as bright and pretty as I can."

"The flowers are so lovely."

"I can't bear a house without flowers."

"What about your own house?"

"My dear, it's empty. I shall have to take you up to High Cross one
day to show it to you. I bought a pair of old cottages just after the war
and converted them. Even though I shouldn't say so, it is very charming. And, of course, it's so handy for Eliot's garage; as it is, living here,
he seems to be perpetually on the road."

"Yes, I suppose so."

I could hear footsteps coming down the hall again; in a moment
the door opened, and Pettifer edged around it, cautiously, carrying a
tray laden with all the accoutrements of mid-morning coffee, including a large silver pot with steam drifting from its spout.

"Oh, Pettifer, thank you . . ."

He came forward, stooped with the weight of the tray, and Mollie
got up to fetch a stool and place it swiftly beneath the tray so that the
old man could put it down before it tilted so sharply that everything
on it went hurtling to the floor.

"That's splendid, Pettifer."

"One of the cups was for Joss."

"He's upstairs working. He must have forgotten about the coffee.
Never mind, I'll drink it for him. And, Pettifer . . ." He straightened,

slowly, as though all his old joints were aching. Mollie took the letter from Ibiza off the mantelpiece where she had placed it for safety. "We thought, all of us, that perhaps it would be the best if you told the Commander about his daughter and then gave him this letter. It would be best, we thought, coming from you. Would you mind?"

Pettifer took the thin blue envelope.

"No, Madam. I'll do it. I'm just on my way up now to get the Commander up and dressed."

"It would be a kindness, Pettifer."

"That's all right, Madam."

"And tell him that Rebecca is here. And that she's staying. We'll have to make up the bed in the attic but I think she'll be quite comfortable."

Again a gleam came into Pettifer's face. I wondered if he ever really smiled, or whether his face had dropped permanently into those lugubrious lines and a cheerful expression had become physically impossible.

"I'm glad you're staying," he said. "The Commander will like that."

When he'd gone, I said, "You'll have a lot to do. Shouldn't I go, and get out from under your feet?"

"You'll have to collect your things from Mrs Kernow anyway. I wonder how we could manage that? Pettifer could take you, but now he'll be occupied with Grenville and I must speak to Mrs Thomas about your room and then start thinking about lunch. Now what are we going to do?" I could not imagine. I was certainly not going to be able to carry all my belongings up the hill from the town. But luckily Mollie answered her own question. "I know. Joss. He can take you and bring you back up the hill in his van."

"But isn't Joss working?"

"Oh, for once we'll interrupt him. It's not often he's asked to put himself out—I'm sure he won't mind. Come along, we'll go and find him."

I had thought that she would take me to some forgotten outhouse or shed where we would find Joss, surrounded by wood shavings and the smell of hot glue, but to my surprise, she led me upstairs, and I forgot about Joss, because these were my first impressions of Boscarva, where my mother had been brought up, and I didn't want to miss a thing. The stairs were uncarpeted, the walls half panelled and then darkly papered above and hung with heavy oil paintings. All was at variance with the pretty, feminine sitting-room which we had left downstairs. On the first-floor landing passages led to left and right, there was a tallboy of polished walnut, and bookcases heavy with books, and then we went on again, up the stairs. Here was red drugget, white paint, again the passages led away to either side, and Mollie took the right-hand one. At the end of this passage was an open door, and from behind it the sound of voices, a man's and a girl's.

She seemed to hesitate and then her footsteps quickened, determined. Her back view became, all at once, formidable. With me following she went down the passage and through the door, and we were in an attic which had been converted, by means of a skylight, to a studio, or perhaps a billiard room, for against one wall was a massive, leather-seated sofa with oaken arms and legs. Now, however, this cold and airy room was being used as a workshop, with Joss in the middle of it, surrounded by chairs, broken picture frames, a table with a crooked leg, some scraps of leather, tools and nails, and a gimcrack gas ring on which reposed an unsavoury-looking glue pot. Wrapped in a worn blue apron, he was carefully fitting beautiful scarlet hide over the seat of one of the chairs, and as he did this, was being entertained by a young and female companion, who turned, disinterested, to see who had come into the room, and was so breaking up this cosy *tête-à-tête*.

Mollie said, "Andrea!" And then, less sharply, "Andrea, I didn't realize you were up."

"Oh, I've been up for hours."

"Did you have any breakfast?"

"I didn't want any."

"Andrea, this is Rebecca. Rebecca Bayliss."

"Oh, yes," she turned her eyes on to me. "Joss has been telling me all about you."

I said, "How do you do." She was very young and very thin, with long seaweedy hair that hung on either side of her face, which was pretty, except for her eyes which were pale and slightly protuberant, and not improved by a great deal of clumsy mascara. She wore, inevitably, jeans, and a cotton tee-shirt which did not look entirely clean and which revealed, with no shadow of a doubt, the fact that she wore nothing beneath it. On her feet were sandals which looked like surgical boots that had been striped in green and purple. There was a leather boot-lace around her neck upon which hung a heavy silver cross of vaguely Celtic design. Andrea, I thought. So bored with Boscarva. And it made me uncomfortable to think that she and Joss had been discussing me. I wondered what he had said.

Now, she did not move, but stayed where she was, legs straddled, leaning against a heavy old mahogany table.

"Hi," she said.

"Rebecca's going to stay here," Mollie told them. Joss looked up, his mouth full of tacks, his eyes bright with interest, a lock of black hair falling over his forehead.

"Where's she going to sleep?" asked Andrea. "I thought we were a full house."

"In the bedroom along the passage," her aunt told her crisply. "Joss, would you do a favour for me?" He spat the tacks neatly into his palm and stood up, pushing his hair back with his wrist. "Would you take her, now, down to Mrs Kernow, and tell Mrs Kernow that she's coming here, and then help her with her suitcases and bring her back up to Boscarva again? Would that be very inconvenient?"

"Not at all," said Joss, but Andrea's face assumed an expression of bored resignation.

"It's a nuisance, I know, when you're busy, but it would be such a help . . ."

"It's no trouble." He laid down his little hammer and began to un-tie the knot of his apron. He grinned at me. "I'm getting quite used to carting Rebecca about."

And Andrea gave a snort, whether of disgust or impatience it was impossible to tell, sprang to her feet and marched out of the room, leaving the impression that we had been lucky to escape without a monumentally slammed door.

And so I was back where I started, with Joss, crammed into the ram-shackle little van. We drove in silence away from Boscarva, through

Mr Padlow's building estate, and on to the slope of the hill that led
down to the town.

It was Joss who broke the silence.

"So, it all worked out."

"Yes."

"How do you like your family?"

"I haven't met them all yet. I haven't met Grenville."

He said, "You'll like him," but the way he said it, he made it sound,
"You'll like *him*."

"I like them all."

"That's good."

I looked at him. He wore his blue denim jacket, a navy polo-necked
sweater. His profile was impassive. I felt it would be easy to be maddened by him.

"Tell me about Andrea," I said.

"What do you want to know about Andrea?"

"I don't know. I just want you to tell me."

"She's seventeen, and she thinks she's in love with some guy she
met at Art School, and her parents don't approve so she's been rusti-
cated with Auntie Mollie. And she's bored stiff."

"She seems to have taken you into her confidence."

"There's no one else to talk to."

"Why doesn't she go back to London?"

"Because she's only seventeen. She hasn't got the money. And I
think she hasn't quite got the courage to stand up to her parents."

"What does she do with herself all day?"

"I don't know. I'm not there all day. She doesn't seem to get up until
lunchtime, and then she sits around watching television. Boscarva's
a house of old people. You can't blame her for being bored."

I said, without thinking, "Only the boring are bored." This had
once been drummed into me by a wise and well-meaning head-
mistress.

"That," said Joss, "sounds uncomfortably sanctimonious."

"I didn't mean it to."

He smiled. "Were you never bored?"

"Nobody who lived with my mother was ever bored."

He sang, "You may have been a headache, but you never were a bore."

"Exactly."

"She sounds great. Exactly my sort of female."

"That's what most men thought about her."

When we got to Fish Lane Mrs Kernow was out, but Joss seemed to have a key. We let ourselves in and I went upstairs to pack my suitcase and my rucksack while Joss wrote Mrs Kernow a note to explain the new arrangements.

"How about paying her?" I asked as I came downstairs, bumping the rucksack behind me.

"I'll fix that when I next see her. I've told her so in the note."

"But I can pay for myself."

"Of course you can, but let me do it for you." He took my suitcase and went to open the door, and there did not seem to be opportunity for further argument.

Once more my belongings were heaved into the back of the little truck, once more we headed for Boscarva, only this time Joss took me round by the harbour road.

"I want to show you my shop . . . . I mean, I just want to show you where it is. Then if you want to get hold of me for any reason, you'll know where to find me."

"Why should I want to get hold of you?"

"I don't know. You might need wise counselling; or money; or just a good laugh. There it is, you can't miss it."

It was a tall narrow house, boxed in between two short fat houses. Three storeys high with a window on each floor, and the ground floor still in a state of reconstruction, with new wood unpainted and great circles of whitewash splashed over the plate glass of the shop window.

As we flashed past it, tyres rattling on the cobbles, I said, "That's a good position, you'll get all the visitors coming in to spend their money."

"That's what I hope."

"When can I see it?"

"Come next week. We'll be more or less straight then."

"All right. Next week."

"It's a date," said Joss, and turned the corner by the church. He put the little truck into second gear and we roared up the hill with a noise like a badly tuned motor bicycle.

Back at Boscarva, it was Pettifer who, hearing our arrival, emerged from the front door as Joss lifted my suitcase from the back of the truck.

"Joss, the Commander's downstairs and in his study. He said to bring Rebecca in to see him just as soon as you arrived."

Joss looked at him. "How is he?"

Pettifer ducked his head. "Not too bad."

"Was he very upset?"

"He's all right . . . now you leave that case, and I'll carry it upstairs."

"You'll do no such thing," said Joss, and for once I was glad that he was being his usual bossy self. "I'll take it up. Where's she sleeping?"

"In the attic . . . the other end from the billiard room, but the Commander did say, right away."

"I know," Joss grinned, "and Naval time is five minutes beforehand. But there's still time to take the girl up to her room, so stop fussing, there's a good man."

Leaving Pettifer still mildly protesting, I followed him up the two flights of stairs that I had already climbed this morning. The sound of the vacuum had stopped, but there was the smell of roasting lamb. I realized then that I was very hungry and my mouth watered. Joss's long legs sped ahead of me, and by the time I reached the slope-ceilinged bedroom which was to be mine, he had set down the suitcase and the rucksack and gone to fling wide the dormer window, so that I was met by a blast of cold, salty air.

"Come and look at the view."

I went to stand beside him. I saw the sea, the cliffs, the gold of bracken and the first yellow candles of gorse. And below was the Boscarva garden which, because of the stone balustrade of the terrace, I had not been able to see from the drawing-room window. It had been built in a series of terraces, dropping down the slope of the hill, and at the bottom, tucked into a corner of the garden wall, was a stone cottage with a slate roof. No, not a cottage, perhaps a stable, with a commodious loft above it.

I said, "What's that building?"

"That's the studio," Joss told me. "That's where your grandfather used to paint."

"It doesn't look like a studio."

"From the other side it does. The entire north wall is made of glass. He designed it himself, had it built by a local stonemason."

"It looks shut up."

"It is. Locked and shuttered. It hasn't been opened since he had his heart attack and stopped painting."

I shivered suddenly.

"Cold?" asked Joss.

"I don't know." I moved away from the window, undoing my coat, dropping it over the end of the bed. The room was white, the carpet dark red. There was a built-in wardrobe, shelves full of books, a washbasin. I went over to wash my hands, turning the soap beneath the warm water. Over the basin was a mirror which gave me back a reflection both dishevelled and anxious. I realized then how nervous I was of meeting Grenville for the first time, and how important it was that he should get a good impression of me.

I dried my hands, went to unbuckle my rucksack, and found a brush and comb. "Was he a good painter, Joss? Do you think he was a good artist?"

"Yes. The old school, of course, but magnificent. And a marvellous colourist."

I pulled the rubber band from the end of my plait, shook the coils free, and went back to the mirror to start brushing. Over my reflected shoulder I could see Joss watching me. He did not speak while I brushed and combed and finally re-plaited my hair. As I fastened the ends, he said, "It's a wonderful colour. Like corn."

I laid down the brush and comb. "Joss, we mustn't keep him waiting."

"Do you want me to come with you?"

"Please."

I realized then that this was the first time I had ever had to ask him to help me.

I followed him downstairs, down the hall and past the sitting-room, to a door which stood at the end of the passage. Joss opened it and put his head around.

He said, "Good morning."

"Who's that? Joss? Come along in . . ." The voice was higher pitched than I had imagined, more like the voice of a much younger man.

"I've brought someone to see you . . ."

He opened the door wide, and put his arms behind me to propel me gently forward into the room. It was a small room, with french windows leading out on to a paved terrace and a secret garden, warm with trapped sunshine, and enclosed by dense hedges and escallonia.

I saw the fire flickering in the grate; the panelled walls covered either with pictures or books; the model, on the mantelpiece, of an old-fashioned naval cruiser. There were photographs in silver frames, a table littered with papers and magazines, and a blue and white Chinese bowl filled with daffodils.

As I entered, he was already heaving himself—with the aid of a stick—out of a red leather armchair, which stood half turned towards the warmth of the fire. I was amazed that Joss did nothing to help him, and I began to say, "Oh, please don't bother . . ." but by then he was on his feet and erect, and a pair of blue eyes surveyed me calmly from beneath jutting brows and bristling white eyebrows.

I realized then that I had steeled myself to finding him pathetic in some way, old, infirm, perhaps a little shaky. But Grenville Bayliss, at eighty, was formidable. Very tall, very upright, starched and barbered, smelling faintly of Bay Rum, he was a credit to his servant Pettifer. He wore a dark blue blazer, of Naval cut, neatly creased grey flannels, and velvet slippers with his initials embroidered in gold. He was also very tanned, his bald head brown as a chestnut beneath the thinning strands of white hair, and I imagined him spending much time in that little sunny secret garden, reading his morning paper, enjoying a pipe, watching the gulls and the white clouds scudding across the sky.

We looked at each other. I wished that he would say something but he simply looked. I hoped that he liked what he saw, and was glad I had taken the time to brush my hair. And then he said, "I've never been in this situation before. I'm not quite sure how we're meant to greet each other."

I said, "I could give you a kiss."

"Why don't you do that?"

So I did, stepping forward and raising my face, and he stooped slightly and my lips touched the smooth clean skin of his cheek.

"Now," he said, "why don't we sit down? Joss, come and sit down."

But Joss excused himself, said that if he didn't start work soon then he would have done nothing all day. But he stayed long enough to help the old man back into his chair, and pour us both a glass of sherry from the decanter on the side table, and then he said, "I'll leave you. You'll have a lot to talk about," and with a cheerful wave of his hand, slipped away. The door closed quietly behind him.

Grenville said, "I believe you know him quite well."

I pulled up a stool so that I could sit and face him. "Not really. But he's been very kind, and . . ." I tried to think of the right word. "Convenient. I mean, he always seems to be there when people need him."

"And never when they don't?" I was not sure if I could entirely agree with this. "He's a clever boy, too. Doing up all my furniture."

"Yes, I know."

"Good craftsman. Lovely hands." He laid down his sherry glass, and once more I was subjected to that piercing blue stare. "Your mother died."

"Yes."

"Had a letter from this Pedersen fellow. He said it was leukaemia."

"Yes."

"Did you meet him?"

I told him about going to Ibiza and the night I had spent with Otto and my mother.

"He was a decent chap, then? Good to her?"

"Yes. He was immensely kind. And he adored her."

"Glad she ended up with somebody decent. Most of the chaps she picked on were just a lot of bounders."

I smiled at the old-fashioned word. I thought of the sheep-farmer, and the American in his Brooks Brothers shirts, and wondered how they would have liked being called bounders. They probably wouldn't even have known what it meant.

I said, "I think she sometimes got a little carried away."

A gleam of humour showed in his eyes. "You seem to have adopted a fairly worldly attitude?"

"Yes. I did. Long ago."

"She was a maddening woman. But she'd been the most enchanting little girl it was possible to imagine. I painted her often. I've still got one or two canvases of Lisa as a child. I'll have to get Pettifer to look them out, show them to you. And then she grew up and everything changed. Roger, my son, was killed in the war, and Lisa was always at loggerheads with her mother, rushing off in her little car, never coming home at night. Finally she fell in love with this actor fellow, and that was it."

"She really *was* in love with him."

"In love." He sounded disgusted. "That's an overrated expression. There's a lot more to life than just being in love."

"Yes, but you have to find that out for yourself."

He looked amused. "Have you found it out?"

"No."

"How old are you?"

"Twenty-one."

"You're mature for twenty-one. And I like your hair. You don't look like Lisa. You don't look like your father either. You look like yourself." He reached for his sherry glass, raised it carefully to his mouth, took a sip, and then replaced the glass on the table by his chair. In such cautious actions did he betray his age and his infirmity.

He said, "She should have come back to Boscarva. At any time we would have welcomed her. Come to that, why didn't *you* come?"

"I didn't know about Boscarva. I didn't know about you until the night before she died."

"It was as though she'd put the past out of her life. And when her mother died and I wrote to tell her, she never even replied."

"We were in New York that Christmas. She didn't get your letter till months later. And then it seemed too late to write. And she was so bad at writing letters."

"You're standing up for her. You don't resent the fact that she kept you from this place? You could have been brought up here. This could have been your home."

"She was my mother. That was the important thing."

"You seem to be arguing with me. Nobody argues with me nowadays. Not even Pettifer. It gets very dull." Once more I was fixed with that blue stare. "Have you met Pettifer? He and I were in the Navy together about a century ago. And Mollie and Eliot? Have you met them?"

"Yes."

"They shouldn't be living here at all, of course, but the doctor insisted. Doesn't make that much difference to me, but it's hard luck on poor Pettifer. And Mollie's got a niece here as well, dreadful child with sagging breasts. Have you seen her?"

I managed not to giggle. "Yes, for a moment."

"A moment would be too long. And Boscarva. What do you think of Boscarva?"

"I love it. What I've seen of it, I love."

"The town's creeping out over the hill. There was a farm at the top, belonged to an old lady called Mrs Gregory. But this builder fellow talked her into selling up to him and now they've bulldozed the fields flat as a pancake and they're putting up houses nineteen to the dozen."

"I know. I saw them."

"Well, they can't come any further, because the farm at the back of this place and the fields on either side of the lane belong to me. Bought them when I bought Boscarva, back in 1922. Wouldn't like to tell you how little it cost me. But a bit of land around you gives you a feeling of security. Remember that."

"I will."

He frowned. "What's your name again? I've forgotten it already."

"Rebecca."

"Rebecca. And what are you going to call me?"

"I don't know. What do you want me to call you?"

"Eliot calls me Grenville. You call me Grenville too. It sounds more friendly."

"All right."

We drank our sherry, smiling, content with each other. Then, from the back of the house, came the sound of a gong being rung. Grenville put down his glass and got painfully to his feet, and I went to open the door for him. Together, we went down the passage towards the dining room and family lunch.

7

xhaustion hit me at the end of that long, eventful day, and unfortunately in the middle of dinner. Luncheon had been a sustaining, homely meal, eaten at a round table set in the bay window of the big dining room. This had been laid with a simple checked cloth, and everyday china and glass, but dinner was a different affair altogether.

The long, polished table in the middle of the room was set for the five of us, with fine linen mats, and old silver and glass sparkling in the candlelight.

Everybody, it seemed, was expected to change in honour of this apparently nightly ritual. Mollie came downstairs in a brocade housecoat the colour of sapphires, which emphasized the brightness of her eyes. Grenville wore a faded velvet dinnerjacket and Eliot a pale flannel suit in which he looked as elegant as a greyhound. Even Andrea, probably under much protest, had put on a different pair of trousers and a blouse of broderie anglaise which looked as though it could have done with a press, or a wash, or maybe both. Her lank hair was tied back with a scrap of velvet ribbon, the expression on her face continued to be one of resentful boredom.

Not in the habit of attending formal dinner parties, I had nevertheless packed a garment which would obviously have to appear every evening as long as I stayed in this house, for I had no other. It was a caftan of soft brown jersey wool, with silver embroidery at the neck and the wrists of the flowing sleeves. With it, I wore my silver bracelets and a pair of hoop ear-rings which my mother had given me for my twenty-first birthday. Their weight, on this occasion, gave me odd comfort and confidence, two things which I badly needed.

I did not want to have dinner with my newly acquired family. I did not want to have to make conversation, to listen, to be intelligent and charming. I wanted to go to bed and be brought something undemanding, like Bovril or a boiled egg. I wanted to be alone.

But there was soup and duckling, and red wine, dispensed by Eliot. The duckling was rich and the room very warm. As the meal slowly progressed I felt more and more strange, disembodied, light-headed. I tried to concentrate on the flames of the candles in front of me, but as I stared at them they separated and repeated themselves, and the voices around me became blurred and unintelligible, like the hum of conversation heard from a distant room. Instinctively, I pushed my plate away from me, knocked over the wineglass, and watched, in hopeless horror, as the red wine spread amongst the shattered splinters of glass.

In a way the accident was a blessing, for they all stopped talking and looked at me. I must have gone quite pale, for Eliot was on his feet in an instant and at my side . . .

"Are you all right?"

I said, "No, I don't think I am. I'm sorry . . ."

"Oh, my dear." Mollie flung aside her napkin and pushed back her chair. From across the table Andrea eyed me with chill interest.

"The glass . . . I'm so sorry . . ."

From the head of the table Grenville spoke. "It doesn't matter about the glass. Leave the glass. The girl's exhausted. Mollie, take her up and put her to bed."

I tried to protest, but not very hard. Eliot drew back my chair and helped me to my feet, his hands firm beneath my elbows. Mollie had gone to open the door, and cooler air moved in from the hall— already I felt better, as though, perhaps, after all I was not going to faint.

As I passed Grenville, I said, "I'm sorry," for the third time; "forgive me. Good night." I bent and kissed him, and left them all. Mollie closed the door behind us and came upstairs with me. She helped me undress and get into bed, and I was asleep before she had even turned off the light.

I slept for fourteen hours, waking at ten o'clock. I had not slept so late for years, and beyond my window the sky was blue and the cold bright northern light reflected from the sloping white-painted walls of my room. I got up, pulled on a dressing-gown and went and had a bath. Dressed, I felt wonderful, apart from the sinking sensation of shame at my behaviour the night before. I hoped they had not all thought that I was drunk.

Downstairs, I finally ran Mollie to earth in a little pantry, arranging a great mass of purple and pink polyanthus in a flowered bowl.

"How did you sleep?" she asked at once.

"Like the dead. I'm sorry about last night . . ."

"My dear, you were tired out. I'm sorry I didn't realize before. You'll want some breakfast."

"Just coffee."

She took me into the kitchen and heated coffee while I made some toast. "Where is everybody?" I asked.

"Eliot's at the garage, of course, and Pettifer's taken the car to Fourbourne to do some shopping for Grenville."

"What can I do? There must be something I can do to help."

"Well . . ." she debated. I looked at her. This morning she wore a cashmere sweater the colour of caramel and a slender tweed skirt. Immaculately made up, with every strand of hair in place, she seemed almost inhumanly neat. "You could go and fetch the fish for me in Porthkerris. The fishmonger rang up to say he'd got some halibut and I thought we'd have it for dinner. I could lend you my little car. Do you drive?"

"Yes, but couldn't I walk down? I like walking and it's such a lovely morning."

"Of course, if you want to. You could take the short cut over the fields and along the cliff. I know—" she appeared to be suddenly struck by inspiration—"take Andrea with you, and then she can show you the way, and show you where the fish shop is. Besides, she never takes

any exercise if she can possibly help it and a walk would do her good."
She made Andrea sound like a lazy dog. I did not particularly relish
the idea of Andrea's company for the entire morning but I was sym-
pathetic to Mollie, being encumbered by this unengaging girl, so I
said that I would do as she suggested, and when I had finished my
breakfast went in search of Andrea whom Mollie had last seen out on
the terrace.

I found her bundled in a rug, lying on a long cane chair in a patch
of sunshine, and peevishly regarding the view, like a seasick passenger on a liner.

"Will you walk down to Porthkerris with me?" I asked her.

She fixed me with her protuberant stare. "Why?"

"Because Mollie's asked me to go and pick up some fish and I don't
know where the shop is. Besides, it's a lovely morning, and she thought
we might go down to the cliffs."

She considered my suggestion, said, "All right," uncoiled herself
from the rug and stood up. She wore the same dirty jeans as yesterday
and a vast black and white sweater which reached below her narrow
hips. We went back to the kitchen to fetch a basket and then set out,
by way of the terrace and the sloping garden, down in the direction of
the sea.

At the bottom of the garden, stone steps led up and over the wall,
and Andrea went ahead of me, but I paused because I wanted to inspect the studio from this new angle. It was, as Joss had said, locked
and shuttered, and somehow desolate, and the great window on the
north wall had been closed off by tightly-drawn curtains so that not a
chink presented itself to any inquisitive passer-by.

Andrea stood on the top of the wall, her gaze following mine.

"He never paints now," she told me.

"I know."

"I can't think why. There's nothing wrong with him." She jumped,
hair flying, down off the wall, and totally disappeared. I took a last
look at the studio and then followed her and we took a trodden path
that led down through small, irregular fields, and came out at last,
through the hazard of some waist-high gorse bushes, to a stile, and so
on to the cliff path.

This was obviously a favourite walk with visitors to Porthkerris, for there were seats set in sheltered view points, and litter bins for rubbish, and notices warning people not to go too near the edge of the cliff which was likely to collapse.

Andrea instantly went to the very edge and peered over. Gulls wheeled and screamed all around her, the wind tore at her hair and the baggy sweater, and from far below came the distant thunder of surf on rocks. She flung her arms wide and teetered slightly as though about to fall over the edge, but when she saw that I didn't care whether she committed suicide or not, she returned to the path, and in single file we walked on, Andrea in front.

The cliff curved and the town came into view in front of us, the low grey houses nestled around the sweep of the bay and climbing the steep hill to the moor behind. We went through a gate, and were now on to a proper road, and so able to walk side by side.

Andrea became conversational.

"Your mother's just died, hasn't she?"

"Yes."

"Aunt Mollie was telling me about her. She said she was a tart."

Painfully, I remained serene. It would have been instant victory for Andrea if I had been anything else.

"She didn't really know her. They hadn't seen each other for years."

"Was she a tart?"

"No."

"Mollie said she lived with men."

I realized then that Andrea was not merely trying to needle me, she was genuinely curious, and there was envy there as well.

I said, "She was very gay and very loving and very beautiful."

She accepted this. "Where do you live?"

"In London. I've got a little flat."

"Do you live alone, or with somebody?"

"No, I live alone."

"Do you go to parties and things?"

"Yes, if someone asks me and I want to go."

"Do you work? Do you have a job?"

"Yes. In a bookshop."

"God, how grim."

"I like it."

"Where did you meet Joss?"

Now, I thought, we're getting down to business, but her face was empty of expression.

"I met him in London . . . he mended a chair for me."

"Do you like him?"

"I don't know him well enough to dislike him."

"Eliot hates him. So does Aunt Mollie."

"Why?"

"Because they don't like having him around the place all the time. And they treat him as though he should call them Sir and Madam, and of course he doesn't. And he talks to Grenville and makes him laugh. I've heard them talking."

I imagined her creeping up to closed doors, listening at keyholes.

"That's nice, if he makes the old man laugh."

"He and Eliot had a terrible row once. It was about some car that Eliot had sold to a friend of Joss's and Joss said it wasn't roadworthy and Eliot called him an insolent, interfering bastard."

"Did you listen in to that one as well?"

"I couldn't help hearing. I was in the loo and the window was open and they were out on the gravel by the front door."

"How long have you been staying at Boscarva?" I asked, curious to know how long it had taken her to dig all these skeletons out of the family cupboards.

"Two weeks. It seems like six months."

"I should have thought you'd have loved coming down."

"For heaven's sake, I'm not a child. What am I meant to do with myself. Go bucket and spading on the beach?"

"What do you do in London?"

She kicked a pebble, viciously, hating Cornwall. "I was at an art school, but my parents *didn't approve—*" she put on a mealy voice— "of my friends. So they took me away and sent me here."

"But you can't stay here for ever. What are you going to do when you go back?"

"That's up to them, isn't it?"

I felt a twinge of pity for her parents, even parents who had somehow raised such an obnoxious child.

"I mean, isn't there anything you *want* to do?"

"Yes, just get away, be on my own, do my own thing. Danus, this fabulous chap I went around with, he had a friend who was running a pottery on the Isle of Skye, and he wanted me to go and help . . . It sounded super, you know, living in a sort of commune, and right away from everybody . . . but my grotty mother shoved her great oar in and spoiled it all."

"Where's Danus now?"

"Oh, he went to Skye."

"Has he written to tell you about it?"

She tossed her head, fiddled with her hair, would not meet my eye. "Yes, actually, long letters. Reams of them. He still wants me to go there, and I'm going to, just as soon as I'm eighteen and they can't stop me any more."

"Why don't you go back to Art School first, and get some sort of a qualification . . . that'd give you time . . ."

She turned on me. "You know something? You talk like all the rest of them? How old are you anyway? You sound like someone with one foot in the grave."

"It's crazy to wreck your life before it's even started."

"It's my life. Not yours."

"No, it's not my life."

Having thus stupendously quarrelled, we continued our walk into the town in silence, and when Andrea did speak again, it was to say, "That's the fish shop," and wave a hand in its direction.

"Thank you." I went in to collect the halibut but she stayed, pointedly, outside on the cobbled pavement. When I emerged again, she had gone, only to appear the next moment from a papershop next door, where she had been buying a lurid magazine called *True Sex*.

"Shall we go back now?" I asked her. "Or do you want to do more shopping?"

"I can't shop, I haven't any money. Only a few pence."

I was suddenly, irrationally, sorry for her. "I'll stand you a cup of coffee if you'd like one."

She looked at me with sudden delight and I thought she was going to gleefully accept my modest offer, but instead she said, "Let's go and see Joss."

I was taken unawares. "Why do you want to go and see Joss?"

"I just do. I often go and see him when I come down to the town. He's always pleased to see me. He made me promise always to go and see him if I'm down here."

"How do you know he'll be there?"

"Well, he's not at Boscarva today, so he must be at the shop. Have you been there? It's super, he's got a sort of pad on the top floor, just like something out of a magazine, with a bed that's a sort of sofa and masses of cushions and things, and a log fire. And at night—" her voice became dreamy—"it's all closed-in and secret, and there's nothing but firelight."

I tried not to gape. "You mean . . . you and Joss . . ."

She shrugged, tossing her hair. "Once or twice, but nobody knows. I don't know why I told you. You won't tell the others, will you?"

"But don't they . . . doesn't Mollie . . . ask questions?"

"Oh, I tell her I'm going to the cinema. She doesn't seem to mind me going to the cinema. Come on, let's go and see Joss . . ."

But after this revelation, nothing would have induced me to go near Joss's shop. I said, "Joss will be working, he won't want to be interrupted. And anyway there isn't time. And I don't want to go."

"You said there was time for coffee, why isn't there time for Joss?"

"Andrea, I told you, I don't want to go."

She began to smile. "I thought you liked Joss."

"That's not the point. He doesn't want us under his feet every time he turns round."

"Do you mean me?"

"I mean *us*." I was beginning to be desperate.

"He always wants to see me. I know he does."

"Yes, I'm sure," I said gently. "But let's go back to Boscarva."

I reminded myself that from the very start I had not liked Joss. Despite his concern and apparent friendliness he had always left me with that strange sensation of disquiet, as though someone were creeping up behind my back. Yesterday I had begun to forget this initial antipathy, even to like him, but after Andrea's confidences it was not hard to whip back to life my first distrust of the man. He was too good-looking, too charming. Andrea could be a liar, but she was no fool; she had pigeon-holed the rest of the family with disconcerting accuracy, and even if there was only a grain of truth in what she said about Joss, I wanted to have no part of it.

If I had known him and liked him better, I would have taken him aside and taxed him with what she had said. As it was, he held no importance for me. Besides, I had other things to think about.

Grenville did not come down for lunch that day.

"He's tired," Mollie told us. "He's having a day in bed. Perhaps he'll join us for dinner. Pettifer's going to take him up a tray."

So the three of us ate lunch together. Mollie had changed into a neat woollen dress and a double string of pearls. She was going, she said, to play bridge with friends in Fourbourne. She hoped that I would be able to occupy myself.

I said that of course I would be perfectly all right. Across the table, we smiled at each other and I wondered if she had really told Andrea that my mother was a tart, or if this was simply Andrea's interpretation of some vague euphemistic explanation that Mollie had given her. I hoped it was the latter, but still I wished that Mollie had not found it necessary to discuss Lisa with Andrea. She was dead now, but once she had been funny and enchanting and full of laughter. Why couldn't she be remembered that way?

As we sat around the table, the day outside changed its face. A wind got up from the west, and with great speed a bank of grey cloud sped over the blue sky, obliterating the sunshine, and presently it started to rain. It was in this rain that Mollie set off for her bridge party, driving her little car, and saying that she would be home about six. Andrea, perhaps exhausted by her morning's exercise, but more likely bored to death with my company, disappeared up to her bedroom with her new magazine. Alone, I stood at the foot of the stairs, wondering how to amuse myself. The silence of the gloomy afternoon was broken only by the ticking of the grandfather clock and small, occupied sounds which came from the direction of the kitchens, and which, investigated, proved to be Pettifer, seated at a wooden table in his pantry and cleaning silver.

He looked up as I put my head around the door.

"Hallo. I didn't hear you."

"How's my grandfather?"

"Oh, he's all right. Just a bit weary after all the excitement of yesterday. We thought it would be better if he had a day with his toes up. Has Mrs Roger gone?"

"Yes." I pulled up a chair and sat opposite him.

"Thought I heard the car."

"Do you want me to help you?"

"That'd be very kind . . . those spoons there need a good rub up with the shammy. Don't know how they get so marked and stained. But, there, I do know. It's this damp sea air. One thing silver really hates it's damp sea air." I began to rub at the thin worn bowl of the spoon. Pettifer looked at me over the top of his glasses. "Funny to have you sitting there after all these years. Your mother used to spend half her life in the kitchen . . . When Roger went off to boarding school there wasn't anyone else for her to talk to. So she used to come and spend her time with Mrs Pettifer and me. Taught her to make Fairy Cakes, Mrs Pettifer did, and how to play two-handed whist. We had great times. And on a day like this, she used to make toast at the old range . . . mind, that's gone now, we've got a new one and good thing too . . . but that old range was cosy, with the fire burning behind the bars, and all the brass knobs polished up lovely."

"How long have you been at Boscarva, Pettifer?"

"Ever since the Commander bought it, back in 1922. That was the year he left the Navy, decided to be a painter. Old Mrs Bayliss didn't like that. For three months or more she wouldn't even talk to him."

"Why did she mind so much?"

"She'd been with the Navy all her life. Her father was the Captain of the *Imperious* when the Commander was First Lieutenant. That was how they met. They were married in Malta. A lovely wedding with an

arch of swords and all. Being with the Navy meant a lot to Mrs Bayliss. When the Commander said he was going to leave they parted
brass rags good and proper, but she couldn't make him change his
mind. So we left Malta, for good and all, and the Commander found
this house, and then we all moved down here."

"And you've been here ever since?"

"More or less. The Commander enrolled at the Slade, and that
meant working in London, so he had this little *pied-à-terre*, just off St
James's it was, and when he went up to London I went too, to keep an
eye on him, and Mrs Pettifer stayed here with Mrs Bayliss and Roger.
Your mother wasn't born then."

"But, when he'd finished at the Slade . . . ?"

"Well, then he came back for good. And built the studio. That was
when he was painting at his best. Lovely stuff he did then, great seascapes, so cold and bright you could smell the wind, feel the salt on
your lips."

"Are there many of his pictures in this house?"

"No, not many. There's the fishing boat over the dining-room fireplace, and one or two little black and white drawings along the upstairs passage. He's got three or four in his study, and then there's a
couple in the room where Mrs Roger sleeps."

"And the one in the drawing room . . ."

"Oh, yes, that one of course. 'Lady Holding a Rose.'"

"Who was she?"

He did not reply; was, perhaps, preoccupied with his silver, rubbing
away at a fork as though determined to flatten the pattern.

"Who was she? The girl in the picture?"

"Oh," said Pettifer. "That was Sophia."

Sophia. Ever since my mother had fleetingly mentioned her I had
wanted to know about Sophia, and now here was Pettifer bringing up
her name as though it were the most natural thing in the world.

"She was a girl who used to model for the Commander. I think she
first worked for him in London when he was a student, and then
she used to come down here sometimes during the summer months,
take lodgings in Porthkerris and work for any artist who was ready
and able to pay her."

"Was she very beautiful?"

"Not my idea of a beauty. But lively, and what a talker! She was Irish, she'd come from County Cork."

"What did my grandmother think of Sophia?"

"Their paths never crossed, any more than your grandmother would have had social dealings with the butcher or the girl who did her hair."

"So Sophia never came to Boscarva?"

"Oh, yes, she used to come and go. She'd be down at the studio with the Commander, and then he'd get tired, or lose his patience with her, and call it a day, and she'd come up the garden and through the back door calling out, 'Any chance of a cup of tea?' and because it was Sophia, Mrs Pettifer always had the kettle on."

"She used to tell fortunes from teacups."

"Who told you that?"

"My mother."

"That's right, she did. And wonderful things she told us were going to happen to us all. 'Course, they didn't, but it was fun listening to her, just the same. She and your mother were great friends. Sophia used to take her down to the beach and Mrs Pettifer would pack a picnic. And if it was stormy weather they'd go on long walks up on the moor."

"But what was my grandmother doing all this time?"

"Oh, playing bridge or mah-jongg most afternoons. She had a very select circle of friends. She was a nice enough lady, but not really interested in children. Perhaps if she'd been more interested in Lisa when she was a child, they'd have had more in common when Lisa grew up, and maybe your mother wouldn't have run off like that, breaking all our hearts."

"What happened to Sophia?"

"Oh, she went back to London, she got married and she had a baby, I think. Then, in 1942, she was killed in the Blitz. The baby was down in the country and her husband was overseas, but Sophia stayed in London because she was working in a hospital there. We didn't hear about it for a long time, till long after it happened. Mrs Pettifer and I felt as though a light had gone out of our lives."

"And my grandfather?"

"He was sorry, of course. But he hadn't seen her for years. She was just a girl who'd once worked for him."

"Are there any more pictures of her?"

"There's pictures of Sophia in provincial art galleries up and down the country. There's one in the gallery in Porthkerris if you want to go and look at that. And there's a couple upstairs in Mrs Roger's bedroom."

"Could we go and look at them now?" I sounded eager and Pettifer looked surprised, as though I were suggesting something faintly indecent. "I mean Mrs Bayliss wouldn't mind, would she?"

"Oh, she wouldn't mind. I don't see why not . . . come on."

He got laboriously to his feet, and I followed him upstairs and along the first-floor passage to the bedroom over the drawing room, which was large and furnished in a very feminine fashion with old-fashioned Victorian furniture and a faded pink and cream carpet. Mollie had left it painfully neat. The two little oil paintings hung side by side between the windows, one of a chestnut tree with a girl lying in its shade, the other of the same girl hanging out a line of washing on a breezy day. They were scarcely more than sketches, and I was disappointed.

"I still don't know what Sophia looks like."

Pettifer was about to reply when, from the depths of the house, came the ringing of a bell. He cocked his head, like a dog listening. "That's the Commander, he's heard us talking through the wall. Excuse me a moment."

I followed him out of Mollie's room and closed the door behind me. He went on down the passage a little way and opened a door, and I heard Grenville's voice.

"What are you two muttering about in there?"

"I was just showing Rebecca the two pictures in Mrs Roger's room . . ."

"Is Rebecca there? Tell her to come in . . ."

I went in, past Pettifer. Grenville was not in bed, but sitting in a deep arm-chair with his feet propped up on a stool. He was dressed, but there was a rug over his knees and the room was cheered by the flicker of a fire. Everything was very neat and shipshape and smelt of the Bay Rum he put on his hair.

I said, "I thought you were in bed."

"Pettifer got me up after lunch. I get bored stiff lying in bed all day. What have you been talking about?"

"Pettifer was showing me some of your pictures."

"I expect you think they're very old-fashioned. They're going back to realism now, you know, these young artists. I knew it would come. You'll have to have one of my pictures. There are racks of them in the studio that have never been sorted out. I closed the place up ten years ago, and I haven't been there since. Pettifer, where's the key?"

"Put safely away, sir."

"You'll have to get the key off Pettifer, go down and nose around, see if there's anything you'd like. Got anywhere to hang it?"

"I've got a flat in London. It needs a picture."

"I thought of something else sitting here. That jade in the cabinet downstairs. I brought it back from China years ago, gave it to Lisa. Now, it belongs to you. And a mirror that her grandmother left her— where's that, Pettifer?"

"That's in the morning room, sir."

"Well, we'll have to get it down, give it a clean. You'd like that, wouldn't you?"

"Yes, I would." I felt greatly relieved. I had been wondering how to bring up the subject of my mother's possessions, and now, without any prompting, Grenville had done it for me. I hesitated and then, striking while the iron was hot, mentioned the third thing. ". . . and there was a davenport desk."

"Hm?" He fixed me with his ferocious stare. "How do you know?"

"My mother told me about the jade and the mirror, and she said there was a davenport desk." He continued to glare at me. I wished all at once that I had said nothing. "I mean, it doesn't matter, it's just that if nobody did want it . . . if it wasn't being used . . ."

"Pettifer, do you remember that desk?"

"Yes, I do, sir, now you come to mention it. It was up in the other attic bedroom, but I can't remember having seen it lately."

"Well, look for it some time, there's a good fellow. And put another bit of wood on the fire . . ." Pettifer did so. Grenville, watching him, said suddenly, "Where is everybody? The house is quiet. Only the sound of the rain."

"Mrs Roger's out to a bridge party. I think Miss Andrea's in her room . . ."

"How about a cup of tea?" Grenville cocked an eye at me. "You'd like a cup of tea, wouldn't you? We haven't had the chance of getting to know each other. Either you're keeling over in the middle of dinner, or I'm too old and infirm to get out of bed. We make a fine pair, don't we?"

"I'd like to have tea with you."

"Pettifer will bring up a tray."

"No," I said. "I will. Pettifer's legs have been up and down these stairs all day. Let's give him a rest."

Grenville looked amused. "All right. You bring it up, and let's have a good big plateful of hot buttered toast."

I was to wish, many times over, that I had never brought up the subject of the davenport desk. Because it could not be found. While Grenville and I ate our tea, Pettifer began to look for it. By the time he came to take the tray away, he had combed the house from top to bottom, and the desk was nowhere.

Grenville scarcely believed him. "You've just missed it. Your eyes are getting as old as mine."

"I could scarcely miss seeing a desk." Pettifer sounded aggrieved.

"Perhaps," I said, trying to be helpful, "it was sent away to be mended or something . . ." They both looked at me as though I were a fool, and I hastily shut up.

"Would it be in the studio?" Pettifer ventured.

"What would I do with a desk in the studio? I painted there, I didn't write letters. Didn't want a desk cluttering the place up . . ." Grenville was getting quite agitated. I stood up. "Oh, it'll turn up," I said in my best, soothing voice, and picked up the tea tray to carry it downstairs. In the kitchen I was joined by Pettifer, upset by what had happened.

"It's not good for the Commander to get worked up about anything . . . and he's going to go after this like a terrier after a rat. I can tell."

"It's all my fault. I don't know why I even mentioned it."

"But I remember it. I just can't remember having seen it lately." I began to wash the cups and saucers and Pettifer picked up a tea towel in order to dry them. "And there's another thing. There was a Chippendale chair that used to go with it . . . mind, they didn't match, but the chair always sat in front of that desk. It had a tapestry seat, rather worn, birds and flowers and things. Well, that's gone, too . . . but I'm not going to tell the Commander that and neither are you."

I promised that I wouldn't. "Anyway," I said, "it doesn't matter to me one way or the other."

"No, but it matters to the Commander. Artistic he may have been, but he had a memory like an elephant and that's one thing he hasn't lost." He added gloomily, "I sometimes wish he had."

That evening when I went downstairs, changed once more into the brown and silver caftan, I found Eliot in the drawing room, alone except for that inevitable companion, his dog. Eliot sat by the fire with a drink and the evening paper, and Rufus was stretched, like some glorious fur, on the hearthrug. They looked companionable, caught in the light of the lamp, but my appearance disturbed the peaceful scene, and Eliot stood up, dropping the paper behind him on the seat of the chair.

"Rebecca. How are you?"

"I'm all right."

"I was afraid last night that you were going to be ill."

"No. I was just tired. I slept till ten o'clock."

"My mother told me. Would you like a drink?"

I said that I would and he poured me some sherry and I went to crouch by the fire and fondle the dog's silky ears.

As Eliot brought me my drink I asked, "Does he go everywhere with you?"

"Yes, everywhere. To the garage, to the office, out to lunch, into the pubs, anywhere I happen to be going. He's a very well-known dog in this part of the world."

I sat on the hearthrug, and Eliot subsided once more into his chair and picked up his drink. He said, "Tomorrow I have to go over to Falmouth, see a man about a car. I wondered if you'd like to come with me, see a bit of the country. Does that appeal to you?"

I was surprised by my own pleasure at this invitation. "I'd love it."

"It won't be very exciting. But perhaps you can amuse yourself for an hour or two while I'm doing business, and then we'll stop at a little pub I know on the way home. They serve delicious sea food. Do you like oysters?"

"Yes."

"Good. So do I. And then we'll come home by High Cross, and you can see where we normally live, my mother and I."

"Your mother told me about it. It sounds charming."

"Better than this mausoleum . . ."

"Oh, Eliot, it's not a mausoleum . . ."

"I was never much of a one for Victorian relics . . ."

Before I could protest further, we were joined by Grenville. At least, we heard him coming, step by step downstairs; heard him talking to Pettifer, the high-pitched voice and the low growl; heard them coming down the hall, the tap of Grenville's stick on the polished wood.

Eliot made a small face at me and went to open the door, and Grenville moved in, like the prow of some great, indestructible ship . . .

"That's all right, Pettifer, I can manage now." I had got up from the hearthrug, wanting to help push forward the chair which he had used the night before, but this seemed to madden him. He was obviously not in a good mood.

"For God's sake, girl, stop fussing around. Do you think I want to sit *in* the fire, I'll burn to death sitting there . . ."

I edged the chair back to its original position and finally Grenville reached it and sank into it.

"How about a drink?" Eliot asked him.

"I'll have a whisky . . ."

Eliot looked surprised . . . "Whisky?"

"Yes, a whisky. I know what that fool of a doctor said but tonight I'm having a whisky."

Eliot said nothing, just nodded his head in patient acquiescence and went to pour the drink. As he did so Grenville leaned round the edge of the chair and said, "Eliot, have you seen that davenport desk around the place?" and my heart sank into my shoes.

"Oh, Grenville, don't start that again . . ."

"What do you mean, start that again? We've got to find the damned thing. I told Pettifer just now, got to go on looking till we've found it."

Eliot came back with the glass of whisky. He drew up a table and set the glass within Grenville's reach.

"What davenport desk?" he asked patiently.

"Little davenport desk, used to be in one of the bedrooms. Belonged to Lisa, and now it belongs to Rebecca. She wants it. She's got a flat in London, wants to put it there. And Pettifer can't find it, says he's been through the house with a toothcomb, can't find it. You haven't seen it, have you?"

"I've never set eyes on it. I don't even know what a davenport desk is."

"It's a little desk. Got drawers down the side. Bit of tooled leather on the top. They're rare now, I believe. Worth a lot of money."

"Pettifer's probably put it somewhere and forgotten."

"Pettifer doesn't forget things."

"Well, perhaps Mrs Pettifer did something with it and forgot to tell him."

"I've already *said*; he doesn't forget things."

We were joined at this moment by Mollie, who appeared, smiling determinedly, as though she had heard the angry voice raised beyond the closed door, and was about to spread oil on troubled waters.

"Hallo, everybody, I'm afraid I'm a little late. I had to go and do some very exciting things to that delicious piece of halibut Rebecca bought for me this morning. Eliot, dear . . ." she kissed him, apparently seeing him for the first time that evening. "And Grenville—" she stooped to kiss him too—"you're looking more rested." Then, before he could contradict her, she smiled across the top of his head at me. "Did you have a good afternoon?"

"Yes, thank you. How was the bridge?"

"Not too bad. I won twenty pence. Eliot darling, I'd love a drink. Andrea's just coming. She won't be a moment . . ." But she finally ran out of defensive small talk, and Grenville instantly opened fire. "We've lost something," he told her.

"What have you lost? Your cuff-links again?"

"We have lost a davenport desk."

It was becoming ludicrous.

"You've *lost* a davenport desk?"

For her benefit, Grenville went through the whole rigmarole. On being told that it was I who had precipitated this crisis, Mollie looked at me with some reproach, as though she thought this a poor way to return her hospitality and kindness. I was inclined to agree with her.

"But it must be somewhere." She took her glass from Eliot, drew up a stool and sat, all ready to work the whole thing out. "It must have been put somewhere for safety."

"Pettifer has looked for it."

"Perhaps he hasn't seen it. I'm sure he should get his glasses changed. Perhaps it's been put somewhere and he's forgotten."

Grenville thumped the arm of his chair with a balled fist. "Pettifer does not forget things."

"In fact—" said Eliot coolly—"he forgets things all the time."

Grenville glared at him. "And what does that mean?"

"Nothing personal. Just that he's getting older."

"I suppose you're blaming Pettifer . . ."

"I'm not blaming anybody . . ."

"You just said he's too old to know what he's doing. If he's too old what the hell do you think I am?"

"I never said that . . ."

"You blamed *him* . . ."

Eliot lost his patience. "If I was going to blame anybody," he said, raising his voice almost to the pitch of Grenville's, "I'd ask a few questions of young Joss Gardner." There was a pause after he'd come out with this. And then, in a more controlled, reasonable voice, he went on. "All right, so nobody wants to accuse another man of stealing. But Joss is in and out of this house all the time, in and out of all the rooms. He knows what's in this place better than anybody. And he's an expert, he knows what it's worth."

"But why should Joss take a desk?" asked Mollie.

"A valuable desk. Don't forget that. It's rare and it's valuable, Grenville just said so. Perhaps he needed the money. To look at him he could do with a bit of extra cash. And he's an expert. He's up and down to London all the time. He'd know where to sell it."

He stopped, abruptly, as though realizing that already he had said too much. He finished his whisky, and went, without speaking, to pour himself a second glass.

The silence became uncomfortable. To break it, Mollie said, briefly, "I don't think that Joss . . ."

"Just a lot of poppycock," Grenville interrupted her savagely.

Eliot set down the whisky bottle with a thump. "How do you know? How do you know anything about Joss Gardner? He turns up, like a hippy, out of nowhere, says he's going to open a shop, and the next thing you've opened up the house to him and given him the job of patching up all the furniture. What do you know about Joss? What do any of us know about him?"

"I know that I can trust him. I was trained to judge a man's character . . ."

"You could be wrong . . ."

Grenville raised his voice and rode over Eliot's, ". . . and it would be no bad thing if you were to take a few lessons in choosing your companions."

Eliot's eyes narrowed. "What does that mean?"

"It means that if you want to be made a fool of, try doing business with that little shyster Ernest Padlow."

If I could have escaped at that moment, I would. But I was caught, jammed into the corner behind Grenville's chair.

"What do you know about Ernest Padlow?"

"I know you've been seen around with him . . . drinking in bars . . ."

Eliot shot a glance at me, and then said, under his breath, "That bastard Joss Gardner."

"It wasn't Joss who told me, it was Hargreaves, at the bank. He came up for a glass of sherry the other day. And Mrs Thomas came in to do my fire this morning, she'd seen you with Padlow, up at that gimcrack nightmare he calls a housing estate."

"Back-stairs gossip."

"You hear the truth from truthful people. It doesn't matter in which direction they live. And if you think I'm selling up my land to that jumped-up little beachsweeper, you're wrong . . ."

"It won't always be your land."

"And if you're so sure it will be yours, all I can say is, don't count your chickens before they're hatched. Because you, dear boy, are not my only grandchild."

And at this dramatic moment, like a nicely stage-managed play, the door opened and Andrea appeared to tell us that Pettifer had told her to tell us that dinner was ready.

8

It was hard to sleep that night. I tossed and turned, fetched a glass of water, paced the floor, looked out of the window, climbed back into bed and tried once more to compose myself, but always, when I closed my eyes, the evening came back to me like a film played over and over, voices drummed in my ears, and would not be stilled.

All right, so nobody wants to accuse another man of stealing. What do any of us know about Joss?

If you want to be made a fool of, try doing business with that little shyster Ernest Padlow. And if you think I'm selling my land to that jumped-up little beachsweeper, you're wrong . . .

It won't always be your land . . .

. . . you, dear boy, are not my only grandchild.

Dinner had been a gruesome meal. Eliot and Grenville had scarcely spoken a word from beginning to end. Mollie, to make up for their silence, had kept up a patter of meaningless conversation to which I had tried to respond. And Andrea had watched us all, a gleam of triumph in her round, seeking eyes, while Pettifer trod heavily to and fro, removing dishes, handing round a lemon soufflé rich with whipped cream, which nobody seemed to want.

When at last it was over, they had all dispersed. Grenville to his bedroom, Andrea to the morning room from whence we presently heard the blare of the television set. Eliot, with no explanations, put on a coat, whistled up his dog and banged out of the front door. I guessed he had gone to get drunk and didn't entirely blame him. Mollie and I ended up in the drawing room, one on either side of the fire. She had some tapestry and seemed quite prepared to sit and sew in silence, but this would have been unbearable. I said, plunging straight in with the apology which I felt I owed her, "I am sorry about this evening. I wish I'd never mentioned that desk."

She did not look at me. "Oh, it can't be helped."

"It was just that my mother had mentioned it to me, and when Grenville spoke about the jade and the mirror, well, it never occurred to me that I'd start such a storm in a tea-cup."

"Grenville's a strange old man. He's always been stubborn about people, he'll never see that there can be two sides to every situation."

"You mean about Joss . . ."

"I don't know why he's so taken with Joss. It's frightening. It's as though Joss were able to exert some hold over him. Eliot and I never wanted him in and out of the house this way. If Grenville's furniture needed to be repaired, surely he could have come and fetched it in his van and taken it down to his workshop, like any other tradesman would do. We tried to talk Grenville out of it, but he was adamant, and, after all, this is his house. It isn't ours."

"But it will be Eliot's one day."

She sent me a cold look.

"After this evening, one wonders."

"Oh, Mollie, I don't want Boscarva, Grenville would never leave a place like this to me. He just said that to win a point; perhaps it was the first thing that came into his head. He didn't mean it."

"He hurt Eliot."

"Eliot will understand. You have to make allowances for old people."

"I'm tired of making allowances for Grenville," said Mollie, viciously snapping at a strand of wool with her silver scissors. "My life has been disrupted by Grenville. He and Pettifer could have come and lived at High Cross; that's what we wanted. The house is smaller and more convenient and it would have been better for everybody. And Boscarva should have been made over to Eliot years ago. As it is, death duties are going to be exorbitant. Eliot is never going to be able to afford to keep it going. The whole situation is *so* unrealistic."

"I suppose it's hard to be realistic when you're eighty and you've lived in a place most of your life."

She ignored this. "And all that land, and the farm. Eliot is simply trying to make the best of it all, but Grenville won't see that. He's never shown any interest, never encouraged Eliot in any way. Even the garage at High Cross, Eliot got that going entirely on his own. At the beginning, he asked his grandfather to help, but Grenville said he wasn't going to have anything to do with second-hand cars, and there was a row, and finally Eliot borrowed the money from someone else, and he's never asked his grandfather for a shilling since that day. You'd think he'd deserve some credit for that."

She was pale with anger on Eliot's account—a little tigress, I thought, fighting for her cub, and I remembered my mother's low opinion of the way in which she had possessed and molly-coddled the young Eliot. Perhaps neither of them had ever grown out of the habit.

To change the subject I told her about Eliot's invitation for the next day. "He said he'd take me into High Cross on the way home."

But Mollie was only momentarily diverted. "You must go in and see the house, Eliot's got the key. I go up most weeks to make sure everything's all right, but really I get so depressed having to leave my darling little house and come back to this gloomy place . . ." and then she laughed at herself wryly. "It's getting me down, isn't it? I must try to pull myself together. But really I'll be glad when it's all over."

When it's all over. That meant when Grenville finally died. I didn't want to think about him dying any more than I wanted to think about Joss coupled with the unsavoury Andrea; any more than I wanted to think about Joss helping himself to a davenport desk and a Chippendale chair, heaving them into the back of his little truck, and selling them to the first dealer who made him a good offer.

What do you know about Joss? What do any of us know about him?

For my part I wished I knew nothing. I turned in bed, thumped at the pillows, and waited, without much hope, for sleep.

It rained in the night, but the next morning it was still and clear, the sky a pale, washed blue, everything wet and shining, translucent in the cool spring light. I leaned out of the window and smelt the dampness, mossy and sweet. The sea was flat and blue as a sheet of silk, gulls drifted lazily over the rim of the cliff, a boat moved out from the harbour, heading for distant fishing-grounds, and so still was the air that I could hear the distant chug of its engine.

My spirits rose. Yesterday was over, today would be better. I was glad to be getting out of the house, away from Mollie's reproach and Andrea's unsettling presence. I bathed and dressed and went downstairs and found Eliot in the dining room, eating bacon and eggs, and looking—I was thankful to see—cheerful.

He looked up from the morning paper. "I wondered," he said, "if I was going to have to come and wake you up. I thought perhaps you'd forgotten."

"No, I didn't forget."

"We're the first down. With any luck we'll be out of the house before anyone else appears." He grinned, ruefully, like a repentant boy. "The last thing I want on a beautiful morning like this is recriminations."

"It was all my fault, mentioning that stupid desk. I said I was sorry last night to your mother."

"It'll all blow over," said Eliot. "These little differences of opinion always do." I poured myself a cup of coffee. "I'm just sorry that you were involved."

We left straight after breakfast, and there was a marvellous feeling of relief to be in his car, with Rufus perched on the back seat, and to be escaping. The car roared up the hill away from Boscarva; the wet road was blue with reflected sky, and the air smelt of primroses. As we climbed up and over the moor, the view spread and dipped before us—there were hills topped by ancient cairns and standing stones, and tiny forgotten villages, tucked into the folds of unexpected valleys where little rivers ran, and ancient clumps of oak and elm stood clustered by narrow, hump-backed bridges.

But I knew that we could not enjoy our day together, that we could not be entirely at ease, until I had made my peace with him.

I said, "I know that it'll blow over, and that perhaps it *wasn't* important, but we have to talk about last night."

He smiled at me, glancing sideways. "What do we have to say?"

"Just that, what Grenville said about having another grandchild. He didn't mean it. I know he didn't mean it."

"No, perhaps he didn't. Perhaps he was just trying to set us against each other, like a pair of dogs."

"He'd never leave me Boscarva. Never in a thousand years. He doesn't even know me, I've only just come into his life."

"Rebecca, don't give it another thought. I'm not going to."

"And, after all, if it is going to be yours one day, I don't see why you shouldn't start thinking about what you're going to do with it."

"You mean Ernest Padlow? What a lot of gossips those old people are, carrying tales and making mischief. If it isn't the bank manager it's Mrs Thomas, and if it isn't Mrs Thomas it's Pettifer."

I made myself sound casual. "Would you sell the land?"

"If I did, I could probably afford to live at Boscarva. It's time I set up on my own."

"But—" I chose my words tactfully—"but wouldn't it be rather . . . spoiled . . . I mean, living there with rows of Mr Padlow's little houses all round you?"

Eliot laughed. "You've got entirely the wrong end of the stick. This wouldn't be a building estate like the one at the top of the hill. This would be high-class stuff, two acre lots, very high specifications as to the style and the price of the houses built on them. No cutting down of trees, no despoiling of the amenities. They'd be expensive houses for expensive people, and there wouldn't be a lot of them. How does that sound to you?"

"Have you told Grenville this?"

"He won't let me. He won't listen. He's not interested and that's it."

"But surely if you explained . . ."

"I've been trying to explain things to him all my life and I've never got anywhere. And now, is there anything else you want to discuss?"

I considered. I certainly didn't want to discuss Joss. I said, "No."

"In that case shall we forget about last night and enjoy ourselves?"

It seemed a good idea. We smiled at each other. "All right," I said at last. We crossed a bridge and came to a steep hill, and Eliot changed down, expertly, with the old-fashioned gear stick. The car poured up the savage slope, its long, elegant bonnet seeming to point straight to the sky.

We got to Falmouth about ten o'clock. While Eliot attended to his business I was turned loose to explore the little town. Facing south, sheltered from the north wind, with gardens already filled with camellias and scented daphne bushes, it made me think of some Mediterranean port, and this illusion was strengthened by the blue of the sea on that first warm spring day, and the tall masts of the yachts which lay at anchor in the basin.

I felt, for some reason, impelled to shop. I bought freesias for Mollie, tightly in bud with their stalks wrapped in damp moss so that they would not wither before I got home, a box of cigars for Grenville, a bottle of fruity sherry for Pettifer, a record for Andrea. The sleeve portrayed a transvestite group with sequined eyelids. It seemed to me to be right up her street. And for Eliot . . . I had noticed that his watch strap was wearing thin. I found a narrow strap in dark crocodile, very expensive, exactly right for Eliot. Then I bought a tube of toothpaste for myself, because I needed one. And for Joss . . . ? Nothing for Joss.

Eliot picked me up, as we had arranged, in the lounge of the big hotel in the middle of town. We drove very fast out of the town and through Truro, and down into the little maze of lanes and wooded creeks that lay beyond until we came to a village called St Endon, where there were white cottages, palm trees and gardens full of flowers. The road wound down towards the creek, and at the very bottom was a little pub, right on the water's edge, with the high tide lapping at the wall below the terrace. Kittiwakes perched along the top of it, their eyes bright and friendly, unlike the greedy, wild gulls of Boscarva.

We sat out in the sunshine, drinking sherry, and I gave Eliot his present, then and there; he seemed inordinately delighted, ripping off the old watch strap right away and fitting on the new, shining leather one, adjusting the little clips with the blade of his penknife.

"What made you think of giving me that?"

"I noticed your old one was worn. I thought perhaps that you might lose your watch."

He leaned back in his chair, watching me across the table. It was so warm that I had pulled off my sweater and rolled up the sleeves of my cotton shirt. He said, "Did you buy presents for everybody?"

I was embarrassed. "Yes."

"I thought you had a lot of parcels. Do you always buy presents for people?"

"It's nice to have people to buy presents for."

"Isn't there anyone in London?"

"Not really."

"No one special?"

"There's never been anyone special."

"I can't believe it."

"It's true." I could not think why I was confiding in him this way. Perhaps it had something to do with the warmth of the day, surprising me by its beneficence, lowering all my guards. Perhaps it was the sherry. Perhaps it was simply the intimacy of two people who had weathered such a storm as the row that had taken place last night. Whatever the reason, it was easy that day to talk to Eliot.

"Why is that?" he asked.

"I don't know. It may have something to do with the way I was brought up . . . my mother lived with one man after another, so I lived with them too. And there's nothing like living at close quarters with people to destroy that marvellous illusion of romance."

We laughed. "That could be a good thing," said Eliot. "But it could be a bad thing, too. You mustn't close up altogether. Otherwise nobody's ever going to get near you."

"I'm all right."

"Are you going back to London?"

"Yes."

"Soon?"

"Probably."

"Why not stay for a bit?"

"I don't want to wear out my welcome."

"You won't do that. And I've hardly spoken to you. Anyway, how can you go back to London and leave all this behind you . . . ?" His gesture included the sky, the sun, the quiet, the lap of water, the promise of the coming spring.

"I can, because I have to. I've a job to get back to and a flat that needs painting, and a life to pick up and start all over again."

"Can't that wait?"

"Not indefinitely."

"There's no reason to go." I did not reply. "Unless," he went on, "you were put off by what happened last night." I smiled and shook my head, because we had promised not to mention that again. He leaned on the table, his chin on his fist. "If you really wanted a job you could get one here. If you wanted a flat of your own you could rent that too."

"Why should I stay?" But I was flattered at being so persuaded.

"Because it would be good for Grenville, and for Mollie, and for me. Because I think we all want you to stay. Particularly me."

"Oh, Eliot . . ."

"It's true. There's something very serene about you. Did you know that? I noticed it that first evening I saw you before I even knew who you were. And I like the shape of your nose, and the sound of your laugh, and the way you can look marvellously ragamuffin one minute, in jeans and with your hair coming all unravelled, and then, the next minute, like a princess in a fairy story, with your plait over your shoulder and that stately gown you wear in the evenings. I feel as though I'm finding out new things about you every day. And this is why I don't want you to go. Not just yet."

I found that I could think of no rejoinder to this long speech. I was touched by it, and embarrassed too. But still, it was gratifying to be liked and admired, and even more gratifying to be told so.

Across the table, he began to laugh at me. "Your face is a picture. You don't know where to look and you're blushing. Come along, finish your drink and we'll go and eat oysters—I promise I'll not pay you any more compliments!"

We lingered over lunch in the small, low-ceilinged dining room, eating at a table which wobbled so much on the uneven floor that Eliot was forced to prop up one of the legs with a scrap of folded paper. We ate oysters and steak and a fresh green salad and drank our way through a bottle of wine. We took our coffee back into the sunshine, and sat on the edge of the terrace wall, watching two boys, sunburned and barelegged, rig up a dinghy and take her sailing out on to the blue waters of the creek. We saw the striped sail fill with some mysterious, unfelt breeze, as the dinghy heeled and went away from us, around the tip of a wooded promontory. And Eliot said that if I stayed in Cornwall, he would borrow a boat and teach me to sail; we would go mackerel fishing from Porthkerris—in the summer he would show me all the tiny coves and secret places which the tourists never found.

At last it was time to go, and the afternoon wound itself in like a long, shining ribbon. Sleepy and replete he drove me slowly back to High Cross, taking the long road that led through forgotten villages and the heart of the country.

When we got to High Cross, I realized that it stood at the very summit of the peninsula, so that the village had two aspects, one north to the Atlantic, the other south to the Channel; it was like being on an island, swept with clean winds and ringed by the sea. Eliot's garage stood in the middle of the village street, a little back from the road, with a cobbled forecourt set about with tubs of flowers, and inside the glass-fronted showroom stood the gleaming, racy cars. Everything was very new and expensive looking and immaculately kept. I wondered, as we crossed the forecourt towards the showrooms, how much Eliot had had to sink into such a venture, and why he had decided that it was a viable proposition to open such a specialized garage in this out-of-the-way spot.

He pulled one of the sliding glass doors aside and I went in, my feet making no sound on the highly polished rubber floors.

"Why did you decide to start your garage here, Eliot? Wouldn't it have been better in Fourbourne or Falmouth or Penzance?"

"Psychological selling, my dear. Get a good name for yourself and people will come from the ends of the earth to buy what you've got to sell." And he added with disarming candour, "Besides, I already owned the land, or at least my mother did, which was an excellent incentive to build the garage here."

"Are all these cars for sale?"

"Yes. As you can see we concentrate on continental and sports cars. We had a Ferrari in last week, but that was sold a couple of days ago. It had been crashed, but I've got this young mechanic working for me, and by the time he'd finished with it it was as good as new . . ."

I laid my hand on the gleaming yellow bonnet. "What's this?"

"A Lancia Zagato. And this is an Alfa Romeo Spyder, only two years old. Beautiful car."

"And a Jensen Interceptor . . ." That was one that I recognized.

"Come and see the workshop." I followed him through another sliding door at the back of the showroom and decided that this was more like my idea of a garage. Here was the usual clutter of dismantled engines, oil cans, long flexes trailing from the ceiling, naked bulbs, tool benches, old tyres and trolleys.

In the middle of all this a figure was stooped over the stripped-down engine of a skeletal car. He wore a welding mask which made him appear monstrous, and worked with the roaring blue flame of a welding gun. The noise of the gun was overlaid by non-stop blaring music from a surprisingly small transistor radio perched on a beam above him.

Whether or not he saw us coming was anybody's guess, but it was only when Eliot switched off the radio that he shut off his gun and straightened up, pushing the welding mask up and back off his face. I saw a thin, dark young man, oil-stained and in need of a shave, his hair long, his eyes sharp and bright.

"Hallo, Morris," said Eliot.

"Hallo."

"This is Rebecca Bayliss, she's staying at Boscarva."

Reaching for a cigarette, Morris looked my way and gave me a nod. I said, "Hallo," just to be friendly, but got no more response. He lit his cigarette, then slipped the fancy lighter back into the pocket of his oily overalls.

"Thought you'd be coming in this morning," he told Eliot.

"I told you I was going over to Falmouth."

"Any luck?"

"A 1933 Bentley."

"What sort of condition?"

"Looked OK. A bit of rust."

"Get the old paint spray out. There was a chap in the other day, wanting one of them."

"I know, that's why I bought it. Thought we'd take the transporter over, tomorrow or the next day, pick her up."

They fell silent. Morris went to his transistor and turned it on again, if anything louder than before. I looked down at the confusion of engineering on which he had been working and finally asked Eliot what sort of a car it had originally been.

"A 1971 Jaguar XJ6 4.2 litre, if you really want to know. And it will be again when Morris has finished with it. This is another that was in a crash."

Morris came back to stand between us.

"What exactly are you doing to it?" I asked him.

"Straightening out the chassis, fixing the wheel alignment."

"What about the brake shoes?" said Eliot.

"It could have done with new brake shoes, but I fixed the old ones to cover us for the guarantee . . . and Mr Kemback rang up from Birmingham . . ."

They began to talk shop. I drifted away, deafened by the sound of rock, went back through the showroom and out into the forecourt where Rufus waited, with dignity and patience, behind the driving wheel of Eliot's car. Together we sat there until we were rejoined by Eliot. "Sorry about that, Rebecca; I wanted to check on another job. Morris is a good mechanic, but he gets shirty if he's expected to answer the telephone as well."

"Who's Mr Kemback? Another customer?"

"No, not exactly. He was down here last summer on holiday. He runs a motel, a garage, just off the M6. He's got quite a selection of old cars. Wants to start a museum, you know, a sort of sideline to the bacon-and-egg trade. He seems to want me to run it for him."

"You mean go and live in Birmingham?"

"Doesn't sound very tempting, does it? Anyway, that's it. Let's go and look at my mother's house."

We walked there, just a little way down the street, then up a short lane and through a double white gate, and the path sloped up to a long, low white house, which had been converted from two ancient thick-walled stone cottages. Eliot took a key out of his pocket and opened the door and inside it was cold, but not musty or damp. It was furnished like an expensive London flat, with pale, thick, fitted carpets and pale walls and sofas upholstered in mushroom-coloured brocade. There were a great many mirrors and little crystal bag chandeliers hanging from the low-beamed ceilings.

It was all charming, and just what I had imagined, and somehow wrong. A kitchen like an advertisement, a dining room furnished with gleaming mahogany, upstairs there were four bedrooms and three bathrooms, a sewing room and a linen cupboard of mammoth proportions, richly smelling of soap.

At the back of the house was a little patio, and then a long garden sloped up to a distant hedge. I looked at the patio and could see Mollie out there, entertaining her friends, with cane furniture set out on the flagstones, and martinis to drink, served from an expensive glass trolley.

I said, "It's a perfect house," and meant it. But I did not love it as I loved Boscarva. Perhaps because it was too perfect.

We stood in the elegant out-of-place drawing room and eyed each other. Our day together seemed to have come to an end. Perhaps Eliot felt this too and wanted to postpone it, for he said, "I could put on a kettle and make you a cup of tea, only I know that there's no milk in the fridge."

"I think we should go home." I was surprised by an enormous yawn, and Eliot laughed at me. He took my shoulders between his hands. "You're sleepy."

"Too much fresh air," I answered. "Too much wine."

I tipped my head back to look up into his face, and we were very close. I could feel his fingers tighten over my shoulders. He wasn't laughing any more, but his deep-set eyes held an expression as gentle as anything I had ever seen.

I said, "It's been a wonderful day . . ." but that was as far as I got, because he kissed me then, and for some time I was not able to say anything at all. When at last he drew away I was so shaken that all I could do was lean limply against him, wanting to cry, feeling a fool, knowing that the situation was fast slipping out of my control. My cheek was against his coat, and his arms around me held me so close that I could feel, like the throb of a drum, the solid beating of his heart.

Over the top of my head, I heard him say, "You mustn't go back to London. You mustn't ever go away again."

9

The shopping which I had done in Falmouth proved to be an unexpected blessing. I must have been inspired, for, without thinking, I provided exactly the small talking point we all needed to smooth over the embarrassment of the previous uncomfortable evening. Mollie was charmed with her freesias; she couldn't grow them at Boscarva, she explained, the winds were too cold, the garden too exposed. She paid me the compliment of arranging them with more artistry than one would have thought possible, and finally giving them the place of honour in the middle of the mantelpiece in the drawing room. They filled the room with their rich romantic scent, and the cream and the violet and the deep pink drew one's eye, quite naturally, up to the portrait of Sophia. The flowers seemed to complement the glowing skin tones and the fragile shimmer of the white dress.

"Beautiful," said Mollie, standing back, but I could not be sure whether she was referring to the flowers or the portrait. "It was sweet of you to bring them. And did Eliot take you to see my house? So now you can understand how I feel about having to live in this great place." She regarded me thoughtfully, her eyes narrowed. "You know, I believe the day has done you good. I could even imagine you've caught the sun. You've got quite a good colour. The air must agree with you."

Pettifer accepted his sherry with dignity, but I could tell that he was pleased. And Grenville was wickedly delighted with his cigars, for the doctor had warned him against smoking and Pettifer had hidden his usual supply. I understood that he was parsimonious about doling them out. Grenville took and lit one instantly, puffing away with immense satisfaction and leaning back in his big chair like a man without a care in the world. Even with Andrea I had for once done the right thing. "*The Creepers!* How did you know they're my favourite group? Oh, I wish there was a record player here, but there isn't and I left mine in London. Gosh, aren't they fabulous, groovy . . . ?" And then she came down to earth again, searching for the price tag. "That must have cost you something."

It was as though, with peace offerings, we had all formed an unspoken pact. Last night was never discussed. There was no mention of the davenport desk, of Ernest Padlow, of the possible sale of Boscarva Farm. There was no mention of Joss. After dinner Eliot set up a table, and Mollie got out the rosewood box containing the mah-jongg set, and we played until bed time, Andrea sitting with Mollie in order to learn the rules.

I caught myself thinking that, if a stranger were to come, unexpectedly, upon us, how he would be charmed by the picture we made, caught, like flies in amber, in the pool of light from the standard lamp, absorbed by our timeless occupation. The distinguished painter, mellow in the twilight of his years, surrounded by his family; the pretty daughter-in-law and the handsome grandson—and even Andrea, for once alert and interested, absorbed by the intricacies of the game.

I had played as a child with my mother, sometimes making up a foursome with two of her friends, and found myself comforted by the remembered touch of the ivory and bamboo tiles, by their beauty, and the satisfying sound they made, like sea pebbles disturbed by the tide, as we stirred them around in the middle of the table.

At the start of each round we built the four walls, two tiles high, and closed them together into a tight square, "to keep the evil spirits out," we were told by Grenville, who had learned to play as a young Sub-Lieutenant in Hong Kong and knew all the traditional superstitions of the ancient game. I thought how easy it would be, how safe, if ghosts and doubts and skeletons-in-the-cupboard could be thus shut out and kept at bay.

The travel brochures and holiday posters of Porthkerris inevitably portrayed a place where the sea and the sky were always a bright and unsullied blue, the houses white with sunshine, the odd palm tree in the foreground lending that suggestion of Mediterranean glamour. The imagination was led, naturally, to visions of fresh lobster, eaten out of doors; artists with beards and paint-stained smocks; and weather-beaten fishermen, picturesque as pirates, sitting on bollards, smoking their pipes and discussing last week's catch.

But Porthkerris, in February, in a north-east gale, had no shred of connection with this nebulous paradise.

The sea, the sky, the very town were grey, the maze of baffling, narrow streets subjected to onslaughts of bitter wind. The tide was high; the waves broke against the sea-wall and splashed across the road, misting the windows of the houses opposite with salt, and filling the gutters with yellow foam, like dirty soapsuds.

It was as though the place were under some sort of a siege. Shoppers were wrapped, buttoned, scarved in every sort of protective clothing, their faces half hidden by hoods or deep coat collars, their bodies bundled into ambiguity, so that men and women all looked alike, gumbooted and shapeless.

The sky was the colour of the wind, the air filled with flying flotsam, old leaves, twigs, scraps of paper, even tiles torn from roofs. In the shops, people forgot what they had come to buy, the talk was all of the weather, the wind, the damage the storm was going to do.

I had come, once more, to shop for Mollie, fighting my way down the hill in borrowed raincoat and rubber boots, because I felt safer on my feet than I would have driving Mollie's insubstantial car. Now that I was more familiar with the town I no longer needed Andrea to show me the way . . . anyway Andrea was still in bed when I left Boscarva, and for once I did not blame her. The day was not inviting and it was hard to believe that only yesterday I had been sitting out, in my shirt-sleeves, basking in a sun as warm as May.

The last of the shopping completed, I emerged from the baker's as the clock in the tower of the Norman church struck eleven. Normally, under such conditions, I would have headed straight back up the hill to Boscarva, but I had other plans. With my head down, the heavy basket over one arm, I made for the harbour.

The Art Gallery, I knew, was housed in an old Baptist Chapel, somewhere in the maze of streets which lay to the north of the town. I had thought that I would simply go and look for it, but as I braved the harbour road, battling with alternate assaults of wind and spray, I saw the old fisherman's lodge which had been converted to a Tourist Information Bureau and decided that I would save myself both time and effort if I made a few inquiries.

Inside, I found an unenthusiastic girl huddled over a paraffin stove; booted and shivering, she looked like the sole survivor of some Arctic expedition. When I appeared she did not move from her chair but said, "Yes?" and stared at me through a pair of unbecoming spectacles.

I tried to feel sorry for her. "I'm looking for the Art Gallery."

"Which one did you want?"

"I didn't know there was more than one."

Behind me the door opened and shut and we were joined by a third person. The girl looked over my shoulder and a faint interest gleamed behind her pebble glasses.

"There's the Town Gallery and the New Painters," she said, much more lively.

"I don't know which I want."

"Perhaps," said a voice behind me, "I can help."

I swung around and Joss stood there, in rubber boots and a streaming black oilskin, a fisherman's cap jammed down on to his head. His face was wet with rain, his hands jammed into the deep pockets of the coat, his dark eyes glinting with amusement. One half of me could see exactly why the sluggish girl behind the counter had suddenly come to life. The other half was maddened by his extraordinary ability to turn up just when I was least expecting him.

I remembered Andrea. I remembered the desk and the chair. I said, coolly, "Hallo, Joss."

"I saw you come in. What are you wanting to do?"

The girl chipped in. "She wants the Art Gallery."

Joss waited for me to enlarge on this and, thus cornered, I did so.
"I thought perhaps there might be some pictures of Grenville's
there . . ."

"You're quite right, there are three. I'll take you . . ."

"I don't need to be taken, I just want to be told how to get there."

"I'd like to take you . . . here—" he removed my heavy basket from
my arm, smiled at the girl and went to open the door. A howl of wind
and a blast of spume-laden air poured in from the outside and a pile
of leaflets flew and scattered from the counter all over the floor. Before we could do any more damage, I hurried out, and the door swung
shut behind us. As though it were the most natural thing in the world,
Joss took my arm and we made our way down the middle of the cobbled road, Joss carrying on a cheerful conversation despite the fact
that the wind tore the words from his mouth, and that, even with his
arm in mine, it was taking all my efforts to progress at all.

"What on earth brings you down to the town on a day like this?"

"You're carrying it. Mollie's shopping."

"Couldn't you have brought the car?"

"I thought I might get blown off the road."

"I love it," he told me. "I love a day like this." He looked as though
he loved it too, wind-whipped and wet and bursting with vitality. "Did
you have a good day yesterday?"

"What do you know about yesterday?"

"I was up at Boscarva and Andrea told me you'd gone to Falmouth
with Eliot. Don't imagine you can keep any secrets in this place. If
Andrea hadn't told me, Pettifer would, or Mrs Thomas, or Mrs Kernow, or Miss Bright-Eyes in the Information Bureau. It's part of the
fun of living in Porthkerris, everybody knows exactly what everybody
else is up to."

"I'm beginning to realize that."

We turned away from the harbour and began to climb a steep cobbled hill. Houses closed in on either side of us, a cat flashed across the
street and disappeared through a crack in a window. A woman in a
pot hat and a blue apron was scrubbing her steps. She looked up and
saw us, and said, " 'Ullo my lover," to Joss; her fingers were like a bunch
of pink sausages, made so by the hot water and the cold wind.

At the end of the street, we found ourselves in a little square which I had not seen before. One side of this was taken up by a large barn-like structure, with arched windows set high along the wall. By the door was a sign, PORTHKERRIS ART GALLERY, and Joss let go of my arm, pushed open the door with his shoulder and stood aside to let me go ahead of him. Inside it was bitterly cold, draughty, totally empty. The white walls were hung with paintings, of all sorts and shapes and sizes, and two great abstract sculptures were marooned in the middle of the floor, like rocks exposed by an ebb tide. There was a table by the door, with neat stacks of catalogues and folders and copies of *The Studio*, but despite this window-dressing the gallery stayed thick with the atmosphere of joyless bygone Sundays.

"Now," Joss put down my basket and took off his cap, shaking it free of rain as a dog shakes its coat, "what do you want to see?"

"I want to see Sophia."

He glanced at me sharply with a sudden turn of his head, but in the same instant smiled and put his hat on his head again, pulling the peak down over his eyes, like a guardsman.

"Who told you about Sophia?"

I smiled sweetly. "Perhaps it was Mrs Thomas. Perhaps it was Mrs Kernow. Perhaps it was Miss Bright-Eyes in the Information Bureau."

"Insolence will get you nowhere."

"There *is* a portrait of Sophia here. Pettifer told me."

"Yes. It's over this way."

I followed him down the length of the floor, our rubber-booted footsteps sounding loud in the emptiness.

"There," he said. I stopped beside him and looked up, and she was there, sitting in a beam of lamplight with some sewing in her hands.

I stared at it for a long time and finally let out a long sigh of disappointment. Joss looked down at me from under the ridiculous peak of his cap.

"What's that sigh for?"

"You still can't see her face. I still don't know what she looks like. Why didn't he ever paint her face?"

"He did. Often."

"Well, I still haven't seen it. It's always the back of her head, or her

hands, or else she's so small a part of the picture she doesn't have a
face at all, just a blob."

"Does it matter what she looked like?"

"No, it doesn't matter. It's just that I want to know."

"How did you know about Sophia in the first place?"

"My mother told me about her. And then Pettifer, and the picture
of her—the one at Boscarva in the drawing room—is so charming
and feminine, one feels she must have been beautiful. But Pettifer
says that she wasn't beautiful at all. Just very charming and attractive." We looked again at the picture. I saw the hands, and the shine
of lamplight on her dark hair. "Pettifer says that art galleries up and
down the country have portraits of Sophia hanging on their walls. I
shall just have to go on from Manchester to Birmingham, to Not-
tingham, to Glasgow, until I find one that isn't of the back of her
head."

"What will you do then?"

"Nothing. Just know what she looks like."

I turned from my disappointment and began to walk back to the
door where my laden basket waited for me, but Joss was there first,
stooping to swing it up and out of my reach.

I said, "I must go back."

"It's only—" he consulted his watch—"half past eleven. And you've
never seen my shop. Come back with me and let me show it off, and
I'll make you a cup of coffee and drive you home. You can't possibly
walk up the hill with this great weight on your arm."

"Of course I can."

"I won't let you." He opened the door. "Come along."

I couldn't go without the basket and he obviously wasn't going to give
it up, so, resigned and reluctant, I went with him, pushing my hands
into my pockets so that he could not take my arm. He seemed in no
way put out by my ungraciousness, which in itself was disconcerting,
but when we got back to the harbour and were once more in the teeth
of the wind, I nearly lost my balance with the unexpectedness of it,
and he laughed and pulled my hand out of my pocket, taking it in his

own. It was hard not to be disarmed by this protective and forgiving gesture.

As soon as the shop came in view, the tall narrow house shouldering up between the two short fat ones, I saw that indeed changes had taken place. The window frames were now painted, the plate glass had been cleaned, and a sign put up over the door. JOSS GARDNER.

"How does that look?" He was full of pride.

"Impressive," I had to admit.

He took a key out of his pocket and unlocked the door and we went into the shop. Packing cases stood about on the flagged floor, and around the walls, shelving was being erected in varying widths, up to the ceiling. In the centre of the room was another structure, rather like a child's climbing frame, and this had already been set out with modern Danish glass and china, cooking pots in bright colours, and brightly striped Indian rugs. The walls were white, the woodwork had been left in its natural state, and this and the grey floor provided a simple and effective background to the bright wares which he had to sell. At the back of the shop an open staircase rose to the upper floors, and beneath this was another door, ajar, leading down into what appeared to be a dark cellar. "Come upstairs . . ." He led the way.

I followed him. "What's that door there?"

"That's my workshop. It's in a dreadful mess, I'll show you that another time. Now this—" we emerged on to the first floor, and could scarcely move for baskets and wickerwork—"I haven't exactly got this straight but, as you can see, this is where you buy baskets for logs, clothes pegs, shopping, babies, laundry, anything you care to put in them."

None of it was very spacious. The narrow house was just a glorified staircase with a landing on each floor.

"Up again. How are your legs? Now we come to the *pièce de résistance*, the owner's palatial living quarters." I passed a tiny bathroom squeezed into the turn of the stairs. And lagging behind Joss's long legs found myself remembering Andrea's yearning descriptions of his flat, and hoping it would not be the way she had described it to me, but entirely different, so that I would know that her imagination had taken control, and that she had made the whole thing up.

Just like something out of a magazine. With a bed that's a sort of sofa and masses of cushions and things and a log fire.

But it was just the way she had said. As I came up the last stairs, my fleeting hope swiftly died. And there *was* something closed-in and secret about it, with the ceiling sloping down to the floor and a dormer window set into the gable with a seat below it. I saw the little galley, enclosed behind a counter, like a bar, and the old Turkish carpet on the floor, and the divan, red-blanketed, pushed against the wall. As she had said, it was scattered with cushions.

Joss had put down my basket and was already divesting himself of his wet clothes and hanging them on an old-fashioned cane hat-stand.

"Take your things off before you die of cold," he told me. "I'll light a fire . . ."

"I can't stay, Joss . . ."

"No reason not to light the fire. And please, take off that coat."

I did, unbuttoning it with frozen fingers, pulling off my damp woollen hat and shaking my plait down over my shoulder. While I hung these up beside Joss's things, he was busy at the fireplace, snapping twigs, balling paper, scraping together the ashes from some previous fire, lighting it all with a long taper. When it was crackling he took some pieces of driftwood, tar-soaked, from a basket by the fireplace, and stacked them round the flames. They spat, and spluttered, and swiftly caught. And the room, by firelight, sprang to life. He stood up and turned to face me.

"Now, what do you want? Coffee? Tea? Chocolate? Brandy and soda?"

"Coffee?"

"Two coffees coming up." He retired behind his counter, filled a kettle and lit the gas. As he collected a tray and cups, I went over to the window, knelt on the seat and looked down through the fury of the storm to the street below, washed by spray as the waves broke over the sea wall. The boats in the harbour bobbed about like demented corks, and huge herring gulls floated over their swinging mastheads, screaming at the wind. Absorbed in the task of making our coffee, Joss moved with economy from one side of the galley to the other, neat-fingered and self-sufficient as a single-minded yachtsman. So occupied, he appeared harmless enough, but the disconcerting point about

Andrea's revelations was that they all seemed to contain an element of truth.

I had known Joss for only a few days, but already I had seen him in every sort of mood. I knew he could be charming, stubborn, angry, and downright rude. It was not difficult to imagine him as a ruthless and passionate lover, but it was distasteful to imagine him with Andrea.

He looked up suddenly and caught my eye. I was embarrassed, caught with my thoughts. I said, quickly, to divert us both, "In good weather you must have a lovely view."

"Clear out to the lighthouse."

"In the summer it must be like being abroad."

"In the summer it's like Piccadilly Underground at rush hour. But that only lasts for two months." He came out from behind his counter, carrying a tray with the steaming cups, the sugar bowl and the milk jug. The coffee smelt delicious. He pulled forward a long stool with his foot, set the tray at one end of it and himself at the other. Thus, we faced each other.

"I want to hear more about yesterday," said Joss. "Where did you go besides Falmouth?"

I told him about St Endon and the little pub by the water's edge.

"Yes, I've heard about it, but I've never been there. Did you get a good lunch?"

"Yes. And it was so warm that we sat out in the sunshine."

"That's the south coast for you. And what happened then?"

"Nothing happened then. We came home."

He handed me my cup and saucer. "Did Eliot take you to High Cross?"

"Yes."

"Did you see the garage?"

"Yes. And Mollie's house."

"What did you think of all those elegant, sexy cars?"

"I thought just that. That they were elegant and sexy."

"Did you meet any of the guys who work for him?"

His voice was so casual that I became wary.

"Who, for instance?"

"Morris Tatcombe?"

"Joss, you didn't ask me here for coffee at all, did you? You're pumping me."

"I'm not. I promise I'm not. It's just that I wondered if Morris was working for Eliot."

"What do you know about Morris?"

"Just that he's rotten."

"He's a good mechanic."

"Yes, he is. Everybody knows that, and it's the only good thing about him. But he's also totally dishonest and vicious to boot."

"If he's totally dishonest, why isn't he in jail?"

"He's already been. He's just come out."

This took the wind out of my sails, but I soldiered bravely on, sounding more sure of myself than I felt.

"And how do you know he's vicious . . . ?"

"Because he picked a quarrel with me one night in a pub. We went outside and I punched him in the nose, and it was lucky for me I hit him first, because he was carrying a knife."

"Why are you telling me this?"

"Because you asked. If you don't want to be told things, you shouldn't ask questions."

"And what am I meant to do about it?"

"Nothing. Absolutely nothing. I'm sorry I brought it up. It was just that I'd heard Eliot had given him a job and I hoped it wasn't true."

"You don't like Eliot, do you?"

"I don't like him, I don't dislike him. He's nothing to do with me. But I'll tell you something. He picks bad friends."

"You mean Ernest Padlow?"

Joss sent me a glance that was full of reluctant admiration.

"You don't waste much time, I'll say that for you. You seem to know it all."

"I know about Ernest Padlow because I saw him with Eliot that first night when you gave me dinner at The Anchor."

"So you did. That's another rotten egg. If Ernest had his way the whole of Porthkerris would be bulldozed into car parks. There wouldn't be a house left standing. And we would all have to go up the hill and live in his fancy little semis which in ten years' time will be leaking, leaning, cracking up and generally bagging at the knees."

I did not reply to this outburst. I drank my coffee and thought how pleasant it would be to have a conversation without being instantly drawn into longstanding vendettas which had nothing to do with me. I was tired of listening to everybody I wanted to like running down the reputations of everybody else.

I finished my coffee, set down the cup and said, "I must get back."

Joss, with an obvious effort, apologized. "I'm sorry."

"Why?"

"For losing my temper."

"Eliot's my cousin, Joss."

"I know." He looked down, turning his cup in his hands. "But, without meaning to, I've become involved with Boscarva, too."

"Just don't take your prejudices out on me."

His eyes met mine. "I wasn't angry with you."

"I know." I stood up. "I must go," I said again.

"I'll drive you back."

"You don't have to . . ." But he paid no attention to my protest, just took my coat from its hook and helped me on with it. I pulled the wet woollen hat over my ears and picked up the heavy basket.

The telephone rang.

Joss, in his oilskin, went to answer it, and I started downstairs. I heard him call, just before he took the receiver off the hook, "Rebecca, wait for me. I won't be a moment . . ." and then, into the telephone, "Yes? Yes, Joss Gardner here . . ."

I went down to the ground floor and the shop. It was still raining. Upstairs I could hear Joss deep in conversation.

Bored with waiting for him, perhaps a little curious, I pushed open the door of the workshop, turned on the light, and went down four stone steps. There was the usual confusion, benches, woodshavings, scraps, tools, vises; over all hung the smell of glue, of new wood, of polish. There was also a clutter of old furniture, so dusty and ramshackle it was impossible to tell whether it was of any value or not. A chest of drawers missing all its handles, a bedside cupboard without a leg.

And then, at the very back of the room, in the shadows, I saw them. A davenport desk, in apparently perfect repair, and alongside it a chair in the Chinese Chippendale style, with a tapestry seat, embroidered in flowers.

I felt sick, as though I had been kicked in the stomach. I turned and went up the steps, turning off the light and closing the door, going through the shop and out into the bitter windblast of that wicked February day.

My workshop's in a dreadful mess, I'll show you that another time.

I walked and then found that I was running up towards the church, into a warren of little lanes where he would never find me. I was running, always uphill, encumbered by the shopping basket, heavy as lead, and my heart pounded in my chest and there was the taste of blood in my mouth.

Eliot had been right. It was too easy for Joss and he had simply taken his chance. It was my desk; it was *my* desk that he had taken, but he had taken it from Grenville's house, flinging the old man's trust and kindness back in his face.

I could imagine killing Joss, and it was easy. I told myself that I could never speak to him, could never bear to be near him again. I had never been so angry in my life. With him; but worse with myself, for having been taken in by his empty charm, for having been proved so totally wrong. I had never been so angry.

I stumbled on up the hill.

But if I was so angry, then why was I crying?

10

I t was a long and exhausting climb back to Boscarva, and I have never
found it possible to sustain extreme emotion for more than ten minutes. Gradually, fighting my way up the hill against the weather, I
calmed down, wiped my tears away with my gloved hand, pulled myself together. In an apparently intolerable situation, there is nearly always something one can do, and long before I reached Boscarva I had
decided what it was. I would go back to London.

I left the shopping basket on the kitchen table and went upstairs to
my room, took off all my drenched clothes, changed my shoes, washed
my hands, carefully re-plaited my hair; thus calmed I went in search
of Grenville and found him in his study, sitting by the fire and reading the morning paper.

He lowered this and looked over the top of it as I came in.

"Rebecca."

"Hallo. How are you this wild morning?" I sounded determinedly
cheerful, like a maddening nurse.

"Full of aches and pains. The wind's a killer even if you never go
out in it. Where've you been?"

"Down in Porthkerris. I had to do some shopping for Mollie."

"What time is it?"

"Half past twelve."

"Then let's have a glass of sherry."

"Is that allowed?"

"I don't give a damn if it's allowed or not. You know where the decanter is."

I poured two glasses, carried his over and set it carefully down on the table by his chair. I pulled up a stool and sat facing him. I said, "Grenville, I have to go back to London."

"What?"

"I have to go back to London." The blue eyes narrowed, the great jaw thrust out; I hastily made Stephen Forbes my scapegoat. "I can't stay away for ever. I've already been away from work nearly two weeks, and Stephen Forbes, the man I work for, he's been so good about it, I can't just go on taking advantage of his kindness and generosity. I've just realized that it's Friday already. I must go back to London this weekend. I must be back at work on Monday morning."

"But you've only just come." He was obviously thoroughly disgusted with me.

"I've been here three days. After three days fish and guests stink."

"You're not a guest. You're Lisa's child."

"But I still have commitments. And I like my job and I don't want to stop working." I smiled, trying to divert him. "And now I've found the way to Boscarva, perhaps I can come again, when I've got more time to spare, to spend with you."

He did not reply but sat, looking old and grumpy, staring into the fire.

He said dismally, "I may not be here then."

"Oh, of course you will be."

He sighed, took a slow, shaky mouthful of sherry, set down his glass, and turned to me, apparently resigned.

"When do you want to go?"

I was surprised, but relieved, that he had given in so easily.

"Perhaps tomorrow night. I'll get a sleeper. And then I can have Sunday to get myself settled into my flat."

"You shouldn't be living in a flat in London on your own. You weren't made for living alone. You were made for a man, and a home, and children. If I were twenty years younger and could still paint, that's how I'd show you to the world, in a field or a garden, knee-deep in buttercups and children."

"Perhaps it'll happen one day. And then I shall send for you."

His face was suddenly full of pain. He turned away from me and said, "I wish you'd stay."

I longed to say that I would, but there were a thousand reasons why I couldn't. "I'll come back," I promised.

He made a great and touching effort to pull himself together, clearing his throat, re-settling himself in his chair. "That jade of yours. We'll have to get Pettifer to pack it in a box, then you can take it with you. And the mirror . . . could you manage that on the train, or is it too big? You ought to have a car, then there would be no problems. Have you got a car?"

"No, but it doesn't matter . . ."

"And I suppose that desk hasn't . . ."

"It doesn't matter about the desk!" I interrupted, so loudly and so suddenly that Grenville looked at me in some surprise, as though he had not expected such bad manners.

"I'm sorry," I said quickly. "It's just that it really doesn't matter. I couldn't bear everybody to start quarrelling about it again. Please, for my sake, don't talk about it, don't think about it any more."

He regarded me thoughtfully, a long unblinking stare that made me drop my eyes.

He said, "You think I'm unfair to Eliot?"

"I just think that perhaps you never talk to each other, you never tell each other anything."

"He'd have been different if Roger hadn't been killed. He was a boy who needed a father."

"Couldn't you have done as a father?"

"Could never get near him for Mollie. He was never made to stick to anything. Always chopping and changing jobs and then he started that garage up three years ago."

"That seems to be a success."

"Second-hand cars!" His voice was full of unjustified contempt. "He should have gone into the Navy."

"Suppose he didn't want to go into the Navy?"

"He might have, if his mother hadn't talked him out of it. She wanted to keep him at home, tied to her apron strings."

"Oh, Grenville, I think you're being thoroughly old-fashioned and very unfair."

"Did I ask you for your opinion?" But already he was cheering up. A good argument was, to Grenville, like a shot in the arm.

"I don't care whether you asked for it or not, you've got it."

He laughed then, and reached forward to gently pinch my cheek. He said, "How I wish I could still paint. Do you still want one of my pictures to take back to London with you?"

I was afraid that he had forgotten. "More than anything."

"You can get the key of the studio from Pettifer. Tell him I said you could have it. Go and nose around, see what you can find."

"You won't come with me?"

Again the pain came into his face. "No," he said gruffly, and turned away to take up his sherry. He sat, looking down at the amber wine, turning the glass in his hand. "No, I won't come with you."

At lunch he broke the news to the others. Andrea, livid that I was going back to London while she had to stay in horrible, boring Cornwall, went into a sullen sulk. But the others were gratifyingly dismayed.

"But do you have to go?" That was Mollie.

"Yes, I really must. I've got a job to do and I can't stay away for ever."

"We really love having you here." She could be charming when she wasn't aggressive and possessive about Eliot, resentful of Grenville and Boscarva. I saw her again as a pretty little cat, but now I was aware of long claws hidden in the soft velvet paws, and I knew that she had no compunction about using them.

"I've loved it too . . ."

Pettifer was more outspoken. After lunch I went out to the kitchen to help him with the dishes, and he minced no words.

"What you want to go away for now, just when you're settling down and the Commander's getting to know you—well, it's beyond me. I didn't think you were that sort of a person . . ."

"I'll come back. I've said I'll come back."

"He's eighty now. He's not going to last for ever. How are you going to feel, coming back and him not here, but six feet under the ground and pushing up the daisies?"

"Oh, Pettifer, *don't.*"

"It's all very well saying 'Oh, Pettifer, *don't.*' There's nothing I can do about it."

"I've got a job. I must go back."

"Sounds like selfishness to me."

"That's not fair."

"All these years he's not seen his daughter, and then you turn up and stay three days. What sort of a grandchild are you?"

I didn't reply because there was nothing to say. And I hated feeling guilty and being put in the wrong. We finished the dishes in silence, but when they were done and he was wiping down the draining board with a damp cloth, I tried to make my peace with him.

"I'm sorry. I really am. It's bad enough having to go without you making me feel a brute. And I will come back. I've said I will. Perhaps in the summer . . . he'll still be here in the summer, and the weather will be warm and we can do things together. Perhaps you could take us out in the car . . ."

My voice trailed away. Pettifer hung his cloth neatly over the edge of the sink. He said, gruffly, "The Commander said you were to have the key of the studio. Don't know what you'll find down there. A lot of dust and spiders, I should think."

"He said I could have a picture. He said I could go and choose one."

He slowly dried his worn, gnarled hands. "I'll have to find the key. It's put away for safe keeping. Didn't want it lying around where any-one could get their hands on it. There's a lot of good stuff down in the studio."

"Any time will do." I could not bear his disapproval. "Oh, Pettifer, don't be angry with me."

He melted then. "Oh, I'm not angry. Perhaps it's me who's being selfish. Perhaps it's me who doesn't want you to go."

I saw him suddenly, not as the ubiquitous Pettifer around whom this household revolved, but as an old man, nearly as old as my grand-father and probably as lonely. A stupid lump came into my throat and

for a terrible moment I thought I was going to burst into tears, which
would have made it the second time that day, but then Pettifer said,
"And don't go choosing one of them nudes, they wouldn't be suitable,"
and the dangerous moment was behind me and we were smiling, friends
again.

That afternoon Mollie lent me her car, and I drove the five miles to
the railway junction and there bought myself a ticket back to London
and reserved a sleeper for the night train on Saturday. The violence of
the wind had dropped a little, but it was still wild and stormy, with
trees down and devastation everywhere, smashed greenhouses, broken branches, and fields of early spring bulbs flattened by the gales.

I got home to find Mollie in the garden at Boscarva, bundled up
against the weather (even Mollie could not look elegant on such a day)
and trying to tie up and rescue some of the more fragile shrubs that
grew around the house. When she saw the car, she decided to call it a
day, for as I put it away and walked back towards the house I met her
coming towards me, stripping off her gloves and tucking a strand of
hair into her head-scarf.

"I can't bear it a moment longer," she told me. "I hate wind, it ex-
hausts me. But that darling little daphne was being snapped to ribbons, and all the camellias have been burnt by this wind. It turns them
quite brown. Let's go in and have a cup of tea."

While she changed I put the kettle on, and set out cups on a tray.
"Where is everybody?" I asked her when she reappeared, miraculously
neat once more, down to her pearls and her matching ear-rings.

"Grenville's having a nap and Andrea's up in her room . . ." she
sighed. ". . . I must say, she really isn't the easiest of girls. If only she'd
do something to amuse herself instead of skulking around in this
tiresome manner. I'm afraid it's not doing her any good being down
here, I didn't think it would, to be quite honest, but my poor sister
was quite desperate." She looked around the comfortable kitchen.
"This is cosy. Let's have our tea in here. The drawing room's so
draughty when the wind's from the sea, and we can scarcely draw the
curtains at half past four in the afternoon . . ."

She was right, it was cosy in the kitchen. She found a cloth and laid
the tea, setting out cakes and biscuits, sugar bowl and silver milk jug.

Even for kitchen tea, it appeared, her standards were meticulous. She pulled up two wheel-back chairs, and was in the act of reaching for the teapot when the door opened and Andrea appeared.

"Oh, Andrea, dear, just in time. We're having kitchen tea today. Do you want a cup?"

"I'm sorry, I haven't got time."

This unexpectedly mannerly reply made Mollie look up sharply. "Are you going out?"

"Yes," said Andrea, "I'm going to the cinema."

We both stared at her like fools. For the impossible had happened— Andrea had suddenly decided to take much trouble with her appearance. She had washed her hair and tied it back off her face, found a clean polo-necked tee-shirt, and even, I was delighted to see, a bra to wear beneath it. Her Celtic cross hung around her neck on its thread of leather, her black jeans were neatly pressed, her clumpy shoes polished. Over her arm was a raincoat and a fringed leather handbag. I had never seen her look so presentable. And, best of all, the expression on her face was neither sulky nor malevolent, but ... demure? Could one possibly describe Andrea as looking demure?

"I mean," she went on, "if that's all right by you, Auntie Mollie."

"Well, of course. What are you going to see?"

"*Mary of Scotland*. It's on at the Plaza."

"Are you going by yourself?"

"No, I'm going with Joss. He rang me while you were out gardening. He's going to give me supper afterwards."

"Oh," said Mollie, faintly. And then, feeling that further comment was expected of her, "... how are you going to get down there?"

"I'll walk down, and I expect Joss will drive me home ..."

"Have you got some money?"

"I've got 50p. I'll be all right."

"Well ..." But Mollie was defeated. "Have a good time."

"I will," she flashed us both a smile. "Goodbye."

The door swung to behind her.

"Goodbye," said Mollie. She looked at me. "Extraordinary," she said.

I was concentrating on my cup of tea. "Why so extraordinary?" I said casually.

"Andrea and . . . Joss. I mean he's always been quite polite to her, but . . . to ask her out . . . ?"

"You shouldn't sound so surprised. She's attractive when she cleans herself up and bothers to smile. Probably she smiles at Joss all the time."

"You think it's all right, letting her go? I mean I do have responsibilities . . . ?"

"Honestly, I don't see how you could have stopped her going. Anyway she's seventeen, she's not a child. She can surely look after herself by now . . ."

"That's just the trouble," said Mollie . . . "That's always been the trouble with Andrea."

"She'll be all right."

She would not be all right, and I knew this, but I could not disillusion Mollie. Besides, what did it matter? It was no business of mine if Joss chose to spend his evenings making firelit love to an adolescent nymphomaniac. They were two of a kind. They deserved each other. They were welcome to each other.

When we had finished tea, Mollie tied a neat apron around her waist and started preparing dinner. I cleared away the cups and saucers and washed them up. As I was drying the last plate, and putting it away, Pettifer appeared, bearing in his hand a large key which looked as though it might unlock a dungeon.

"I knew I'd put it somewhere safely, found it in the back of a drawer in the Commander's bureau . . ."

"What's that, Pettifer?" Mollie asked.

"The key to the studio, Madam . . ."

"Heavens, who wants that?"

"I do," I said. "Grenville said I could go down and choose a picture to take back to London."

"My dear child, what a task you'll have. The place must be in the most terrible mess, it hasn't seen the light of day for ten years."

"I don't mind." I took the key which weighed heavy as lead in my hand.

"Are you going now? It's getting dark."

"Aren't there any lights?"

"Oh, yes, of course, but it's very cheerless. Wait till tomorrow morning."

But I wanted to go now. "I'll be all right. I'll put on a coat."

"There's a torch on the hall table, you'd better take that as well, the path down the garden is quite steep and slippery."

And so, buttoned into my leather coat, and armed with the torch and the key, I set off, letting myself out of the house by the garden door. The wind from the sea was still violent, carrying with it squalls of thin, cold rain, and I had to struggle to get the door closed behind me. The dismal afternoon was turning early to darkness, but still there was enough light to pick my way cautiously down the sloping garden, and I did not turn on the torch until I reached the studio when I needed its beam to find the keyhole.

I fitted the key and it turned reluctantly, needing oil; the door swung inwards, creakingly. There was a damp and musty smell, a suggestion of cobwebs and mould, and I quickly put my hand inside and felt for the light switch. At once a single naked bulb, high in the roof, sprang to a chill and insubstantial life, and I was surrounded by leaping shadows, for the draught caused the long flex to swing to and fro like the pendulum of a clock.

I went in and shut the door behind me and the shadows, slowly, were stilled. Around me, dust-covered shapes loomed in the half-light, but across the room was a standard lamp, with a crooked, broken shade. I picked my way over to this, found the switch and turned that on, and at once everything looked a little less forlorn.

I saw that the studio had been designed on two levels with a sleeping gallery at the south end, reached by a stair like a ship's ladder.

I went half-way up the ladder and saw the divan and the striped blanket. Over the bed was a window tightly shuttered, and a pillow had shed feathers, perhaps the work of some marauding mouse. The remains of a small dead bird lay, twig-like and dehydrated, in the corner of the floor. I shuddered slightly at the desolation, and descended again to the studio.

The wind banged and rattled at the huge north window. A complicated contraption of strings and pulleys worked the long curtains, and I struggled with these for a moment, but was finally defeated by their mechanics and left the curtains closed.

In the middle of the floor was a model's throne, with a sheeted shape in the middle which proved to be an ornate gilt chair. The mice had been at the seat of this, too—scraps of red velvet and horsehair were scattered about, along with mouse-droppings and a great deal of dust.

Under another sheet I found Grenville's workbench; his brushes, his trays of paint-tubes, palettes, knives, bottles of linseed oil, piles of unused canvases, grimy with age. There was also a little collection of *objets trouvés*, small things which, perhaps, had taken his fancy. A sea-polished stone, half a dozen shells, a bunch of gulls' feathers, probably collected for the practical purpose of cleaning his pipe. There were curling, faded snapshots, of nobody I recognized, a blue and white Chinese ginger jar filled with pencils, some bottles of fossilized Indian ink, a scrap of sealing wax.

It was like prying, as though I were reading another person's diary. I put back the sheet and went on to the true purpose of my visit, which was the stack of unframed canvases standing around the wall, each with its face turned inwards. These had been dust-covered too, but the sheets had slipped, draping themselves about the floor, and as I dislodged the first pile my fingers touched cobwebs, and a huge, disgusting spider went scuttling across the floor and lost itself in the shadows.

It was a slow business. Five or six at a time, I lifted out the pictures, dusted them off, leaned them in rows against the model's throne, shifting the rickety standard lamp so that the light should shine on them. Some were dated, but they were stacked away in no sort of chronological order, and for the most part I could tell neither when nor where they had been painted. I only knew that they compassed the whole of Grenville's professional life and all his interests.

There were landscapes, seascapes—the ocean in all its moods—charming interiors, some sketches of Paris, some that looked like Italy. There were boats and fishermen, street scenes of Porthkerris, a number of rough charcoal sketches of two children, whom I knew were Roger and Lisa. There were no portraits.

I began to make my selection, setting aside the pictures which I found particularly engaging. By the time I had reached the final pile, there were half a dozen of them propped against the seat of a sagging couch, and I was dirty and cold, with grimy hands and cobwebs clinging to my clothes. With the good feeling of a task nearly completed I went to sort out the last pile of canvases. There were three pen and ink drawings, and a view of a harbour with yachts at anchor. And then . . .

It was the last canvas and the biggest of all. It needed two hands and all my efforts to lift it out of its dark corner and turn it around to face the light. I held it upright with one hand and stood back, and the face of the girl leapt out to meet me, the dark, tip-tilted eyes smiling with a vitality undimmed by the dust of the years that passed. I saw the dark hair and the bumpy cheekbones and the sensuous mouth, not smiling, but seeming to tremble on the brink of laughter. And she wore the same fragile white dress, the dress that she had worn for the portrait that hung over the fireplace in the drawing room at Boscarva.

Sophia.

Ever since my mother had mentioned her name I had been fascinated by her. The frustrations of never knowing what she looked like had only increased my obsession. But now that I had found her and we were face to face at last, I felt like Pandora. I had opened the box and the secrets were out, and there was no way in the world of packing them back and locking the lid once more.

I knew that face. I had talked to it, argued with it; seen it scowl and smile; seen the dark eyes narrowed in anger and glint with amusement.

It was Joss Gardner.

11

All at once I was bitterly cold. It was dark now and the studio was icy, but as well I could feel the blood drain from my face like water out of a basin; I could hear the laboured thumping of my own heart, and I started, violently, to shiver. My first instinct was to put the portrait back where I had found it, pile some other canvases on top of it and hide it, like a criminal trying to conceal a body, or something worse.

But in the end I reached for a chair and arranged it carefully, so that it supported Sophia's portrait like an easel, and then I backed away on shaking legs and carefully lowered myself on to the sagging seat of the aged sofa.

Sophia and Joss.

Sophia the enchanting, and the baffling Joss, whom I had finally learned was not to be trusted.

She went to London, she got married, she had a baby, I think, Pettifer had told me. Then in 1942 she was killed in the Blitz.

But he had not mentioned Joss. And yet Joss and Sophia were so obviously, inextricably linked.

And I thought of my desk, my mother's desk that she meant me to have, hidden away at the back of Joss's workshop.

And I heard Mollie's voice. *I don't know why Grenville's so taken with Joss. It's frightening. It's as though Joss were able to exert some hold over him.*

Sophia and Joss.

It was dark now. I had no watch and I had lost all track of time. The wind drowned all other sound, so that I did not hear Eliot coming down the garden from the house, picking his way through the darkness because I had taken the torch. I did not hear anything until the door burst open, as though on a gust of wind, causing the light to start up its demented swinging, and frightening me nearly out of my wits. The next instant Rufus bounded in and flung himself up on the sofa beside me, and I realized that I had company.

My cousin Eliot stood in the open doorway framed in darkness. He wore a suede jacket and a pale blue polo-necked sweater and he had slung a raincoat around his shoulders like a cloak. The cruel light drained all the colour from his thin face, and turned his deep-set eyes into two black holes.

"My mother told me you were down here. I came to . . ."

He stopped, and I knew that he had seen the portrait. I couldn't move, I was too petrified with cold, and anyway, now it was too late to do anything about it.

He came into the studio and closed the door. The leaping shadows, once more, were slowly stilled.

We neither of us said anything. I held Rufus's head, instinctively seeking comfort in his soft, warm fur, and watched while Eliot shrugged off his raincoat, dropped it across a chair, and came slowly to sit beside me. His eyes never left the portrait.

At last he spoke. "Good God," he said.

I said nothing.

"Where did you find that?"

"In a corner . . ." My voice came out as a croak. I cleared my throat and tried again. "In a corner, behind a lot of other canvases."

"It's Sophia."

"Yes."

"It's Joss Gardner."

There was no denying it. "Yes."

"Sophia's grandson, do you suppose?"

"Yes. I think he must be."

"Well, I'll be damned." He leaned back, and crossed his long, elegant legs, suddenly relaxed, like a knowledgeable art critic at a private view.

His obvious satisfaction puzzled me, and I did not want him to think that I shared it.

I said, "I wasn't looking for it. I've been wanting to know what Sophia looked like, but I had no idea there was a portrait of her down here. I just came to look for a picture because Grenville said I could have one to take back to London."

"I know. My mother told me."

"Eliot, we mustn't say anything."

He ignored this. "You know, there was always something funny about Joss, something unexplained. The way he turned up in Porthkerris, out of the blue. And the way Grenville knew that he was there; the way he gave him a job, and the run of Boscarva. I never trusted Joss farther than I could see him. And the desk disappearing—the desk that should have come to you. It was all fishy beyond words."

I knew that I should tell Eliot then that I had found the desk. I opened my mouth with the intention of doing just this thing, and closed it again because somehow the words would not be spoken. Besides, Eliot was still talking and had not noticed my incipient interruption.

"My mother swore he had some sort of a hold over Grenville."

"You make it sound like blackmail."

"Perhaps, in a modified form, it was. You know, 'Here I am Sophia's grandson, what are you going to do for me?' And Pettifer must have known as well. Pettifer and Grenville have no secrets from each other."

"Eliot, we mustn't say that we found the picture."

He turned his head to look at me.

"You sound anxious, Rebecca. On Joss Gardner's behalf?"

"No. On Grenville's."

"But you like Joss."

"No."

He pretended to be amazed. "But everybody likes Joss! Everybody, it seems, has fallen under his spell of boyish charm. Grenville and Pettifer; Andrea is besotted by him, she never leaves him alone, but I think there may be something just a little physical in that attraction. I thought that you were bound to have joined the club." He frowned. "You *did* like Joss."

"Not now, Eliot."

He began to be intrigued. He shifted his position slightly, so that we half-faced each other on the sofa, his arm along its carved back, behind my shoulder.

"What happened?" he asked.

What had happened? Nothing. But I had never felt quite easy about Joss, and all the coincidences that seemed to tie our lives together. And he had stolen my mother's desk. And he was now, at this moment, carrying on his clandestine affair with the unsavoury Andrea. At the very idea of this, my imagination was apt to turn and run.

Eliot was waiting for my reply. But I only shrugged and shook my head hopelessly and said, "I changed my mind."

"Could yesterday have had anything to do with it?"

"Yesterday?" I thought of sitting with Eliot on the sunbaked terrace of the little pub; of the two boys sailing their dinghy down the blue waters of the creek; and finally Eliot's arms, encircling and holding me, the feel of his kisses, and the sensation of losing control, of sliding over a cliff.

I shivered again. My hands, cold and grimy, lay in my lap. Eliot put his own over them and said, in some surprise, "You're freezing."

"I know, I've been here for hours."

"My mother told me you want to go back to London." We seemed to have dropped the subject of Joss and I was thankful for this.

"Yes, I have to go."

"When?"

"Tomorrow night."

"You never told me."

"I didn't decide until this morning."

"You seem to have changed your mind, and made a lot of decisions all in one day."

"I hadn't realized how the time had flown. I've been away from work for nearly two weeks."

"Yesterday, I asked you to stay."

"I have to go."

"What would make you stay?"

"Nothing. I mean . . . I can't . . ." I was stammering like a fool, but I was too cold, too dirty and too tired for such a conversation. Later, perhaps, I would be able to cope . . .

"Would you stay if I asked you to marry me?"

My head shot up. Something like horror must have shown on my face, for he put back his head and laughed.

"Don't look so shocked. There's nothing shocking about getting married."

"But we're cousins."

"That doesn't matter."

"But we don't . . . I mean . . . You don't love me."

It was an appalling thing to say, but Eliot took it in his stride.

"Rebecca, you are stammering and stuttering like a shy schoolgirl. Perhaps I do love you. Perhaps I would have loved you for a long time before asking you to marry me, but you've precipitated this situation by suddenly announcing out of the blue that you're going to go back to London. So if I'm going to say it at all, I'd better say it now. I want you to marry me. I think it would work very well."

Despite myself, I was touched. No one had ever asked me to marry them before, and I found it flattering. But even as I listened to Eliot with one part of my mind, the other part ran round in circles like a squirrel in a cage.

Because there was still Boscarva, and the land that Eliot needed to sell to Ernest Padlow.

You are not my only grandchild.

". . . it seems ridiculous to say goodbye and walk out of each other's lives when we've only just met each other, and there are so many good things going for us."

I said quietly, "Like Boscarva."

His smile froze slightly around the edges. He raised an eyebrow. "Boscarva?"

"Let's be honest and truthful, Eliot. For some reason you need Boscarva. And you think that Grenville might leave it to me."

He took a deep breath as though to deny this, hesitated, and then let it all out in a long sigh. His smile was rueful. He ran a hand over the top of his head.

"How cool you are. The Ice Princess all of a sudden."

"You need Boscarva so that you can sell the farm to Ernest Padlow to build his houses."

He said, carefully, "Yes." I waited. "I needed money to build the garage. Grenville wasn't interested so I approached Padlow. He agreed and the security was the Boscarva farm. Gentleman's agreement."

"But it wasn't yours."

"I was sure it would be. There was no reason why it shouldn't be. And Grenville was old and ill. The end could have come any day." He spread his hands. "Who would have imagined that three years later he'd still be with us?"

"You sound as though you want him dead."

"Old age is a terrible thing. Lonely and sad. He's had a good life. What is there for him to cling on for?"

I knew that I could not agree with Eliot. Old age, in Grenville's case, meant dignity and purpose. I had only just got to know him, but already I loved him and he was part of me; I could not bear to think of him dying.

I said, trying to stay practical, "Isn't there some other way you could pay off Mr Padlow?"

"I could sell the garage. The way things are going I might have to do that anyway."

"I thought you were doing so well."

"That's what everybody's meant to think."

"But if you sold the garage, what would you do then?"

"What do you suggest I should do?" He sounded amused as though I were a child with whims to be indulged. I said, "How about Mr Kemback, and the car museum in Birmingham?"

"What an uncomfortably good memory you've got."

"Would working for Mr Kemback be such a bad thing?"

"And leave Cornwall?"

"I think that's what you should do. Make a new start. Get away from Boscarva and . . ." I stopped, and then thought, *in for a penny, in for a pound*, ". . . and your mother." I finished in a rush.

"My mother?" Still that amusement, as though I were a beguiling fool.

"You know what I mean, Eliot."

There was a long pause. Then, "I think," said Eliot, "you have been talking to Grenville."

"I'm sorry."

"One thing's for certain, either Joss or I will have to go. As they say in Westerns, 'This town ain't big enough for the two of us.' But I'd rather Joss went."

"Joss is unimportant. He's not worth taking a stand over."

"If I sold the garage and went to work in Birmingham, would you come with me?"

"Oh, Eliot . . ."

I turned away from him and came face to face once more with Sophia's portrait. Her eyes met mine and it was as though Joss sat there, listening to every word we were saying, laughing at us. Then Eliot put his hand beneath my chin and jerked my head around so that once more I was forced to meet his eye.

"Listen to what I'm saying!"

"I am listening."

"We don't have to be in love with each other. You know that, don't you?"

"I always imagined it was important."

"It doesn't happen to everyone. Perhaps it won't ever happen to you."

It was a chill prospect. "Perhaps not."

"In that case," his voice was very gentle and reasonable, "would a compromise be such a bad thing? Wouldn't a compromise be better than a nine to five job for the rest of your life and an empty flat in London?"

He had touched me on the raw. I had been alone for too long, and the prospect of staying alone for the rest of my life was frightening. Grenville had said, *You were made for a man and a home and children.* And now they were all there, waiting for me. I had only to reach out my hand, to accept what Eliot was offering me.

I said his name, and he put his arms around me, and drew me very close, kissing my eyes, my cheeks, my mouth. Sophia watched us and

I did not care. I told myself that she was dead, and Joss I had already put out of my life. Why should I care what either of them thought of me?

Eliot said at last, "We must go." He held me away from him. "You must have a bath and wash all those dirty marks off your face, and I must get the ice out of the fridge, and be all ready and dutiful to pour drinks for Grenville and my mother."

"Yes." I drew away from his arms, and pushed a lock of hair out of my face. I felt deathly tired. "What time is it?"

He looked at his watch, the strap that I had given him still shining and new. "Nearly half past seven. We could stay here all night, but unfortunately life has to go on."

I got wearily to my feet. Without looking at the portrait I took it up and put it back in its hidden, dusty corner, along with the cobwebs and the spiders, its face to the wall. Then I picked up other pictures, at random, and piled them around and against it. Everything, I told myself, was just as it had been before. We tidied up in a cursory fashion and covered the canvases with the fallen dust-sheet. Eliot switched off the standard lamp, and I picked up the torch. We went out of the studio, turning off the light and closing and locking the door. Eliot took the torch from me, and together, following the bobbing circle of light, we went up the garden, stumbling a little over hidden verges and tussocks of grass, mounting the shining wet steps of the terrace. Above us the house loomed, lighted rooms glowing behind drawn curtains, and all around us was the wind and the silhouettes of leafless, tormented trees.

"I've never known a storm to last so long," said Eliot, as he opened the side door and we went inside. The hall felt warm and safe, and there was the good smell of the chicken casserole that we were to have for dinner.

We parted, Eliot heading for the kitchen, and I upstairs to shed my filthy clothes, draw a bath and wallow in warm, scented steam. Relaxed at last I thought about nothing. I was too tired to think. I would fall asleep, I decided, and probably drown. For some reason the idea of this did not alarm me.

But I did not fall asleep, because as I lay there, I heard, above the noise of the wind, the sound of an approaching car. The bathroom faced over the back of the house, the drive and the front door. I had not bothered to draw the curtains and the headlights of the car flashed for a second against the dark glass. A door banged, there were voices. Thus disturbed, I climbed out of the bath, dried myself and started across the passage to my room, but stopped dead when I heard the raised voices carrying up the stairwell from the hall.

". . . found her half way up the hill . . ." a man's voice, unrecognized. And then Mollie, ". . . but my dear child . . ." This was interrupted by a wild cacophony of sobbing. I heard Eliot say, "For heaven's sake, girl . . ." And then Mollie again. "Come in by the fire . . . come along now, you're all right. You're safe now . . ."

I went into my room, pulled on my clothes, buttoned the neck of the brown caftan, brushed and plaited my hair, all in the space of moments. I painted on a layer of lipstick—there was no time for more—thrust my bare feet into sandals and ran downstairs, screwing on my ear-rings as I did so.

As I reached the bottom of the stairs Pettifer appeared through the kitchen door with a face like a thundercloud and bearing in his hand a glass of brandy. It was indicative of the gravity of the situation that he had omitted to put it on a silver salver.

"Pettifer, what's happened?"

"I don't know what's happened, exactly, but it sounds as though that girl's having hysterics."

"I heard a car coming. Who brought her home?"

"Morris Tatcombe. Says he was driving home from Porthkerris when he found her on the road."

I was horrified. "You mean *lying* on the road? Had she been hit by a car, or something?"

"I don't know. Probably just had a tumble."

At the far end of the hall the drawing room door burst open and Mollie came towards us, half running.

"Oh, Pettifer, don't stand talking, hurry with the brandy." She saw me standing, quite at a loss. "Oh, my dear Rebecca, what a terrible thing, quite terrible. I'm going to ring the doctor." She was at the telephone, thumbing through the book, unable to see because she had somewhere mislaid her glasses. "Look it up for me, there's a dear. It's Doctor Trevaskis . . . we ought to have it written down somewhere, but I can't find . . ."

Pettifer had gone. I took the telephone book and started to look for the number. "What's happened to Andrea?" I asked.

"It's the most ghastly story. I can hardly believe it's true. What a mercy Morris found her. She could have been there all night. She could have died . . ."

"Here it is. Lionel Trevaskis. Porthkerris 873."

She put a hand to her cheek. "Oh, of course, I should know it off by heart." She lifted the receiver and dialled. While she waited she spoke to me, swiftly. "Go and sit by her, the men are so useless, they never know what to do."

Mystified and oddly reluctant to know the details of Andrea's unhappy experience, I nevertheless did as she asked me. I found the drawing room in something approaching a shambles. Grenville, apparently nonplussed, stood in front of the fireplace with his hands behind his back and said nothing. The rest of them were grouped around the sofa; Eliot had given Morris a drink, and they watched while Pettifer, with commendable patience, was trying to trickle some brandy down Andrea's throat.

And Andrea . . . despite myself I was shocked and frightened by her appearance. The neat sweater and the pressed jeans in which she had set out so gaily were soaking wet and smeared with mud. Through the tear in the jeans I could see her knee, cut and bleeding, vulnerably childlike. She had lost, it seemed, a shoe. Her hair clung, like seaweed, to her skull, her face was blotched with crying, and when I said her name she turned her head to look at me from pathetic, streaming eyes; I saw with horror the great bruise on her temple, as though she had been savagely struck. The Celtic cross on its leather thong was also lost; torn off, perhaps, in some unthinkable struggle.

"Andrea!"

She gave a great wail and heaved herself over to press her face into the back of the sofa, spilling the brandy as she did so, and knocking the tumbler clean out of Pettifer's hand.

"I don't want to talk about it. I don't want to talk about it . . . !"

"But you must!"

Pettifer, exasperated, collected the glass and went from the room. I told myself that he had never liked the girl. I took his place beside her, sitting on the edge of the sofa, trying to turn her shoulders toward me.

"Did somebody do this to you?"

Andrea flung herself back at me, her body convulsed. "Yes!" She screamed at my face as though I were deaf. "Joss!" And with that she dissolved once more in a welter of sobs.

I looked up at Grenville and was subjected to a stony, unblinking glare. His features might have been carved from wood. I decided there was no help to be expected from that quarter. I turned to Morris Tatcombe.

"Where did you find her?"

He shifted, one foot to another. I saw that he was dressed as though for a night on the town. A leather jacket, decorated with a rash of embroidered emblems, and spotted with rain, skin-tight jeans and boots with high heels. Even with high heels the top of his head scarcely reached to Eliot's shoulder, and his long hair hung damp and lank.

He tossed this back, a gesture both aggressive and self-conscious.

"Half way up Porthkerris Hill. You know, where the road narrows and there isn't a pavement. She was half way up the bank, half in the ditch. Lucky I saw her, really. Thought she'd been hit by a car, but it wasn't that. Seems she had this row with Joss Gardner."

I said, "He asked her to go to the cinema with him."

"I don't know how it all started," said Morris.

"But this, it seems—" said Eliot gravely—"is how it ends."

"But . . ." There had to be some other explanation. I was about to tell them this when Andrea let out another wail, like some aged sibyl keening at a wake, and I lost my temper.

"Oh, for goodness sake, girl, shut up!" I took her by her shoulders and gave her a little shake so that her head bobbed on the silk cushion like a badly stuffed rag-doll. "Stop making that dementing noise and tell us what happened."

Words began to spill out of her mouth, made ugly with weeping. (I thought briskly, *at least she isn't missing any teeth,* and hated myself for my own hard heart.)

"I . . . we . . . went to the cinema . . . and wh . . . when we came out, we went to a pub, and . . ."

"Which pub?"

"I don't know . . ."

"You must know which pub . . ."

My voice rose in impatience. Behind me, Mollie, whom I had not heard come into the room, said, "Oh, don't shout at her. Don't be unkind."

I made an effort and tried again, more gently.

"Can't you remember where you went?"

"No. It was d . . . dark . . . and I . . . couldn't see. And then . . . and then . . ."

I held her firmly, trying to calm her "Yes. And then?"

"And Joss had a lot of whisky to drink. And he wouldn't bring me home. He wanted me to g . . . go back to his flat with him . . . and . . ."

Her mouth went square, her features dissolved into uncontrollable weeping. I let her go and stood up, backing away from her. At once Mollie took my place.

"There," she said. "There, there." She was more gentle than I, her voice as soothing as a mother's. "Now there's nothing more to worry about. The doctor's on his way, and Pettifer's putting a nice hot bottle in your bed. You don't need to tell us any more. You don't need to talk about it any more."

But, perhaps calmed by Mollie's manner, Andrea seemed anxious to make a clean breast of it, and, through interminable sobs and gasps, we were to hear the rest of the story.

"And I didn't want to go. I . . . I wanted to come home. And I . . . left him. And he came after me. And . . . I tried to run, and I tripped on the p . . . pavement, and my shoe . . . c . . . came off. And then he c . . . caught me, and he be . . . began shouting at me . . . and I screamed and he *hit* me . . ."

I looked at the faces around me, and the same horror and consternation, in varying degrees, was mirrored upon them. Only Grenville appeared coldly, deeply angry, but still he did not move, he did not say a word.

"It's all right," Mollie said again, her voice shaking only a little. "Now, everything's all right. Come along, upstairs."

Somehow Andrea, wilted and bedraggled, was eased off the sofa, but her legs would not hold her weight, and she started to collapse. It was Morris who, standing nearest to her, stepped forward and caught her before she fell, swinging her up, with surprising strength, into his puny arms.

"There," said Mollie, "Morris will carry you upstairs. You'll be all right . . ." She moved towards the door. "If you'll come this way, Morris."

"OK," said Morris, who did not appear to have much option in the matter.

I watched Andrea's face. As Morris moved, her eyes opened and looked straight into mine, and our glances clashed and held. And I knew that she was lying. And she knew that I knew she was lying.

Leaning her head against Morris's chest, she began to cry again. Swiftly, she was borne from the room.

We listened as Morris's burdened footsteps went down the hall, started up the staircase. Then Eliot said, with masterly understatement, "An unsavoury business." He glanced at Grenville. "Shall I ring the police now or later?"

Grenville spoke at last. "Who said anything about ringing the police?"

"You surely don't intend to let him get away with it?"

I said, "She was lying."

Both men looked at me in some surprise. Grenville's eyes narrowed and he was at his most formidable. Eliot frowned. "What did you say?"

"Some of her story may be true. Most of it probably is. But still, she was lying."

"How was she lying?"

"Because as you said yourself, she was besotted with Joss. She wouldn't leave him alone. She told me that she'd been often to his flat, and she must have been, because she described it to me and every detail was right. I don't know what happened this evening. But I do know that if Joss wanted her to go back with him, she'd have gone like a shot. No arguments."

"Then how," asked Eliot smoothly, "do you account for the bruise on her face?"

"I don't know. I said I don't know about the rest of her story. But that bit, for sure, she made up."

Grenville moved. He had been standing for a long time. Slowly, he went to his chair and lowered himself carefully into it.

"We can find out what really happened," he said at last.

"How?" Eliot's question came out like the shot of a gun.

Grenville swung his head around and fixed his gaze on Eliot.

"We can ask Joss."

Eliot let out a sound, which in old-fashioned novels would have been written as "Pshaw."

"We shall ask him. And we will be given the truth."

"He doesn't know what the truth means."

"You have no justification for making such a statement."

Eliot lost his temper. "Oh, for God's sake, does the truth have to be thrown in your face before you recognize it?"

"Don't raise your voice to me."

Eliot was silent, staring in disbelief and disgust at the old man. When at last he spoke, it was in scarcely more than a whisper. "I've had enough of Joss Gardner. I've never trusted him nor liked him. I believe he's a phoney, a thief and a liar, and I know that I'm right. And one day you too will know that I'm right. This is your house. I accept that. But what I will not accept is his right to take it over, and us with it, just because he happens to be . . ."

I had to stop him. "Eliot!" He turned to look at me. It was as though he had forgotten I was there. "Eliot, please. Don't say any more."

He looked down at his glass, finished the drink in a single mouthful. "All right," he said at last. "For the moment, I won't say any more."

And he went to pour himself another whisky. As he did this, with Grenville and I watching him in silence, Morris Tatcombe came back into the room.

"I'll be off then," he said to the back of Eliot's head.

Eliot turned and saw him. "Is she all right?"

"Well, she's upstairs. Your mother's with her."

"Have another drink before you go."

"No, I'd better be off."

"We really can't thank you enough. What would have happened if you hadn't seen her . . ." He stopped, the unfinished sentence conjuring up visions of Andrea dying of exposure, exhaustion, loss of blood.

"Just lucky I did." He backed away, obviously anxious to be off, but not quite sure how to get there. Eliot put the stopper into the decanter, left his freshly filled glass on the table and came to his rescue.

"I'll see you to the door."

Morris ducked his head in the general direction of Grenville and myself.

"Night, all."

But Grenville had hauled himself to his feet with massive dignity. "You've handled things very sensibly, Mr Tatcombe. We're grateful to you. And we would be grateful, too, if you would keep the girl's version of what happened to yourself. At least until it has been authenticated."

Morris looked sceptical. "These things get around."

"But not, I am sure, through you."

Morris shrugged. "It's your affair."

"Exactly. Our affair. Good night, Mr Tatcombe."

Eliot led him away.

Grenville laboriously settled himself once more in his chair. He passed a hand over his eyes, and it occurred to me that such scenes could not be good for him.

"Are you all right?"

"Yes. I'm all right."

I wished that I could confide in him, tell him that I knew about Sophia, and Joss being her grandson. But I knew that if there were any telling to be done, it had to come from him.

"Would you like a drink?"

"No."

So I left him alone, busying myself in tidying the cushions on the flattened sofa.

It was some time before Eliot re-appeared, but when he did he seemed quite cheerful again, the sudden row which had flared between him and Grenville now quite forgotten. He went to pick up his drink. "Good health," he said, raising his glass to his grandfather.

"I suppose we're in debt to that young man," said Grenville. "I hope one day we'll be able to settle it."

"I shouldn't worry too much about Morris," Eliot replied lightly. "I should think he's quite capable of settling it for himself. And Pettifer has asked me to tell you both that dinner is ready."

We ate alone, the three of us. Mollie stayed with Andrea, and in the middle of dinner the doctor arrived and was taken upstairs by Pettifer. Later, we heard him talking to Mollie in the hall, then she showed him out and came into the dining room to tell us what he had said.

"Shock, of course. He's given her a sedative, and she has to stay in bed for a day or two."

Eliot had gone to pull out a chair for her, and she sank into this looking exhausted and shaken. "Imagine such a thing happening. How I'm going to tell her mother, I can't think."

"Don't think about it," said Eliot, "till tomorrow."

"But it was such an appalling story. She's only a child. She's only seventeen. What could Joss have been thinking of? He must have gone out of his mind."

"He was probably drunk," said Eliot.

"Yes, perhaps he was. Drunk and violent."

Neither Grenville nor I said anything. It was as though we had entered into some sort of an unspoken conspiracy, but this did not mean that I had forgiven Joss, nor condoned anything that he had done. Later, probably, when he had been interrogated by Grenville, the whole truth would come out. By then I would probably be back in London.

And if I was still here . . . Slowly, I ate a little bunch of grapes. This could be my last dinner at Boscarva, but I truly did not know whether I wanted it to be or not. I had reached a cross-roads, and had no idea which was the way I should take. But soon I was going to have to make up my mind.

A compromise, Eliot had said, and it had sounded tepid. But after the histrionics of this evening, the very words had a solid ring to them, sensible and matter-of-fact, with their feet planted squarely on the ground.

You were made for a man and a home and children.

I reached for my wine glass and, glancing up, saw that Eliot watched me across the polished table. He smiled, as though we were conspirators. The expression on his face was both confident and triumphant. Perhaps, while I was thinking that I would probably end up by marrying him, he already knew that I would.

We were back in the drawing room, sitting around the fire and finishing our coffee, when the telephone started to ring. I thought that Eliot would go to answer it, but he was deep in a chair with the paper and a drink, and managed to linger so long that it was Pettifer who finally took the call. We heard the kitchen door open and his old feet go so slowly across the hall. The ringing stopped. For some reason I glanced up at the clock on the mantelpiece. It was nearly a quarter to ten.

We waited. Presently the door opened and Pettifer's head came around the edge of it, his spectacles glinting in the lamplight.

"Who is it, Pettifer?" asked Mollie.

"It's for Rebecca," said Pettifer.

I was surprised. "For me?"

Eliot said, "Who's ringing you at this hour of the day?"

"I've no idea."

I got up and went out of the room. Perhaps it was Maggie, wanting to tell me something about the flat. Perhaps it was Stephen Forbes, wondering when I was going to return to work. I felt guilty, because I should have been in touch with him, letting him know what I was doing and when I planned to go back to London.

I sat on the hall chest and picked up the receiver.

"Hallo?"

A small, mouse-like voice began speaking, sounding very far away.

"Oh, Miss Bayliss, we were passing, and he was lying there . . . my husband said . . . so we got him up the stairs and into the flat . . . don't know what happened. Covered in blood and he could hardly talk. Wanted to call the doctor . . . but he wouldn't let us . . . frightened leaving him there on his own . . . there ought to be somebody there . . . said he'd be all right . . ."

I must have been exceptionally slow and stupid, but it took me a little time to realize that this was Mrs Kernow, calling me from the phone box at the end of Fish Lane, to tell me that something had happened to Joss.

was amazed and gratified to find myself in a state of almost total calm. It was as though I had already been prepared for this crisis, been given my orders and told what to do. There were no doubts and so no indecision. I must go to Joss. It was as simple as that.

I went up to my bedroom and got my coat, put it on, did up the buttons, came downstairs again. The key of Mollie's car lay where I had left it, on the brass tray in the middle of the table in the hall.

I picked it up, and as I did so the drawing room door opened and Eliot came up the passage towards me. It never occurred to me that he would try to stop me going. It never occurred to me that anyone or anything could stop me going.

He saw me, bundled into my old leather coat. "Where are you off to?"

"Out."

"Who was that on the telephone?"

"Mrs Kernow."

"What does she want?"

"Joss has been hurt. She and Mr Kernow were walking home along the harbour road, they'd been visiting her sister. They found him."

"So?" His voice was cold and very quiet. I expected to be intimidated, but I was not.

"I'm going to borrow your mother's car. I'm going to him."

His thin face hardened, the skin drawn tight over the jutting bones. "Have you gone out of your mind?"

"I don't think so."

He said nothing. I slipped the key into my pocket and made for the door, but Eliot was faster than I, and in two strides was in front of me, standing with his back to the door and with his hand on the latch.

"You're not going," he said pleasantly. "You don't really think I'd let you go?"

"He's been hurt, Eliot."

"So what? You saw what he did to Andrea. He's rotten, Rebecca. You know he's rotten. His grandmother was an Irish whore, God knows who his father was, and he's a womanizing bastard."

The ugly words, which were meant to shock me, slid off my back like water from a duck. Eliot saw this and my unconcern infuriated him.

"Why do you want to go to him? What good could you do? He won't thank you for interfering, if it's thanks you're looking for. Leave him alone, he has no part of your life, he's none of your concern."

I stood watching him, hearing him, without making sense of anything he said. But I knew, all at once, that it was over, the uncertainty and the indecision, and I felt light with relief, as though a great weight had been lifted from my shoulders. I still stood at the crossroads. My life was still a confusion. But one thing had made itself abundantly clear. I could never marry Eliot.

A compromise, he had said. But, for me, it would have been a poor bargain. All right, he was weak, and probably not the most successful of businessmen. I had recognized these flaws in his character and had been prepared to accept them. But the welcome he had shown me, the hospitality, and the charm which he could turn on and off like a tap, had blinded me to his vindictiveness and the frightening strength of his jealousy.

I said, "Let me go, Eliot."

"Supposing I say that I won't let you go? Supposing I keep you here?" He put his hands on either side of my head, pressing so tightly that it felt as though my skull would crack open, like a nut. "Supposing, now, that I said I loved you?"

I was sickened by him. "You don't love anyone. Only Eliot Bayliss. There's no room for anyone else in your life."

"I thought we decided that it was you who didn't know how to love."

His grip tightened. My head began to pound and I closed my eyes, enduring the pain.

"When I do—" I told him through clenched teeth—"it won't be you."

"All right then, go . . ." He let me loose so suddenly that I nearly lost my balance. Savagely he turned the handle and flung the door open, and instantly the wind poured in, like some monstrous creature that had been waiting all evening to invade the house. Outside was the dark and the rain. Without another word, not stopping to look at Eliot, I ran past him and out into it, as though to some sanctuary.

I had still to get to the garage, to struggle with doors in the darkness, to find Mollie's little car. I was convinced that Eliot was just behind me, as frightening as an imagined bogy man, waiting to jump, to catch me, to stop me from getting away. I slammed the car door shut, and my hand shook so much I could scarcely get the ignition key fitted. The first time I turned it, the engine did not start. I heard myself whimpering as I pulled out the choke and tried again. This time the engine caught. I put the car into gear and shot forward, through the darkness and the rain, up the puddled driveway with a great spattering of gravel, and so at last out and on to the road.

Driving, I regained some of my previous calm. I had eluded Eliot, I was going to Joss. I must drive with care and good sense, not allow myself to panic, not risk a skid or a possible collision. I slowed down to a cautious thirty miles per hour. I deliberately loosened my death-like clutch on the driving wheel. The road ran downhill, black and wet with rain. The lights of Porthkerris came up towards me. I was going to Joss.

Now, the tide was at full ebb. As I came out on to the harbour road, I saw the lights reflected in wet sand, the boats drawn up out of the reach of the storm. Overhead tattered scraps of cloud still poured across the sky. There were people about, but not very many.

The shop was in darkness. Only a single light glowed from the top window. I parked the car by the pavement and got out and went to the door and it opened. I smelt the new wood, my feet brushed through the shavings which still lay about the place. From the light of the street lamp outside I could see the staircase. I went up it, cautiously, to the first floor.

I called up, "Joss!"

There was no reply. I went on, up into the soft light. There was no fire and it was very cold. A squall of rain swept the roof above me.

"Joss."

He was lying on his bed, roughly covered by a blanket. His forearm lay across his eyes, as though to shut out some unbearable light. When I spoke he lowered this, and raised his head slightly to see who it was. Then he dropped back on to the pillow.

"Good God," I heard him say. "Rebecca."

I went to his side. "Yes, it's me."

"I thought I heard your voice. I thought I was dreaming."

"I called up, but you didn't reply."

His face was in a terrible mess, the left side bruised and swollen, the eye half-closed. Blood had trickled and dried from a cut in his lip, and there did not seem to be any skin on the knuckles of his right hand.

"What are you doing here?" He spoke muzzily, perhaps because of the lip.

"Mrs Kernow rang me."

"I told her not to say anything."

"She was worried about you. Joss, what happened?"

"I fell amongst thieves."

"Are you hurt anywhere else?"

"Yes, everywhere else."

"Let me see . . ."

"The Kernows bandaged me up."

But I stooped over him, gently drawing back the blanket. As far as his rib-cage he was naked and below this tenderly swathed in what looked like strips torn from an old sheet. But the ugly bruising had spread up and on to his chest, and on his right side the red stain of blood had started to seep through the white cotton.

"Joss, who did this?"

But Joss did not answer me. Instead, with a strength surprising in one so hurt, he put up an arm and pulled me down so that I was sitting on the edge of his bed. My long, blonde plait of hair hung forward over my shoulder, and while he held me with his right arm, his left hand was occupied in slipping off the rubber band which held the ends together, and then, using his fingers like a comb, he loosened the strands, unravelling them, so that my hair hung like a silken tassel, brushing on to his naked chest.

He said, "I always wanted to do that. Ever since I first saw you looking like the head girl of . . . what was it I said?"

"The head girl of a nicely run orphanage."

"That's it. Fancy you remembering."

"What can I do? There must be something I can do?"

"Just stay. Just stay, my darling girl."

The tenderness in his voice . . . Joss, who had always been so tough . . . dissolved me. Tears sprang into my eyes and he saw these and pulled me down, so that I lay against him, and I felt his hand slip up beneath my hair and close around the back of my neck.

"Joss, I'll hurt you . . ."

"Don't talk," he said, as his seeking mouth found mine. And then, "I've always wanted to do this, too."

It was evident that none of his infirmities, his bruises, his bleeding, his cut lip, were to deter him in any way from getting exactly what he wanted.

And I, who had always imagined that loving was something to do with fireworks and explosions of emotion, discovered that it was not like that at all. It was warm, like sudden sunshine. It had nothing to do with my mother and the endless procession of men who had invaded her life. It was cynicism and preconceived ideas flying out of an open window. It was the last of my defences gone. It was Joss.

He said my name and he made it sound beautiful.

Much later, I lit a fire, piling on the driftwood so that the room was bright with flickering firelight. I would not let Joss move, so that he lay with his dark head propped on his arms, and I felt his eyes following every move I made.

I stood up, away from the fire. My hair fell loose on either side of my face, and my cheeks were warm from the fire. I felt soft with content. Joss said, "We have to talk, don't we?"

"Yes."

"Get me a drink."

"What do you want?"

"Some whisky. It's in the galley, in the cupboard over the sink."

I went to find it, and two glasses. "Soda or water?"

"Soda. There's a bottle-opener hanging on a hook."

I found the opener and took the cap off the bottle. I did this clumsily and it fell to the floor, rolling in the maddening manner of such things into a dark corner. I went to retrieve it and my eye was caught by another small and shining object, lying half under the kickboard beneath the sink. I picked it up and it was Andrea's Celtic cross, the one that she had worn on a leather thong around her neck.

I kept it in my hand. I poured the drinks and took them back to Joss. I handed him one, and knelt on the floor beside him.

I said, "This was under the sink," and showed him the cross.

His swollen eye made it difficult for him to focus. He squinted at it painfully.

"What the hell's that?"

"It's Andrea's."

He said, "Oh, to hell." And then, "Get me some more pillows, there's a good girl. I could never drink whisky lying down."

I gathered up a couple of cushions off the floor, and propped him against them. The action of sitting up was agony for him and he let out an involuntary groan.

"Are you all right?"

"Yes, of course I'm all right. Where did you find that thing?"

"I told you. On the floor."

"She came here this evening. She said she'd been to the cinema. I was working downstairs, trying to get the shelving finished. I told her I was busy, but she just came up here, as though I'd never said a word. I followed her up and told her to go home. But she wouldn't go. She said she wanted a drink, she wanted to talk . . . you know the sort of drivel."

"She's been here before."

"Yes, once. One morning. I was sorry for her and I gave her a cup of coffee. But this evening I was busy; I had no time for her and I wasn't sorry for her. I said I didn't want a drink. I told her to go home. And then she said that she didn't want to go home, everybody hated her, nobody would talk to her, I was the only person she could talk to, I was the only person who understood."

"Perhaps you were."

"OK, so I was sorry for her. I used to let her come and get in my way when I was working at Boscarva, because there wasn't much else I could do about it, short of bodily throwing her out of the room."

"Did you do that this evening? Throw her out?"

"Not in so many words. But finally I'd had enough of her batty conversation and her totally unfounded belief that I was ready, willing and eager to jump into bed with her, and I lost my temper and told her so."

"What happened then?"

"What didn't happen? Screams, tears, accusations, routine hysteria. I was subjected to every sort of vilification. Face slapping, the lot. That was when I finally resorted to force, and I bundled her down the stairs and threw her raincoat and her beastly handbag after her."

"You didn't hurt her?"

"No, I didn't hurt her. But I think I frightened her, because she went then, like the hammers of hell. I heard her clattering down the stairs on those ghastly clogs she wears, and then I think she must have slipped because there was the most frightful thumping and bumping as she went down the last few stairs. I shouted down to make sure she was all right, but then I heard her running out of the shop and slamming the door behind her, so that I imagined she was."

"Could she have hit herself on anything? Bruised her face when she fell?"

"Yes, I suppose she could. There was a packing case full of china standing at the bottom of the stairs. She could have collided with that . . . Why do you ask anyway?"

I told him. When I had finished he let out a long, incredulous whistle. But he was angry too.

"The little bitch. I think she's a nymphomaniac, do you know that?"

"I've always thought so."

"She was always talking about some guy called Danus, going into the most gruesome of intimate details. And the bloody cheek of telling everyone that I had asked her to go to the cinema with me. I wouldn't ask her to empty a dustbin with me . . . What's happened to her now?"

"She's been put to bed. Mollie got the doctor."

"If he's worth his salt he'll have diagnosed self-induced hysteria. And he'll prescribe a good walloping and send her back to London. And that'll get her out of everybody's way."

"Poor Andrea. She's very unhappy."

As though he could not keep his hands off it, he reached out to touch my hair. I turned my head and kissed the back of his hand, the lacerated knuckles.

He said, "You didn't believe her, did you?"

"Not really."

"Did anyone else?"

"Mollie and Eliot did. Eliot wanted to call the police but Grenville wouldn't let him."

"That's interesting."

"Why?"

"Who was it who brought Andrea home?"

"I thought I'd told you. Morris Tatcombe . . . you know, the boy who works for Eliot . . ."

"Morris? Well I'll be . . ." He stopped in midsentence, and then said again, "Morris Tatcombe."

"What about him?"

"Oh, Rebecca, come along. Pull yourself together. Use your wits. Who do you think gave me this beating?"

"Not Morris." I did not want to believe it.

"Morris and three others. I went along to The Anchor for a glass of beer and a pie for my supper, and when I was walking home, they jumped me."

"You knew it was Morris?"

"Who else would it be? He's always had this grudge going for me ever since we last crossed swords and he ended up on his backside in the gutter. I thought his putting the boot in this time was just a continuation of our running feud. But it seems that it wasn't."

Without thinking I began to say, "Eliot . . ." and then stopped, but it was too late. Joss said quietly, "What about Eliot?"

"I don't want to talk about Eliot."

"Did he tell Morris to come after me?"

"I don't know."

"He could, you know. He hates my guts. It fits."

"I . . . I think he's jealous of you. He doesn't like your being so close to Grenville. He doesn't like Grenville being so fond of you. And . . ." I looked down at my drink, turning the glass in my hand, feeling suddenly nervous. "There's something else."

"From your expression one would think you'd murdered somebody. What is it?"

"It's . . . the desk. The desk downstairs in your workroom. I saw it this morning, when you were telephoning."

"I wondered why you'd suddenly gone cantering out into the rain. What about it?"

"The desk and the Chippendale chair. They come from Boscarva."

"Yes, I know."

His calmness shocked me. "You didn't *take* them, Joss?"

"*Take them?* No, I didn't take them. I bought them."

"Who from?"

"A man who runs an antique shop up beyond Fourbourne. I'd been to a sale about a month ago, and I dropped in to see him on the way back, and I saw the chair and the desk in his shop. By then I knew all Grenville's furniture and I knew they'd come from Boscarva."

"But who took them?"

"I regret to have to shatter your innocence, but it was your cousin Eliot."

"But Eliot knew nothing about them."

"Eliot most certainly did. They were in one of the attics, as far as I remember, and he probably imagined they'd never be missed."

"But why . . . ?"

"This is like playing the truth game. Because Eliot, my love, my darling child, is head over heels in debt. That garage was financed by Ernest Padlow in the first place, it cost a bomb and it's been losing money steadily for the past twelve months. God knows what use fifty pounds would have been to Eliot, a mere drop in the ocean one would have thought, but perhaps he needed a little ready cash to pay a bill or put on a horse or something . . . I don't know. Between you and me, I don't think he should be running his own business. He'd be better working for some other guy, being paid a regular salary. Perhaps, one evening, when you're sitting over drinks at Boscarva, you could try and persuade him."

"Sarcasm doesn't suit you."

"I know, but Eliot makes me edgy. Always has done."

I felt, obscurely, that I must stand up for Eliot, make excuses for him.

"In a way, he thinks that Boscarva and everything in it already belong to him. Perhaps he didn't feel it was . . . stealing . . . ?"

"When did they realize the things were missing?"

"A couple of days ago. You see, the desk belonged to my mother. Now it belongs to me. That's why we started to look for it."

"Unfortunate for Eliot."

"Yes."

"I suppose Eliot said I'd taken them."

"Yes," I admitted miserably.

"What did Grenville say?"

"He said that you'd never do a thing like that."

"And so there was another monumental row."

"Yes."

Joss sighed deeply. We fell silent. The room was growing cold again, the fire beginning to die down. I got up and went to put another log on it, but Joss stopped me.

"Leave it," he said.

I looked at him, surprised. He finished his drink and put the empty glass down on the floor beside him, and then pushed back the blanket and began, carefully, to get out of bed.

"Joss, you mustn't . . ."

I flew to his side, but he pushed me away, and slowly, with infinite caution, got to his feet. Once there, he grinned triumphantly down at me, a bizarre sight, bruised and battered, and dressed in bandages and a crumpled pair of jeans.

"Into battle," he said.

"Joss, what are you going to do?"

"If you'll find me a shirt and a pair of shoes, I'll get dressed. And then we're going to go downstairs, and get into the truck and drive back to Boscarva."

"But you can't drive like that."

"I can do anything I want," he told me, and I believed him. "Now find my clothes and stop arguing."

He would not even let me take Mollie's car. "We'll leave it there, it'll be all right. Someone can fetch it in the morning." His own little truck was parked around the corner, up a narrow alley. We got in, and he started the engine and backed out on to the road, with me giving directions because he was too stiff to turn around in the seat. We headed up through the town, along streets that had become familiar to me, over the cross-roads and up the hill.

I sat, staring ahead, with my hands clasped tightly in my lap. I knew that there was still something else we had to talk about. And it had to be now, before we reached Boscarva.

For some reason, as though he were immensely pleased with life in general, Joss has started to sing.

> *"The first time ever I saw your face*
> *I thought the sun rose in your eyes*
> *And the moon and stars . . ."*

"Joss."

"What is it now?"

"There's something else."

He sounded shocked. "Not another skeleton in the cupboard?"

"Don't joke."

"I'm sorry. What is it?"

I swallowed a strange obstruction in the back of my throat.

"It's Sophia."

"What about Sophia?"

"Grenville gave me the key of the studio so that I could go and choose a picture to take back to London. I found a portrait of Sophia. A proper one, with a face. And Eliot came to find me, and he saw it too."

There was a long silence. I looked at Joss but his profile was stony, intent on the road ahead. "I see," he said at last.

"She looks just like you; or you look just like her."

"Naturally enough. She was my grandmother."

"Yes, I thought that was probably it."

"So the portrait was in the studio?"

"Is . . . is that why you came to live in Porthkerris?"

"Yes. Grenville and my father fixed it between them. Grenville put up half the capital for my shop."

"Your father . . . ?"

"You've met him. Tristram Nolan Gardner. He runs an antique shop, in the New Kings Road. You bought a pair of balloon-back chairs from him. Do you remember?"

"And he found from my cheque that I was called Rebecca Bayliss."

"Right. And he found out, by cunning question and answer, that you were Grenville Bayliss's granddaughter. Right. And he found out that you were catching the train to Cornwall last Monday. Right."

"So he rang you up and told you to meet the train."

"Right."

"But why?"

"Because he felt involved. Because he thought you seemed lost and vulnerable. Because he wanted me to keep an eye on you."

"I still don't understand."

"You know something?" said Joss. "I love you very much."

"Because I'm being stupid?"

"No, because you're being marvellously innocent. Sophia wasn't only Grenville's model, she was his mistress as well. My father was born at the beginning of their relationship, long before your mother arrived. Sophia married, eventually, an old friend she'd known from childhood days, but she never had any more children."

"So Tristram . . . ?"

"Tristram is Grenville's son. And Grenville is my grandfather. And I am going to marry my half-cousin."

"Pettifer told me that Sophia meant nothing to Grenville. That she was just a girl who'd worked for him."

"If it meant protecting Grenville, Pettifer would swear that black is white."

"Yes, I suppose he would." But Grenville, in anger, had been less discreet. " 'You are not my only grandchild!' "

"Did Grenville say that?"

"Yes, to Eliot. And Eliot thought he meant me."

We had reached the top of the hill. The lights of the town were far behind us. Ahead, beyond the huddled shapes of Ernest Padlow's housing estate, lay the dark coastline, pricked with the tiny lights of random farms, and beyond it the black immensity of the sea.

I said, "I don't seem to remember you asking me to marry you."

The little van bumped and lurched down the lane towards Boscarva. "I'm not very good at asking things," said Joss. He took his hand off the wheel and put it over mine. "I usually just tell people."

As once before, it was Pettifer who came out to meet us. As soon as Joss switched off the engine of the van, the light in the hall went on, and Pettifer opened the door, as though he had known instinctively we were on our way.

He saw Joss open the car door and ease himself out, in obvious discomfort and pain. He saw Joss's face . . .

"For heaven's sake, what happened to you?"

"I had a difference of opinion with our old friend Morris Tatcombe. I probably wouldn't look like this except that he had three of his chums with him."

"Are you all right?"

"Yes, I'm fine. No bones broken. Come on, let's go in."

We went indoors and Pettifer closed the door.

"I'm glad to see you, Joss, and that's the truth. We've had a proper how-do-you-do here and no mistake."

"Is Grenville all right?"

"Yes, he's all right. He's still up, in the drawing room, waiting for Rebecca to come home."

"And Eliot?"

Pettifer looked from Joss's face to mine.

"He's gone."

Joss said, "You'd better tell us about it."

We ended up in the kitchen, around the table.

"After Rebecca had gone, Eliot went down to the studio and came back with that portrait of Sophia. The one we looked for, Joss. The one we never found."

I said, "I don't understand."

Joss explained. "Pettifer knew Sophia was my grandmother, but no one else did. No one else remembered her. It was all too long ago. Grenville wanted it to stay that way."

"But why was there only one picture of Sophia with a face? There must have been dozens Grenville painted of her. What happened to all of them?"

There was a pause while Joss and Pettifer looked at each other. Then it was Pettifer's turn to explain, which he did with much tact.

"It was old Mrs Bayliss. She was jealous of Sophia . . . not because she had any notion of the truth . . . but because Sophia was part of the Commander's other life, the life Mrs Bayliss didn't have no time for."

"You mean his painting."

"She would never have anything to do with Sophia, more than a frosty good morning if she happened to meet her in the town. And the Commander knew this, and he didn't want to upset her, so he let all the pictures of Sophia go . . . all except for the one you found. We knew it was somewhere around. Joss and I spent a day looking for it, but we never turned it up."

"What were you going to do with it if you found it?"

"Nothing. We just didn't want anyone else to find it."

"I don't see why it was so important."

Joss said, "Grenville didn't want anyone to know about what happened between him and Sophia. It wasn't that he was ashamed of it, because he'd loved her very much. And after he's dead, it won't matter any longer, he doesn't give a damn who knows then. But he's proud, and he's lived his life according to a certain set of standards. We probably think they're old-fashioned, but they're still his own. Does that make sense to you?"

"I suppose so."

"Young people now," said Pettifer heavily, "talk about a permissive society as though it were something they'd invented. But it's not new. It's been going on since the beginning of time, only in the Commander's day it was handled with a little more discretion."

We accepted this meekly. Then Joss said, "We seem to have gone off at a tangent. Pettifer was telling us about Eliot."

Pettifer collected himself. "Yes, well. So down to the drawing room Eliot went, and stormed in, with me behind him, went straight to the mantelpiece, and dumped it up there, alongside the other picture. The Commander never said a word, just watched him. And Eliot said, 'What's that got to do with Joss Gardner?' Then the Commander told him. Told him everything. Very quiet and very dignified. And Mrs Roger was there too, and she just about threw a fit. She said all these years the Commander had deceived them, letting Eliot believe that he was his only grandson, and he'd get Boscarva when the Commander died. The Commander said he'd never said anything of the sort, that it was all surmise, that they'd simply been counting their chickens before they were hatched. Then Eliot said, very cold, 'Perhaps now we can know what your plans are?' but the Commander said that his plans were his own business, and *quite right* he was too."

This little bit of championship was accompanied by Pettifer's fist coming down with a thump on the kitchen table.

"So what did Eliot do?"

"Eliot said in that case he was going to wash his hands of the whole lot of us . . . meaning the family, of course . . . and that he had plans of his own and he was thankful to be shed of us. And with that he collected a few papers and a brief-case and put on his coat and whistled up his dog and walked out of the house. Heard his car go up the lane and that was the end of him."

"Where's he gone?"

"To High Cross, I suppose."

"And Mollie?"

"She was in tears . . . trying to stop him doing anything stupid, she said. Begging him to stay. Turning on the Commander, saying it was all his fault. But of course, there wasn't anything she could do to stop Eliot. There's nothing you can do to stop a grown man walking out of the house, not even if you do happen to be his mother."

I was torn with sorrow and sympathy for Mollie.

"Where is she now?"

"Up in her room." He added gruffly, "I made her a little tea tray, took it up to her, found her sitting at her dressing-table like something carved out of stone."

I was glad I had not been here. It all sounded very dramatic. I stood up. Poor Mollie. "I'll go up and talk to her."

"And I—" said Joss—"will go and see Grenville."

"Tell him I'll be there in a moment or two."

Joss smiled. "We'll wait," he promised.

I found Mollie, white-faced and tear-stained, still sitting in front of her frilled dressing-table. (This was in character. Even the deepest excesses of grief would not cause Mollie to fling herself across any bed. It might crease the covers.) As I came into the room, she looked up, and her reflection was caught three times over in her triple mirror; for the first time ever, I thought that she looked her age.

I said, "Are you all right?"

She looked down, balling a sodden handkerchief in her fingers. I went to her side. "Pettifer told me. I'm so very sorry."

"It's all so desperately unfair. Grenville's always disliked Eliot, resented him in some extraordinary way. And of course, now we know why. He was always trying to run Eliot's life, come between Eliot and me. Whatever I did for Eliot was always wrong."

I knelt beside her, and put my arm around her, "I really believe he meant it for the best. Can't you try to believe that too?"

"I don't even know where he's gone. He wouldn't tell me. He never said goodbye."

I realized that she was a great deal more worried about Eliot's abrupt departure than she was about the evening's revelations concerning Joss. This was just as well. I could comfort her about Eliot. There was not a mortal thing I could do about Joss.

"I think," I said, "that Eliot may have gone to Birmingham."

She looked at me in horror. *"Birmingham?"*

"There was a man there who wanted to give him a job. Eliot told me. It was to do with second-hand cars. He seemed to think that it might be quite interesting."

"But I can't go and live in *Birmingham*."

"Oh, Mollie, you don't have to. Eliot can live on his own. Let him go. Give him the chance of making something of his life."

"But we've always been together."

"Then perhaps it's time to start living apart. You've got your house at High Cross, your garden up there, your friends . . ."

"I can't leave Boscarva. I can't leave Andrea. I can't leave Grenville."

"Yes, you can. And I think Andrea should go back to London, to her own parents. You've done all you can for her, and she's miserable here. That's why all this happened, because she was unhappy and lonely. And as for Grenville, I'll stay with him."

I came downstairs at last, carrying the tea tray. I took it into the kitchen and put it on the table. Pettifer, sitting there, looked up at me over the edge of his evening paper.

"How is she?" he asked.

"All right now. She's agreed that Andrea should go home, back to London. And then she's going back to High Cross."

"That's what she's always wanted. And you?"

"I'm staying here. If that's all right with you."

A chill gleam of satisfaction crossed Pettifer's face, the nearest he could get to a look of delight. There was no need for me to say more. We understood each other.

Pettifer turned his paper. "They're in the drawing room—" he told me—"waiting for you," and he settled down to the racing page.

I went and found them, backed by the two portraits of Sophia in her white dress, Joss standing by the fire, and Grenville deep in his chair. They both looked up as I came in, the long-legged young man with his villainous black eye, and the old one, too tired to pull himself to his feet. I went towards them, the two people I loved most.